new bedlam

new bedlam
bill flanagan

A Novel

The Penguin Press • New York • 2007

Thanks to the MTV Networks alumni association, especially Tom Freston, Judy McGrath, John Sykes, Jeff Gaspin, Lauren Zalaznick, Brent Hansen, and Bill Roedy. Special thanks to Herb Scannell for all the Bonanza episodes. Thanks to Ramon for the makeup, the Haveys for the carp, Fred for "Over the Rainbow," and Gordon for the raccoon story. Chip Young first speculated on who slept with whom on Gilligan's Island. Richard Reed invented the Holdster. Thanks to Jeff Rosen for the wise advice on A&R—better late than never, Jeff. Thanks to Andrew and Jeff at the Wylie Agency for riding shotgun and to Scott Moyers for telling me where the book was. Love to Susan, Kate, Sarah, and Frank. RIP Arch and Jeri MacDonald.   —W.F.F.

THE PENGUIN PRESS
Published by the Penguin Group
Penguin Group (USA) Inc., 375 Hudson Street, New York, New York 10014, USA • Penguin
Group (Canada), 90 Eglinton Avenue East, Suite 700, Toronto, Ontario, Canada M4P 2Y3
(a division of Pearson Penguin Canada Inc.) • Penguin Books Ltd, 80 Strand, London
WC2R 0RL, England • Penguin Ireland, 25 St Stephen's Green, Dublin 2, Ireland (a division of Penguin
Books Ltd) • Penguin Books Australia Ltd, 250 Camberwell Road, Camberwell, Victoria 3124, Australia
(a division of Pearson Australia Group Pty Ltd) • Penguin Books India Pvt Ltd, 11 Community Centre,
Panchsheel Park, New Delhi—110 017, India • Penguin Group (NZ), 67 Apollo Drive, Rosedale,
North Shore 0745, Auckland, New Zealand (a division of Pearson New Zealand Ltd) • Penguin Books
(South Africa) (Pty) Ltd, 24 Sturdee Avenue, Rosebank, Johannesburg 2196, South Africa

Penguin Books Ltd, Registered Offices: 80 Strand, London WC2R 0RL, England

First published in 2007 by The Penguin Press, a member of Penguin Group (USA) Inc.

Copyright © Bill Flanagan, 2007
All rights reserved

Grateful acknowledgment is made for permission to reprint an excerpt from "Bonanza Theme," by Jay Livingston and Raymond B. Evans. © Copyright 1959, Jay Livingston Music, Inc./ASCAP. Copyright renewed. International copyright secured. © 1959 St. Angelo Music. All rights administered by Universal Music Corp./ASCAP. Used by permission. All rights reserved.

Library of Congress Cataloging-in-Publication Data
Flanagan, Bill.
New Bedlam : a novel / Bill Flanagan.
p. cm.
ISBN-13: 978-1-59420-050-2
I. Title.
PS3556.L313N49   2007
813'.54—dc22   2006034934

Printed in the United States of America
1   3   5   7   9   10   8   6   4   2

DESIGNED BY GRETCHEN ACHILLES AND AMANDA DEWEY

FOR MY SISTERS,

SARAH AND ELLEN

new bedlam

part one
networking

1.

Bobby Kahn fired people. It was the only bad part of a job he loved. If you asked him about it he would say the same five words each of the other twenty-four network vice presidents uttered when you asked any of them: "It comes with the turf." That's how they talked. They were proudly unoriginal. It is why they made good television executives.

The truth was that this bit of the turf caused Bobby to sleep badly the night before and feel lousy for a couple of days after. Even when he was firing someone he disliked, even when it was he who had made the decision, he hated it.

He had worked out a technique. He never actually told people that they were out. He never said, "You're fired," or, "We have to let you go," or even, "I'm afraid the network has decided to make some changes." Instead Bobby began the conversation as if the firing were something both of them already knew about, as if the chopped head had heard the bad news the day before and now the two of them were digesting it together, as comrades.

Every person in every job has at least imagined what it would be like to be sacked. Bobby connected to that. He recognized all the reactions: stiff-upper-lipped resolution, uncorked rage, weepy self-recrimination, embarrassment, resentment, fear of financial ruin, and the horrible confirmation of the primeval paranoia that all of one's worldly success was predicated on fraud.

Bobby knew all of his compensatory obligations, too, from hand-on-the-shoulder commiseration to eyebrow-cocked incredulity to head-shaking "What's this place coming to?" empathy.

He gave them as much time as they wanted. He let them vent. He let them be brave. He let them be angry. He said as little as he could get away with. He kept his answers vague and his face set. Bobby figured that what the person being fired wants most is dignity. She wants to not be embarrassed in front of her coworkers. He wants to not be ashamed in front of his children.

If someone had been at the network a long time or was far enough up the org chart, Bobby would offer a paper consultancy or an independent production deal. At least through the end of their existing contract, sometimes beyond. For someone more junior he might dangle the chance of coming back later in another position.

"This place is a revolving door," Bobby would say. "The only way to move up here is to go somewhere else for a while and do great stuff and then come back at a higher salary."

The chopped head did not need to believe any of it. Bobby was kindly offering a cover story. He was collaborating in an alibi.

He always allowed a few minutes at the end to recall the happy times he and the firee had shared in better days gone by. Without saying anything that could be used against him in a wrongful dismissal suit, Bobby would shake his head sadly and wonder vaguely what bad days were ahead for this screwed-up network if this was the sort of talent they were letting slip away.

With a repertoire like that you'd think Bobby would have been better prepared when they came and fired him.

Howard Temple fired Bobby. Howard was the network's President of Programming and Production, East Coast. He was a friendly back-slapper with a big gut and a decent handicap, yellow hair and red skin. Howard and Bobby had played golf that weekend. Bent over the sink splashing water on his face, Bobby realized that the whole time they were telling jokes and talking about the fall schedule, Howard knew that he was going to walk into Bobby's office on Monday and cut his nuts off. He was sick all over again.

Howard felt bad. He had argued for Bobby in the boss's office. He had lost. The word was, "The posse's getting close. We need to throw them a body." Howard certainly didn't want that body to be his own. He would make sure Bobby had a good exit package. Bobby Kahn had made the network a lot of money, and anyway, Howard liked the kid.

What could he do? Howard was just one little loop in a long helix. Yes, he was called President of Programming, but that title was deceiving. In ancient days, in the 1980s, the number of network vice presidents had expanded to where it seemed like there was a Vice President of Paper Cups and a VP of Parking Spaces. This led to a creeping inflation in the number of senior vice presidents, until by the early nineties there were SVPs slipping Chinese menus under the door. By the midnineties the title executive vice president began worming into the contract vocabulary, a solid gold star on the upper management epaulet. By the turn of the century, however, EVPs were ubiquitous, and so the network began bestowing presidencies on whoever ran a main department. Each coast had a President of Programming and Production. There were Presidents of Sports, Sales, and News. There was a President of Talent Relations and a President of Business Affairs. To Howard's resentment, there was now a President of Public Relations. At some point in the next contract-negotiation cycle some glory-hogging lawyer would win his client the title Emperor of Affiliate Relations and the whole personnel department would explode.

All of these fake presidents reported to the real president, the President of the Network. He reported to the Chairman of the Network. The chairman was himself only one of a tableful of direct reports to the Chief Operating Officer of the bigger company that owned the network. The COO reported to the chairman of that bigger company. It was like one of those Russian dolls with a dozen smaller dolls inside it. It reminded Howard of an old *Twilight Zone* episode in which the Earth turns out to be an atom on a slide on the microscope of a giant child on a much bigger planet. To be a mere President of Programming in such a scheme was to be the little monkey at the far left of the evolutionary chart.

None of this had ever bothered Bobby Kahn. He loved his job too much to worry about anything but the work. Bobby had the confidence born of early success. He mentored. He spoke to college classes. He gave informational interviews to interns.

Bobby's ambition was born before he had second teeth. His dad managed a department store, but had started out as an electronics repairman, and Bobby inherited his love for technology. As a child in Massapequa, Long Island, Bobby awaited the arrivals of the new TV and stereo models the way other boys looked forward to the rollout of new cars. After his parents split up and Bobby saw less of his dad, TV was what they talked about.

Bobby knew from an early age he was going to work in television. He subscribed to *TV Guide* for the articles. He lay awake nights thinking of how he would counterprogram each network's schedule to combat whoever was dominant. He knew how ABC could break NBC's "Must See TV" stranglehold. He knew how CBS could cop some of Fox's youth appeal. He even had ideas for how PBS could double its pledge drive.

As a kid he did errands at the local ABC affiliate. In college he interned at one of the broadcast networks every summer. He answered phones and collated receipts for important men. He made a good impression. He was hired in the spring of his senior year and skipped commencement to get a jump on the job.

He was a natural. He flew up through Finance and made the side step into Scheduling at the right time—age twenty-five. That put him close to where he wanted to be: Programming and Production. By twenty-eight he was Executive in Charge of Production on three soap operas and a daytime talk show. It was not a creative job—he oversaw budgets and acted as messenger between the network and the producers—but it got him in the mix. He watched each episode scrupulously, gave notes promptly, and did not express any resentment when his suggestions were ignored.

Before Bobby was thirty he had his first hit, a game show he spotted in turnaround from daytime and grabbed for prime time. It was called *I'll Eat Anything!* and it was a summer phenomenon. The more pundits howled about a new low in America's public discourse, the bigger the ratings grew.

Bobby looked at his pale face in the lavatory mirror. He had invested everything he had in this job and after ten years it was gone. For what? All because he just had to win that last Friday night. They already had Sweeps sown up, but Bobby wanted a little more bubble in the champagne. So he looked the other way when the producers of *Lookers,* his biggest hit, fudged a little reality in their reality show. So what? The sweet girl won and the nasty girl lost. It was what America wanted. But that nasty girl was nasty off camera, too. She was a sore loser. She had to go whining to the press, and just like that, Bobby's lifetime of good work was destroyed.

He rinsed his mouth. He cleaned himself up. He got his breathing back to normal. He flashed through scenarios like he was clicking through channels. He tucked in his shirt and knocked on Howard Temple's door.

Howard was turned in his chair, speaking on his phone in a low, weary voice. Bobby recognized the tone at once. Howard was indulging in the Sacker's Prerogative. He was sadly telling his wife or a pal or some other confidant about what a rough day he was having, what a hard duty he'd had to perform firing that poor sap Bobby Kahn. Recognition stiffened Bobby's resentment. Here was the executioner looking for empathy, the soldier complaining about the burden of his atrocities. It was a form of subtle machismo. Poor me, it's so hard to be a powerful man with the lives of incompetents in my mighty hands. My grim duty exacts a terrible burden on my sensitive soul.

The pot-bellied hypocrite was milking sympathy for himself out of the pain he rained on Bobby! Although every part of him was struggling to suppress bitterness or personal animosity, Bobby could not help regarding his mentor at that moment as a pompous prick.

Bobby coughed. Howard looked up from the phone call. He covered the receiver and spoke like a gentle teacher calling on a handicapped child.

"Yes, Bob?"

"Howard, I'm sorry I reacted badly. Just taken by surprise." Howard began to tut-tut but Bobby cut him off. "Listen, I don't need severance, I don't need a production deal, I don't even need my contract paid out." Howard protested but Bobby pressed on. He felt a little of his old confidence. It was like when he rolled over Howard to get *Hollywood's Hidden Brothels* on the air.

Bobby said, "All I need, Howard, is for you to keep my leaving a complete secret for four weeks. I mean absolute J. Edgar Hoover, Price Waterhouse–level security. Who knows already?"

"Well, Bobby, I'm not sure. I mean, I suppose Personnel knows, and the executive committee. Obviously the brass knows."

"Press?"

"I doubt it."

"Wayne? Bruce? The other SVPs?"

"No."

"Then do this for me, Howard. Please. Get everyone who already knows to put a lid on it for four weeks. I'll get out of the office, you can say I'm on vacation. Let me find another job before this gets into the *Hollywood Reporter*. Just give me a shot at finding something else. Otherwise, this will kill me in the industry."

Bobby could see that Howard was unsteady. This firing was a PR move. The network wanted the scandal to go away quick. To sit on the announcement would be to invite more heat. Upstairs wanted a head right now.

"Come on, Howard," Bobby said. He said it with attitude. His juice was coming back. "You need me to take the blame for the *Lookers* scandal. If I go down quietly, you're off the hook. If I go down ugly, it just gets worse. And you know with me gone, you're the guy it gets to. Give me four weeks to find a soft place to land and I'll swallow that sword for you. Whether I find another job or not, I'll swallow it. You can get the Wise Men to wait that long for their chunk of meat."

Howard thought about his options. Bobby knew how it was. Once in a while a firee reacts in a way you don't expect. Then you have to improvise. But you can't stall, you can't let him get the upper hand. You can't let him leave the office with any questions still hanging, or you'll spend the next six months in litigation. You'll spend the next six months arbitrating "One More Thing"s.

Bobby figured that what Howard wanted most right then was to have Bobby out of the room. The older man seemed to be rolling something around in his mouth. He said, "Two weeks. I can't possibly get you more than that."

"Done deal. Two weeks, Howard. For real. Any whisper of this anywhere, any phone calls from colleagues asking me if I'm okay, any sign of sympathy from the security guard, and I am going to make the quiz-show scandals of the 1950s look like *Sesame Street.*"

"I don't like you threatening me, Bobby."

"I don't like you firing me, Howard. We all got stuff we don't like."

Bobby left fast. His adrenaline was up, his mouth tasted like tin. He shouldn't have been nasty at the end, but what the hell? He was fighting for his life. How long could he trust Howard to sit on this? Maybe one week. Long enough to shift the blame. Bobby had to move quickly if he was going to find another job in television while he was still a boy innovator, a young visionary, the unwed father of reality TV.

2.

That evening, while Bobby Kahn limped out to Massapequa to tell his fiancée, Marsha, that she would need to let some of the air out of her extravagant wedding plans, a thin man named Moe stood on a toilet in a locked stall in a public restroom in a small Native American museum in Pawcatuck, Connecticut.

The man squatted with his trousers up and a foot on either horn of the horseshoe-shaped seat. He had been crouched like this for two hours. After thirty minutes his legs had cramped painfully. After an hour and a half his grim determination was rewarded with numbness—an anesthesia which opened his awareness to another discomfort: He needed very much to urinate. The bowl seemed to beckon him. Moe shook off the temptation like a thirsty sailor resisting the salty sea. He was on a mission and would not falter. A ring of perspiration crept out from the rim of his curly toupee and settled along his pale, sloped forehead, just above the continuous eyebrow that stretched like a caterpillar from one side of his thin skull to the other. Moe breathed softly through his mouth. The pain in his urinary tract subsided. The voice from the bowl receded.

As Bobby Kahn drove out of the Midtown Tunnel and onto the Long Island Expressway, he was hit by successive waves of anxiety, dread, and shame. The bravado he had summoned in Howard Temple's office gave way. How could he tell the woman who loved him that he was a bum?

He counted down the exits to Massapequa like a condemned man watching the clock tick toward his execution.

Across Long Island Sound and up the New England coast, silence held dominion upon the Native American museum as Moe maintained his vigil. Only a few miles from Moe, two other men stood in the grand foyer of the Mystic Aquarium, studying a great black manta ray. The fish swam back and forth, languid and majestic in the window of an enormous tank.

The short, red-haired one vibrated with excitement. He wore a black turtleneck, black peacoat, black corduroy slacks, and black track shoes. His name was Kenny King and he was committing a crime. He could not have been more enthusiastic. It was Kenny who put Moe Notty in the toilet stall with orders to neither stir, sit, nor be seen until the Native American museum was locked for the night. Kenny would linger here at the aquarium with his confederate Sammy Bignose until they were sure the museum was closed and enough time had passed that there was no chance of some crafty Indian staying late and interfering with their felony.

It was almost time. Soon Kenny would buzz Moe's pager twice as a signal to sneak out of the restroom and unlock the back door. Kenny had been planning this robbery for weeks. He was the brains of the outfit.

While Kenny shivered and twitched in anticipation of the impending burglary, Sammy Bignose was entranced by the manta ray. Each time the dark creature swept by in its endless circle, slowly waving its great cape, Sammy was drawn further into hypnotic reverie.

"I wouldn't mind to be a fish," he thought as the manta glided past on a stream of bubbles. "Swim all night. . . . Coast. . . . Never get thirsty. . . . Never have to lift up anything heavy. Food swims right in your mouth. Just keep going, keep moving. Float sometimes. Not a bad life."

Sammy Bignose was as dim as his friend and coworker Moe Notty, but very few people recognized it. Moe breathed through his mouth and wore a bad hairpiece and smelled like a wet dog. Sammy Bignose had good manners and white teeth and a neat shag haircut and a round rosy face. He smiled often and had a good word for everyone. You had to get to know Sammy to realize how thick he was. Sammy himself didn't know it. His mother and sisters did but they never told him.

The only regret Sammy had in life was his unfortunate nickname. He was christened Santos Bigenos. It didn't take long for neighborhood wise guys to start calling him Bignose. Sammy's nose was not especially big, but he had given up protesting. His nose was inarguably irregular. It sloped to the left, like a skier changing his mind halfway down the hill. In profile, it descended from his head like a broken staircase. Santos Bigenos had been called Sammy Bignose for so long now that he hardly heard it anymore. He did note, admiringly, that the manta ray had no nose at all.

Kenny King jabbed Sammy Bignose in the ribs, breaking his reverie.

"Time to MOOOOVE," Kenny whispered with a taut grin that bared rows of tiny teeth. The conspirators walked briskly to the exit. Sammy looked back once at the manta ray.

When they reached the parking lot Kenny broke into a trot. He pulled out an electric key and beeped the locks on his black Land Rover. He hoisted himself up into the front seat like a small cowboy bounding onto a tall horse. Sammy Bignose, his faithful Tonto, took the seat beside him.

"Remember what we talked about, Ken," Sammy Bignose said gently. "Play it cool. Drive slow. Don't draw attention."

Kenny nodded, but excitement was flooding his system. He shifted the sport-utility vehicle into gear and tore out of the parking lot, spitting dirt and gravel.

Kenny killed his headlights while still on the main road. The Land Rover passed the museum and circled around and parked in the lot of the Big Pig mini-mart a block away.

As Kenny King and Sammy Bignose were sliding out of their get-away car, Bobby Kahn was pulling into the driveway of his fiancée's mother's home on Long Island. Bobby looked through the picture window at the sight of Marsha and her sister and her mom smiling and chatting over a thick bridal magazine. Bobby took a moment to burn the picture into his memory before he walked in and ruined it.

Inside the toilet stall of the Pawcatuck Native American museum, Moe remained crouched like a soldier waiting in ambush.

Behind the museum, Kenny drew a black knit wool cap from his pocket and pulled it over his head. Sammy Bignose was surprised to see that Kenny had cut two eyeholes into the cap.

"Whoa, Ken. We goin' in masked?"

Kenny turned the cap back up. "Just in case. Might have to run. Don't want the pigs to make us!"

"Make us what?"

"Identify us! What if there's hidden cameras?"

"Huh. I kinda wish you'd told me. I woulda brought a mask, too."

Kenny reached in his jacket and pulled out a pair of sunglasses. "Put these on." Sammy did so. Kenny nodded assurance, but he thought that if there were a security camera, Sammy's nose would give him away. "You got the bag?"

Sammy patted a mailman's sack slung by his hip.

"Let's go!"

In the silent men's room, Moe's buzzer beeped twice. The sudden noise startled him. He lost his balance and put one foot in the toilet. He made a watery path to the back door, which he unlocked and threw open.

He was shocked to look into the wild eyes of a masked man. He drew back, and saw his friend Sammy in sunglasses.

"Let us in!" the masked man cried. It was Kenny. Moe fell back and let his two comrades inside.

"Why you wearin' sunglasses, Sammy?"

"No names!" Kenny hissed.

"Why you wearin' a mask, Ken?"

Kenny made a sound like he was strangling and gestured toward a long glass casket on the other side of the room.

"Your leg's wet, man," Sammy said softly to Moe. "You okay?"

Moe nodded quickly. He didn't want to have to explain to Kenny that he stepped in the toilet. It was the kind of thing Kenny would bring up forever.

Kenny's attention was on the glass casket. Within lay the bones of what was alleged to have been an ancient Mohegan Indian. The disposition of the skeleton had come to Kenny's attention through newspaper accounts of protests from the Native American community over the disrespect indicated by putting a dead Indian's bones on public display. Had the Pawcatuck Native American museum been run by whites, the skeleton would have already been reinterred.

The argument was complicated by the museum's being operated by descendants of Wampanoags and Pequots, while the protesters were from families involved in the operation of the nearby Narragansett gambling casino. The Museum Indians called attention to the dubious genealogies of the Casino Indians, many of whom resembled the Portuguese, Cape Verdian, and even Swedish settlers with whom the Narragansetts' blood had mingled. That the administrative director of the casino, Frank Strongbow, had been born Francis O'Connor was a further impediment to fraternity between the tribes.

Insults were thrown back and forth, disparaging accusations about who were the real Indians and who were the exploiters. The Museum Indians mocked the Casino Indians for decorating their gaming rooms with Big Chief stereotypes, selling tobacco in "Smoke Signal Shops," and peddling souvenir tomahawks, peace pipes, and feather headdresses.

The Casino Indians accused the Museum Indians of envy. There was a lot of bad blood all around. As had happened so often in the history of relations between Native Americans and colonists in New England, the feuding and divisions between the tribes opened the door for dishonest white men to come in and loot the wampum. Kenny King was one such white man.

In Massapequa, Bobby's fiancée was not taking his bad news well. It could have occurred to her that this might be a moment to cast aside her own disappointment, embrace her future husband on his hard day, and stroke his brow while vowing that these material things did not matter. It did not. She demanded in increasingly hysterical tones to know what he had done wrong. Why he had made everyone at his job hate him. Had he done this deliberately to ruin the wedding into which she had poured so much time and attention? Under the heat of these accusations, Bobby's guilt began to bake into anger.

In Pawcatuck, Kenny was a little pissed himself. His diamond glass cutter was not doing the job the way he had seen it done by covert operatives on *24*. He was scratching the glass brutally, but it was not slicing neatly like cardboard under a razor. His suction cup was not sticking. His breath was fogging up the glass casket, and he was sweating like a hamster in a sock.

"Want me to try, Ken?" Sammy Bignose offered.

"No names!" Kenny grunted. He had one foot on the floor and the other on the sarcophagus. To gain leverage, he lifted his foot off the floor, lay on his belly on the casket, and pushed the glass cutter down with both hands. He was face to face with the skeleton. There was some give. The blade pushed through the glass with a small pop. Kenny smiled and began to draw the blade along. There was a shiver and a lurch and then to his horror he heard a sharp snap like a shotgun. A web of cracks bloomed beneath him. He fell through the glass with a crash, landing on the bones of the last Mohegan.

Kenny screamed and Moe and Sammy ran to haul him out. They got him on his feet and brushed him up and down to see if he was cut as he shook uncontrollably. He appeared not to be hurt, there was no blood or visible rips in his black clothes. Kenny regained his equilibrium and realized that if any policemen, Wampanoag warriors, or nosy neighbors were within the sound of his screams, he and his crew had better beat it quick or get caught vandalizing a historic corpse.

Kenny ordered Sammy to load the bones into his mail sack fast, and the three burglars made for the back door. They could not bring themselves to move slowly through the parking lot.

As they reached the car, Kenny turned to Sammy. "Did you do the dog?"

"Dog?"

"The dog, Sammy! Your only part of the job, remember?! Tell me you put the dog in the display case!"

Sammy resented the suggestion that this was the only part of his job—as if he had not shared equally in the risks and responsibility for the entire mission. But he knew Kenny, and he knew that Kenny would get petulant as the embarrassment of his panic in front of his subordinates sunk in.

Sammy reached in his mail sack, pushed aside the Mohegan bones, and pulled out a small stuffed toy bulldog dressed in a blue and white Yale University sweater.

"I forgot the dog, Kenny."

"Dammit, Sammy! How could you screw that up! Moe and I executed our responsibilities like clockwork. Well, move fast. You gotta go back in."

"Oh come on, Kenny! The cops will be here any second. . . ."

"Better move fast, then!"

Sammy knew not to argue. He handed Moe the bag of bones and ran back into the museum with the toy dog. Once inside, though, he did not put the dog in the casket as Kenny wanted. He tossed it on the floor and ran out again. Partly it was fear that the police would show and Kenny would take off without him. But it was also the sort of subtle resistance Kenny inspired in all of the employees he bullied and mocked. Something in Kenny made people who worked for him want to screw up in little ways he could never prove.

The SUV was already rolling when Sammy opened the back door and climbed in.

"Dog placed properly?" Kenny called from behind the wheel.

"Dog in place," Sammy answered.

"Skeleton on board and accounted for?"

"Skeleton on board," Moe replied. Kenny was too nervous to talk anymore. He went down the side streets at sixty miles an hour and hit eighty going up the on-ramp to the interstate. Only when the black

Land Rover had crossed from Connecticut into Rhode Island did his anxiety break into elation.

"We did it!" Kenny cackled. "EEEE hee hee hee hee! Moe, nobody saw you go into the restroom?"

"I don't think so, Ken."

"EX-cellent. Now you know, Sam, it's so important that you put that bulldog in the display case where the bones were. That's gonna make sure the cops never suspect us."

Sammy grunted. He knew that Kenny was now going to try to rewrite how the whole thing went down, leaving out the part where he got scared and started screaming, giving himself all the credit. Fine with Sam. He knew how Kenny was. He was used to it.

"See, when the cops see the Yale bulldog, they're gonna think this was the work of Skull and Bones." Kenny had to do the speech again. Sammy thought Kenny often believed he was on television and had to give occasional plot summaries, like TV detectives do after commercial breaks.

"Skull and Bones are famous for stealing skeletons. They keep them in a secret vault in New Haven. They've got Abe Lincoln, Annie Oakley, some mummies, all kinds of famous bones down there."

Moe squinted in confusion. He said, "Abraham Lincoln's skeleton is in a fraternity house in New Haven? I thought he was in the Lincoln Memorial."

"Well, no one can PROVE Skull and Bones has him," Kenny said. "But the government knows. See, Skull and Bones' members are, like, the Bushes and the head of the CIA and the Trilateral Commission, Kissinger, the Clintons, the people who own the *New York Times,* the Saudis. If the cops think Skull and Bones stole this skeleton, they won't ask too many questions. It's like *The X-Files.*"

Kenny looked over his shoulder at Sam and said, "So, Sammy, putting that bulldog in there was really important. When we use these bones, no one will make the connection with the Indian museum. The authorities will blame it on Yale and that'll be the end of it."

Sam knew that this was Kenny's way of offering a peace pipe. He was giving Sammy credit for an important part of the mission they had accomplished together. Sammy smiled. The only friends Kenny had were the people who worked for him.

They got off the highway at the Wyoming, Rhode Island, exit, took the back roads down to the ocean, and followed the shore road home. They drove into the village of New Bedlam and dropped Moe at his mother's house. Next was Sammy at his condo. Kenny gave him an elaborate series of high-fives and knuckle brushes.

Kenny King drove past the Hungry Horse Tavern, the Steak & Shake, the hardware store, the fish market, the bakery, the French Catholic church, the Italian Catholic church, and the Portuguese Catholic church and turned toward the marina. He pulled into the first reserved parking space in front of the old Victorian house that was headquarters of King Cable Television.

Upstairs in his office he slid the stolen bones into narrow cloth sheaths designed for golf clubs. He gathered the sheaths and slipped them into an old golf bag. He opened a closet door, bent down, and pried up two boards from the floor. He lowered the bones of the Mohegan into the hole, replaced the planks, and covered his hiding place with a small green rug and a framed pastel painting of the stars of the television series *21 Jump Street*.

Down the coast and across the Sound, Bobby Kahn walked out of a familiar house for the last time. He looked back at the picture window. His fiancée was crying in the arms of her sister and mother. Her lack of sympathy for Bobby had culminated in a series of recriminations that ended with her accusing him of not having ever wanted to marry her at all. Bobby, hurt and humiliated and beaten down from a terrible day, had not elected to deny it. He had only meant to give back a little of what he was getting, but it had gone too far. In the end, he would have had to go back into the room with all the angry relatives and humble himself in front of them, and he just did not have it in him to do that.

Somehow, to his astonishment, he didn't even feel that bad. Standing outside the picture window looking in, he was reminded of the way he sometimes used to feel when he canceled a beloved TV series: a little sad to see it go, a little sensitive that the actors would not like him anymore, but also proud of his power and the cool detachment he could summon to wield it.

3.

obby collapsed into his airplane seat exhausted. He had fought with his taxi driver over the best route to take to beat the rush-hour traffic to JFK and was sure that the cabbie had driven into the worst bumper-to-bumper construction mess in the five boroughs out of spite.

Check-in did nothing to sooth his anxiety. The airline was practicing tough love with its corporate passengers and the woman behind the counter refused to upgrade Bobby to first class on air miles alone. The full cost of a first-class ticket was two thousand, two hundred and eight dollars, and did he wish to purchase one? Bobby pointed out that he was already holding an eighteen-hundred-dollar business-class ticket and as he had many thousands of frequent-flier miles, a platinum card, and flew this airline at least twice a month, she should just give him a seat up front if one was sitting empty.

He knew the airlines were having tough times and trying to force business travelers to spend full fare; the unspoken subtext was, hey, it's not YOUR money. In this case, though, it was. Bobby had paid for his own ticket to Los Angeles, the first time he could remember doing that since college, and he was determined to use his miles to get the rest of the way up the plane. It was not a matter of luxury. He was flying to California under the pretext of network business to try to drop in on as many potential new employers as possible. He had lined up lunch with a sitcom producer, dinner with a big syndicator, and a tentative golf game with a former subordinate now doing well at a rival network. Bobby was going to have to shovel a lot of schmooze in the next few days, and he could blow the whole thing if anyone from the industry saw him sitting anywhere but first class.

"You know," he said to the clerk with what sweetness he could summon, "my company spends about a hundred thousand dollars on this airline every week. I've always found you folks pretty reasonable about bumping me up if there's an empty seat in first."

"It's not first, sir, it's premium."

"Premium."

She clicked through her computer screen. She seemed to be taking longer than necessary. Finally she said, "We do have one seat open in premium. How would you like to pay for it?"

Bobby pointed again to his Platinum Miles card on the counter. The woman said, "It will cost you ten thousand air miles plus a same-day access fee of seventy-five dollars."

"Fine," said Bobby. She took a phone call. Bobby boiled. Eventually she printed out a green and white computer card, drew lines through it, scribbled all over its face, and told him he better hurry, the flight was about to board and it was at the very last gate at the farthest archipelago of the terminal.

He thanked her for taking such good care of him and smiled.

By the time Bobby cleared security, he had heard the final boarding call for Flight 104 to Los Angeles. He hopped down the corridor and into the tunnel with his bag, his overcoat, his belt, and his unlaced shoes in his hand. His wristwatch, keys, pen, and other items that might ring a bell were all shoved in the pocket of his suitcase, from which nickels, dimes, and quarters were falling and bouncing onto the airport carpet.

His stress fell away when he reached the first-class cabin. His seat was deep and wide. He checked to make sure the armrest contained all the amenities. A personal movie screen. A computerized flight map. A set of fancy padded headphones the size of Mickey Mouse ears. He had not lucked into one of the mobile couch pods that swing around on a turret and allow you to camp out for your flight in a space-age pup tent, but his seat did recline all the way back to flat.

After settling himself he glanced around the cabin. He saw no familiar faces, no opportunities. As the flight attendants closed the cabin doors, he realized that first class was almost deserted. At least he would have privacy. He pulled out his mobile phone for a last check-in before he had to switch off. His voice mail contained nothing important, no last-minute messages from the LA moguls he was hoping to see when he landed. Also, no message from his ex-fiancée, Marsha. No doubt then—this was not a spat, this was not a fight to be fixed. His marriage was off.

Bobby took comfort in how badly Marsha took the news. She pretty much accused him of conspiring to get himself fired so he would not have to pay for a wedding in Tuscany. He now had someone to condemn for his misery besides himself. Every man who suffers a setback in his professional life looks for a way to blame his wife. Marsha made it easy.

She was a weight he no longer needed to bear. He had to be able to move fast now, sleep rough, improvise, and live off the land. What he needed now was—was *nimbility* a word?—he needed nimbility. He was on a plane to California and he would not come back without a new job in broadcasting. He would not come back without a map of his next five years.

The seat-belt light came on. Bobby straightened his chair and a tall man suddenly loomed next to him.

"Mind if I climb over?" the man said. He motioned toward the window seat next to Bobby. Where did this guy come from? Bobby wondered. They closed the door of the plane five minutes ago.

The man looked like a tennis pro or a sailboat captain. He had thick black hair, pale blue eyes, and a long, lean frame. He was wearing no overcoat, just a tailored blue suit and white shirt. He had a red kerchief in his breast pocket. His long feet were wrapped in fancy sandals. He carried only a small leather satchel.

The man slid into his chair and did not buckle his seat belt as the plane started down the runway. As soon as the wheels were off the ground, while they were still climbing at a hard angle, the man stood again and said, "Mind if I just stash my jacket in the overhead?" Bobby pulled back his feet. They were at a forty-five-degree incline and shaking. The man strolled into the aisle as if he were walking up the steps to his house. Perhaps a stewardess waved to admonish him—all Bobby saw was the man flash his enormous white teeth in a smile and point with casual elegance to someone down the aisle.

The guy even smelled good. Maybe he was a sportscaster. When the plane straightened out, the stranger looked around the cabin and said, "Lot of empty seats. I might move over." With that he was gone.

The tall man settled into a seat in the next to last row, checked to see that the flight attendant was not looking, and switched on his mobile phone. He checked his voice mail. A couple of confirmations of meetings in LA, a reminder from his wife about a birthday party, and three messages from his lunatic stepbrother Kenny about some top-secret endeavor that could not be discussed over the phone. God knows what scheme Kenny and his lunkheads had set off on this time. He deleted the messages.

His phone said, "One new message has been added since the start of this session." He hit the button.

"Skyler, hi, it's Ann. Sorry I missed you. I really wanted to talk to you before you go into those meetings in California. I have some ideas for the sort of properties we should add to Eureka. Call me back, okay? Bye."

Skyler King had been avoiding his sister, Ann, all week. Skyler's family controlled a lucrative cable TV service monopoly in the Northeast. They also owned three local shoestring cable channels that no one watched and only got carried because they owned the distribution network. Skyler had told his partners and the people who worked for him that he was going to California to look at new TV formats. That was true but that was not his priority. Skyler was going to LA to talk to media consultants and interview television executives. He was looking for a head of programming, a new boss to run his family's cable networks.

He needed someone with a special combination of attributes. He needed someone very good and very desperate.

Bobby focused on the work ahead of him. He had a lot to do when he landed. He was scared that word of his firing would arrive before he did. He had taken a big chance the day before with a headhunter who called him for a recommendation on an ex-colleague.

"Tell me about Bill Foster," the headhunter said after the usual chitchat.

"Good guy, works hard," Bobby said. "What's the job?"

"Head of scheduling and promos."

"Which network?"

"Well, Bob, I can't say."

"See, I think Foster would be great at CBS, probably okay at NBC or ABC. If it's CW or Fox, it might be more of a stretch."

"Why do you say?"

"I mean, Foster's a great guy. He and I worked very well together. I think he'd be good for anything."

"But why would he be better at one of the old places?"

"Listen, Tom, this is not in any way a put-down of Foster."

"No."

"It's just an observation about his taste."

"That's valuable."

"Foster doesn't really like the way the business has gone. He's a pro, he gets it, he'll do what he has to do—but he has not embraced the new era with open arms. He still thinks of the reality shows, the T&A, as something you have to do in order to justify, I don't know, paying for *Nightline* or something. Foster has refined taste. He came up in the days of *Cosby* and *Cheers.* He's not thinking multiplatform."

"That's a very useful insight, Bob."

"I mean," here Bobby stuck out his toe to let the lion lick it, "we all feel that way sometimes. It would be nice if you could still get a rating with a news documentary or *M*A*S*H,* but those days are gone. Sometimes I look around here and I wonder if the fellows upstairs really understand that we are not living through an aberration. TV is never going to go back to being scripted sitcoms that run for eight years and shows about private eyes."

"No."

"Frankly, Tom, I sometimes think I wouldn't mind running one of the young networks, getting in with some people who are not so set in their ways."

The headhunter took a moment. "But you'd never leave there, right?"

"Of course, it's been home to me for ten years. But between you and me, Tom, if the right thing came along, I would look at it seriously. I don't know if I want to spend my entire career in one place."

Bobby worried he'd gone too far. He added, "Of course, these guys have been great to me. I mean, I have a lot of loyalty to Howard. I'm just shooting my mouth off."

"Well, listen, would it be okay if I called you once in a while to feel you out on things?"

Bobby clenched his fist. "Well, sure. You know, it doesn't hurt to talk."

Once you floated your name down the headhunter river it was only a matter of days before everyone in the business knew you were in play. Maybe that was a good thing. It was all new to Bobby. Hope jostled with a dread of humiliation in his mind.

He checked his itinerary. He had to cover a lot of ground. A party for one of the stars of the network's top drama at the home of a Beverly Hills philanthropist. A meeting with the costar of a successful sitcom on another network who had a new show to pitch. A network press tour in Pasadena. And six or seven tentative breakfasts, lunches, and drinks with friends and former associates, any of which might turn into a job opportunity. He had to keep his attitude up.

God, he hated feeling like a beggar.

He flipped through his personal movie choices, settled on *Two and a Half Men*, and went right to sleep.

4.

alifornia brought out competing emotions in Bobby Kahn. A
child of television, he always got a charge driving down the
streets where Rockford chased the crooks and the 90210 kids
went to high school. He could not drive past Melrose Place without
slowing down to see if Heather Locklear was on the balcony in a
teddy.

As a television professional, though, he drew a line between real
network executives like himself, who worked in New York and bought
the programs and looked at the business objectively, and LA poseurs
who made and sold the programs and nine times out of ten gave in to
delusions of celebrity by association.

There was an old media proverb: At some point the fellow who
owns the airline starts thinking he can fly the plane. It was Bobby's
experience that television executives in Los Angeles almost always
ended up imagining they were the Talent. Maybe it was proximity to
all the loose blond women, maybe it was spending too much time in
the sun. Bobby had seen it again and again. Take a sensible executive
from New York, leave him in California for six months, and he starts
dressing like a TV cop and driving a hot rod and kissing people he
doesn't know. After a year comes the hair weave. Two years, the chin
tuck. Then you're looking at liposuction. Pretty soon you're arguing
to keep failing shows on the air for all kinds of dubious reasons. It had
been the ruin of many a good man.

There was some part of Bobby that wanted to test his will against such coercion. He always thought that any exec who came to LA and did not lose his head would have a tremendous advantage. But he was a New Yorker, with all of the New Yorker's prejudices. He hoped that this trip to the West Coast would allow him to find a new job back in Manhattan. If not, if he had to stay here for a year or two until he recovered his power, well, he might get a tan but he would never, ever get a trainer.

He checked back with his office in New York to see if any of his tentatives had confirmed. His secretary, Carol, was not there. Even in the best of times she viewed his business trips as permission to spend the day roaming the halls, gossiping in the kitchenette, and going out for muffins. He dialed the number for voice mail.

"You have nineteen new messages.

"Message one. Eight fifteen a.m. today." This was before Carol would have arrived; the message had gone straight to phone mail.

"This is for Bob Kahn. This is Michael Barnett's office calling. Mr. Kahn, Mr. Barnett is sorry but he will not be able to have lunch with you this week. He is going to Africa on Safari." Click.

"Message two. Nine eleven a.m. today." Carol still wasn't in.

"Bobby, Rob Benson! Good to hear from you. Listen, I'm booked up all week with this press tour, but I wonder if you might be able to get together today when you get in? I'm around till about two thirty. Call me."

Damn, Bobby thought, it's after three now. I wish Carol had gotten that one.

He clicked through all his messages. Each told him of another time when Carol was not at her desk, not answering the phone, not being where she was paid to be. Some of the messages were very important, some were not, but none of them had found anyone on the other end of the line when they called the office of a man who was very anxious to be seen as an important executive.

Message eighteen had been left at two thirty p.m. It was Carol. "Bob, it's me. It's been really quiet here, the phone has hardly rung. Your mother called but I told her you were out of town and she said she'd call you on your cell. Someone from the ACLU called to see if you were coming to that dinner at the Waldorf. That's about it. It's been really quiet. I'm going to go to lunch now, so if you can't find me that's where I am."

Bobby wondered if she knew he was being fired. After all, she had to think about her job, too. Maybe she was going on interviews. If Carol knew, he might as well take out an ad in *Variety.* She'd tell anyone who called. If she were ever at her desk when the phone rang.

He made it to his first meeting five minutes early. He was having drinks with two agents and a supporting actress from a popular comedy on another network. She had a series idea, apparently. It could not be too good, Bobby figured, or her own network would want it. Still, this was the trip where he was keeping his ears open. Maybe if her idea was strong, Bobby could attach himself to it. He was keeping his antennae erect.

The young agents were on time for the meeting. The actress was almost thirty minutes late. She did not apologize. One of the agents said she had been on the set all night. They made small talk in front of Bobby to show how close they all were. She ordered tea with honey and sent it back before Bobby suggested they talk business.

"Madeline has come to us with a concept we think is very exciting," said Agent One.

"It's something I thought of myself," Madeline explained.

"The agency heard it and, frankly, we fell off our chairs," Agent Two said.

Bobby was really trying to maintain a positive attitude, but these two boy agents rubbed him the wrong way. They were all of a type— pumped up, arrogant, tucked into designer suits that might have worked on Saturday night at the singles bar but smelled desperate at a Tuesday meeting.

Bobby watched them with the sound turned off. They talked across each other and eyed the actress as if worried she might forget they were there. They slid their business cards across the table like Atlantic City blackjack dealers. He sure did need a job, but could he really spend every day with people like this?

They were letting the actress talk now. Bobby turned up the sound.

"So the idea is, like, *Star Search* in a prison. You take all these hard criminals with tattoos and scars and, like, one tells jokes and another sings 'Over the Rainbow.'"

"You hear their stories, too," Agent Two said.

"Get the background on their crimes," Agent One added. "Their life stories, what drove them to do what they did. Like those packages on the Olympics that tell you who the athlete is and make you really want to root for him."

"And at the end of the season," the actress went on, "you have, like, a face-off between all the weekly winners, and whoever gets the most votes from the audience at home gets a parole."

"Well," Agent One said, "that's up to the governor, I suppose, but I dare say that if the people of America are voting to give one of these guys a second chance . . ."

"And there's every possibility of a recording contract or acting role," Agent Two said, "so it's not like the winner's going to have to steal again. . . ."

"Recidivate," Agent One said. "That's a word, right?"

For all their practiced aplomb, the young agents carried with them an air of suppressed hunger. It made Bobby feel cocky by comparison. As they laid out their pitch they could hear how stupid it sounded. These were men who rehearsed their confidence in front of a mirror. Bobby imagined they went home to studio apartments in Century City with no furniture except a bed, barbells, and a flat-screen TV.

They waited for Bobby to say something. It was hard to know where to begin.

"You'd be in this?" he said to the actress.

"Well, I could make special appearances," she said cautiously.

"And do publicity," Agent Two said quickly. "Madeline would be available for press and promotion and be on the show as needed."

"She is executive producer," Agent One explained.

"Along with our boss, of course."

"And Dick Dalva. You know him. Real pro. Did those ice-skating specials for CBS, created the America First Awards. He'd handle a lot of the day-to-day."

"I mean, I could be," Madeline said.

"Madeline's got obligations to *The Northups*, of course," Agent One said, referring to the series on which she played the sexy bad daughter.

"So you're not leaving *The Northups*," Bobby said.

They all laughed and chattered "No" at the same time. Bobby wondered if she was getting fired, too. They all looked at him again.

"Well, gee," he said carefully. "It's an interesting idea. I have a couple of practical concerns." They leaned toward him and stared. "First, I'm not sure this is a moment in America where people are feeling a lot of sympathy for convicted criminals. I mean, what if the victims of these . . . contestants object to the premise of making stars out of them?"

Madeline said, "The Bible teaches us to forgive and forget. These people are just like you and me except they made one mistake."

Bobby rolled that around for a moment. "That's a very generous attitude, Madeline. But it's possible many viewers will be less understanding. It just seems to me like the potential for bad publicity is pretty severe."

"No such thing as bad publicity," Agent One said with a forced laugh. It was starting to dawn on him that the meeting was a bust and he wanted to get out of there.

"Then," Bobby said, lowering his voice, "there's the race issue."

Madeline and the agents looked at him stupidly. He'd have to say it. "Well, isn't the prison population disproportionately black? I don't think a penitentiary talent show is going to have a whole lot of 'Over the Rainbow.' I think it will be a lot of gangster rap."

"With real gangsters!" Agent Two said. "That's a hook right there!"

"I don't know," Bobby said. "Do you have any footage for me to look at?"

They shook their heads. "We wanted to bring it to you first," Agent Two told him. "We want whoever options this project to have input into the pilot from day one."

"I could be on it more often," Madeline said suddenly. At last she sensed that the pitch was not going well.

"Look," Bobby said, signaling the waiter to bring the tab. "It sounds like something that might work better for FX than for us, but I'm very open to hearing more about it and looking at any footage you put together."

They got out of the restaurant as fast as they could, with false smiles and bone-squeezing handshakes.

Bobby got back in his car and checked his phone mail again. Four more messages, no sign of his secretary. What a discouraging way to begin his secret job search. He decided to check into his hotel and take a swim. He had that Beverly Hills suck-up session at eight. There would be a lot of powerful people there. He had to be at his best.

As he pulled away he saw Madeline the actress yelling at Agent One on the corner as he tried to placate her. A short Mexican woman in a track suit was standing a few feet away from them, holding up her cell phone to take a photo of the fight.

5.

kyler King stood at the window of the living room of his suite on the sixth floor of the Beverly Hills Four Seasons Hotel, talking on his cell phone while assessing himself in a mirror. He was getting a few streaks of white in his thick black mane, which he rather liked. He was bored with being great-looking. He wanted to be dignified.

"Captain Hook can fly, honey? Wow, that must have been scary. I wish I'd seen that movie. Do you think we can rent it again so I can watch it with you? Great. Okay, Maudie, put Mommy on, okay? Thanks, sweetie. I love you."

He took three steps toward the closet. The connection crackled and was lost. How come that always happened in expensive hotels? he wondered. Skyler had a theory. The advent of mobile phones had cost the hotel industry millions of dollars in phone charges. Skyler suspected some hotels were fighting back with low-level electronic signals designed to disrupt cell-phone service. Why not? No law against it. Damn clever really. He moved to the window and called back his wife.

He raised his arm and sniffed. He smelled good.

In an airy beachfront home in New Bedlam, Rhode Island, Claudia King took the phone from her daughter and said hello to her husband.

"Annie's here," she told him. "You want to say hi?"

Oh hell, Skyler thought, she caught me. His half sister, Ann, was a nice kid, but Skyler felt about her the way a man of the world might feel about an illegitimate child. It was easy to forget she existed, and often inconvenient when she showed up.

Annie's British accent came over the line. "Hello, Sky! How are you? How's California?"

"I'm on to some interesting stuff here. Couple of big ideas I'm anxious to talk with you about. For the channels."

Skyler hoped that Annie's being out of college now would not mean she would start taking her partnership in King Cable too seriously. He already had to handle their bullying father and the lunatic Kenny. Skyler did not need any more cooks at the stove.

Annie said, "You're buying up U.S. rights to foreign programs or something? Looking for the next Pop Idol?"

"Maybe so," Skyler said. He was walking around the room trying to find a spot where his phone would fail. Never when you need it. "I'm just snooping around. Anyway, I'll fill you in when I get back. Claudia told you we're having the big party on the Fourth."

"I wouldn't miss it."

"Great. Is Claudia still there?"

His wife was gone. He could hear the kids squealing in the background and general pandemonium in the New Bedlam kitchen. Claudia had walked away and left him with his half sister.

"Guess I lost them," Skyler said. "Well okay, Annie. I'm late for a meeting, but I can't wait to bring you up to speed back at the reservation. So long now." And he was gone.

Annie knew that was probably the longest conversation she would have with Skyler all summer. She reminded herself that she was a grown woman now, an equal partner. Annie's father might have given her a channel as a pacifier, a tax dodge, or a consolation prize for having ignored her since she was five years old. That didn't matter. Annie was determined to claim what was hers, including her place in the King family. She had as much right to be in New Bedlam as any of them. Her big brother would have to get used to taking her seriously. King Cable was her business, too.

She thought of what one of the producers at Eureka! The Arts Channel had said about Skyler: "Your brother's got a whole lot of Noblesse and zero Oblige."

Half an hour later Skyler climbed into the BMW convertible he had ordered delivered to the hotel and took off for the home of Rita McVinney, philanthropist, author, and widow of Hollywood super-agent Russ "The Bishop" McVinney. A child bride in the great man's old age, Rita had become the Pamela Harriman of Beverly Hills: hostess, political activist, and arbiter of good taste. Rita was throwing a party tonight for Mark Cutler, the handsome star of the hit TV series *Court of Appeals.* The party was ostensibly to celebrate the acclaim Cutler was winning for his first major film role. It was likely that it was being paid for by the television studio that produced *Court of Appeals* as part of their efforts to keep their leading man from bolting to the big screen. It would be the way of television to toast and fete the charismatic Cutler's success in public, while privately making sure his representatives knew that any attempt by him to leave *C of A* before his five-year contract had been honored would result in a lawsuit so enormous, a smear campaign so dirty, and a blacklisting so thorough as to shame Roy Cohn.

Driving through the warm LA evening with the top down and his sunglasses on, Skyler felt like Steve McQueen. His lawyer had put him in touch with another lawyer who set up this invitation and told him who he needed to meet. Skyler knew that King Cable would be a tough sell to the kind of executive he hoped to attract, but he had great confidence in his own charisma. Skyler had been talking less attractive people into doing what he wanted his whole life. And, God above, if there was one thing he loved about Hollywood, it was the desperate need of the homely people to make the beautiful ones like them.

As Skyler drove west, Bobby Kahn approached Mrs. McVinney's from the other direction. Bobby had checked into his usual room at Shutters on the Beach in Santa Monica. He swam, showered, and checked his voice mail four more times, but no one was looking for him. Even the Shutters restaurant, where he could usually find at least one or two showbiz big shots, was void of all honchos. He drank a beer at the bar as slowly as he could and gave up hoping someone would walk in and hire him. There was nothing for Bobby to do but head to Beverly Hills.

As he drove out of the hotel an Eagles song came on the car radio. Something about the music and the buzz from the beer and the sun setting over the ocean cheered him up. Okay, so suppose he had to move to Los Angeles for a while. How bad would that be? He was single now, right? Young TV exec in a bachelor pad on the Pacific? He was carried up by a feeling he sometimes got when he was overtired in California: "What's so bad about this? Who says life has to be hard? Why *can't* it be sunny all the time?"

He passed a car wash with a neon marquee like a movie theater. "TONIGHT—ON THE HOSE—DENNIS LAMENDOLA and working the soap machine J. D. HORNOFF."

That's what's remarkable about this place, Bobby figured. The best-looking kid in every high school in America gets told over and over, "You're so attractive, you should go to Hollywood." And about one out of ten of them believes it. Thousands and thousands of boys and girls with no acting talent, no connections, nothing to go on but good looks arrive here and find a place to live and get a job to tide them over till they get discovered. They work in a market or flip burgers or pump gas or wash cars. After a while, they realize that they're never going to get in the movies. But they marry other good-looking losers and have beautiful kids and eventually they get to manage the market or run the burger joint or open their own gas station. When they do they put up neon lights or name it after a classic movie or hang up pictures of famous actors behind the counter, and they feel a little like they're part of it after all. And the funny thing is, they are.

Bobby checked himself in the mirror. Marsha always told him he was handsome. He liked thinking so. God knows, though, she was wrong about everything else.

Luxury cars were parked all along the winding side streets of a green and prosperous neighborhood where uniformed valets ran up and down trying to make sure that none of the well-exercised power brokers had to walk more than ten feet. It looked like a particularly festive funeral procession. Skyler pulled his rented car up tight along-side a Bentley, boxing it in, and left the keys in the ignition in case anyone had to move it.

He strolled past little knots of rich people on the front lawn and into a home that looked like an old mosque captured by the Spanish and decorated by Zorro. A three-story foyer rose up to reveal balustrades and little bridges. A string quartet was playing on one of the bal-conies, hung up there like ornaments on a Christmas tree. Servants circulated with trays of champagne, red wine, and sparkling water. A chef was shredding beef off what looked like a baseball bat made of meat. Straight ahead the charming hostess was hanging on the arm of the charismatic television star whose success they were all there to celebrate.

Skyler went straight up to them and introduced himself. He told her she had a lovely home and told him he was a big fan. Two or three more polite volleys and he was able to move on into the billiards room, where he could begin sniffing out moguls.

Outside, Bobby Kahn searched for a parking place. Look at that, some jerk just double-parked in front of that Bentley and walked away. He was going off California again. He needed another beer.

When Bobby came into the billiards room, Skyler was chatting with the wife of Mrs. McVinney's tae kwon do instructor and looking for an escape. The two men made eye contact and half nodded. Each thought he knew the other from somewhere but was not sure. Bobby assumed Skyler was an actor. Skyler thought he might have seen Bobby's picture in the paper.

Skyler waited for the woman talking to him to pause for a breath. He said, "Say, can I get you another drink?" Her glass was full. "I'll be right back."

He walked toward Bobby and put out his hand. "Hi. Skyler King."

"Bob Kahn. How's this party looking, Skyler?"

"Watch out for the lady I was talking to. She has some real estate she wants to unload."

Bobby smiled and took a sip of his beer. He surveyed the room. One or two familiar faces, including the head of daytime scheduling at his own place, who seemed surprised to see him. Nobody important yet.

"So how's life in California?" Bobby asked the tall man. How did he know him? Was he on *Desperate Housewives*?

"Seems pleasant. I'm an East Coast boy."

"Me too."

"How do you know Rita?"

"I don't really. Cutler is with our network. *Court of Appeals*."

"Ah, and what do you do at the network, Bob?"

Bobby explained that he was Senior Vice President of Programming. Skyler seemed impressed. Who was this guy? Bobby wondered. Maybe one of those auteur producers? Maybe HBO?

"You in the business?" Bobby asked.

"When I come to a bash like this, I sometimes wonder," Skyler said. Bobby looked at Skyler's watch. He was rich anyway.

They were interrupted by a man with long white hair in an expensive suit and a T-shirt.

"Skyler?" the man said. "Scott Brebner!"

"Oh, Scott!" Skyler smiled. This was the friend of his lawyer who had set up his schedule. "Good to see you. You know Bob Kahn?"

Bobby didn't think so but the white-haired man recognized Bobby's name.

"I don't know if we've ever actually met," Brebner said, "but we travel in the same circles. You do some work with my colleague Tom Jackson, don't you, Bob?"

Goddamn it, Bobby thought. Tom Jackson the headhunter. Was word already out? Did this stranger know Bobby was looking for a job? How many people at the party had heard? The West Coast scheduling guy from the network still had not come over to say hello. Had he sniffed rumors Bobby was out? Had everyone? Was this whole trip a fool's errand? If he could not trust his old friend Howard to protect his job, why the hell would he trust him to keep his secret?

He had to say something. "Tom and I just spoke a couple of days ago."

"Yes," Brebner said. He turned his attention back to Skyler. "Now, Sky, there's a couple of people here I want you to meet. I just saw Randall Maine in the bar. He did some good work for Turner."

Bobby knew Randy Maine. Randy had come to see him looking for a job months ago. Who was this guy Skyler?

"Nice meeting you, Bob," Skyler said as Brebner took him by the elbow.

"You, too," Bobby said, and raised his beer in salute. "By the way, Skyler. What do you do?"

"I run a little cable operation in New England and upstate New York."

Bobby relaxed. That was it. Cable operator. Small-time. "What's the company?" he asked.

"King Cable," Skyler King said. "Cape Cod, New Hampshire, part of Vermont, Rhode Island, up by Rochester and Syracuse, central Mass."

"That's a lot of territory."

"Yah. It's fun, you know? Get to know the different communities."

Sounds like my idea of hell, Bobby thought. He'd never heard of King Cable but he could imagine the lay of it. In the late seventies you could buy the cable rights to small towns for next to nothing. Any local entrepreneur with a chain of convenience stores or a healthy mattress franchise could lay down a couple of hundred grand and pick up exclusive rights to Schenectady, Worcester, or Asbury Park.

Big cities got hung up in years of litigation and bribery, but out in the boondocks you could buy cable rights for a bag of seeds. Over the next twenty years, those investments grew to be worth millions, then tens of millions, and finally hundreds of millions of dollars. From water to TV, the last two decades of the American century were devoted to the proposition that the public could be persuaded to pay for what it had always gotten for free. Guys like this Skyler here lucked into little empires. As cable grew they were sitting on expanding monopolies. A hundred new networks sprang up and paid the local cable landlords to carry their shows. At the same time, customers paid them for the service.

Lucky hicks who made their first money selling water beds woke up and found themselves media barons. As if that was not sweet enough, they got to hold on to some of the airtime to sell their own commercials. It started as cheap spots for the corner pizza parlor on local access shows, but within a few years the hillbillies were selling time on CNN and Nickelodeon. Money poured in from three directions.

Eventually even the broadcast networks had to deal with them, as all television began traveling through that little black box. The only viewers left who did not have cable were too poor to matter. The network had people to deal with these mouth-breathers. It had nothing to do with Bobby. He hoped the Internet or the phone companies or the satellite dishes would soon finish them off. As far as he was concerned, most small-town cable operators were greedy knuckle-draggers who had lucked into a twenty-five-year bonanza. The sooner the system moved past them, the better.

Bobby Kahn still had a distance to fall.

6.

Over the next three days, Skyler was steered to meetings and chats with eleven different television professionals who might be bold, hungry, or desperate enough to consider moving to Rhode Island to run King Cable. It was a disappointing exercise. The ones who wanted the job were all unimpressive, and the ones who looked like they might have had a fresh idea since *Laugh-In* did not want the job once they heard the details.

One fellow suggested he would consider taking it on if he could work from his home in Malibu and fly in for a couple of days a month. By the last day of his trip, Skyler was almost ready to consider it, but besides lacking commitment, the sun-baked old fart just rubbed him the wrong way. When Skyler told him he had three kids, the jerk looked startled and said, "With the same wife?" He wanted written assurances that he would have complete autonomy and the power to make decisions without the permission of the King family. Skyler was happy to imply anything, but to ask for guarantees in writing suggested a lack of subtlety. Skyler said no.

The last item on his itinerary was a drive south to Laguna to visit a show-and-tell presentation by packagers and independent producers of successful foreign TV franchises available for licensing in the USA. There was an honorable tradition of American hits springing from British seeds, from *All in the Family* and *Sanford and Son* to *Survivor* and *American Idol.* Brebner had suggested that one New

Zealand entrepreneur who would be there might be a good fit for King Cable. Skyler did not hold out much hope, but he had nothing to lose.

He drove out of Los Angeles, past the dinosaur oil fields, through the Orange County sprawl, past the eruptions of family discount motels that marked the route to Disneyland. Approaching Laguna the landscape turned the unnatural green of a pool table and began to roll and fall strangely, as if someone had thrown a fuzzy emerald rug over a collection of bowling balls and watermelons. There was something half formed and prehistoric about rural California, as if the humans had arrived a thousand years before God had the place ready.

Well, Skyler figured, that's why they were still plagued with earthquakes, mudslides, and wildfires. The locals were lucky pterodactyls didn't swoop up out of the La Brea tar pit.

West Coast culture made him laugh. Skyler considered that one of his great gifts was the ability to suffer fools gladly, to enjoy the silliness life presented rather than be annoyed by it. Look at Kenny! He elicited nothing but exasperation in Ann and Claudia and disdain from the old man, but Kenny was a source of endless amusement for Skyler. And those sidekicks of his, Bignose and Moe! The rest of the office referred to them as The Bizarros. It was worth having them on the payroll just for the comic relief. And they kept Kenny occupied so he didn't gum up the rest of the operation.

Kenny and Skyler had formed their first business partnership when they were still in college. King Concepts was incorporated to make and market a poster of two porcupines mating over the slogan "Love Hurts." It was a dorm-room smash. Variations on the poster— sometimes the porcupines were cartoons, sometimes actual nature photos—sold for years. A T-shirt deal doubled the profits. Even after settling lawsuits from classmates and acquaintances who claimed to have come up with the idea or contributed to the poster design, Skyler and Kenny split eighty thousand dollars from King Concepts' initial venture.

A follow-up poster, "Dope Springs Eternal," did less well, but it did not lose money. King Concepts only went under when Kenny persuaded Sky to move into fashion accessories. The Holdster was a sort of purse for men, a pistol-shaped leather pocket hung from the belt to carry wallet, keys, pen, comb, glasses, and whatever else the fashion-conscious male might want to keep at hand but out of his tight trousers. The manufacturing costs of the Holdster depleted the porcupine poster profits, and when the men of America were unmoved by the suggestion that they strap accoutrements to their legs, King Concepts went belly-up, leaving behind a barn full of leather sheaths.

A washout at twenty-one, Kenny kept looking for the next big idea, and he kept treating the uninterested Sky like an active collaborator. When cable TV began worming its way through the walls of the suburbs, the partners both saw their opportunity. They went to old Dominic King for funding. They had been bound together ever since.

The road into Laguna slithered between the hills toward the sea. Coming into the town, Skyler was struck by how different this oceanside village was from New Bedlam. The Atlantic shore had its share of tacky tattoo parlors, go-kart tracks, and pickup bars, but they were kept at a civil distance from the beautiful old homes, quaint inns, and expensive restaurants.

He parked his car in front of an art gallery displaying what appeared to be the same sort of sunset-and-seagull paintings you could buy in any tourist town in New England. Skyler saw that half the paintings seemed to have been copied out of old *Playboy* magazines.

He leaned in to look closer. A pink pastel sun cast long shadows on a yellow beach in the center of which a young woman with breasts bigger than her head was reclining nude and arch-backed on a blanket. Sky wondered if the artist was the same one who used to airbrush the sides of Kenny's van.

He found the hotel where the foreign TV pitches were taking place. Skyler poured himself a coffee, took a chair, and sat through several of the presentations. He saw no impending *All in the Family*, not even a next *Who Wants to Be a Millionaire*. He began keeping one eye on the screen while scanning through a newspaper someone had left. There was a lot of adult animation from Asia, most of which relied on either women with inhuman proportions fighting monsters or fuzzy cartoon animals having their eyes poked out and legs sawed off.

Skyler sat through three hours of caustic, crude, and violent content and saw nothing that struck him as even competently gross. It all seemed to have been created by horny teenage boys. He thought, I should bring Kenny some screeners.

He came to attention when the New Zealand producer who Brebner had told him about finally got up to pitch his new concept. It was a format, he said, that had already enjoyed great success in Brazil and the Philippines. It was a live-action contest called *Love Race*. Skyler leaned forward. He allowed himself a flicker of hope. If this fellow really did have a hot idea, and if he turned out to be the one to take over the King channels, well, maybe they could hit the ground running. Maybe he'd come to New Bedlam with his first hit in hand. Sister Annie might recoil at something called *Love Race*, but if the show were a hit it could bring new viewers to her classier fare.

The lights went down. *Love Race* came up. Over terrible hip-hop music three gawky young men—one Latino, one Asian, one blond—

ran around a small track, jumped through a hoop, and swung on three ropes across a little stream.

There was a quick cut to three young women laughing and pointing. Then the three men, against a bright yellow and red kiddie-show background, stripped off their clothes while comically bouncing around the room, knocking into one another, and stumbling to get out of their pants and shoes.

Skyler was surprised that they stripped naked. Swinging dicks on TV. He wondered if *Love Race* really ran like this in Brazil. The three young men, still laughing and joking over the blaring music, walked behind a red banner that hid their genitals. They faced the camera. A game-show host led the three young women—all of whom were clothed—onto the set to inspect the boys and make lewd comments. Then the host sat the women across the room, turned to the camera, and pulled out a suggestive pink popgun.

So far the noisy soundtrack seemed to have been designed to obscure that none of the dialogue was in English. But now an American voice was dubbed in as the host shot off his popgun and shouted, "Ready! Steady! LOVE RACE!"

To Skyler's wonder, the three young men behind the red banner that covered the space between their bellies and their knees began frantically masturbating while the host cheered and the three women struck sexy poses. The hip-hop got louder and sillier until buzzers blared and confetti fell and the host announced that one of the young men had won. The girls clapped, the two losers smiled good-naturedly, and a black man dressed as a British judge in black robes and white wig stepped out of nowhere to inspect something behind the banner which the viewer could not see and to raise the damp hand of the winner.

If Skyler had seen *Love Race* at a stag party or in a foreign hotel, he would have laughed and shaken his head, but to have flown across the country and then driven all the way down here for this annoyed him. He did not bother to meet up with the New Zealander. He did not care to shake that hand. On the way back to LA, he phoned Brebner and expressed his disappointment.

"Sorry about that, chief," Brebner told him. "But listen, I have a name that might change your mind. This is a big one. You met Bob Kahn at Rita's last night, remember?"

"What, the guy at the bar? He was drunk, Scott. For God's sake, I told you already—"

"No, no. That was Randy Maine. No, Kahn was the fellow you were talking with when I came in. Nice-looking kid. Big development honcho in New York."

"Oh, him. If he's so hot why would he be interested in King?"

"I hear things. You read about that business with *Lookers*?"

"Remind me."

"It was in all the papers, *Time* and *Newsweek*. Turned out someone was rigging the results. Big scandal. Condemnations in Congress and everything."

"Was this guy behind it?"

"I don't know. It's like Milli Vanilli, you know? Everyone knew but no one knew. Well, someone is going to have to take the rap, and if I were a betting man, I'd say Bob Kahn is the likely fall guy. This is a very, very able television executive, Sky. Before this he was on the fast track to a presidency. Could be bargain time."

Skyler was intrigued. He had manufactured enough fall guys in his time that he took no offense at either Bobby's alleged crime or the network's throwing him overboard to cover it up. As far as Skyler was concerned, all that meant was that he might be able to take advantage of someone else's bad break to grab the sort of executive he was after. The opportunity fit Skyler's view of himself as a man who was luckier than the next guy and quick to cash in on it.

"He'll have to move to Rhode Island," Skyler said. "And I want a two-year commitment. Unbreakable."

"From both sides?"

"Well, if he turns out to be mentally ill, Scott, I'll pay him off. You think we can get him?"

"Won't be cheap."

"How much?"

"He'll ask for a million."

"He won't get it."

"He's worth it, Sky. What would you pay?"

Skyler would have to split the salary between himself, Ann, and Kenny. That wouldn't be so bad. Leave the old man out of it for now.

He said, "I'll go to seven-fifty—but Brebner, don't start there. Okay? If he's on the ropes he might bite for less. Maybe he has family in New England or something. Where is he from anyhow?"

"Native New Yorker. I'll see if I can get him, Sky."

Skyler hung up. He felt better now. Maybe he had met his man after all. Maybe this trip had been worthwhile. If he'd known, he'd have paid more attention to Kahn at the party. He seemed all right, from what Skyler could remember. He was presentable, he spoke well, he appeared to have a brain. He chuckled. Three points right there that would make Kenny nervous. Three points that would distinguish Bobby Kahn in New Bedlam.

7.

ack in New York, Bobby could not kid himself that Howard
had honored their secrecy pact. When he walked into the
men's room, colleagues stopped laughing and averted their
eyes. A fellow he used to work with phoned out of nowhere and asked
if he needed anything. He found he was not being copied on e-mails.

When he walked into the Four Seasons restaurant, he felt as if he
had a bell around his neck. It seemed to him they made him wait
longer than they ever had before, and gave him a table behind a pole.
Each day's job-hunting lunch was more anxious than the last. He was
reduced to eating with Ted Blender, a producer of daytime chat shows
and one of the dumbest guys in the industry. Blender said to Bobby
with bisque running off his chin, "Hey, what's going on over there
anyway? I hear they're interviewing all over for a new head of programming. Are you getting a promotion or something?"

Bobby knew they'd have to name his replacement soon. In a *Wall
Street Journal* article about the continuing fallout from the *Lookers*
meltdown, the president of the network said that the investigation was
ongoing and an anonymous insider said that a "major housecleaning
was imminent." What buzzards. They canceled his show when it was
pulling down a twelve point five! How much more blood could anyone demand?

His options were contracting fast. Only a week before, he had
wondered if he could condescend to live in Los Angeles for a year.

Now he would not hesitate. He needed that soft place to fall, to do his time in exile so he could wash off the stink and come back into the big league in a year or two. But if he didn't find that soft place quick, he would never find it at all.

He was thirty-three. Young in most jobs but late middle age for a television executive. TV execs peaked early, like major-league pitchers. No secret why. Successful programmers were successful because, in addition to any other talents, they liked TV. They shared the taste of the eighteen-to-thirty-four demographic. Movie moguls could be eccentric, record bosses could be criminals. Even magazine editors could work at being weirdos. But successful television executives, though they might be smart, had to be well-adjusted, statistically average, spiritually suburban Americans who did not go on vacation in places where people spoke foreign languages and who really cared that Ross ended up with Rachel.

Bobby knew that he was at the age when an unmarried Manhattan-dwelling programmer who took a big fall might not get back up again. He was in danger of slipping off the statistical center. He'd been making a little too much money for a little too long. His tastes were getting a little too refined. It happened to the best of them. At some point you find yourself not caring about Ross and Rachel. You start going to foreign films. You see a play when you don't have to, when it doesn't even star a TV actor on sabbatical. You hit thirty-five and you still don't have kids.

So here he was, having breakfast with the headhunter, in the foyer of a trendy hotel so far downtown there was no chance of being seen by anyone from any of the networks. He felt like a traveling salesman sneaking off to meet a hooker.

"Bob."

"Tom."

"Thanks for coming."

"No sweat."

"Bob, remember we talked about my keeping my eye out for something new for you? Something cutting-edge?"

Bobby began to protest but swallowed it. What the hell, why pretend? He let Tom Jackson talk.

"There is a very interesting little company looking for a chief executive. Three small networks, privately owned, looking to go national. One's an arts channel, one is a sort of classic-TV thing, and the third is a placeholder, a sort of sci-fi deal. They are fully funded, staffed, and already have distribution in five or six states with a strong base to expand quickly."

"We're talking cable."

"Yes."

"Basic?"

"Basic in some areas, up the dial in others, but with a strong, secure base. The company owns the platform in several states. They are looking for someone to oversee a period of rapid growth with heavy investment."

"Do I know these networks? Would I recognize their names?"

"They are not on in Manhattan yet. You know how that is. But they are very well established in New England and parts of upstate. You met one of the principles in California. Skyler King? King Cable?"

Oh for God's sake, Bobby thought. If you're going to drag me downtown for this petty bullshit you can pay for the six-dollar orange juice.

What he said was, "That's nothing that would interest me, Tom. I am a professional. I have a pretty strong track record in this business. I don't know exactly who or what made you think I would be interested in—"

"Bob," the headhunter broke in with force, "you need a new podium. You need a chance to show that you can take something small and grow it. Let's be blunt, Bob. You need a lifeboat and a place where you can prove you've still got it."

Bobby was surprised to hear it laid out like that. No one had said anything straight to him since his fiancée told him to fuck himself.

"That might be partly true," he stammered, "but I have a lot of friends in this business. I'm not at the point where I have to consider—"

"You're not at that point, Bob, you're past it. They've filled your job. Willie Brand from Lifetime. The contract is finished, everyone knows. It will hit the papers in a few days. Then you are Nixon. Agnew, even. You are the fall guy for the whole *Lookers* mess. Radioactive."

Bobby couldn't speak. Tom Jackson went on.

"Let me head off those ingrates at the pass. Do the deal with King Cable before Skyler King gets wind that you're in trouble. Lock down a contract while you're at premium value. Then you and King get to the press first. Spin it as a bold move by a young visionary who sees the future and is ready to step away from the tired old broadcast behemoth and hook his leash to the new paradigm."

"You've written the press release already."

"It's a great parachute, Bob. A chance to be the ringmaster of your own circus. A real no-lose opportunity."

"I'd need a million a year to even consider it."

"You'll get there. But start slow. This is a big step for them, too, you know. They're a family business, father and sons. They know they need professional leadership to pull off their ambitions, but there's going to be a little sticker shock."

"What'll they pay?"

"They're thinking five hundred grand," Jackson said. Bobby

snarled. "I think I can raise that by half. Here's the thing. Look to the IPO. This is all about taking advantage of satellite and the digital platforms to position their networks across the whole spectrum, across the whole country. You get the three networks looking good, generate some press, build up the profile, they take the company public in a year or two, and you walk away with a huge win. Millions."

Bobby stared down at his fruit slices. If he did this, at least he'd have a story to tell. At least he'd have a place to stand until he could get back on his game. At least he'd have an income.

"I don't want anything to do with their local cable business, though. I'm not a shoe salesman."

"Absolutely. You're doing the networks, creative. Nothing to do with the old business."

"What are these channels called?"

"The arts channel is called Eureka. You've heard of it?" Bobby shook his head no. "The classic-TV thing is called BoomerBox. Shows for baby boomers." Bobby had never heard of that either. Jackson put down his napkin and started talking about setting up a meeting with Skyler King to work out timing and getting that press release ready and drawing up a deal memo and how much Bobby was going to love Rhode Island and what a short hop it is from Manhattan.

Bobby cut him off. "What's the third one called?"

Jackson pretended not to understand. He said to let him get the check.

"The third channel," Bobby said. He could not bring himself to call these obscure stations "networks." "What is the third channel called, the science-fiction one?"

"The Comic Channel."

"Stand-up comics?"

"No. It's the Comic Book Channel."

"Bullshit."

"The Comic Book Channel."

"What, you mean like *Matrix, E. T., Battlestar Gallactica* . . . ?"

"It's the Comic Book Channel, Bob. It's a channel about comic books."

"Who watches that?"

"A surprisingly large and affluent demo."

Bobby stopped kidding himself then. It was like he was in the Donner party and too hungry for pride. Tom Jackson said that Skyler King would fly down to New York to see him within twenty-four hours. There was no reason they could not have a deal worked out by the weekend and hit the press with this on Monday. Catch Howard and the network with their pants around their ankles.

Bobby insisted on paying the check. He said so long and walked out into the SoHo sunlight. I will come back from this, he told himself. I will take whatever dirt I am given to work with and use it to build a castle. I will make Howard and the network and all of them see what they lost when they turned their backs on me.

8.

A fat man and a skinny man were sitting on a bench in a small park overlooking the harbor in New Bedlam, Rhode Island. They were having a casual debate while taking their lunch. The fat man had strands of long greasy hair plastered across an egg-like dome. His moon face, thin, droopy mustache, and round eye-glasses combined to make him look vaguely Chinese, although he was in fact of Mediterranean heritage. His name was Todd Antonocio. He was talking rapidly while chewing too much sandwich.

"Kirby was childish," he said. "All the square fingers and inflated tendons. I'll grant you, it was a lovely childishness. Now you'll say Picasso was childish. But I say Picasso mediated his childlike instincts with an adult insight and sexuality. Kirby just spilled it all over the page. It took great inkers to reign him in, give that enthusiasm some balance, some context. And whatever you think of Lee, come on. It was the juxtaposition of Lee's down-to-earth attitude and wise-guy jargon that created the frame in which Kirby's illustrations gathered their power. Take away Lee's superego and it's all id, all flailing fists and triple-jointed legs with no sense of proportion. It's the difference between the Thing interacting with a crabby old lady on the subway and Kamandi the Last Boy on Earth fighting a talking bear."

The skinny man looked at his companion, brushed a crumb of wet bread from his cheek, and bit off a piece of his celery stick. He chewed for a very long time and swallowed before he spoke. "I disagree. Of course Kirby was childish, he was working in a children's medium. He succeeded on a preverbal level. That is the gig. That is why he was a great comic-book artist. All Lee did was scrawl adolescent graffiti on the margins of work that would have better stood without it. Let Lee loose in a museum with a Magic Marker and he would have happily scribbled 'It's clobberin' time!' across the face of *Guernica*. But that would not have made him a collaborator, and it would most certainly not have made him co-creator."

The thin man snapped off another piece of his celery stalk, punctuating his point. The man's name was Albert E. Freud. Like his companion, he was an executive of the Comic Book Channel. Albert was five foot one and weighed 110 pounds. He always dressed in a jacket and tie, and although he was thirty-four years old, he still bought his clothes in the boys' department. With his full head of black hair falling over his face, he could have ridden any school bus in the city and not raised an eyebrow until he opened his mouth and spoke in his resonant baritone voice.

Albert Freud made thirty thousand dollars a year from the Comic Book Channel and a bit more from a column he wrote for *Graphic Novel Journal,* a bimonthly magazine of comics criticism. Put that together with the stipends he got from speaking at comic-book conventions and his occasional pieces for Civil War and model-airplane publications, and he lived very comfortably on the left side of a two-family home he had inherited from his grandmother. He ate little and was able to trade the free comics he got in the mail for the reprints he wanted. Albert Freud's career was an ongoing annoyance to his biology-teacher father and socially ambitious mother, and that suited him, too.

Today was Wednesday, the day Freud and Antonocio taped their weekly panel discussion program, *Comix Quorum,* a cornerstone of

the CBC lineup. *Comix Quorum* was the only serious discussion program on the Comic Book Channel. But for this oasis of intelligence,
the entire lineup would consist of second-rate movies, Japanese manga,
Johnny Quest marathons, the occasional Max Fleischer festival, and
faded reruns of *Wonder Woman, The Green Hornet,* and *The Incredible Hulk.*

Today, like many days, *Comix Quorum* had no guests. That did
not bother these two at all. Their topic today, "Lee & Kirby—Who
Did What?," was old stuff, but it was what the fans wanted. E-mails
would fly as aging Marvel Zombies and lonely fanboys weighed in
with their own passionate contributions to the debate.

Albert disdained superheroes and their audience. He would have
rather been talking about the deficiencies he had found in the new
hardcover reissues of Winsor McCay's early-twentieth-century *Little
Nemo* Sunday strips. But television was a popular medium. It was one
of the reasons Albert did not own a TV. He would have to settle for a
brief mention of McCay squeezed into the final minute of the broadcast, in the "Picks and Pans" segment when he and Todd got to mention sequential art projects too esoteric for the body of the program.

The two men gathered up their litter and headed back to the
King Cable studio, a black room on the first floor of the seaside Victorian house.

As they approached the building, they were alarmed to see the
wall explode out of the house next door with a boom. Todd thought
of Galactus belting the Silver Surfer. "Great Krypton!" he shouted.

A wrecking ball swung to a stop in the open space where the top
floor of the double-decker house next to King Cable had been.

"Guess they're knocking down that flea trap next door," Todd said.

"Either that or Fin Fan Foom has returned from his watery
grave."

"Do you think the Kings own it? Maybe they're expanding the studio."

"Great, a bigger black room."

They entered their workplace. Employees of the various King channels were pressed against the east windows of the offices, watching the wrecking ball turn the building next door to splinters.

Kenny King's voice emanated from the top of the stairs like the chattering of a wounded gibbon. "Motherfucker!"

Little Albert turned to Todd. "I would venture a guess the Kings do not own that property."

As president and creator of the Comic Book Channel, Kenny was Todd and Albert's boss. The two had a private nickname for Kenny: "Harry O," for Harry Osborn, the sniveling son of the evil but powerful Green Goblin.

Now Kenny screamed for everyone to evacuate the building. Albert and Todd walked back outside, crossed the street, and looked up to see Kenny on the roof, throwing shingles at the crane next door and howling threats. His two cretins, Moe Notty and Sammy Bignose, were anchoring him so he did not fly over the edge in his rage.

"You're violating an INJUNCTION!" Kenny screamed. "You and your boss are going to JAIL!"

If the wrecking crew heard Kenny screaming over the rumble of the machines and destruction, they did not show it. The ball kept swinging. The house next door came down. Two policemen put up sawhorses to block the street in front of the demolition. Kenny came out of the building and argued with the police, who nodded and did nothing. Kenny charged into the construction site and climbed onto the base of the crane, but the demolition crew pulled him down and the cops dragged him away and told him if he tried anything like that again they'd lock him up. Kenny disappeared down the street.

Most of the King Cable staff left work and went home, but Freud and Antonocio sat in the diner across the road and watched the drama play out. Close to suppertime a long black Lincoln Town Car pulled up to the police barrier and a very wide man in a black suit, white shirt, and black gloves stepped out of the front seat, moved the wooden barrier, got back in the car, and drove straight up to the police cruiser. A short, lean man with hair like white wire stepped out. He was dressed in a thin black raincoat that fell almost to his feet. He went up and said something to the cops. They looked unsure. He said something to the wide man and the wide man handed one of the policemen a mobile phone. The policeman listened for a moment. The policeman gave back the phone, went into the demolition site, and told the crew to stop working.

The crew did as they were told. There was almost nothing left of the house anyway. They packed up for the night and the cops did the same. They picked up their sawhorses and drove away.

Kenny King got out of the back of the black car and walked up to the old man and his wide driver. The three of them stood at the edge of the rubble, surveying the hole where the house next door used to be.

Then the driver moved the car and Kenny and the old man walked across the street into the diner where the Comic Book experts were observing the drama. It was as if two characters in a movie had stepped off the screen and into the audience.

Kenny was subdued. The old man was unreadable. They went to the counter and ordered coffee. Kenny seemed to be coming back from somewhere far away. He focused on the room around him as if he were waking from a dream. He saw his two employees staring at him from a table by the window.

"No show today, boys," he said to them. "We'll tape *Comix Quorum* tomorrow, okay?"

The two critics nodded. The old man turned and looked at them without interest. He had skin like leather, a face like an ax, and narrow eyes that seemed to have no whites at all.

"Dom," Kenny said. "You remember Al and Todd? They do the Comic Book show for us?" The old man took a sip of coffee and neither spoke nor blinked. "You guys know Mr. King, right?"

"Nice to see you, sir," Albert Freud said. "Whatever you said to those policemen sure seemed to work." Albert left the opening out there. The old man turned his back to them and poured an avalanche of sugar into his coffee.

Kenny said, "We told them their house was on fire," and grimaced, trying to make a smile.

Dominic King did not often appear at King Cable. He had other businesses. The television thing was run by his children, and he took no more interest in it than he had in their grades or hobbies when they were growing up. Todd Antonocio had heard stories about Dominic King for years. He owned used-car lots and Laundromats, a tow truck operation, and a string of garages. His real last name was Italian, but he had changed it when he moved down here from Providence. Some people said he had made his first money in vending-machine operations, which meant Mafia, but that was what the Irish said about any Italian who did well in Rhode Island. Just like any Irish family with money was said by the Protestants to have been bootleggers.

Antonocio could see that it pained Kenny to have had to call in the old man. It made Kenny look weak. Antonocio did not know much about Dominic King, but anyone could see that this was not a man with sympathy for weakness. Todd had a nice gig going at Kenny's Comic Book Channel. He really hoped this was not the beginning of Dominic King taking a more active role in the family business.

9.

S kyler King did not call his wife, Claudia, when his plane landed. He went right to the airport garage, picked up his car, and headed home. Driving into New Bedlam, he was startled to see only a busted frame and a pile of wet lumber where the old house next door to his office had been.

Christ, he thought. Fancy Clancy went ahead and knocked down his tenement. Kenny's head must be exploding. Hope he didn't drag the old man into it.

He slowed down to look into the demolition site, its perimeter marked by strips of yellow police tape, orange "Do Not Enter" signs, and legal notices. Four neighborhood kids played at the site's edge near a tough-looking woman in a khaki uniform poking around with a flashlight.

Sky pulled over and rolled down his window to have a look. The uniformed woman walked over to the car. He saw the letters RIWPNRCA on her jacket. Rhode Island Wildlife Protection and Natural Resources Conservation Authority. She said, "Help you, sir?"

"Hello there." Sky flashed his perfect white teeth. "I own this building." He gestured toward the King Cable Victorian. "I've been out of town. What happened here?"

"Not my place to say, sir. You one of the King family?"

"I am."

"Yes, sir, Mr. King. I believe you might want to get over to the town hall. There is a hearing under way to determine the disposition of this project. I am only here to keep the peace."

Oh my bleeding ass, Skyler thought. What miserable mess has Kenny cooked up now, and why are park rangers patrolling the main street as peacekeepers? We got one injunction to stop work on Clancy's demolition. If Kenny had left it to me I could have gotten another and another and another until Clancy got the message and accepted a reasonable offer to sell us the property. But no, they can't let the lawyers handle it. I leave for one week and come back to the Hatfields and McCoys.

Skyler turned on his cell phone. It began to twitch and buzz. He checked. He had seventeen unplayed messages. He turned it off again and drove to the town hall, a nineteenth-century building with a large belfry and a tower clock that had been losing a minute a day since 1955. He dragged himself up to the second-floor public hearing room just in time to hear the presiding officer of the New Bedlam town council telling Kenny to sit down and let Mr. Catalano speak.

Skyler tried to slip into a back seat without being seen. There were five impatient-looking town reps at a table in the front of the room, fifteen or twenty people in the audience, and—to Skyler's horror and amazement—a Providence television news crew shooting the proceedings.

Dan Clancy was a prominent local contractor, political contributor, and pain in the King family's neck. A big Irishman, red of hair and complexion, Clancy shared a mutual hatred with Sky's father that went back decades and exceeded normal business rivalry. Sky had always tried to stay out of it. Kenny was not so restrained.

Old Clancy, redder than ever, was seated behind a table on the left side of the room facing the council. Steve Catalano, a well-liked local lawyer, was standing next to Clancy and addressing the councilmen.

"I hope the honorable representatives will not allow Mr. King's hysteria to muddy a very clear issue. Mr. Clancy sought and was granted all the proper permissions to tear down his old tenement in order to construct in its place a new building, which will enhance the waterfront of our town and all the property around it, including Mr. King's business. The new property, Melville Manor, will provide luxury condominiums for year-round and summer residents of our village, as well as adding valuable retail space to Main Street and the seafront area.

"We believe that Mr. King's earlier stop-work order and injunction against Mr. Clancy was merely a delaying tactic without substantial merit."

Kenny jumped out of his seat as if to speak, but the chairman banged a gavel and told him to sit down or he'd have him tossed out. Kenny fell back into his chair.

Lawyer Catalano continued. "Look, folks, that's old news. Fair or not, Mr. Clancy honored the court's decision, he made good on all the conditions—valid or not—outlined in Mr. King's complaint, and he lived up to the full requirements of the stop-work order and went beyond the specifics of the notice to cure. The end date of that order was reached, the safety and structural integrity of Mr. King's property was assured, and then in full compliance with the letter and the spirit of that injunction, Mr. Clancy went ahead and demolished his old tenement to make way for work on Melville Manor. Furthermore, above and beyond any obligation in law or ethics, Mr. Clancy has offered to send his own crew into the King building to repair any further cracks or damages Mr. King claims to have incurred as a result of Mr. Clancy's work."

The lawyer looked at the council with a smile and shrugged. "I ask you folks, what more in the world could Mr. Clancy do? We are talking about replacing an old eyesore with a beautiful new structure. Mr. Clancy is being magnanimous in the face of what any neutral on-looker would have to characterize as harassment from Mr. King."

Skyler thought about sneaking back out. No one had seen him yet, and nothing good was going to come of this. At least the old man was not in the room. If Dom got involved, it could turn into Sacco and Vanzetti.

Kenny sat slumped at his table like a man defeated. Catalano sat down. The chairman put his hand on his microphone and whispered with the other council members for a minute. Then he leaned forward and said, "Mr. King? Are you prepared to accept Mr. Clancy's new offer and the ruling of this council?"

Kenny struggled to his feet. He slouched like a little boy dragged in front of the principal. He spoke softly with his hands in his pockets and his eyes down.

"I guess I don't have a lot left to stand on," he said. "I would like to state for the record that my only concern is for the protection of my property and the integrity of our historic waterfront. . . ."

Clancy and Catalano were whispering to each other. The council members were glancing at their watches and closing up their files. The case was over.

Then Kenny said, "I would only ask, out of respect to all con-cerned and so that we can get on with our lives and put this behind us, that the delegation from the Rhode Island Historical Society," Kenny waved to a bespectacled trio of two women and a man seated behind him, "and my own engineer and the state Wildlife Protection and Natural Resources Conservation Authority be allowed to quickly examine the site and oversee the rest of the demolition and construction to make sure there is no further negative impact on the coastal environment or the surrounding buildings."

The council members looked confused. Catalano climbed to his feet and said, "Folks, this is one more delaying tactic—"

"No, Steve," Kenny said quickly. "I promise it's not. I just want to make sure we have some objective outside agency keeping an eye on this so that we don't all end up back here in a month. I'll pay the costs myself, okay? Dan can go ahead and put up his building. I just want a clean referee to make sure everything's on the up-and-up."

For the first time Dan Clancy rose to his feet. He looked at the council and then looked Kenny in the eye. "Fine with me," he said. "I want to do this on the fair and square." And in a grand gesture the big Irishman strode across the room and shook Kenny's hand.

The council moved on to an argument about municipal liability for lawn jockeys decapitated by town snowplows. Catalano and Dan Clancy left by a side door. Kenny, as if reluctant to surrender the spotlight, picked up some papers very slowly, said a sad farewell to his experts from the historical society, and headed with eyes downcast along the outer aisle and toward the back door of the council room. Just before he exited, he caught sight of Skyler and for a moment seemed to struggle to suppress a grin.

Uh-oh, Skyler thought, what have I missed?

He caught up with Kenny outside. Sammy Bignose and Moe were waiting in Kenny's black Land Rover.

"Tough break," Skyler said.

"Uh-huh," Kenny said. He was smiling.

"Something I don't know?" Skyler asked.

"Maybe."

"Something I don't want to know?"

"Possibly."

Skyler knew to break it off before Kenny got him involved. "Okay, just make sure it won't come back to our door, right? I have some big plays in motion right now and we cannot afford any embarrassments."

Kenny grinned.

Skyler said, "You know about the birthday party on the Fourth."

Kenny nodded.

"Okay," Skyler said warily. "See you then."

Kenny and his crew drove off.

Three days later Skyler got a phone call at home from the local newspaper, asking for a comment on the big archaeological news from Main Street, New Bedlam. Skyler hung up without speaking and left his house. He drove to the demolition site. Two police officers and the tough lady ranger from the state Natural Resources Conservation Authority stood in front of Dan Clancy, who seemed determined to get his hands around the neck of the bespectacled man from the Rhode Island Historical Society who had been seated behind Kenny at the town council meeting.

Skyler made his way to one side of the site, where a local TV news crew was aiming its camera down into the hole. Skyler tapped a reporter on the shoulder and asked what the big news was.

"Indian burial ground!" the reporter said. "This construction crew was digging the foundation for a new building when they hit a skeleton. They stopped work and called the authorities. Looks like they uncovered an ancient Mohegan graveyard."

"No kidding."

Skyler looked up at the windows of the King Cable offices, whose view of the harbor was now unobscured down to the first floor. He saw faces pressed against the glass watching the brouhaha.

"They're going to bring up the bones and examine them up in

Providence," the reporter said. "If they check out, they'll be reinterred with a proper ceremony, and this lot will be taken by the state and turned into a historical site."

"What do you know?" Skyler said. He kept searching the facade of King Cable. His eyes fell on Kenny at a window on the top floor, fanning his right hand in front of his mouth and holding the splayed fingers of his left behind his head.

What the hell is he doing? Skyler wondered. Then he got it. He was making feathers with his fingers and going *woo woo woo* like Apaches in an old TV show. Skyler did not know how Kenny had come up with an ancient skeleton to plant in Clancy's construction site, and he did not want to know. He just hoped Kenny could keep from bragging about it.

He walked back around the front and saw the red-faced Dan Clancy being cajoled into his car. He looked like he was about to have an aneurysm.

This was why the Kings kept Kenny. He had an idiot savant's talent for devising ways to manipulate government bureaucracy to the King family's service. It was fun, but at this point the rewards were not worth the risks. King Cable was a multimillion-dollar business and Skyler knew what had to happen to make Wall Street and the rest of the business world recognize its potential.

That was why he was bringing in Bobby Kahn.

part two
king cable

10.

Skyler leaned on a wooden deck rail decorated with wet bathing suits, cell phone to his ear, his eyes fixed on the ocean. He told Bobby Kahn he could be his houseguest until he found a place in New Bedlam, and asked him if he had looked at the tapes he had sent down. Bobby said he had, and had lots of notes. He hoped Skyler knew how big a job turning these channels around was going to be. Skyler said Bobby would have full authority to do whatever needed to be done. They wished each other a nice holiday and said good-bye.

Plumes of fireworks bloomed up and down the far shore of Narragansett Bay. Newport's display had begun. Bristol and Warren were lighting up the sky. New Bedlam would be kicking off any minute. Kenny had relieved Skyler of duty supervising the hamburgers and hot dogs cooking on the outdoor grill. Skyler's two little daughters, Maude and Amy, were digging in the sand at the edge of the water in the last thin minutes of daylight.

He looked through the sliding screen doors to the lights inside the house where his wife, Claudia, was decorating the long farmer's table with birthday ribbons for his daughter Maude. His nine-year-old son, Jeremy, was sitting on the end of the dock below him waiting for skyrockets. Skyler liked fireworks; they were one of the few things in life that did not look better on TV.

Skyler observed with satisfaction that all three of his children had their mother's sun-starched blond hair. With every generation the Kings were becoming more Waspy, more Yankee, breeding out the old man's guinea blood. Skyler had his father's thick black hair but his mother's fair skin and blue eyes. He got his height from his mom's father, Sky Koenig. Old Sky had been an army aviator, war hero, and small-town physician. He was better bred than to complain aloud when his favorite daughter married an Italian used-car salesman, but even as a child Skyler picked up on the distance between his ill-bred father and the Koenigs' easy class.

Ten years after she had married Dominic, people in the neighborhood still referred to Skyler's mother as Betty Koenig. She did not correct them. Dominic took the insult as he took every other slight—in silence and with what his son recognized as a mental bookkeeping. Dominic maintained a tally on everyone he knew, quietly checking off debits and credits.

When Dominic left Betty—no small scandal in New Bedlam's Catholic community at the time—Skyler didn't believe it was because he preferred to move in with Kenny's dimwit divorced mother. Dom was banging her anyway, he didn't need to leave Betty for that. No, Sky always figured his mother had simply posted one petty offense too many and Dominic moved her into the foreclosure column. He packed his suitcase and moved to the next block.

People in the neighborhood assumed it was tough on Skyler, but the truth was it wasn't bad at all. The house was a lot nicer with Dominic gone. For Skyler, just fifteen, it was a license to a personal, sexual, and financial freedom he'd never have known with Dom perched at the head of the stairs. And as everyone agreed that Kenny's mom was a poor match for Betty in looks, smarts, and personality, Dom was universally declared the loser even before the judge gave Betty the house and half of what was already a modest fortune. She just went back to being popular Betty Koenig, and Skyler was granted a built-in excuse when he stayed out all night or broke some girl's heart or failed to turn in his homework. His father's desertion gave Skyler nothing but leeway.

As for the old man, he moved through his wives like Caesar advancing north out of Italy. Betty was German and Kenny's mom was French. Dominic's third wife was an Irishwoman living in England, Annie's mother. If Dom marries again, Skyler thought, she'll probably be an Eskimo. Breeding the Wop blood out.

Kenny started shouting that the burgers were ready. Grandma Betty appeared with a birthday cake and Annie snapped photographs. The annual Maude-and-Claud Fourth of July birthday barbecue was one of the occasions when even Annie would not complain about Kenny hanging around. Everyone was welcome, with the obvious exception. It was family tradition that Grandpa did not come. Birthdays and Christmas were Grandma's privilege. Sometime in the next month Dom would show up and take Maude to the mall, where he would bring her to a movie and buy her some expensive gift.

Kenny sidled up to Skyler with a hot dog in each hand. He whispered, "Talk to Annie yet?"

"No. I figure later, after the cake and presents."

"Got it. Lemme know if you need me to soften her up."

Skyler winked at him, the co-conspirator. Claudia called for hamburgers and Kenny ran off to deliver them.

Skyler had sold Bobby Kahn on the job at King Cable and the salary and moving up to New Bedlam. The last small matter that needed tweaking was convincing Kenny and Ann to sign off on the new man's duties and salary before the announcement hit the trades.

Kenny was easy. Skyler appealed to both his vanity and his sneakiness by positioning it as something he and Ken knew had to be done and would have to work together to sell to Annie.

Kenny wanted to meet Kahn, to sign off on him. That would present no problem, just as long as Kahn did not realize that Kenny considered himself to have veto power over his appointment.

Annie was going to take a little more maneuvering. On the plus side, she was much smarter than Kenny, so she should respond to logic. On the down side, she was capable of a very un-King-like loyalty to principles and to people outside the family. Skyler had to tread carefully to be sure Annie saw hiring Bobby Kahn as an opportunity for her arts channel, not as a potential loss of control for her.

Of course, that was a lie. Someone had to pry Annie's fingers from the wheel. Watching Eureka! The Arts Channel was like being trapped in a college course on the history of pottery in which the windows did not open and the professor talked like Beowulf.

Sky's BoomerBox channel was what it was—reruns of old shows for fortysomethings and their children. Kahn could blow it up, paint it green, turn it into nude mud wrestling if it would improve revenue. Skyler did not care. It was an investment and it meant no more to him than his General Electric stock or the rental properties he owned in Cranston and Warwick. Unlike Kenny and Ann, Skyler did not derive any part of his self-image from having a TV channel.

Kenny's station was just like Kenny. The Comic Book Channel. The geek tree house of the airwaves. It had grown out of a cable access show Kenny and a couple of his pals used to do and it showed. Nobody watched it who did not get excited arguing about how Batman fit all those weapons in his belt. As long as Kenny could sit in his office and keep having those arguments with his maladjusted staffers, he would not notice what Bobby did on the air.

King Cable had lucked into millions of dollars by being in the right place at the right time, by being the only place people living in areas they controlled could get *Six Feet Under* and the Cartoon Network and most ball games. But their monopoly was being challenged. New avenues of distribution were opening up—satellite, broadband. People were downloading TV shows onto computers and cell phones. Programmers no longer talked about "viewers"; they talked about "users." Cable TV was in danger of becoming an interim technology, like the streetcar.

When Skyler was little, Dominic told him what his own father had said about the streetcars. When they put down the tracks in the 1890s, everybody said, "Oh my God! The future is here! The twentieth century has arrived! From now on, the whole country will ride streetcars forever!" By 1925 they were tearing up the streetcar tracks. Automobiles had come from behind and knocked them off. The future was over already.

Skyler was still a relatively young man, but he had seen a lot of streetcars come and go. Quad sound. Super Eight movie cameras. Cassettes and eight-tracks. Videotapes. If you got in early you made millions. If you stayed in too long you lost it all.

If King Cable were to avoid going down like the eight-track tape, they had to get out of distribution and into content. They had to grow their channels into real networks that customers would pay to subscribe to, whatever the distribution system. No one who worked for him had the experience or aptitude to lead such a transition. But Bobby Kahn did. And once Bobby Kahn was in, he'd bring in other people like him.

And if in doing that he had to break a few eggs, well, that was the nature of business. If Kahn said some of Kenny and Ann's subordinates had to go, they would have to go. The old man was not getting any younger, and Skyler could not allow these properties to float along as hobbies any longer.

Skyler's sister appeared next to him on the rail.

"The food's on the table," she said. "Want to call in the troops?" Just then the fireworks display at the country club down the beach kicked off. The kids oohed and shouted. Kenny came running to the doorway.

The New Bedlam Fourth of July barrage began. Bombardments lit up across the sky. Rocket trails, crests and blooms of flame and light came riding down on booms and echoes. A shower of embers rained over the bay. The kids were delighted. Skyler peered through the smoke at what he took to be a skyrocket, then Venus, but which revealed itself to be the red taillight of a plane.

He pointed it out to his sister. "Way up there. Too high to be local. Coming in across the Atlantic like you."

"Remember last summer when I arrived on the Fourth?" she said. "I came down the coast looking for the house when all these glowing flowers sprang up along the shore. Pop, pop, pop. It took me the longest time to realize they were fireworks! So strange and beautiful from twenty thousand feet. We landed with explosions going off all around us. It was lovely."

Skyler wanted to take advantage of the warm moment.

"Say, Ann," he said. "I want to mention something to you. About the networks. I don't know how much you've been following all the developments with broadband, but we have a shot right now to move our channels into a lot more homes. Millions of homes. All across the country. It's a real once-in-a-lifetime opportunity, but to do it we need to bring in one or two executives with national broadcast experience."

"To do what, Skyler?"

"Well, to help you and me and our folks understand how to take this thing to the next level."

"Consultants, you mean."

"Possibly, yes. But right now there's this guy Bob Kahn I've gotten to know. Real mover and shaker. Big network guy from New York. Very successful, very well respected. He sees a lot of potential in King, in Eureka, especially. I don't know for sure if we can get him—he's a big name, articles in *Time*, *Newsweek*, all the papers. But I would love to make a bid for him. I get the feeling he might be willing to do it out of enthusiasm for the brands."

"Really. He likes the Comic Book Channel?"

"Well, let's say he would take that on as the price of admission. I really want to see what his ideas are for BoomerBox, and I think he could really help us come up with a defining vision for Eureka."

"So he would report to me."

Ann was too sharp for this, and Claudia was yelling for everyone to come in.

"Ann, this is a guy who programs a broadcast network, who makes a million dollars a year. I think he might just be up for the challenge of moving here and showing us how to bring our very modest channels to national attention. But we would have to give him the authority to do what needs to be done. You would still be president of Eureka. I would still be president of BoomerBox, and Kenny would still be president of CBC. We'd make this guy chief executive or chancellor or something. Obviously we'd still own what we own. But there's no shot of getting him to quit the huge job he has and relocate to New Bedlam if we don't give him some room to do what needs to be done. I haven't even mentioned it to Dom yet. This just came up. I found out he might be available. But we have to move fast. If I can get him up here, will you meet with him?"

"What's his name?"

"Kahn. Bob Kahn."

"Can, like can-do? Or Con, like con man? Or Khan, like Genghis?"

"You'll like this guy."

"That's what you told me about Claudia's cousin Brutus."

"Bruce." Skyler laughed. "You're never going to let me live that down, are you?"

"He put his tongue in my ear at her mother's funeral!"

"He was wracked with grief. What do you say?"

Annie smiled. "Bring out your golden boy. I'll meet him."

"Thanks, Sis. And do me a favor? Don't mention this to Kenny yet, okay?"

11.

kyler had suggested that Bobby take the train from New York to New Bedlam, but he wanted to drive. He needed to be ready for a quick getaway. He followed Route 95 to the Rhode Island line and then cut across a series of country highways until he came to the ocean. New Bedlam was the small fishing town between the small fishing towns of Jerusalem and Galilee. Sky told Bobby that "New Bedlam" was a corruption of the name that the first settlers had intended to bestow—New Bethlehem. That sounded to Bobby like something the Chamber of Commerce cooked up, like the "George Washington slept here" plaque on the local Ramada Inn.

On the outskirts of the town, Bobby passed through a ring of convenience stores, gas stations, and motels that could have been duplicated anywhere in the United States. The only thing that struck him as out of the ordinary was the number of doughnut shops. Bobby had never seen so many in such close proximity. There were Bess Eatons, Allie's, Honey Dews, Krispy Kremes, and a half-dozen Dunkin' Donuts in a two-mile stretch. These people must like lard, Bobby figured.

The fast-food chains fell away as he pulled into the village. Bobby took a left where he should have taken a right at a statue of a World War I soldier and found himself on a narrow street of well-preserved old houses built close together and separated from the road by only about twelve inches of sidewalk. He made a couple of lefts and found his way back to the main road, a street from a Norman Rockwell painting, with a small white brick library, an old red town hall with a high clock tower, a number of churches, a grade school, a barbershop, and several small restaurants. Bobby stopped at a light and looked up at a statue of an old fisherman in full rain gear holding a ship's wheel against a gale. On a large plaque on the statue's base were the names of New Bedlam sailors lost at sea.

The directions to the Kings' house were easy. It was a beautiful home, an old New England farm. Skyler's wife, Claudia, served steak and lobster, and afterward the two men sat up for hours while Bobby talked about his ideas for the channels based on his initial research. Skyler acted interested.

Bobby slept until after eleven in the morning. He could not remember when he had last slept that long or that late. He was groggy and it took him a few moments to remember where he was. Claudia and Skyler were both gone, but a pretty housekeeper gave him coffee. Still full from the late dinner, he took an apple from a basket of fresh fruit on the kitchen counter and went outside.

He found himself on a green hill looking down across a series of short meadows divided by old stone walls, ending in the Atlantic Ocean. The sea was whipped with whitecaps. Past a long L-shaped jetty, a half-dozen sailboats formed a chevron against the waves.

Bobby doubted he was much more than ninety miles from his hometown. Because the people of Long Island and the people of Connecticut historically wanted nothing to do with one another, every proposal to build a bridge between the two places for the last hundred years had been defeated. As a result, southern New England and Long Island, while in sight of each other across the water, had grown up as different as twins separated at birth.

A seagull could fly from where Bobby now stood in New Bedlam, Rhode Island, to eastern Long Island in thirty minutes. The pilot of the small plane passing over his head now would look down and see both places at once. But to get from here to there by road would demand a journey of six hours—across southern Rhode Island and all of Connecticut, almost to New York City, over one of the New York bridges, and then all the way back east for ninety miles. Part of the year a ferry ran from New London to the northeast tip of Long Island, but even that would only cut ninety minutes off a New Bedlam to Massapequa commute.

Bobby's old neighborhood was a place of strip malls, train tracks, plat houses, diners, laundries, convenience stores, and low-rent apartment complexes, strung together by webs of electric and telephone wires. Now he was on a sea-swept lawn by a shingled mansion, and a girl in high boots and jodhpurs was riding her dappled mare across the green fields and up the hill toward him like *National Velvet*.

He snapped back to this universe. A young woman on a big horse was heading his way. She half stood in her stirrups, crouching, as the horse came galloping toward the first stone wall. Bobby winced. The horse stretched its legs and lifted off into the air, sailing over the wall and coming down on Bobby's side. It seemed to pick up speed as it came uphill and cleared the second wall, now close enough to where Bobby stood that he could hear the thud and shudder as it landed. Horse and rider slowed to a trot, turned halfway, and followed the wall up to the crest of the hill where Bobby was standing.

The rider was tall, thin, and fair-skinned. Her yellow blond hair was pulled up in a knot. She had a long face and high cheeks and very pale eyes with lashes so blond that they almost vanished. She looked down at Bobby. "You're the network man. The programming genius."

Bobby studied her and saw Skyler in her aristocratic features, the good skin, and lean frame. "You're another King," he said.

"I'm Ann King," she said. "Skyler is my half brother."

"Boy, there are a lot of you. Is Kenny a half brother, too?"

Even the horse seemed offended. "Kenny," she said the name as if it tasted bad, "is not my brother."

"Stepbrother."

"Kenny is not my stepbrother, he is not my half brother, he is nothing to me at all."

"Your father's stepson."

"No, he is not. He is nothing."

Ann King climbed down off her horse. She handed Bobby the reins. The horse looked at Bobby like he was stupid. Even the animals here are snobs, Bobby thought. Ann took a ribbon from her hair, shook it out, and tied it again. She was pretty, Bobby thought, in a Virgin Queen kind of way. He was glad to see that on the ground she was no taller than he was. Out of those big boots, he might even have an inch on her. She took back the reins.

She said, "Kenny is the grubby little child of a local woman to whom my father was briefly married between Skyler's mother and mine."

"But your father adopted him."

"In fact he did not. My father very specifically declined to adopt Kenny. Perhaps that was one area of contention between Kenny's mother and him. Or not. From what I know of Kenny's mother, she was not much concerned with anyone's welfare but her own."

"Then why does Kenny have your father's name?" he asked. "Why is he a King?"

Ann stretched her neck and looked away like these were matters strangers did not discuss. Then she looked Bobby in the eyes. "Kenny rather pathetically petitioned the court to have his surname changed to King when he was fifteen years old. He claimed the boys at school teased him for having a name different from his mother's."

"Okay."

"It was obvious nonsense. Half the boys at St. Blais had different names than their mothers. None of the boys at school knew Kenny's mother's name because Kenny had no friends. As for their teasing him, I suspect it had more to do with his being a pudgy, whining, uncoordinated, nose-picking, masturbating tattletale than with his surname. As far as they knew, Kenny's surname was Wanker."

Why, Bobby wondered, is this woman talking with an English accent? He was a little intimidated by her, and fascinated by her neck. She had the longest neck he had ever seen on a human being. It should have made her look like a goose, but somehow it made her look like a fairy queen from a children's book. She was nothing like the women he usually went for, but she struck him as really sexy. Maybe it was the little whip.

"Okay, so what's the real reason Kenny changed his name to King?"

"Isn't it apparent? He wanted to be one of us. That none of us wanted him did nothing to discourage it. Kenny wanted to be my father's son. Most of all he wanted to be Sky's brother. That was true since they met. Kenny used to follow him around like a little dachshund. Skyler would make Kenny do tricks for his friends. If Skyler wanted a candy bar he would send Kenny into the canteen to steal it for him. Skyler would eat the candy and Kenny would get caught and punished."

"Sounds like Kenny had a sad life."

Ann King snorted like her horse. "Kenny is a sad little man. But following my brother around has made him wealthy. He can hire people to laugh at his jokes now. So I suppose his plan worked out. Now people have to pretend they like him."

"Not you, though."

"I'm wealthy, too." She swung back up into her saddle. She was going overboard to be snide, he thought, but he didn't want her to leave.

"You have a British accent," he told her.

"I'm English."

"But Sky isn't."

"He's American. Our father moved to England when he married my mother."

"He left America?"

"Astonishing, isn't it?" She widened her eyes, mocking him. "Have you spent much time abroad, Mr. Kahn?"

She knew his name! "Not really. I've been to Canada, the Cayman Islands."

"Never been to Europe?"

"Not really."

"Never been to England?"

"I'm a See America First guy."

"Well, of course. Who needs Paris when you have Boise?"

"You been to Boise, Ann?"

"No, but I could find it on a map. Could you?"

"You're pretty tough."

"I'm not."

"But you don't like Americans."

"My father is American."

"You like your father?"

"Doesn't every girl?"

"What's he like?"

For the first time Ann King hesitated. She looked down at Bobby and over toward the sea. She pulled on the reins and her horse turned to take her away. "Actually, he's a bit like you."

Bobby watched her ride down the hill, jumping walls as she went. That is a woman, he said to himself, beyond all the usual demographic data.

12.

oe Notty was looking everywhere for Sammy Bignose. He found him in the cove behind the King Cable office, standing in the surf up to his waist, wearing swim trunks and the jacket from a wet suit. He was bent forward, with his head underwater.

Moe called Sammy's name but got no response. For a minute or two Moe stood on the sand, flustered. He had big news and he wanted not only to share it with his buddy, but to absorb from his response the measure of how he should react to it.

Unable to raise his friend's attention, Moe took off his shirt, sneakers, and socks, rolled up his jeans to the knees, and waded out toward Sammy, shouting his name the whole way.

Sammy was in a better place. He was breathing through a snorkel and looking through a diving mask at a population he had never recognized lived right alongside his own, right out his window.

Lookit all the little fish, Sammy was thinking. Hey, little green guy! Hurry up, your momma's got to get all those babies home.

His visit with Kenny to the Mystic Aquarium had excited in Sammy a newfound fascination with aquatic life. He had always taken fish for granted, but in the last week he had borrowed a Jacques Cousteau video from the New Bedlam public library, gone for a ride on a glass-bottom boat, and patrolled the aisles of the local fish market with the scholarly focus of Darwin in the Galapagos.

Although under strict instructions from Kenny not to return to

Connecticut for at least six months after the Indian museum incursion, Sammy had sneaked back down to the aquarium on Sunday and spent the day contemplating the marine world.

He had passed thirty minutes staring at a translucent jellyfish, a glowing floating brain trailing a few feathery tendrils. Sammy intuited that this was the closest thing to a being of pure consciousness nature had conspired to construct. He imagined his own brain, unhitched from his skull and floating out into the amniotic ether.

It pleased him to consider himself untethered from the earth except by a wispy film of tissue, riding the currents, his long jelly fingers attuned to each fluctuation of the environment, lapping with the pulse of the ocean of which he was extension and inhabitant, victim and master, feeder and food.

Sammy had no words to share these insights with his friends and family, nor did he want to. They would not understand. This was a private vocation, one that moved him to come here on his lunch hour and sink his head beneath the surface, to map each new Atlantis from the diving bell of his fascination.

At once, his aquatically attuned senses shouted warning. Something large moved in the water around him! Sammy panicked. For an instant he felt at the mercy of prehistoric predators, as fragile as the gray jellyfish bobbing in his skull.

"Wake up, Sam! You're gonna drown in there!"

Sammy raised his head. Through his foggy mask he beheld a fractured image of a white figure flapping its arms. He took off the mask and saw Moe, his pale skin sickly in the midday sun.

"Moe?" he came back to the surface world. "Why are you wearing pants in the water, Moe?"

Moe had indeed walked in up to his waist in his blue jeans. Sammy wished Moe wouldn't do stuff like that.

"What are you doin', Sam? I was yellin' and yellin'."

"Why? What's wrong?"

"I thought you had the bends or somethin'."

"Moe, I'm standing in water up to my belly button. I can't get the bends."

"Not the bends. What do you call it, like when Popeye starts seein' mermaids?"

"Rapture of the deep." Sammy was mastering the vocabulary of the Jacques Cousteau videos.

"Yeah, that's what I thought you had."

"Okay, thank you for coming to my rescue."

"I thought you had, like, when they put you in a tank and you can't hear anything."

"Sensory deprivation."

"Yeah."

"I don't have sensory deprivation, Moe. What did you want me for?"

Moe recalled his mission. "He's here!"

"Who?"

"The guy."

"What guy?"

"The new guy!"

"Oh."

Both men looked up at the grand old house where King Cable resided. They studied the upper windows. Bobby Kahn was in that house. He was a strange and powerful television executive from New York City who was moving up here to change the way things worked. That sounded ominous to Sammy and Moe. The way things worked was fine by them.

"What's he seem like?"

"Kinda weird. He wasn't smiling."

"You talk to him?"

"No. Kenny told me to lay low for a while."

"What else does Kenny say?"

"Kenny's in with him now. They're talkin' with the door closed."

"Well, it's Kenny's channel. He owns it."

"Yeahhhh." Moe sounded unsure.

"Come on, Moe. Kenny's not going anywhere! I mean, how much does this new guy really know about comic books? You think he could run the channel without Kenny?"

"I guess not."

"Kenny told me this guy is like an efficiency expert. He'll be looking at ways to get the channels on more systems around the country."

Moe still looked nervous. Sammy Bignose lowered his voice and talked out of the side of his mouth.

"Know what Kenny told me?"

"What?"

"This guy's not really gonna have much to do with the Comic Book Channel. This guy is really here to make changes in Eureka."

Sammy knew his friend well. Moe smiled.

"You think they might get rid of Judith?"

Sammy nodded like he was telling a child that Santa Claus was moving in for the summer. Sammy and Moe feared and disliked Judith Garlac, a conspicuous Eureka executive who could insult them in ways it took weeks to decipher. She once spent months calling them Hamadryas and Theropithecus, which she told them were Greek gods of wine and merriment, until one day they looked them up online and found they were kinds of monkeys.

"I wouldn't be at all surprised if Judith got shit-canned," Sammy said. "I think it's possible Kenny could end up taking over the whole thing."

"BoomerBox, too?"

"It's possible. The family knows what a good job Kenny does. I figure this new guy might be a first step toward Kenny moving into his dad's seat."

Sammy had succeeded in restoring his friend's confidence. Some of those people at Eureka were conceited. They treated Moe like dirt. A tough guy from New York coming in to shake things up could only be good news for Sammy and Moe. One thing Sammy was sure of: Wherever Kenny King went, he would make sure Moe and Sammy went with him.

Up in Kenny's office, Bobby Kahn looked out the window at the ocean. "There are two men in the water with their clothes on," Bobby said.

Kenny looked. It appeared that Moe was in the ocean in his pants and Sammy was next to him in a shirt. The two of them were supposed to be in the basement running off copies of a Frederick's of Hollywood TV special and staying out of sight. Anything he told them to do . . .

"You know those guys?" Bobby asked.

"I think I recognize them," Kenny told him. "Couple of local morons."

13.

obby kind of liked the old Victorian house by the water. His first impression was that it felt like an inn, and the people who worked at King Cable seemed like an odd collection of guests crossing paths during a summer holiday. The front part of the building was the original house where Bobby and the Kings had their private offices. The back was a modern addition disguised to look like part of the old building, with conference rooms and an edit bay and a large office space with cubicles. The top floor of the old house was higher than the addition, which gave the rooms on the fourth floor of the Victorian unimpeded views of the ocean.

Kenny had the biggest office on the fourth floor and he had decorated it with a nautical theme, somewhat subverted by his statues of Wonder Woman, Vampirella, and Lara Croft, and by a framed poster of two copulating porcupines.

Bobby Kahn sat with his back to the porcupines, wrapping up a pleasant conversation with Kenny. Kenny felt good about Bobby. Smart guy, obviously full of ideas. He was going to tell Skyler to go ahead and hire him, and if Annie didn't agree they would just have to sit her down and tell her the facts of life. You can't come floating in here and tell the guys who built the place how to make business decisions.

Kenny and Ann's latest attempt to be cordial to each other had lasted less than twenty-four hours. Things were fine at the birthday party; she almost acted like a human being. Then the next day Kenny just happened to walk into her bedroom when she was putting on her bathing suit, and she got all freaked-out and called him a Peeping Tom and brought up the whole old business of the knothole in the cabana. Like the statute of limitations hadn't expired on that one already. Boy, Kenny thought, for someone who was given everything without working for any of it, that Ann could really be a bitch.

All of the challenges Bobby faced in fixing King Cable—convincing rival cable systems that they had to pay to carry their dubious channels, creating an appealing environment for advertisers, enticing competent TV executives to move to the boondocks to work for low money, expanding and improving their shaky affiliate relations, soliciting the attention of the national press, and, oh yes, coming up with some breakout-hit programming—paled next to the challenge of walking into the conference room for his first weekly meeting with the executives of the Comic Book Channel.

When he took inventory of King Cable's assets, Bobby's instinct was to shut down the Comic Book Channel and sell the space to infomercials. He was very sorry to learn that it was the personal bailiwick of Kenny King. The Comic Book Channel not only reflected Kenny's aesthetic, it was his clubhouse. He had staffed the channel with people who shared his interests and were obligated to laugh when he burped and to eat lunch with him. Most important, the Comic Book Channel allowed Kenny to write off on his income tax the substantial expense of maintaining a vast collection of rare comic books and fantasy memorabilia.

Skyler had explained all this to Bobby as if finding a way to make the Comic Book Channel profitable were no more of a challenge than fixing a weak lead-in on an otherwise stable Sunday-night schedule. It seemed likely to Bobby that even if he were given a hundred million dollars, five years, and the best creative minds in the television business, he could never make a success out of the Comic Book Channel for one simple reason: There would never be a substantial number of people in the United States who wanted to watch a television channel about comic books. And that was not even taking into consideration the lack of interest from advertisers in paying to have their products associated with a demographic that had little income, less prestige, and scant hope of marrying or producing children.

Kenny King seemed to have plucked the CBC executive team from *Star Trek* conventions, superhero chat rooms, and the stool behind the counter at the local comic-book store. On one side of the conference table sat the King Cable staffers who shared duty across channels—the research, acquisitions, marketing, and ad sales reps. Across from them sat the sticky-fingered, flabby, and badly groomed executives whose professional attentions were devoted exclusively to the Comic Book Channel.

Bobby had been working hard to memorize their names. There was Boris Mumsy, a chubby black kid no more than twenty-two with a failed Afro that cascaded up and down in mounds. Boris peppered his speech with expressions from old Marvel Comics, *Mad* magazine, and TV reruns. He called his peers "True Believers" and "the usual gang of idiots" and liked to say "Bang! Zoom!" to emphasize a point. Boris began each meeting with Hostess Cup Cakes or Drakes Ring Dings and a bottle of Pepsi in front of him on a paper towel.

Boris seemed at least moderately well adjusted compared to Albert E. Freud, a skinny, bespectacled cynic with a pointed face, wire-rim glasses, and oily hair that he combed from a low part on the left side of his head into a long flap of a bang that crossed his brow and fell below his right ear. If tubby Boris was basically amiable, thin Albert was miserable. He appeared to Bobby to be the smart kid who'd been beat up in the schoolyard one time too many and had retreated into a defensive nastiness. Albert gave the impression of hating everyone else in the room and perhaps even comic books, too, although he sure seemed to know a lot about them.

Most creepy because he was so much older—Bobby figured him for forty—was Todd Antonocio, a short, balding man with a Fu Manchu mustache and an air of effeminate condescension toward Bobby and the TV professionals across the table. Todd appeared amiable enough, but he brushed away every suggestion that came at him with the "Oh don't be silly" manner of an old schoolmarm pestered by ignorant children.

When Bobby said, "I think we have to take a hard look at the numbers we're getting on this *Comix Quorum*," Todd waved his hand and said, "The *Quorum* is very important to CBC's image and to maintaining communication with our core audience. I understand you don't feel part of that conversation, Bob, but trust me—you'll understand when you've been here awhile. It's important."

Bobby looked around the table. The Comic Book Channel geeks nodded as if that was the end of that. The TV folks stared into space, counting the minutes until this meeting was over. At the other end of the table, Kenny King was grinning.

Bobby had to establish his authority. He could not let this bullshit pass.

"Sorry, Todd," Bobby said. "That's not how it works. *Comix Quorum* is not important to CBC's image because CBC does not have an image. Unphotogenic people sitting around a badly lit table talking about obscure comic-book trivia might work on your Web site, but it's bad television. I don't care how cheap it is to produce. Whatever it costs is too much. I will not waste money, effort, or airtime on that kind of programming."

Albert Freud muttered, "Told you," and snickered.

Boris Mumsy chewed twice as fast.

Todd Antonocio turned in protest to his patron, Kenny King, who was still grinning.

Bobby moved to head off Kenny stepping in. He turned to the woman in charge of audience research. "What are the ratings on *Comix Quorum*, Khefa?"

"Lowest on the channel. Too low, actually, for Nielsen to record."

"Right," Bobby said. "Which is part of our problem making a case for CBC to advertisers."

"Well, that's about right, Bob." Gary, who ran ad sales, spoke up. "We've been running public affairs spots in there, and some make-goods, but even the local merchants aren't really looking for placement in the *Quorum*."

Old Todd shook off his indignation at being talked back to and said firmly, "You don't get it. The show is not a big ratings performer but it is very important to our core audience. It is where they get to put a face on the Comic Book Channel."

"That's the problem, Todd," Bobby said. "It's a really bad face! Here's what I want all of you to think about. The core audience for the Comic Book Channel as it exists today is not sufficient to justify a business. Please let that sink in. The viewers you spend so much time worrying about are not the viewers we need to attract to make this channel viable. We need to reach out to a whole new constituency. And chances are that new constituency will not only not want to watch *Comix Quorum*—they will want to turn off the TV as soon as they see it. Okay? Got it?"

The table was silent. Kenny finally weighed in: "I know this is a new way of working, guys, but Bobby has the big picture in mind.

We gotta think outside the box now. We're gonna invest a lot of dough in growing this channel and we might have to say good-bye to some of our old loyalties."

Thank God, Bobby thought. He had primed Kenny on all this in private, but he was not certain Kenny had accepted it, or would stick by Bobby in front of the room. Bobby did not know why Kenny King inspired such hostility in his non-sister Ann and such eye-rolling condescension from many of the other people Bobby had met in his first days at King Cable. Sure, the guy was a little needy, a little hungry to please, but from what Bobby had seen he was neither a fool nor nearly as odd as some of the other characters roaming the halls.

Bobby did not know that the real reason Kenny backed him was because snobby Todd had always blocked Kenny's efforts to join the *Comix Quorum* panel.

Todd shut up and sulked. Bobby felt a wave of satisfaction from the TV side of the table. They might never turn the Comic Book Channel into a successful business, but it would at least be fun to watch Bobby slap these creeps around.

14.

The King family homestead was, like everything involving the Kings, a complicated legal entity. A picturesque New England farm, it looked to an outsider such as Bobby Kahn as if it had been in the family since colonial times. It was easy to imagine prior generations of King women waiting in the upstairs window for the whaling ships to come home.

In fact, the old farm had been purchased by Dominic and Betty King when she was pregnant with Skyler. Dom would have preferred something modern, a ranch house with a gravel lawn so he didn't have to think about cutting grass. But Betty wanted a home, a place where a menagerie of children and animals could tumble and play in bucolic safety. And Dominic did like that by having chickens and goats he could write off the property as a working farm.

Betty wanted an arcadia by the sea and Dominic indulged her. As their fortune grew they bought up surrounding lots and properties. A rundown house next door was remade into a quaint guest cottage. An old dairy barn was restored and filled with chickens, ducks, rabbits, and two sheep, April and May. When the owner of The Crow's Nest bar finally agreed to sell Dom his property, the Kings were able to extend their domain up to the ocean. They tore up the parking lot and planted grass, knocked down the tavern, and used the wood to build fences and a tree fort for Skyler. A long adjacent garage was restored to its original status as a horse barn.

By the time the horse barn was complete, the marriage was over. Betty kept the house and land while Dominic moved on, first to Kenny's mother and then to his subsequent conquests. Skyler spent his teenage years sharing the house with his mom and a legion of carpenters, handymen, and landscapers.

It was only when Skyler was out of college and married that his mother surprised everyone by announcing her intention to sell the property into which she had lavished so much care and move to Florida. No one could argue with the economics—in twenty-five years the value of oceanfront property in Rhode Island had increased twenty times.

Not wanting to let the place go but also not wanting to pay what it was worth, Skyler invented a scheme to keep the house and get someone else to pay for it. Skyler proposed that a King family trust be set up to buy the house from Betty, using funds from the King business empire. The owners of the trust were the owners of King Cable—Skyler, Ann, Kenny, and old Dom. Taxes and routine costs of upkeep were to be paid by the trust. They drafted further agreements that the property could only be sold to an outsider if all the owners agreed, and every effort would be made to keep the property in the family as long as even one of them wanted it.

Dom made it clear he wanted nothing to do with living in the house, which made it easy on everyone. Betty moved to Captiva Island in Florida, but came back to Rhode Island each summer, staying in her old home from May until September. Annie, while she was still in school, had arrived each June and stayed through August. She got along fine with Betty. Their relationship benefited from the historic interregnum of Dom's brief marriage to Kenny's mother between Betty and her own mum. Now Annie was going to live in the house year-round and pressed Betty to stay through Christmas.

Skyler and his wife, Claudia, used the family house for social occasions—Thanksgiving, Christmas, and a ritual New Year's Eve party—but they mostly lived in their beach house two miles away. In theory they moved back to the farm each autumn when Betty and Annie left, but in practice it was too much of a pain to shift their three kids and their dogs two miles up the road. Even the horses wintered in Virginia.

The odd man out, as always, was Kenny. No one had ever invited Kenny to live there, and although he was on paper a co-owner, he was not brave enough to suggest it. During the awkward teenage period when Skyler's dad left Betty to shack up with Kenny's mom, Betty had been deeply generous to the embarrassed Kenny, treating him as if no foolishness that went on between grown-ups could ever interfere with her affection for Skyler's little chum.

Now Kenny often appeared at the house to patrol the fences, chat with the caretaker, and roll the tennis court. Occasionally he could be seen in the early morning attacking a cluster of brambles with a scythe or charging up a thicket of briars on a rider mower. Once, when a hornet's nest laid havoc to the children's tennis games, Kenny was spotted crossing the south lawn with a shotgun. Before Skyler and Claudia could register what they had just seen, a blast shook the property and little Jeremy came racing into the house shouting that Uncle Ken had just blown the hornets to oblivion.

So it was Kenny who took Betty's lament about the gunk in her millpond seriously. When she pointed it out to Skyler, he shrugged and said, "You should have somebody look at that, Ma."

When she brought Annie out to see how the pretty pond was clogged with bacteria, Annie just said, "I suppose it's nature's way," and rode off on her horse.

Butts the caretaker said it was too bad the pond was so backed up, but it was part of a whole ecosystem of streams and swamps and wetlands and there was no way to go in there without filing all sorts of environmental-impact statements and getting permission from several different state and municipal bureaucracies, all of which would take months even if there were no court challenge, and anyway, what can you do? Drain the thing and dredge it and then try to fill it again clean? That would cost a fortune and take months and who knew if it would even work or what was causing it? Everyone Betty consulted told her she would just have to live with a congealed millpond.

That point, the point at which polite discussion and legal remedies hit a wall, is where the Kings turned to Kenny.

Excited by the assignment, Kenny sat in his King Cable office trolling the Internet for information on how best to combat bacteria clusters in freshwater ponds. He was not surprised to discover that while the overregulated northern states relied on nature to clean up its own mess, down south the citizens had developed methods for beating nature at its game with little sympathy for federal regulations or the Druids who wrote them.

At a secret meeting at an old wooden table in the hayloft of the King family barn, Kenny laid out to his henchmen Sammy and Moe the parameters of their next adventure.

"Carp," Kenny said.

Moe looked at Sammy. Sammy smiled and said nothing. Kenny nodded and grinned. "These redneck scientists in Arkansas have developed a special breed of bacteria-eating carp! Is that amazing? They can't cure cancer but . . . Anyway—you get these carp when they're little, still in the egg. You dump them in an infested pond, and they eat through all the gunk." Kenny looked from face to face. Sammy was still grinning vacantly. Moe's nose was running.

"GET IT? These carp are hungry crap-eating bastards! You dump the eggs in the pond, the eggs hatch, and the shit-eating carp grow to like two feet long and munch through all the bacteria! It's clean, it's easy, and it's ALL NATURAL."

"Is it legal?" Moe asked.

"Depends. It's legal in Arkansas for damn sure. It's big business down there. You ever seen the ponds in Arkansas? Spotless. Good fishing, too."

"Ken," Sammy said, still smiling. "One question. Don't you end up with a pond full of two-foot carp? I mean, maybe that's not a bad thing but—"

Kenny leaped for joy. "This is the beauty part!" he cried. "This is the miracle of American ingenuity!" He ran out of the room. Moe looked like he was going to speak but Sammy shushed him. Let Kenny play this out.

Kenny ran back in trailing a long sheaf of computer printouts.

"The carp are castrated!" he cried.

He waited for a response. Sammy and Moe traded glances and then Moe said, "Wow, those scientists in Arkansas do some fine detail work. How do they do that, Ken? Do they take, like, tweezers or—"

"NO NO NO!" Kenny's eyes were rolling back in his head he was so happy. "They BREED them so they're sexless! The carp are genetically engineered so they can't reproduce. They are simply sexless gunk-eating machines!

"I've ordered a small truckload of these castrated cannibal carp eggs from Arkansas. The truck can only bring the eggs through certain states, the closest of which is Ohio. Day after tomorrow, we are going to drive out to the Ohio-Pennsylvania border and meet that truck and load those eggs into our van and drive them back to New

Bedlam and introduce those fish into the fetid green waters of my mom's millpond and stand back and watch those monsters do their stuff. It's going to be like *Alien* around here!"

On their way home Bignose and Moe looked at each other.

"That was weird."

"Yeah."

"Not the fish."

"No."

"Kenny called Skyler's mother 'my mom.'"

"Don't tell anybody, okay?"

"I won't."

15.

W as Skyler calling from a racetrack? There was a strange roar in the background and his voice came in and out. He seemed to be asking Bobby how the new job was going and if Bobby had seen the great blurb in the *Hollywood Reporter* and the item in the *Boston Globe* about the surprising move of the young New York network hotshot to the feisty New England cable upstart.

Bobby had seen all that. He didn't want to tell Skyler that these tiny items—single sentences in crammed media columns—meant nothing to the bigger world. At the network he got a thick stack of xeroxed articles every day, all of them talking about something he or his colleagues were doing. He rarely looked at them.

He was, however, happy that they had blindsided his old boss Howard and the network with the announcement he was quitting to take over King Cable. That had been sweet. One nice thing about dealing with such a small company was that contract, title, and salary negotiations that would have taken six months in Manhattan were wrapped up in two phone calls and one face-to-face session with Skyler. Maybe, Bobby told himself, the whole business would work that way. Maybe he'd find King Cable quick and responsive in a way the lumbering broadcast networks could never be. Maybe the reality would actually live up to the rhetoric.

Skyler's voice came back on the phone: "You've met with the BoomerBox guys?"

"Well, yeah," Bobby said. "I met with scheduling, marketing, and ad sales. As far as I can tell, you don't have anyone really running that channel." He realized Skyler might take this as an insult; on paper Skyler was president of BoomerBox. "Day-to-day," he added quickly.

Skyler showed no offense. "That's exactly right, that's why I need you to be merciless in there. Leah schedules BoomerBox and pretty much makes the creative decisions by default. Jerry Hellman helps Leah with the promos. It's pretty bare bones."

"Don't Leah and Jerry schedule the other channels, too?"

"CBC yes, Eureka no." There was a sudden whooshing noise in Bobby's ear. Skyler's voice went away and came back again: ". . . sat down with the Comic Book Channel yet?"

"Yes."

"Charismatic crew, aren't they? How about Eureka?"

"I'm going in there with all of them in half an hour. First staff meeting. You want to join us?"

"I wish I could, Bob," Skyler said with no pretense of sincerity, "but I'm about to jump out of a plane."

Bobby assumed he was joking, but after saying good-bye he looked out his window and saw two orange parachutes wafting toward the meadows outside of town.

Coming into the conference room, Bobby smelled something ugly. Had a wet animal died in the wall? Did someone broil a mouse in the microwave? He was about to say, "What stinks in here?" but something in the faces of the people around the table stopped him.

Their expressions fluctuated between dread and annoyance, like ninth-graders facing the math teacher on a February Monday. Nothing in their demeanor suggested anything he said would not be interpreted in the worst way. He looked for a place at the table. It hit him that what

he smelled might be one of them. No matter how much they hate being here with me, he thought, I hate being with them more.

The upper management of Eureka! The Arts Channel was eight
pasty people who looked like they could benefit from some vita-
min C. Ann King had taken a seat at the middle of the table, her
thick blond hair pulled back and a pair of Ben Franklin glasses guarding the tip of her nose.

Eureka's general manager, Judith Garlac, was perched at the head
of the table like a stern bird. Judith had been the steward of Eureka
while Ann was in college. Bobby had met her briefly and been unable
to engage her in conversation. Judith made it clear that she considered herself regent to an underage queen.

Judith had taken the power chair and flanked herself with two assistants, one typing into a computer and the other spreading out folders and scribbling into a ring-bound notebook. Guarding her forward
frontier was a small phalanx of paper coffee cups and an old tea mug
wrapped in a knit cozy. Everything in her manner signaled to Bobby
and to the room that this was still her command, Bobby was a guest.

A wide woman in an untucked black shirt and a broad purple
skirt was patting the empty seat next to her. Bobby sat down. She
smiled and greeted him as if they were dear old friends—former
dorm buddies, maybe, or summer neighbors. He had never seen her
before. She rubbed his shoulder and he flinched. She whispered in his
ear, "Don't worry, they won't bite."

Judith passed a note to her secretary and looked up at Bobby for
the first time. She smiled. No one else did, except the crazy woman
snuggling up against him. Judith said, "We were just going over the
August stunt plan. Did you see my fax?"

Bobby admitted he had not and asked if she would e-mail it to him.

"We don't trust e-mails," Judith said. Still no movement from the grim faces. Bobby looked across the table at Ann King. Her face was blank, as if she were watching TV.

"What's the August stunt?" Bobby asked.

Judith nodded to a damp man in a tweed suit that looked like it was adhering to his skin.

"*Seven Days of Shakespeare,*" he recited. "Some of the Bard's best and best-loved plays as interpreted by cinema's great legends."

Silence fell over the table. Bobby waited to see if anyone would break it. At last he said, "What's in it? Kenneth Branagh?"

A woman whose head was barely above the table raised her hand cautiously. Judith nodded at her. The woman had long, stringy hair and a face that seemed to be all nose, with eyes on either side of her head, like a trout.

"We couldn't get any Branagh," she said in a thick New England accent. Bobby knew she was the head of acquisitions, but he could not recall her name. "We have Orson Welles's *Throne of Blood* and the *Midsummer Night's Dream* from CBS with Diana Rigg and Richard Chamberlain."

"Isn't that from, like, 1968?" Bobby asked the room.

The damp man said, "Rarely seen. Good press hook."

Trout Woman lifted her head above the table and said, as if reading from a card, "Very much a Most Requested Rarity. Dr. Kildare and Mrs. Peel. Sooo sexy."

Time for Bobby to go to work. "I'm not sure anyone under retirement age will care about that," he said. "Also, isn't that on videotape? Is it even in color?"

"This is the sort of discovery our audience expects from us," Judith said, still smiling. "They will gladly overlook some technical imperfections to spend a few hours with a lost treasure."

"Well, I don't know," Bobby said. He had not intended to come out swinging, but there was more self-deception going on here than he had expected. "I'm looking at the numbers on this channel, and, folks, they don't tell a pretty story. I mean, right of the decimal is one thing, but for most of the last three months you guys are struggling to crack a point one! Look at this. What did you have on last Sunday night at ten p.m.?"

There was a great shuffling of papers and feet before Trout Woman peeked up from under the table like Kilroy and said, "'Tapestries: A History.'"

"What's that about? Carole King?"

A chinless man with curly brown hair spoke up. "It's about medieval tapestries."

"You put on a show about curtains? In Sunday prime?"

"It's performed well before," the chinless man said. He was defensive.

"Well, folks, you must have burned that one out, because in all my time in television that is the first prime-time show on any channel I have ever seen achieve a total zero. Not a rounded zero. Not zero point zero two four. I chased this down. 'Tapestries: A History of Old Curtains' achieved the rarely seen perfect box of eggs—zero point zero zero zero. If anybody left their TV on to keep the cat company and that thing came on, the cat got up and changed the channel."

No one laughed, although the crazy fat woman next to him rocked back on her haunches a little and nudged his leg.

"Come on, guys! You don't want to look at numbers like that any more than I do. You are smart people, you have a smart channel. But this is not school. You don't get points for being smart. You get points for putting on shows that people watch."

Ann King finally spoke. "Running 'Tapestries' at that time was a mistake."

Judith jumped in—she was going to shut this down. "'Tapestries' always did well for us, but it was overplayed. We should have rested it. We won't make that mistake again. If you look at the overall weekend, though, it wasn't bad. Quarter to quarter, we're up in all demos."

Now Bobby leaned forward and smiled. He said, "I'm afraid we're only up quarter to quarter because last quarter was so bad that the news in Serbian would have been an improvement. We gotta pull together, guys. We gotta think smart about how we promote, how we schedule, and most of all, what we spend our money putting on our air."

Judith was too sharp to argue the inarguable. She shifted tactics. She said, "Tell us, Bob, how do we make *Seven Days of Shakespeare* work better?"

Bobby was ready. He did not want this first meeting to turn into a debate. He needed these people to sign on to his vision. The crazy woman shimmying next to him slid over her copy of the stunt proposal so he could see it. But she kept one hand on the edge of it so he'd have to share.

"Okay," Bobby said. "I'm looking at a lot of very high and inside programming. I mean, gee whiz, guys, you've got Kurosawa in here."

"We were lucky to get that," the chinless man snapped.

Bobby thought, Who is this mental patient? He continued: "What about that Steve Martin movie where he played the only guy in Los Angeles who loved Shakespeare? What was that called?"

"*Roxanne?*" the trout woman ventured.

"*Roxanne* is Edmond Rostand!" the chinless man told her with all the anger he could not point at Bobby. "It's *Cyrano!*"

"Fine," Bobby said. "Call it *Shakespeare and His Friends.* Try to get *Roxanne.*" Bobby said to the trout woman, "That's a good call." She beamed. The chinless man flushed.

"Let's think fresh," Bobby said. "How can we make this more fun? What kind of hook can bring in some new eyeballs?"

Trout Woman was blooming now. She was showing some neck. She said, "How about Mel Gibson's *Hamlet*?"

This was too much for the man with no chin. His thermostat blew. "Showtime has that tied up for the next four years! To even try to buy a window on that would cost more than our budget for the quarter!"

Trout Woman sank like a periscope. Bobby said, "You never know. We might have something we could swap."

"I do know," the chinless man said.

"Okay, fine," Bobby said. "But what about seeing if there's a 'Making of Mel Gibson's *Hamlet*?' I'll bet there is. I'll bet it's on DVD. If we could get that—and maybe a couple of others, maybe the making of that Ethan Hawke *Hamlet* and—who else?"

"Branagh!" said the crazy fat woman, and she pinched Bobby's arm.

"Okay," he said. "That's an awful lot of *Hamlet*—what else is there? Leonardo's *Romeo and Juliet*, there must be a doc about that."

The tweedy damp man spoke. "There was a movie about *Othello* set in a California high school!"

"*O*," said the chinless man with contempt. "It was called *O*. Unwatchable."

"Like Kurosawa's a crowd-pleaser?" Bobby said. He realized he was going to have to take this nasty little guy down. Tough luck, but it always happens. It's like the first day in prison: You have to pick a fight with someone or they'll make a Mary out of you.

"Here's the thing, guys. If we can get one week's use of these 'making-ofs' for cheap, we suddenly have a lot of star power to put in the promos. I mean, if you cut the 'To be or not to be' speech from

Olivier saying the first few words to Branagh to Hawke to Mel to, I don't know, Homer Simpson, you've got a hell of a promo. It shows the range of what we've got—"

"Except we don't actually have it," the chinless man said.

"—and it shows an attitude, a sense of humor. It says, Hey, this ain't the boring old Shakespeare. This is something special. That's what a good promo does."

Judith Garlac wanted to take back control of her minions. She said, "I think there's a lot we can take away from that. Thank you, Bob. Denise and Mark, let's grab a minute after this and talk strategy. Now, moving on—"

"Wait, hold on, excuse me, Judith," Bobby said. "Before we move on. That thing I said about *The Simpsons.* They must have done some Shakespeare parodies."

"*Frasier* did!" the crazy wide woman said right in Bobby's ear. The glares from her comrades bounced off her.

"Yeah, okay." Bobby smiled. He was in his game now. "Do you guys remember the episode of *Gilligan's Island* where Gilligan was Hamlet and the Skipper was . . . who's the fat guy?"

"Hamlet, if you go by the text," Annie said. Judith smiled at her, like a proud tutor.

"Polonius," the madwoman said gleefully.

"Yeah, yeah," Bobby said. "And Mrs. Howell was the mother—"

"Gertrude!" cried the giddy fat lady. Bobby felt like he should throw her a fish.

"Let's get that episode, and some other sitcom takes on Shakespeare. This could be fun, this could get a lot of press."

The chinless man's head had turned into a cartoon thermometer. He almost spat. "This is not what we do! Eureka does not run *Gilligan's Island*!"

"Eureka didn't *used* to run *Gilligan's Island,*" Bobby said. "We're throwing out the old rules."

Bobby's words had barely landed on their ears when a terrible smell rose in the conference room. He glanced around. No one else was reacting, but he could see in the fluttering of eyelids and tapping of pencils that they smelled it, too. Someone had let rip a silent fart.

Bobby struggled to maintain his concentration. He looked around. "Is there anyone here from ad sales?" He asked. There was not. "Why not?" he asked.

"This is the creative meeting," Judith said. "We try to respect the separation of church and state."

This was too much for Bobby. "What separation of church and state! This is TV! We're here to sell ads! We sell ads by racking up ratings! We rack up ratings by putting on shows people want to watch! This is not a campus book club!"

A second blast of silent fart hit Bobby. He carried on. "There is no separation of church and state in this enterprise. We are the Taliban." Nobody smiled.

Bobby had not set out to admonish Judith Garlac in front of her subordinates. He tried to be conciliatory. "I have the greatest respect for what you guys have accomplished with the resources you've been given. But moving forward, we have the opportunity—"

"Bob," Judith said. "I wish you wouldn't say 'guys' when more than half the room is women. It's a little inappropriate."

Right there, Bobby knew. Judith Garlac would never accept him. Too bad for her. Bobby Kahn fired people. Judith was going to have to go. He glanced at Ann King. If she wanted to sit at the grown-ups' table she would have to accept that it was time to lose the babysitter. Bobby did not come to this godforsaken Mayberry to fail.

Judith was still talking. She didn't know she was dead. She was saying, "We know quite a lot about Eureka's core audience. These are people who don't respond to much of what mainstream TV has to offer. Some of your ideas are terrific fun, Bob, and would probably work well at CBS or NBC, but the Eureka Golds, as we call our heaviest tune-ins, would be appalled by seeing the Simpsons or Gilligan or, quite frankly, Mel Gibson show up on their channel."

Thanks for the setup, Bobby thought. Now I get to beat down the greatest fallacy in television—the sin of superserving the wrong audience. It is the sure prescription for failure. Bobby turned to Khefa, the research chief. He said, "Who are the Eureka Golds?"

Khefa looked uncomfortable. She spoke as if she were reading from a cue card: "The most frequent viewers of the channel are the ones who most like the shows we put on."

Bobby looked across the table at Ann King, catching her eye. Ann said, "Well, I suppose we could also say that about the Kangaroo Channel, couldn't we?"

"Right," Bobby said. Ann got it, thank God. If he could separate her from her regent, Judith, he might bring her around to his way of thinking. He turned to the rest of the room. "The worst thing we could do is put all our effort into pleasing an audience that is too small and, frankly, too old to interest the advertisers we need to satisfy. We need to attract new viewers, younger viewers, better-looking viewers if we can. . . ." Nobody laughed.

"Relying only on what your heaviest viewers want is suicide if those viewers constitute an audience too small to keep the network afloat." He looked around. He didn't need agreement. Comprehension would be enough. "We have to come up with stuff that will bring in new eyes. I want Eureka moments to be passed around virally on mobile phones. I want our Gilligan/Hamlet/Simpsons promo to show up on YouTube."

This was answered by the silent eruption of the worst fart yet. Everyone in the room acted as if it were as natural as a spring breeze.

Bobby was finished for the day. He asked for DVD copies of the Shakespeare programs they had in hand and for Acquisitions to look into what else they could get. The group rose and left the room. Ann King did not make eye contact with Judith Garlac, who said nothing to anyone as she gathered her papers. Clearly Judith was used to running this kingdom; Ann's coming home to claim her throne shook her as much as Bobby's arrival did. Bobby thought there was a fifty–fifty shot Judith would quit before he could fire her.

The heavy woman in black and purple put her hand on Bobby's and said in a near whisper, "I have been waiting for so long for someone to say that. Thank you."

I dunno, he thought as he headed into the hall, make your allies where you can find 'em, I guess.

The angry chinless man passed by them. He was almost pressed against the wall, walking at an awkward angle, in an effort to stay as far from Bobby as he could. He had his head down and his eyes almost closed. As he passed, Bobby caught the dead-animal smell. Chinless was the mad farter!

Bobby waited until he and the smell were gone and then said to the wide woman, "Who is he?"

She was delighted to conspire. "Mark Findle. He does clearances."

"And is he the . . ." Bobby fumbled. He waved his hand in front of his nose.

"Yes! They all assume it's uncontrollable, but I have my doubts!"

"You mean the guy just sits there and . . . lets it rip?"

"I think it's deliberate," the woman said. "I've noticed a pattern!"

Bobby nodded and followed her down the stairs. He missed New York like Starksy missed Hutch.

16.

obby's office was nice, at least. He took command of what had
been a conference room on the top floor of the great Victorian
house. A bay window looked down on a cove filled with sailboats. An antique oak table served as his desk. He had three television
monitors in a row against the wall. The pictures were on, the sound
off. He had a leather couch and a pair of stuffed chairs arranged
around a low coffee table covered with oversized gift books no one
had ever opened.

The three TVs were tuned to the three channels owned and operated by King Cable. It was a depressing panorama. Eureka was broadcasting a documentary about Dutch paintings. The Comic Book
Channel was running what Bobby prayed would be the final install-
ment of *Comix Quorum*. BoomerBox had a rerun of *Petticoat Junction*.

Bobby stared at the screens. It was Monday morning. It was hard
to face the job he had taken on. The printouts, notes, phone slips,
and cold coffee spread out across the table proved that when he left
the office Friday evening he had been full of fire. He had been doing
so many small things that the enormity of the job ahead had been ob-
scured by the activity.

But after a couple of days away from it, the challenge was intim-
idating. It was not possible to cancel every show on all three channels
and fire every person working there at the same time. Short of that,

though, he could not imagine how to get started with this salvage operation.

He muttered a little mantra: "Low Impact Monday, Low Impact Monday." It was something one of the vice presidents at the network used to say at the start of every week. This fellow was older, in his forties, a crook-spined lifer in the dark hole of Research. When Bobby would come roaring back from the weekend full of ideas and enthusiasm, the man would shuffle toward the coffee machine and tell him, "Bob, you need to husband your enthusiasm. Always strive for a Low Impact Monday. Ease yourself back into the work week. Take a long lunch, leave a little early, schedule nothing for Monday evening. It's the only way to do this for a long while without getting a hernia of the spirit."

Bobby had figured the man's spirit had herniated anyway, but this morning he understood. Maybe if he minimized his work today, if he really took it easy on himself, he would build up enough steam by tomorrow to plow into the massive task in front of him. Right now, he could not imagine ever seeing the end of this mine shaft.

His mood had sunk so low he was almost glad to see Kenny King bound in. Then Kenny spoiled it by speaking.

"Whoa, bro! Look at the big honcho at his biiiiig desk! Look at that window! Got the TVs goin', got the power chair! Hey, everybody! BOBBY KAHN IS ON TOP OF THE WORLD!"

"Had some coffee this morning, Ken?"

"I AM BUZZING ON BOBBY THE K!" Kenny scrunched up his face and made some weird Tom Jones dance move. Bobby wondered if he was going to jump up on his desk. If he did that, Bobby decided, he would punch him in the nuts.

"Listen to this, bro." Kenny leaned across Bobby's table and exhaled milk breath. "Big Daddy is in town and he wants to meet you A—S—A—PEEEE!"

How did this nut make it through junior high school? Bobby wondered. If he'd been in seventh grade in Massapequa he'd have been drowned in the boys' toilet the first day. "Who's the big daddy?" Bobby asked.

"The King of Kings!" Kenny shouted. "The big D!" He started warbling and strumming an invisible guitar. "Dominica-nica-nica, Daddy Dominic's in town! He wants to meet young Bobby and give Kenny boy his crown!"

Dominic King. The mysterious father. Bobby was anxious to meet the man whose money he was spending, whose empire he was charged with expanding, who had somehow bred this family.

An hour later Bobby and Kenny walked along a short stretch of broken sidewalk to The Red Tide, a shingled restaurant with a pink wooden swordfish over the door and lobstermen drunk at the bar. It was not quite noon. Kenny greeted a couple of the drunks by name. They did not acknowledge him.

Dominic King was reading the newspaper at a table by the window. He had a half-eaten plate of some sort of breaded meat in front of him. Silverware for three lay on paper place mats decorated with drawings of anthropomorphic quahogs licking their lips at the chef's specials. There were three water glasses, all of which the man reading the paper had drunk from.

"Daddy Dom!" Kenny announced. "This is Bobby Kahn, our big-shot TV executive who escaped NYC and has discovered the good life in little baby Rhode Island and says he will never go back!"

The man behind the newspaper looked up at Bobby as if he had asked if he wanted more bread. Dominic King had curly silver hair with thick black eyebrows on a hard narrow face. His skin was dark to begin with and darker from the sun. He was small and muscular, like someone who had spent years hauling rope. Bobby offered his hand. Dominic shook it without enthusiasm. He had almost no fingernails.

Kenny took one of the free chairs and drank from one of the half-empty glasses. Dominic gestured for Bobby to sit, too. A waiter brought over two plates of fish and chips. Dominic said, "I ordered for you."

Kenny dug in and talked with his mouth full. "Bobby and I have a million good ideas for the channel," he said, spitting bits of fish. "We're thinking of doing some made-for-TV movies which we could spin into licenses for action figures and video games—"

Dominic turned to Bobby. He said, "You have people up here?"

"No," Bobby said. "My family's on Long Island."

"Married?"

"No."

"Good."

"Hey, Dom," Kenny said, "you think Bobby might want to go out with Miss Quigly? She's pretty hot, huh?"

"Go get me some vinegar," Dominic said. He turned back to Bobby. "Why did you leave a big job in the city to come up here and work at this clam shack?"

Bobby read the old man's eyes. If he tried to tell him he believed passionately in the prospects of King Cable, he'd laugh in his face. But if he admitted he needed the job, he'd get no respect. So he said, "I was tired of being a cog in a big machine. I needed to run something on my own."

The old man nodded. That made sense to him.

"You go to college?"

"Yes."

"I didn't go to college," Dominic said. It was like a door had opened. He had decided Bobby was okay to talk to. "My mother wanted me to. She said, Become a pharmacist. I said, What, Ma, and stand behind a counter all day selling ointments to old ladies? Not me. I worked on cars. I liked that. She said, You'll be a grease monkey all your life. I said, Maybe. But I'll be doing work I enjoy."

Kenny started picking at Bobby's French fries. Dominic kept talking.

"By the time I'm twenty I open my own garage, right off the highway in Pawtucket. I do foreign engines, Japanese, you name it. Most places at the time only know how to do Ford, GM. I fix them all, whatever drives in, I can handle it. You know what I call my business?"

"What?"

"King Motors. You know why?"

"That's your name."

"Not yet it isn't. What? These ones didn't tell you? You think King's my real name? I look like a King to you? I'm born Dominic Coutu. You think the snobs on the east side are going to trust their Bentleys to a guinea named Dom Coutu? Oh no. But D. C. King of King Motors, he gets all the business."

"So you changed your name."

"Later. After my mother died. After I made so much money I didn't care. I had garages all over Rhode Island, Massachusetts. King Motors, King Used Cars, King Car Wash. I was very prominent."

"When we were kids," Kenny told Bobby, "Dom was on TV all the time. Commercials." Here Kenny began to recite in a booming announcer's voice, "Old car not running? Come see the King! Trouble with your engine? Come see the King! Finance issues keeping you out of the auto of your dreams? Come see the King!"

Kenny finally had his stepfather's attention. The old man fixed his eyes on him and said, "Your head is full of this crap." He turned back to Bobby and said, "He was a little blob, sitting in front of the television all day. Wouldn't go outside and play like a boy."

Kenny turned red but kept smiling. "Good thing for you. I got us into the TV business."

Dominic said to Bobby, "You know my son Skyler?"

"Sure."

"This one was always tagging along behind Skyler. From when they were this big. Like a puppy dog. When they're in college, they come to me."

"It was my idea," Kenny said.

"They come to me and Skyler says, Dad, we got a business proposal for you. You know what it is? They want me to loan them money to buy cable rights to Johnston, Cranston, East Providence. I said, What is this? They said, Cable television. Pay TV. I say, Who in the fuck is going to pay money for TV? They say, It's the new thing. You pay every month, you get a hundred channels. I say, What's on these hundred channels? Oh, they say, twenty channels of sports, ten channels of news, operas, movies, every ball game anywhere in the country you could want to see.

"I say, What's this miracle gonna cost me? They say, We can get the exclusive rights to three cities for two hundred thousand. I say, Dollars? Yes! How you gonna pay me back? Oh, we'll sell advertising. You two? Yes. Who's gonna buy it? Every bakery, every restaurant, every politician running for office. They'll all get to advertise on TV like you did, Dad, with King Motors.

"I say, This I want to see. I want to see you two lazy college boys knocking on the back door of Pickles Bakery to sell TV time to the guy making cupcakes. They say, Oh, Pop, we'll give you two minutes of free ads for the car washes and garages every hour. You take the money you're spending on TV commercials now and put it into this, and we not only get more ads, we own the stations."

"So you lent them the money."

"Almost. I put up the two hundred grand. I kept the stations in my name as collateral. Good thing, too."

"Funny how that worked out," Kenny mumbled.

Dominic carried on: "The day they hooked them up in the house, I went, What the hell? Some guy is running wires, thick as plastic clothesline, into the living room. He's drilling a hole in the wall. Skyler says, Dad, that's what makes it cable TV, it comes in a cable. I'm saying, What, people who get free television through the air are gonna pay to have it pumped into their house in a garden hose? I have my doubts.

"So they hook it up, they turn it on, I sit there with my clicker, and what? Twenty channels of sports? All the ball games? I don't think so. I got twenty channels of static and about ten channels showing *Green Acres* and *Car 54, Where Are You?*—the same old crap I already got on the old channels except the old channels are free! Now I'm thinking, Skyler's been hanging around with this one so long his stupidity rubbed off.

"I start screaming at them, For this I paid two hundred thousand dollars! I keep clicking around. Then I see this naked fat guy sitting on an inner tube—"

"Water bed," Kenny corrected.

"Squatting there with his gonads hanging out. What the hell! Now we're in the porno business or what? That's what I paid for— *Green Acres* and fat men with their dicks on display! I tell you, I was never so disgusted. Disgusted with my son, disgusted with this one, and disgusted with cable TV."

"It was a new world," Kenny said.

"Finally I calmed down enough, I said to them, You two are going to make this right. I don't know how, but I promise you this—you will make it right or you will never share in any of my money again for as long as you live."

"Motivation," Kenny said.

Bobby absorbed the emotional politics of the relationship. The old man was a hard-ass. Kenny wanted his approval. He was never going to get it.

"It worked out pretty well, though," Bobby said finally.

"Thank you," Kenny grunted.

"I tell you what turned it around," Dom said. "*Bonanza.*"

"Really."

"I told them, First thing you do you get rid of the dicks. No nudity on King Cable. Next thing, What have I bought for two hundred thousand dollars? I start looking at what's on these channels, what's NOT on. There's a show I always loved."

"*Bonanza?*"

"Yes! You know why? That's a show about family. And it's not some schmuck with no job riding a horse from town to town. It's not about a cop who lives in some house no cop could afford who gets shot in the shoulder every week and never takes a bribe. It's not some nonsense about a talking pig or a talking mule or a talking car or my wife's a witch or my wife's a genie or my wife's a mule or any of that foolishness. No, *Bonanza* is about a man who has made a lot of money and he's not ashamed of it. And he's been married many times, which is his prerogative."

"Ben Cartwright's wives DIED, Dom," Kenny said. "He didn't cheat on them and get divorced. . . ."

"So he says," Dom declared ominously. "You don't know the real story."

"It's fiction, Dom."

The old man ignored Kenny and continued, looking straight into Bobby's eyes like he was giving him the secret key to a successful future: "Ben Cartwright is a self-made man who maybe got his hands dirty, but he makes no apologies for that. Sometimes he has to shoot someone who comes on his land. That's the way it is. His son Adam says, 'Pa, send for the sheriff.' But he doesn't need that bullshit. He gets a gun and takes care of his own business. When Skyler was little we used to watch that show together every Sunday night. *Bonanza*. A man and his sons and the empire they built."

"Like you," Bobby said.

"Yes."

"And Skyler was Adam Cartwright."

"I see some similarities," Dom said. "But Adam went away to sea, was never heard from again. Ungrateful."

Kenny's mania was rising again. His mouth wiggled into a grin and his eyes got round with excitement. "I guess Bobby here is like Candy, the hired hand who becomes almost part of the family!"

"We'll see," Dom said carefully.

"And I'm Little Joe!"

"You," Dom looked half-amused at his stepson. "You're barely Hop Sing!" Kenny's face fell and for the first time Dominic King seemed happy. He leaned over to Bobby and said, "I made them run *Bonanza* on our channels twice a day, at five in the afternoon and at ten o'clock at night. I put all my King Motors ads in those runs. That's when this business really took off. Whatever these ones tell you, it was *Bonanza* that gave King Cable the cash flow to survive the first two years. After that, things got easier."

"Sure, Dom," Kenny said with exaggerated sarcasm. "It was all you. You and the Cartwrights. Nothing to do with me working my

ASS off selling ads up and down Route 95, working the phones, chasing down deadbeats, bringing in the actual CASH. That had nothing to do with our success."

"Cable TV really took off," Dominic said as if this was something Bobby wouldn't have heard about. "Between 1980 and 1984 we got TNT, CNN, MTV. The thing started happening. I took all the money I made—"

"I," Kenny repeated.

"I took all the money I made and put it right into buying up more towns. We spent two years fighting off all challengers to hook up Providence and Newport. Then we moved out toward the Cape. Fall River, New Bedford, Hyannisport."

"Speaking of Cartwrights," Kenny said.

"The Kennedys were a weak imitation of the Cartwrights!" Dom declared. "The old man and the three sons. Nixon was Paladin. His time was over."

"By 1985 King Cable controlled TV access in large parts of four New England states and some of upstate New York," Kenny said. "I could tell you every city. I went to the town hall meetings, I lobbied the local councils, I gave free cable to more mayors, board members, overseers, and newspaper editors than Ted Turner."

Bobby got the picture. When the Kings were building their cable empire, Kenny was the salesman, lobbyist, and bagman. He carried the dough to pay the bribes to get King Cable the contracts that became worth many millions of dollars, as television went from a free commodity to a leased service.

It explained a lot. Skyler had the vision and the old man had the money, but they needed someone to do the dirty work. Kenny was the fat kid who ate worms for a dime. He was desperate to be accepted. He'd do anything to be part of Skyler's family. Skyler got

Kenny to do the jobs Skyler would not stoop to do, jobs he didn't want to know about.

Kenny had served the Kings well. He knew where the family's dirty laundry was because he was the one who soiled it. They could never get rid of him.

Bobby studied Kenny picking at the last bits of fish batter and licking his fingers. It was possible he was smarter than the Kings, but his emotional dependence on them made him functionally dumber. Kenny longed for the family's acceptance and Skyler knew how to dangle it in front of him. The old man could not care less. He never would.

The bartender brought a check. Dominic wrote his name on it and stuck it under his plate. Kenny got up and said, "Gotta run, Dom. Phone conference with California."

Bobby stood and offered the old man his hand. Dominic grabbed his wrist and said, "It's good you're here. One thing I need you to do for me. I paid for all the *Bonanza*s. Three hundred and fifty episodes. These ones haven't run them in years. I want you to put them back on the air. All the sex and ugliness on television now. Young people should see these shows."

"The licenses may have expired," Bobby said. He didn't want to have to run forty-year-old Westerns on his channels.

"They have not," Dominic said. "Three hundred and fifty hours of the highest-rated television series of all time are gathering dust. I want you to get it back on."

They said good-bye and Kenny and Bobby walked back to the office. It began to rain, a sun shower. Bobby had a big enough job beating these bad channels into shape with a free hand. If he was going to have to program according to what the boss's father wanted to watch in his Barcalounger, there was no way to make it work.

"That's our dad," Kenny said gaily. "Welcome to King World!"

"You think we could just run him off copies of *Bonanza* and he could leave the rest of the world alone?" Bobby said.

"Dom is not happy," Kenny said, "unless everyone eats what he's eating."

17.

When they got back to the office, Kenny told an obvious lie about having to meet an independent producer and took off for the afternoon. Bobby walked upstairs to his office and found Annie King in a bad mood. Bobby had accepted Judith Garlac's resignation without consulting Annie. The King sister was sore. Bobby had already accepted that whatever slight chance he might have of finding romance with this long-necked English girl had to take a backseat to fixing her family's business. She liked him less every day.

In a chair against the wall behind Annie slumped pudgy Boris Mumsy, from what Bobby had seen the only African American in New Bedlam, Rhode Island. Boris had made an appointment with Bobby to present a list of ideas for the Comic Book Channel.

The old Bobby Kahn would have sent Boris away and placated Ann as quickly as possible and got her out of his office. In his new life, however, Bobby's resources were limited. These were his executives. Why should he take on their burdens? Who's the boy wonder here? Let them help HIM.

"Ann," Bobby said, "I asked Judith if she had spoken to you about quitting. She obviously did not want to. I don't know why, you'll have to ask her. Boris, if you will put your new show ideas in an e-mail, I will give them my full attention and get back to you with comment. Now, why don't both of you come in? I would like your advice."

Both looked taken aback. Ann eyed Boris like a hawk contemplating a hedgehog. Boris leaned away from her.

"It's come to my attention that we have over three hundred episodes of *Bonanza* in our library," Bobby said, settling into his chair
and glancing at his e-mail. "We need to figure out a smart way to use
that resource. I don't want to just run them as is. Can either of you
think of a stunt or a special or some way to package these shows that
will hook viewers and make a statement about the channels and
maybe generate a little press?"

"Bob," Ann said, "this is nothing to do with Eureka. If we could
take a minute to discuss—"

Bobby cut her off. "I don't know, Ann, Eureka might benefit from
some classic American gunslinging. Now come on, this is too small an
organization to put up walls between good ideas. You are my best
minds. Let's focus on this for a minute."

Boris Mumsy twisted. His eyes seemed to roll off in different directions. Then he said, "Robert Altman directed a lot of *Bonanza*s.
He got fired for making Hoss and Little Joe talk at the same time."

Annie looked at Boris as if he had just announced that Thomas
Jefferson invented cheese fries.

"See," Bobby said, "I never knew that. That's a good hook. Ann,
wouldn't you say some of Eureka's viewers would be interested in a
rare look at the television apprenticeship of one of America's great
film directors? What else, Boris?"

Boris Mumsy's eyelids were fluttering. He began to talk very
quickly. His face was lit with the satisfaction of a man ending a long
constipation with an explosive evacuation.

"Guy Williams, who played Zorro, did a season on the show as
Will Cartwright, Ben's nephew, when they first got the idea that Pernell

Roberts was going to quit. Then Pernell Roberts agreed to stay and so Guy Williams went and did *Lost in Space* and then Pernell Roberts quit after all, so they were screwed."

"Hmm, fascinating," Bobby said. He wondered what an X-ray of Boris's brain would look like. "That might be useful somewhere, but it's not as good as the Altman thing. What else?"

"You know, Ben Cartwright was a cabin boy in the War of 1812 and when Adam was a baby Ben was a sea captain in New Bedford and he gave Herman Melville the idea for *Moby Dick,* and then Adam's mother died and Ben roamed the West as a drunken bum until Hoss's mother cleaned him up and married him and she was Swedish and Hoss means 'Big Man' in Swedish, not 'Horse,' but she was killed by an arrow through the heart in an Indian attack and he took the two little boys out West in the Gold Rush and hit it rich and built the Ponderosa, and Joe's mother was a French woman from New Orleans who might have been a prostitute, they sort of fudged that, but—"

Bobby's head was clicking like a turnstile. "Go back to the War of 1812. Any other stuff like that?"

Annie looked like she was going to take a swing at someone.

Boris said, "Wellll, you know, Mark Twain was friends with the Cartwrights. He got the idea for *Tom Sawyer* at the Ponderosa. And during the Civil War, Ben had the vote to decide if Nevada would join the Union or the Confederacy and because of the Ponderosa's rich natural resources whichever side he joined was going to win the war, so he was under a lot of pressure from both the North and South and then he got wounded and had to give his vote to Joe, who was in love with a Southern girl—"

Annie couldn't stand it anymore. "Bob!" she snapped. "This is really not very useful! If you don't mind, I have work to do."

"This *is* our work," Bobby said. "How do you know all this stuff, Boris?"

"*Bonanza* was on every day after school when I was a kid," he said.

Yeah, Bobby thought, and you weren't outside playing baseball with your many pals, were you, you poor slob. All he said out loud was, "Thanks to Dominic King and his local car dealership."

Bobby reflected on one of the marvels of the television age: Thanks to endless syndicated reruns, children growing up in the sixties, seventies, eighties, and nineties all shared the same useless reference points. They could not name the vice presidents they'd lived through, but they could name every member of the Brady Bunch.

"Okay," Bobby said, "how do we take all this Cartwright alternative American history and make something out of it that will bring a lot of eyeballs and a lot of press to King Cable?"

"The Altman thing is interesting," Annie said glumly. "If Truffaut worked on *Little House on the Prairie* we might have something."

"Nah," Bobby said. "Ninety percent of viewers never heard of Robert Altman and ninety-nine percent don't care. But I like this Mark Twain, Moby Dick, Civil War stuff. Do you think we could chop up all these weird historic bits and make one big Ken Burns–type TV biography of Ben Cartwright, like he was a real person?"

Boris nodded enthusiastically. Annie exhaled. This was not the moment to protest but she promised herself that moment would come.

Bobby said, "You remember when they did that special television extended version of *Godfather I* and *II* where they recut the scenes in chronological order and added new bits and—"

"The Corleones moved to the Ponderosa!" Boris blurted.

"What?"

"In *Godfather II*, when they sell the house in New York and move west to take over the gambling in Las Vegas. They build a big estate on Lake Tahoe. That's where Michael kills Fredo. That was in the same place where the Ponderosa was."

"These are not real people!" Annie cried. "Bob, I have to go."

Boris Mumsy looked Ann King in the eye for the first time. He spoke with new confidence: "They are not real people, Ann, but their stories are set in real locations. Each episode of *Bonanza* opens with a burning map showing the location of the Ponderosa. It covers a great area just east of Reno, Nevada, and bordering the entire north side of Lake Tahoe. The same place the Corleones moved to a hundred years later."

A thoughtful silence descended, which Boris ended by crying, "Bang! Zoom!"

Bobby was delighted. A little because he had become Anne Sullivan to Boris Mumsy's Helen Keller. A little because Ann King had been put in her place so sweetly. But most of all he was delighted because he believed he had a stunt that would help brand one of his channels and make a statement about the new King Cable, while also giving the big boss what he wanted: respect to the Ponderosa.

"So tell me this," Bobby said. "How else can we compare the Cartwrights to the Corleones?"

Boris ran out of the room and came back in with two bags of M&M's. He poured them into his mouth while pacing back and forth between Bobby's office door and the picture window.

"Three sons!" he shouted. "Tough dad! They get in lots of gunfights! Move from the East Coast to Lake Tahoe!"

"Yeah," Bobby said, "the American myth. Loyal sons who kill their dad's enemies and come home for dinner around the family table. We need more."

"A metaphor for American capitalism," Ann said cautiously. "It was a useless contribution, but Bobby nodded as if it were strong. Get her into the game.

"The two older sons die and the little one no one took seriously ends up inheriting the whole thing," Boris said. He dribbled a little bit of chocolate on his shirt when he said it.

"Whoa," Bobby said. "Say that again."

"Well, it's all about Adam and Sonny at first," Boris said. "Then Adam is lost at sea and Sonny gets shot in the toll booth, so it goes to Hoss and Fredo, but Hoss dies saving a little girl from drowning—"

"I didn't know that," Ann said.

"And Fredo gets shot and dumped in the lake, so Michael Corleone and Joe Cartwright end up in charge of the empire."

Ann allowed herself a little laugh. "Sounds like the Kennedys," she said.

"Yeah," Bobby said. "Dominic was funny. He said the Kennedys were copying the Cartwrights."

They were all silent for a moment. Boris was circling the room like a lost duck looking for a place to land.

Bobby said, "It's exactly like the Kennedys, actually."

Annie nodded. "The father who built the empire. The three sons, the first two are killed—"

Bobby said to Boris, "When did *Bonanza* come on anyway?"

"Every day at five."

"No, no, I mean originally."

"Sunday night at nine."

"What *year*, Boris?"

"Oh. Late fifties. 1959."

"That's weird," Bobby said. "Before Kennedy was president. That's really strange." He began to laugh. "Boris, this is great. Ann, I'd like to put some of your production guys on this. We'll need Acquisitions to look into getting a window on the *Godfather* movies, and we gotta start buying up every Kennedy movie: *The Missiles of October; PT109; The Greek Tycoon; Young Joe, the Forgotten Kennedy!*"

"You know," Ann volunteered, "we might be able to work *The Brothers Karamazov* into this, too."

Bobby said, "Hmm, could be, Ann. Send me a fax on that one."

It might have been diplomacy, it might have been hypocrisy, but Bobby chose to accept Ann's contribution as sincere support. He wanted the head of marketing in here right away.

He reached for his phone and hit "O." A robot woman's voice said, "Welcome to the phone mail system. Please say the name of the employee you wish to reach."

"Abe Tottle."

The robot voice said, "Did you say, 'Jerry Hellman'?"

"No."

"Did you say, 'Gail Suberti'?"

"No."

"Sorry. Please say the name of the employee you wish to reach again, or if you wish to speak to the operator, say 'Operator.'"

"Operator."

"Did you say, 'Kenny King'?"

Bobby put down the phone and walked to the door of his office and asked his assistant to go get Abe Tottle.

When the freckled Tottle arrived and saw the strange alliance convened, he registered a curiosity bordering on mild alarm.

"Abe," Bobby said proudly. "BoomerBox is going to plan, launch, and execute a full-on month-long superstunt for third quarter. I want promotions, newspaper articles, drive-time radio call-in shows, full-page ads in *USA Today*, and billboards on every bus shelter along Madison Avenue."

"Great," Tottle said. "I'll sell all our homes to pay for it. What is the campaign?"

"Kennedys, Cartwrights & Corleones!" Bobby said proudly. "Three generations of America's First Families!"

Tottle shook his head and smiled. Annie showed some pride in having been part of a successful brainstorm, and Boris Mumsy's bent spine uncurled to reveal a self-confident young TV executive.

Bobby Kahn did not know for sure if it was a good idea or an idiotic release of pent-up tension, but for the first time since he lost his job in New York he was enjoying a day at work.

18.

There were two approaches to the King house. There was a paved road that turned to white gravel as it got near the front door, with forks off toward the barn and the guesthouse. Everyone from the mailman to dinner guests came up that way.

Bobby drove to the house by the back way, a muddy road that wound through an uncut meadow, past a small green pond, and along a stone wall until it ended behind the house in a dirt patch where several generations of King automobiles had lived and died. This was the approach used by the family and those friends who didn't have to knock. A row of half-tended shrubs protected people in the house from having to see what looked like the morning after a demolition derby. Along with four working cars—two new SUVs, an Audi station wagon, and a dusty Mustang convertible with the keys in the ignition—sat the rusting bones of a 1957 Thunderbird, a huge gray DeSoto that looked like something Humphrey Bogart drove to a rubout, a John Deere tractor missing one wheel, and a bird-shit-stained yellow Karmann Ghia with the seats removed and a family of cats living inside.

Bobby was vaguely aware that using the back entrance marked him as an intimate of the Kings, not merely an employee, though he hated banging the bottom of his BMG on the rutted road to take advantage of the privilege. He had found an apartment in an oceanfront condominium complex one town over, but he still had most of his clothes in the King guesthouse.

He parked and walked past the cats chewing over a dead bird and came around the hedge to the side porch, where Annie, Skyler, and Skyler's wife, Claudia, were drinking iced tea and playing cards. The two women barely acknowledged Bobby when he said hello. Skyler looked up and back fast, as if he were afraid of being cheated.

"Be with you in a minute, Bob," Skyler said, gesturing toward the door to the kitchen. "Grab a Lorna Doone."

Bobby stepped from sunlight into shadows. He clicked a switch on the wall, but only a faint light came on. A dozen lamps disguised to look like candles in glass bells were mounted on the walls, but only two of them worked. He figured he could fix that if someone gave him a screwdriver and a soldering iron.

He found the cookies and put them on a china plate and brought them back out to the card game.

"What are you playing?" Bobby asked.

"Casino, King family pastime," Claudia said. "You better learn. But be careful, they change the rules if you start to win."

"I'm going to leave these sore losers to their bitterness," Skyler said. He got up and the two men walked away from the porch onto the grass.

"I had my first sit-down with Eureka," Bobby said. "Strange crew."

"Careful what you say to Annie," Skyler said. "Bring her along gently. Let her feel like she's in on the decisions. She's upset that you shit-canned Judith."

Bobby began to defend himself, but Sky shook his head. "She'll get over it. What's the takeaway on Eureka?"

"Ann's a little proprietary right off," Bobby said. "That's to be expected. That's fair. She's smart and she'll learn fast. Some of her staff, though, strike me as shaky."

"Talking about me?" Annie asked. She had come up on them quietly. She looked at Bobby. "Did you really have time to get to know these people and assess their strengths and weaknesses and evaluate the contributions they had made and the talents—"

"Hey, Annie," Skyler said. "I have to be able to ask Bob for his gut reactions and he has to be able to give them to me without worrying about someone keeping score. Now, can he and I talk freely or do we need to get out of here?"

Annie said nothing. She seemed very young next to Skyler. Before she turned to go she gave Bobby a look that was half warning and half imploring: Don't tell my big brother I don't know what I'm doing.

Bobby suddenly saw the way to get Annie on his side: Treat her as Skyler's equal. She was the classic late child, the kid who thought she had missed all the good stuff and would always be playing catch-up. Bobby doubted that there had really been a lot of good stuff to miss with the Kings, but he would happily conspire to make Annie feel like she deserved a seat at the grown-ups' table. He said, "I'd love it if I could sit down with you this week, Ann, and get your input. You know more about this than I do."

She left happy.

When Annie was gone Bobby said, "Who's the fat woman who tried to sit on my lap the whole meeting? Old hippie type, you know, probably got a house full of cats and candles. Kept agreeing with everything I said before I said it."

"Ah ha ha ha. Abigail! Abigail Plum, Eureka's auteur, aka Abigail Plump, aka Flabby Abby. Creator, producer, executive producer, writer, and interviewer of the channel's top-rated series, *FootNotes*—in which Abigail uses her unique gifts of empathy to get today's leading lights in literature, theater, film, and pottery making to open up about their creative process. A rare bird, our Abigail."

"Wait, Kenny told me about this. Did they do a parody of her on *Saturday Night Live*?"

"Some claim she helped inspire one of their sketches, 'some' being only Abigail herself and a couple of the trolls who work for her. No one else believes anyone at *Saturday Night Live* ever heard of her. Kenny likes to repeat the story, though."

"Is she any good? Is her show good?"

"You'll tell me. It's the most popular thing on Eureka. But that's like saying it's the most nutritious doughnut."

"And the pissed-off little man with no chin? Pasty? Round shoulders and an enormous ass?"

"Ah, Mark Findle." Skyler laughed. "He's a pip, isn't he? Nasty. Had a wife. Poor woman looked like she was scared to talk. Finally left him for a milkman. Who knew where she found a milkman in this day and age? Really ticked him off. I heard he put all her clothes in his front yard and set fire to them. Later found out she had money in one of the pockets. Angry, angry guy. Totally unemployable."

"Well, that raises the question—"

"Hey, get rid of him if you need to. Do what has to be done. Get that channel working, Bob. No sentimentality."

"I mean, this guy Findle—he's in charge of clearances, right? That's a job that requires a lot of glad-handing, a lot of schmoozing. It's hard to imagine him being good at it."

"Yah, well, truth to tell, Bob, I think Eureka has been sort of a bottom-feeder. I mean, the stuff they put on, I don't think anyone's fighting over the third-run rights to old Moscow Ballet specials, you know?"

"Exactly. But that's got to change and I need a good clearance person and a great head of acquisitions, someone who has real relationships, who can get us programming that people will want to watch. I don't want to judge anyone too quickly, but I just can't imagine Findle developing the sorts of skills we need in the time we have."

"And you haven't mentioned the rippers."

"Geez! Thank you! I didn't think I was the only one who noticed."

"Oh no. Hard to miss. He fumigates a room. Annie claims it was a by-product of some drastic weight-loss program he went on when his wife left him. He drank bottles of this purple pudding all day and dropped fifty pounds in about four weeks. That's when the farting started. They're all too sensitive to bring it up. After four or five years, though, we began to suspect it was not entirely involuntary."

"I'd like to consider seeing who else is available with that skill set," Bobby said.

"You won't find someone else who can cut gas like Chinless Findle," Skyler said. They laughed like two buddies in a beer commercial.

19.

kyler, Ann, and Kenny were surprised to see a sort of friend-
ship forming between Bobby Kahn and old Dominic. There
was no real precedent for Dom reaching out to anyone he had
not known for decades. It was hard for his children to know what to
make of it.

If Bobby was sometimes appalled by the old man, he was also
sometimes impressed. Dominic could not have been more different
from the network suits who thought of themselves as self-made men
but were in fact salaried functionaries who had never risked anything
that mattered. Dom had clawed up with his fingers and teeth and
made no apologies for not caring which fork he used. You could say a
lot of bad things about him, but he had less hypocrisy in him than
anyone Bobby had ever known.

The more time they spent together, the more Bobby saw that he
could learn from the old man. Dom knew money, Dom knew people,
Dom knew how to manipulate local laws and federal tax rules to his
ends. All that was interesting to someone of Bobby's disposition. He
came to understand over time that what Dominic King really knew
was how to hate. Whether that was useful or not, Bobby wasn't sure,
but it was interesting to observe.

Dom had a deep catalog of hatreds, general and personal. He
hated know-it-alls, he hated condescension, he hated goody-two-
shoes. He hated people who talked too much and Amtrak and the

Catholic church. He hated whining, canned spaghetti, and arrogant waiters. He did not simply dislike these people, institutions, and commodities. He hated them. The snotty waiter might leave work to find that a sharp key had been dragged along the side of his parked car. The monsignor might wake to learn that a legal challenge had been filed to his legitimate request for a building permit. The canned spaghetti might return to the market through a glass window.

Old age had not dimmed Dom's fires. If anything, rage at his body's diminishing capacities had stoked the furnace. Fury was the fuel he fed on. It focused his mind and gave him power.

Dom didn't know French and he didn't know calculus. He would not have been able to name a philosopher if he caught one crapping in his corncrib. Who was his congressman? Like he gave a flying frig. But hatred, this he would know. And it worried him that his children did not share his capacity.

Oh, the girl, Annie, she was a flower child anyway. What did she know? A kid. Let her get married a couple of times and she'd locate her loathing. It was Sky who worried him. Sky was a grown man with children of his own. His lack of enmity struck Dom as a real weakness. Everything had come too easy to Sky. Always got someone else to do the dirty work. That was fine as a convenience but it was bad for his character. Sometimes a man needs to get his own hands soiled, if only so he can know in his gut how the world really works. Sky knew it in his head, but that might not be good enough if things went south. Sooner or later, Dom believed, things always go south.

In the library of Dom's loathing, there was a lit spot on a high shelf saved for the Newport contractor Dan Clancy. "Fancy Danny Clancy," Dom called him with spite in front of as many people as he could as often as possible. Sometimes he referred to him as Nancy Clancy, an odd aspersion to cast on a man of rigorous masculinity.

The barb was doubly sharp as many of the people to whom Dom disparaged Clancy knew that long ago Dom had cuckolded him. The implication was medieval; had Clancy been a real man Dominic King could not have seduced his wife.

Dom could be a real jerk about stuff like that.

It galled him that Clancy had forgiven his adulteress wife and taken her back. For years afterward it infuriated him when the pair of them and their freckled children would march up to communion every Sunday and made a show of dropping a fat wad in the collection basket. It made him fume to see newspaper photographs of them laughing together on the lawn of some Newport charity function. In his less rational moments, Dom wished he'd had gonorrhea so he could have passed it along to them.

It was an old enmity, but like a bad tooth it still ached. Dom had hated Clancy long before he took his wife across her ironing board, itself many years now gone. Dom had hated Clancy since the contractor first made money and began carrying himself like an old Yankee mill owner. As Clancy went from paving parking lots to throwing up garages to building banks to winning municipal contracts in Newport and Providence, he acted like the Lord Mayor of Dublin come back as a jackass. He tried to buy himself into society by giving over his ludicrous home to political galas and sponsoring teams of retards in the Special Olympics.

What poor excuse for a man waves his money around like a bouquet?

Worst of all, in the days before Dom's contempt was communicated, Clancy used to call on him for donations to this or that pathetic cause. "The unwed mothers need our support," he whined, "if we're ever to turn them from the course of vile abortion. Can I look to you for a thousand, Dominic?"

"You can look to my ass, Dan, to see what comes out of it."

Dan Clancy really earned Dom's contempt when Clancy Construction merged with Cianci Brothers Realty of North Providence to become Clancy & Cianci. The pig-nosed, red-faced Irishman got in bed with Dom's brother Italians to leech off more of the state and city construction contracts and buy up fields and meadows all along the ocean to throw up crappy housing developments with fairy names like "Longfellow Acres" and "Walden Court."

The Ciancis with whom Clancy partnered were no kin to Buddy Cianci, the notorious mayor of Providence whose twenty-year reign over Rhode Island's capital was interrupted only by occasional felony convictions. These were Ciancis from a whole other part of Italy. But of course everybody assumed they were relations, and Clancy & Cianci never worked too hard to correct the misapprehension. How many extra millions had been shoveled into their dump trucks because out-of-state imbeciles thought they were buying favor with the mayor? How many kickbacks intended for Providence City Hall made their way into Dan Clancy's Sunday envelope? And did the pale-eyed prig ever have the honesty to turn it back to whichever poor dipshit sent the bribe up the wrong hose? No, no, no. Mr. Propriety was too busy posing for pictures holding a shovel at the groundbreaking of the new children's hospital.

Professionally, Clancy and Dom had crossed spears for the first time in the eighties when Dom was seeking to grease the city of Providence to give him a lucrative tow-truck contract. Tow trucks and snow removal had begun as a sideline to Dom's limousine rental business, itself an outgrowth of his car lots. Dom had made an informal consortium with two other tow-truck operators to lobby the city to install parking meters on the unregulated streets of downtown. Such an innovation would bring increased revenue to the city, provide a boon to downtown parking garages, regulate the traffic flow, and re-move the spectacle of ugly junk heaps sitting for days or even weeks in front of struggling businesses. The bulk of the money made from tow fines would further fatten the city's purse. But the fees paid out of those fines to the tow-truck operators would be a substantial wind-fall, too.

It was a pleasant scenario for everyone. Almost everyone, anyway. The whimpering of a few small merchants and restaurants that it was tough enough to lure consumers away from the suburban malls and into downtown without towing their cars was lost amid the song of imagined cash registers ringing all the way from Providence City Hall to King Towing.

It was to have been a sweet deal indeed. But somehow, when the en-velopes containing the bids were opened, Dominic King and his part-ners had been underbid by a last-minute and unforeseen competitor—a new entity called Emerald Road Service Inc., incorporated that very week in nearby Smithfield, and owned by a small group of local busi-ness executives organized by Daniel Clancy.

And what was the difference between bids in this contract worth millions of dollars over the next ten years? Why, by a most remarkable subtlety of reckoning, Emerald Road Service had managed to submit an estimate for its services only two hundred and fifty dollars cheaper than that offered by Dominic King and his group.

It cost Dom money, it cost Dom the respect of his partners, and it cost Dom his inroads with the Cianci administration. The last was not necessarily the choice of the mayor, but once a man screws you like that there's no going back.

It was in the wake of this humiliation that Dom set about seduc-ing Clancy's wife, a job no easier for her being unattractive. Dom had not reckoned on Clancy taking her back, or her going, or the two of them acting now like it had never happened as a new generation of red-haired grandchildren belly-flopped into the Clancy gene pool.

It really pissed him off.

Understanding as he did the reciprocal protocols of hatred, Dom had long waited for a retaliatory volley. For years Clancy merely passed him by with cold contempt, hardly even bothering to badmouth him. A woman might have assumed that Clancy had moved on emotionally, that whatever malice he bore Dom in his heart he had cleansed in the holy waters of forgiveness. A woman could afford to think that way.

It worried Dom that his own son Skyler might even think that way sometimes, like a woman.

Dom knew that a man who had scratched up from the bottom could never think that way. He knew Clancy was waiting for him. It could be a pipe in an alley, or it could be a whisper to the IRS. Dom did what he always did—he watched where he stepped.

Part of him was relieved when the shot was finally fired. When that wrecking ball flew through the air and splintered the old double-decker house that abutted King Cable, it had swung from the arm of a crane owned by Clancy & Cianci. Dom's foe had shown his teeth at last. He had bought up the land around Dom's lovely seaside Victorian and was going to dig a deep basement, fill it with cement, pile up gray cinderblocks five stories high, cover Dom's windows, devalue his property, and open some kind of low-rent, public-service needle exchange/homeless shelter/soup kitchen/leper bath right smack up against the King family's respectable business.

Dom had walked with Kenny through the King Cable house. There were new cracks snaking across the plaster. The grouting was coming loose. Shelves were tipping, tapes were sliding, fragile electronic equipment was being knocked around.

Dominic had known this was just the first shot. When they started digging it would get much worse. A slip or two, a pipe cut, a power line punctured, a cesspool backed up. That was nothing. Petty harassment. The real damage would come when they got underground. These old shorefront houses were all built on sand. You start digging under one, the sand moves, the foundations crack, the walls begin to heave and shift. Maybe you apologize and act magnanimous and plaster those fissures right over and throw in a new coat of paint. In exchange, of course, for a settlement paper laying out the limits of responsibility, indemnifying the new builders against any future claims for damages by the owners of the old and frankly, Your Honor, dubious adjacent structure.

Dominic knew how this would play out. Two, three, five years from now his house would fall down with his business inside, maybe with one of his kids in it. And Fancy Dan Clancy would be in the legal clear.

Skyler had wanted to call in more lawyers and get another writ to stop the work. Like Clancy would have not already bribed the zoning board.

Skyler thought he knew how the world worked, but he didn't know. In that last battle with Fancy Dan, it had been Kenny the redheaded stepchild who played dirtier than the fat Irishman to whom he bore an uncomfortable physical resemblance.

A smile crossed Dominic King's face like a razor slicing skin. An Indian graveyard? How fuckin' funny was that? It had to be Kenny. If Dom had any doubts he lost them the night the environmentalists shut down Clancy's excavation.

That night Dominic walked up to the top floor of his seaside Victorian mansion and made his way to the widow's walk. There he found

Kenny King, flanked by his two drooling puppets, Moe and Bignose, standing on the rail on which he had lined up empty beer bottles, pissing over the side into the empty cab of Dan Clancy's crane.

The two goons cowered when they saw the old man, but Kenny went right on urinating, cursing the absent construction crew in a maniacal cackle.

It was perhaps the only time in his life when Dominic had thought, "I wish Skyler could be a little more like Kenny."

20.

Skinny Albert Freud and tubby Todd Antonocio entered the King conference room for the weekly Comic Book Channel staff meeting to find their companion Boris Mumsy and, to their surprise, a full complement of King Cable executives, including Khefa from ratings, Abe from marketing, Jerry from promos, and the boy wonder himself, Bobby Kahn. It crossed Albert Freud's mind that this might be the inevitable day someone came in and closed the Comic Book Channel and he would be forced to go back to dental school.

"Sit down, guys," Bobby Kahn said. "I want to get going."

Albert saw that Bobby was acquiring a suntan. He's taking to our seaside ways, he thought. The sun left no stain on Albert or Todd. They were white as bleach. Even Boris was pretty pale for a black man. The staff of the Comic Book Channel might not score well in a push-up contest, but they were under no threat from melanoma.

Bobby called the meeting to attention.

"I know you have to run through your agenda," Bobby said, "but I want to get all of you thinking about a new priority. Boris has come up with a terrific stunt idea for Eureka."

He filled the room in on "Kennedys, Cartwrights & Corleones."

Bobby went on: "I've been looking at just the initial footage, the writing, the clips that are coming in, and I've got to tell you, this feels big to me. I think Eureka is going to get a lot of bang out of this. It's smart, it's funny, it can help put us on the map. Now my challenge to you guys is, what is the equivalent stunt for the Comic Book Channel? What can we come up with that will spin old acquisitions in a new way? Come on, guys, let's jam on this a little right now and then I would ask all of you to form breakout groups and get back to me with some formal ideas."

"How about a weekend of *Wonder Woman*?" Khefa suggested. No one said anything.

"What do you see that being?" Bobby asked.

"Like, all the best episodes of *Wonder Woman* in a single weekend."

No one spoke. Bobby was determined to coach here. "No bad ideas, people. Let's talk it through. Was there ever a *Wonder Woman* movie? Anything?"

"There was a cartoon show," Khefa said.

"How about other female superheroes?" Bobby asked. "There was *The Bionic Woman*, right? Okay, this is how I need you to think. Who else? *Xena the Warrior Princess*. A *Supergirl* movie."

"*Sheena, Queen of the Jungle*," Todd offered.

"I don't think we want to go black and white," Bobby said. "Needs to be in the memory of the core. This could work, be good for female viewers, balance the demos a little. What is the male/female split on Comic Book Channel, Khefa?"

"Ninety-seven percent male," Khefa replied.

There was an awkward silence in the room.

"Okay," Bobby said, "maybe we don't *start* with a female stunt. What else? Come on, folks, this is your channel. What do your core viewers respond to?"

Albert Freud suggested a five-part series on EC Comics, *Mad* magazine, and the McCarthy-era crusade against horror comics led by the right-wing psychologist Fredric Wertham. Bobby looked at him as if he had frogs coming out of his ears.

"Too high and inside," Bobby said. "Look, of the stuff you do, what raises the needle? Boris?"

Boris said, "Batman."

Albert rolled his eyes. Bobby asked Boris to elaborate.

"Really, anytime we do anything on Batman the numbers go up," Boris said. "We had those movie specials and they always did really well, repeated forever. And when we had the artist who did the Joker limited series on *Comix Quorum*, we got the best numbers ever."

Bobby slapped the desk. "THAT'S what I need to know!" He looked over at Khefa, who nodded, verifying Boris's stats. "And look how much material there is to draw from! There's the *Batman* movies, with all the attendant promo material, there's the old TV show—"

Todd moved to protest that the sixties *Batman* TV series was a blight from which the comic-book culture took decades to emerge, but Albert put a hand on his wrist to silence him. It was like in the school cafeteria, when too passionate an expression of conviction about the *The Doom Patrol* might attract a slap from a passing jock. Todd recognized Albert's warning at once. Bobby Kahn was that teenage jock in a new incarnation. The Comic Book Channel staff would have to moderate their passions around him. Boris had clearly been the quickest to figure this out. He was already speaking Bobby's language, like the nerd who did the bully's homework.

"There's tremendous material on Batman," Boris said. "He's one of those iconic characters that even people who never read comics have opinions on. We could start now collecting comments from any celebrities we interview on any of the other channels. If Abigail's interviewing Meryl Streep about her new movie, throw in a question about Batman at the end. Store 'em up and use 'em as bumpers."

The rest of the group looked at Boris Mumsy as if he had levitated into the air and floated over the table. When had the stuttering black kid with the fluttering eyelids gained this confidence? When had he ever offered an opinion about anything other than which Green Lantern had the coolest costume? Next thing you knew he'd be going out with girls!

Bobby Kahn approved. He said, "That's the thinking we need, people! I like it a lot. Warners is doing another *Batman* movie, right? They'll help us get material. There must be old junket interviews with George Clooney and Michael Keaton and Christian Bale. Those would be cheap and could be the basis for a new special. How long has Batman been around?"

"1939," Albert said quickly. He wanted to get in on this.

"Wow," Bobby said. "That's a lot of history right there!"

"There were early movie serials, too," Boris said. "Black-and-white stuff from the forties. Really goofy."

"Great," Bobby said. "That'll be good for press, but don't spend too much time there. Make sure you keep coming back to the new movie. That'll keep the studio happy, too."

"I can interview Frank Miller," Todd suggested. "The guy who did *The Dark Knight Returns.*" Bobby looked at him blankly. "That was the graphic novel that redefined the character for a new generation."

Bobby nodded. "Just make sure you use plenty of graphics and remember, keep coming back to the movies. The audience we want to reach doesn't know anything about the comic books. Make sure you get lots of footage of Michelle Pfieffer and Halle Berry in their Catwoman costumes, too. Don't be too gay about this."

Bobby regretted saying it as soon as the phrase left his lips. At the network using a derogatory term like *too gay* would have got him hauled off to the Human Resources dungeon and sentenced to a weekend of diversity training. Here it was worse. The staff of the Comic

Book Channel might or might not be homosexual, but each of them had probably been called "fag" since sixth grade.

It was Albert Freud who saved Bobby with an unexpected wise-crack: "Holy homosexual subtext, Batman!"

Everyone laughed. Bobby smiled and said weakly, "Not that there's anything wrong with it, Boy Wonder."

"I'll take care of it," Boris announced. He stood from the table and said to Bobby, "We'll work up an outline for the Batman project. I think we can come up with something special."

Todd leaned toward Albert as Boris strode from the room. "Boris has been bitten by a radioactive spider," he whispered.

21.

When he arrived in New Bedlam, Bobby gave up his social life like a man going into a monastery. At first he went back to New York most weekends, then only on Sundays, and lately just once or twice a month. There was too much work to be done at King Cable to waste time on the weekends. He had sublet his apartment in Manhattan and moved most of his belongings into his mother's attic on Long Island.

Bobby didn't mind keeping his mother at a safe distance. She had her sisters and her daughter to keep her occupied. Bobby's mom had no real conception of where Rhode Island was. She thought any land north of the Whitestone Bridge was populated by lumberjacks.

Initially concerned that her son had sent himself into exile to mourn a broken heart, she had insisted that Bobby ask out the daughter of one of her friends. They had hit it off okay, and in his first disconnected weeks at King Cable, Bobby had come home to take the young woman out a couple of times. They had even kissed in his car, like teenagers, but he stopped it there. He had to make this new job work and a weekend girlfriend on Long Island would only distract him. It was an obligation he could not assume.

After a summer in New Bedlam, though, the prospect of finding some female companionship began to nudge into his program planning. He had a brief fling with a woman who worked at a gym he had joined, but she turned out to have both a small daughter and an ex-husband who taught kung fu.

As a man's libido rises, his discretion sinks. On a hot August Saturday, Bobby agreed to go with Kenny to a bar in Newport where, Kenny swore, the women had neither scruples nor bras. Some shred of his normal restraint warned Bobby that taking romantic advice from Kenny was like getting safety tips from the cast of *Jackass,* but he rationalized that he was only going to unwind and have a couple of beers and—anyway—the channels were starting to head in the right direction. It was healthy to blow off some steam.

As soon as Bobby got in the front seat of Kenny's Land Rover— Bignose and Moe were already in the back—he wondered if he was really in such need of female companionship as to justify this company, and if this company might not preclude any shot at romance. They pulled out of New Bedlam like the cast of *Happy Days,* with a Green Day CD blasting and beer bottles splashing as a wild-eyed Kenny hit every bump on the Jamestown and Newport bridges.

Kenny had the self-absorption of an adolescent, along with a teenager's lack of filters on his mouth or libido. He was not a kid, though. Kenny was sliding toward middle age. His youthful freckles were beginning to look like sun damage.

Kenny had always had a thick skin when it came to chasing women. He did not mind rejection. He figured it into his calculations. Kenny's philosophy, imparted to Moe and Sammy Bignose like the secret of the genome, was that in any bar on any Friday you had to expect twenty rejections for every one invitation to sit down, five sit-downs for every phone number, three phone numbers for every date, and a total of eight dates with as many as four separate women for every successful culmination of sexual congress.

Of course, the statistics varied according to the height or depth of one's standards. In Kenny's experience, ugliness was less of an issue than an amateur might expect. Homely women often had elaborate defenses. Many beautiful woman had unseen vulnerabilities. At fifteen minutes to closing time, looks told you nothing, so you might as well hit on the pretty ones first. What did change the odds was age. While there were no sure things, women over forty hanging around bars on the weekend were the easier fish to land, regardless of how attractive, smart, or well-off they might be. Kenny had recently found himself trolling those waters. It scared him. The women he slept with were important to him as a mirror reflecting his own value and attractiveness. Lately it was tough to look in that mirror.

Not that Kenny shared any of this with Bobby. What he said to Bobby as they roared into a parking lot on a hill behind a big barroom was, "Code of Men, Bob: What happens at the Rhode House stays at the Rhode House!" He locked the car and hurried down the hill like a sailor landing at a free bordello.

Richard's Rhode House was a warehouse-size saloon with early rock-and-roll records hanging from the ceiling and murals of dead rock stars lined up like saints along the wall. Bobby recognized a blue Jimi Hendrix praying over a flaming guitar, and a ghostly Jim Morrison floating in a coffinlike bathtub. Most of the others, old black men and mad-eyed rockabilly rebels, he did not know. Bobby was not a big rock-music fan. He liked Billy Joel, Madonna, and though he would not admit it to these guys, Broadway show times.

The room was filled to what looked like three times the fire capacity. A very large band—ten or twelve men with horns—was making an ear-bleeding racket from a stage on the far side of the room. Kenny paid a cover to a bearded, toothless man at the door, refused to let Bobby contribute, and bullied his way up to the bar to get each of them a Guinness in a plastic cup. Sammy and Bignose vanished into the crowd.

Bobby's eyes got used to the room and his ears got used to the sound. A lantern-jawed front man in ruffled shirt and tight pants was bellowing through a barrage of oldies. "Expressway to Your Heart," "It's Not Unusual," "Do Wah Diddy Diddy," "Hitch-Hike," "Boom Boom (Out Go the Lights)."

Kenny was doing some mutant version of the Hully Gully while his beer splished and splashed. Bobby chugged his drink fast, before it got knocked out of his hands. He leaned toward Kenny and shouted, "So this is Rhode Island nightlife!"

Kenny was peering around the room like a hunting dog. He saw something and without a word shot into the crowd. When Bobby spotted him again, he was on the staircase, halfway up to the balcony, his shirttails flying and his hair in his wet red face, dancing with a tattooed woman in an "I'm with Stupid" T-shirt. A mustachioed bouncer was trying to get his attention and move him off the stairs, but Kenny was oblivious.

Bobby swam back to the bar and got another drink. The band finished an especially frantic reading of the Supremes' "Come See About Me" and a chant rose from the crowd.

"Shoe shots! Shoe shots! Shoe shots! Shoe shots!"

The singer feigned puzzlement. He looked around at his bandmates, who shrugged and acted confused. The singer walked to the edge of the stage, leaned over, and cocked an ear to the audience.

"SHOE SHOTS! SHOE SHOTS! SHOE SHOTS!"

Light seemed to dawn on the singer's face. He mimed a gesture like raising a cup to his lips. His expression said, "You mean THIS?"

Acclamation moved through the room. The chanting was now unanimous. Kenny King, his arm around the tattooed lady on the stairs, had his left shoe in his hand and was swaying with the room, shouting.

"SHOE SHOTS! SHOE SHOTS! SHOE SHOTS!"

To the delight of the crowd, the singer on stage asked for a shoe from the front of the audience. Thirty sneakers, sandals, and boots were waved up at him. He selected a petite pointy-toed high heel offering. He waved to his trombone player, who appeared at his side with a bottle of red wine.

Oh come on, Bobby thought to himself, they're not really going to do this. . . .

The trombone player filled the shoe with wine, politely demurred from taking the first sip, and then led the audience in chanting "SHOE SHOTS! SHOE SHOTS! SHOE SHOTS!" as the singer tipped the shoe to his lips and chugalugged the whole thing.

He wiped his mouth with the back of his hand, raised the empty shoe into the air like the head of a slain enemy, and tossed the shoe back to a big-haired woman while the band behind him kicked into an impassioned rendition of James Brown's "I Feel Good."

Nero in his decadence would have blushed at the frenzy that followed. All over Richard's Rhode House young men and women who tomorrow would be going to school, working in banks, operating heavy machinery, and behind the wheels of automobiles were filling each other's shoes with liquor and beer, passing them around, and guzzling down booze, toe jam, and sock string with wild abandon.

Bobby must have looked alarmed and alone. A young woman with a shock of blond hair falling across her left eye looked at him and laughed. He looked back at her with what he hoped she would read as boyish hurt.

"Don't rub it in," he said.

"You're new here." She smiled. She had a nice smile and big teeth, like a rabbit's.

"It shows, huh? I just moved here. I'm trying to fit in."

She laughed again. "It's not working!" Bobby tried to look sad, and she added, "That's a good thing."

Bobby thought she was pretty cute. She had a kind of modified boy's haircut that made her look like Tinker Bell. She was dressed in a black sleeveless T-shirt and jeans. She wore jade earrings shaped like teardrops. She did not fit any obvious stereotype.

"You've hurt my feelings," Bobby said.

"I don't think so." She stuck out her hand. "I'm Kim."

"I'm Bob Kahn."

"Hello, Bob."

"You from Newport, Kim?"

"Yep. Don't hold it against me."

"It's a beautiful place," Bobby said. Then he felt silly for saying that and asked her, "Can I buy you ten drinks?"

She gave him a look that made him think she might end the conversation right there. He tried to recover. "Better yet, how about you buy me a drink. I'm the lost New Yorker here."

She asked what he was drinking and disappeared toward the bar. Bobby lost sight of her. After five minutes he thought she was not coming back, but after ten she reappeared with four plastic cups hanging from her fingers. Two were filled with Guinness and two with Jameson's whiskey. They tipped cups and drank.

"Thanks, Kim," he said.

"Be glad I didn't make you drink it out of my shoe," she replied. "That's how we select mates around here."

They tried to talk above the noise. Bobby told her he was a TV executive—mentioned the network, said he was running King Cable. She nodded. He thought he had passed another hurdle. She said she was teaching school for now, but really she was a painter. She showed in some of the local galleries.

Wow, Bobby thought, I managed to find a smart one.

They danced to a Jackson Five song. Bobby was an uncomfortable dancer, but the room was so crowded he only had to hold up his arms and sway. At one point in the dance he caught sight of a bare-chested Kenny waving his shirt over his head. When the band took a break, he and Kim stood in the middle of the floor, sweaty and smiling.

She was facing him directly, her hands on his forearms. They stared at each other for about five seconds and he leaned forward and kissed her.

She kissed him back. They stood looking at each other for another moment, until someone slammed into Bobby's back. Kim shouted, "Let's go!" and they made their way toward the door.

The streets of Newport were full of tourists. Groups of teenagers passed by eating pizza and ice cream cones. Drunks tumbled out of waterfront bars. High rollers, pie-eyed from cocktails, zigzagged out of fancy restaurants talking loudly on their way back to their boats.

Bobby thought of trying to take the young woman's hand but decided against it. How old was she? Twenty-six, twenty-seven? He stole a look at her. She was pretty, all right, not TV beautiful but classy. She could have come in on one of those yachts.

"How did you become interested in television?" she asked him.

"I just always liked it, even as a kid," Bobby said. "I wasn't school smart. I mean, I did okay but my mind was elsewhere."

Kim nodded and smiled.

"I played Little League and stuff like other kids, but I remember when I got to be about eleven, all of a sudden it became really serious. Everybody got all worked up about winning. If you dropped the ball it wasn't just a game anymore, people got mad at you. That took the fun out of it for me. I just didn't care that much."

"But why TV?"

"Well, you know. I grew up on Long Island in the 1980s. We weren't spending weekends at the museum. TV is what we had. I mean, people always put down TV but what are they putting down? There are plays on TV, the greatest films, science programs, every kind of sport. The national elections are decided on television. Television eats any other form you put near it. It ate politics, it ate baseball, it ate music. I never understood how people can say, 'Oh, I hate television, I prefer the theater!' Well, TV is theater. What do you think the difference is between going to Broadway to see some Neil Simon play and watching Seinfeld? Except that Seinfeld is a lot less expensive and twice as funny."

"Not all theater is Neil Simon," Kim said.

"No, of course not. But not all TV is junk, either. I mean, I'd put a good episode of *Homicide* up along most drama on Broadway. Almost any *Sopranos* rerun is better than most movies. No magazine interview is going to be better than Charlie Rose, I think. I mean, look. *I Love Lucy, The Honeymooners,* that's real American theater performed in front of a live audience and it still works just as well after fifty years. To me, that's art. It really is."

The schoolteacher took that in. Bobby was surprised he had expounded like that. The liquor must have hit him harder than he realized. He determined to dial back.

"I'll tell you what's really strange," Kim said. "Has it occurred to you ever that when we watch those old comedies, Jackie Gleason and Lucy and all those, we are watching dead people? And that all those people we hear laughing in the unseen audience are dead now, too? Sometimes I'll hear a single laughing voice on one of those old programs and it will occur to me, is there someone who knows that's her mother who was at that taping of that episode of *I Love Lucy*? Does she sit up listening to see if she can hear her mother's laughter?"

Bobby laughed. "Here's something weirder. They used a lot of those old audience tapes from *Lucy* and *The Honeymooners* and even old radio shows in the laugh machines they used to sweeten the soundtracks on shows for years after. So when *The King of Queens* makes a joke and you hear people laughing—"

"It may be the laughter of people who died before we were born." Kim looked at Bobby grimly and then broke into a wide grin.

Bobby whistled the theme from *The Twilight Zone*.

"So you made your dream come true."

"I guess. I mean, to me, as a kid, I'd stay up late and watch Johnny Carson and it just seemed like the way life should be. Everybody was attractive, everybody was witty, everybody was doing really interesting things. And they'd hang out together on Johnny's couch at midnight and smoke cigarettes and crack each other up, while a roomful of spectators laughed at everything they said and applauded them just for walking in."

"Ah," Kim said.

"I mean, what could be better than that?" They had reached a wharf lined with taffy stands, ice cream shops, and a fudge factory, all closed for the night. They kept walking.

"It must have been great in the old days," Bobby said as they reached the end of the wharf and looked out at the boats moored in the harbor. "When there were only three channels and everybody in the country was watching the same thing. That's why older people get that look in their eye when they talk about the Kennedy assassination or the Beatles on *Ed Sullivan.* TV's still at its best when it helps bring people together, when it forms communities. We saw that when the space shuttle blew up, or when the World Trade Center came down."

"The community of tragedy," Kim said.

"That's when we need it most."

Bobby was feeling uncharacteristically emotional. His was not a profound soul, but what there was of it he had bared.

Now he had to face the uncomfortable prospect of finding the drunken Kenny and getting a ride back to New Bedlam. Kenny might be very hard to find, and driving with him when he was sober was harrowing enough. Navigating twenty miles and two steep bridges back to the oceanfront town with a plastered Kenny behind the wheel seemed like hitching a lift with a kamikaze.

Bobby said, "I guess I have to go find my ride. Kim, I'd really like to see you again. Would it be okay if I called you tomorrow?"

She looked him up and down like she was weighing his assets and debits. "I have a car," she said. "I can drive you home later if you want to come over to my place and watch TV."

22.

A nnie called the conference room to order by tapping on her Eureka coffee mug.

"The mayor of Providence has declared September first Abigail Plum Day."

Bobby had a headache. There had been more drinking at Kim's apartment. His memory was a little fuzzy. He hoped he had not drunk out of her shoe. He became aware that the room was waiting for him to say something. He knew "Why Abigail Plum?" would be a mistake. So he said, "That's wonderful news. Congratulations, Abigail. How did this come about?"

Ann said, "The mayor recognized that Abigail is not only a great Rhode Islander, but increasingly a broadcaster of national prominence."

Bobby's eyes fell on Abigail. She was grinning, flushing, blushing, beaming, and hugging herself. She appeared to be inflating like a Macy's balloon.

"This is SO unexpected!" Abigail squeaked. "This is an honor not only for me but for all of my wonderful hardworking genius staff who make *FootNotes* the success that it is. We are a team. Team, team, team."

There was polite applause. Abigail raised her right hand a little, showing the back of it to the room, like the queen of England.

"It would be so nice, Bob," Abigail said when the applause ended, "if you would come sit in on one of our productions. We are about to tape an intimate and revealing conversation with acclaimed poet and novelist Mark Hamburger. Although we usually observe a strict essential personnel-only rule during these interviews, I would like very much to have you there."

Oh God, Bobby thought, why me? "That's great, Abigail, I'd like to do that."

"Friday."

It was like she had his leg in her teeth.

"Uhh . . ."

"Professor Hamburger will be at my house Friday morning at ten sharp. I will arrange for you to join us."

Bobby could not think of an excuse. Abigail batted her eyelids at him with an epileptic enthusiasm. He swallowed and could have sworn he felt a thread go down his throat.

At lunch he tried to coax Skyler into going with him, but the handsome prince of King Cable was having none of it.

"Oh no no. I keep a wide berth between myself and Plump Abby," Skyler said. "You'll be flying solo on this one, pal. Hey, nice job on the upstairs hall light, by the way. I think that wiring was put in by Edison himself."

"Where did she come from anyway?" Bobby said. "She's not really made-for-television. Visually."

"Blame Canada," Sky said. Something on the far horizon from his office window had caught his attention. He was out of his chair and across the room studying the ocean. "My God, I think that's a triple-masted schooner."

"Sky? Abigail?"

"Yah. I think Flabby Abby's a wetback. Don't tell Kenny or he'll call the border patrol. She was doing some public radio show in Montreal or Toronto. Maybe it was Nova Scotia, actually. Anyhow, she and

Annie met up at some Cable in the Classroom convention or something and next thing I knew she'd snuck across the border in the trunk of an ice cream truck. Nice lady, you know. Lives in her own world. Pretend intellectual. Gets *The New Yorker* but doesn't finish the articles. Broadway shows and Miramax movies. Thinks *Frasier* is sophisticated because the characters talk about opera. Wouldn't know a real idea if it came covered in chocolate sauce."

"So why is she on our air?"

"Hey, Flabby Abby does alright. Best numbers on Eureka. Also, it's the one show we syndicate. Goes on some public TV stations in Utah or Idaho or some godforsaken place where they don't know the difference. I think we sell it in parts of Canada, too. We take in more on it than it costs us to make."

"Well, that's the general business model, isn't it?"

"Yeah, but *FootNotes* actually delivers. Who's the guest?"

"Some writer named Hamburger?"

"No idea. Probably an adjunct professor at the community college. Written a book on Mayan embroidery or something. It would be great, Bob, if you could use some of your network connections to help Abigail land some real guests."

Now I'm a talent booker, Bobby thought.

Friday morning he got in his car and drove forty miles north. He followed typed directions to an address on the east side of Providence, a section of Victorian houses and stone mansions set on steep hills. It looked to Bobby like a neighborhood where Vincent Price would brick someone up in a wall.

Abigail Plum had a hell of a house. Bobby drove past it, backed up, and checked the address twice before he believed the four-story brownstone with the steep slate roof was the right place. How could she possibly afford this on a Eureka salary? Was Flabby Abby running a brothel on the side? He climbed a winding stone stairway and pressed a buzzer in the belly of a little plaster Pegasus.

The door was opened by a frail, ash-pale man in slippers and a turtleneck. His hair sat on his head like mistletoe; it appeared to have been colored by shoe polish. He looked at Bobby without interest and said nothing.

"I'm Bob Kahn. Here for Abigail Plum?"

The man stepped back, leaving the door open. He called out, "Tell her he's here!"

Bobby stepped inside. He was in an old-fashioned front hall dressed up with antique oil paintings, an empty umbrella stand, and a large wooden statue of a dancing elephant. Most of the hall was taken up by the long staircase that rose in front of him. A young woman peeked over a railing at the top of the stairs.

"Hi, Bob!" she called. She looked about twenty-five with short brown hair. Bobby had never seen her. "I'm Candida. Come on up."

Climbing the stairs, Bobby put his hand on a thick black cable bound to the banister with heavy electrical tape. When he reached the second floor the cables, cords, and wires multiplied like a nest of snakes, winding toward a large parlor.

Candida stuck out her hand. "Professor Hamburger will be here any minute. Can I get you coffee? Juice?" Bobby stood in the entrance of the parlor. A man with a shaved head in an old army jacket was taping squares of cardboard to a raised klieg light. A black woman even younger than Candida was looking through the viewfinder of a portable video camera mounted on a tripod.

"Where's Abigail?"

"Abigail is preparing," Candida said. "She doesn't speak to anyone before she initiates a 'conversation.'"

Bobby looked up and down the long room. It looked like a series of different sets, a dollhouse with the walls between rooms removed. There was a sequence of green wallpaper that ended a third of the way down the wall, giving way to dark oak bookshelves, which ended before a long portion of the room in which the plaster was painted dark red and hung with slightly out-of-focus Impressionist imitations.

The opposite wall was equally eccentric, passing from yellow and blue panels to raw wood like a beach house to a patch of wall where the lights and camera were focused. Here a stack of hardcover books was piled on an old rolltop desk. On top of the books someone had propped a vase with a drooping lily. Pressed against the wall behind the desk was a false bookcase, a theatrical prop only about two inches thick.

"Why are you shooting in Abigail's house?" Bobby asked Candida, who was reading a light gauge.

"Abigail engages all of her conversations in her home," Candida whispered. "It's part of what gives *FootNotes* its special intimacy."

Yeah, Bobby thought, probably gives Flabby Abby a fat tax write-off, too. Pays for the brownstone.

The doorbell rang with gothic authority. Candida clip-clopped down the stairs to answer it and returned a minute later leading a gaunt man in an old suede coat. He had a long, creased face and a silver mane pushed behind big ears and falling down far below his collar.

"Bob Kahn of Eureka," Candida said. "This is Mark Hamburger."

"Nice to meet ya, Bob." Hamburger stuck out a gnarly hand. Bobby was surprised that the professor/poet/novelist had the voice and manner of a cowboy. He reminded him of some old television character. It would come to him.

Hamburger said, "You work for Abigail?"

Bobby smiled and waited for Candida to explain that he was Abigail's boss's boss, but the silence stretched to awkward. Bobby said, "I work for King Cable. We own Eureka."

"Ah so," Hamburger said amiably. "One of the suits, eh?"

Candida steered Hamburger into a short leather armchair that faced the false bookcase. The lamp and camera were pointed at the back of the author's head. Bobby had been on a lot of sets, but this was an angle he had never seen. Were they documenting the writer's bald spot?

Candida took out a compact and swabbed Hamburger's face with makeup. She offered him a bottle of water. She attached a clip mic to his lapel and slipped on headphones and asked him to count to ten while she hovered over a suitcase tape recorder.

With the technology set and the author made up and facing the wall, Candida called for the windows to be closed and the air conditioning shut off. Gonna get pretty swampy in here, Bobby thought.

There was a moment of pregnant stillness. A gust of florid perfume proceeded the entrance of Abigail Plum, who descended the staircase carrying a cat.

"Mark!" The professor had to crane around in his chair to see her. "Welcome back to my home! You've met my colleague Robert Kahn." She handed the cat to Candida, who passed it to the man with the shaved head in one smooth motion.

"Sure have!" He began to rise but Abigail swept forward, raising her hand like a traffic cop.

"Stay seated, please!"

"How do ya want me?" he asked.

"What I am envisioning," Abigail said, her fingers entwined under her chin, "is you sitting as you are, as if interrupted in contemplation, turning to speak to us over your shoulder."

Hamburger twisted himself over the arm of the chair.

"Like this?"

Abigail said to Candida, "He's so good." She said to Hamburger, "Exactly. Can you hold that position? Is it comfortable?"

Is she nuts? Bobby thought. The guy is contorting himself. Who taught her about television?

"Wal," Hamburger said, "it might not be how I'd normally entertain company, but if it works for you, I'll give it a shot."

Bobby figured, This lonesome wrangler wants to sell some books.

"It's a fascinating process, this program," Abigail said. Was she putting on an English accent?

Abigail continued: "In order to achieve intimacy we must sometimes conspire with artifice. I am sure there are parallels with this in your own work, Mark." Hamburger tried to speak but Abigail shushed him. "Please, hold your thoughts for the tape. I promise you, this setting will read to the viewer as unmediated. As true."

She turned to Bobby but continued to speak as if addressing a seminar.

"I am so bored with that deadly two-white-faces-conversing-in-front-of-a-black-backdrop scenario. Of course as a student I adored Suskind and Cavett but that format is SO tired by now it really might as well be Jay Leno."

She said Jay Leno's name like it was diarrhea. This bothered Bobby. Who is she to condescend to a superstar? Who are these pretentious nobodies?

She waved her hand at the books piled on the desk at the edge of the camera's frame.

"Do you like the books I've selected for your environment?" she asked Hamburger. "Two of yours. LOVE the new one, by the way. One by Jack Hawkes. Sentimental choice for me, he was my first guest you know. A genius and a gentle soul. I have Geoffrey Wolff's

Providence and a signed first edition of *Death in the Afternoon.* That combination felt to me like Mark Hamburger."

The professor nodded and smiled. "A stirring syllabus," he said.

Bobby saw Candida toss a glance at the man with the shaved head. The black woman looked away. Abigail's crew must goof on her when she's not around, Bobby thought.

Hamburger was going to put up with all of it. The professor was willing to let this stubby little cowgirl put her brand on his butt if it helped get him on the front table at Barnes & Noble.

Everyone got shushed. Candida patted the professor's brow with a Kleenex. Abigail closed her eyes and drew in her breath. The interview began.

Abigail: "Mark Hamburger. Welcome. Your new novel, *No Other Troy,* strikes me as a meditation on the difficulty of maintaining a belief in the possibility of redemption in a universe in which God is silent. Is that how you see it?"

Bobby smiled. Davy Crockett had to chew on that for a minute.

"Wal," Hamburger said finally, "I suppose we all need something to get us out of bed in the morning. For some folks it's God, some it's work." He turned sly. "For some it's someone who makes us want to stay in bed for a couple of days." The randy old snake was looking for book sales all right. Abigail missed the opening to talk about sex; she was looking down at a card with her next question.

Hamburger said, "I suppose we're all on a mission of some kind."

Bobby realized who he reminded him of: Mister Ed.

Candida stopped shooting. Abigail looked up. Candida gave her some signal. Abigail leaned forward and said to the professor in a stage whisper, "Mark, I'm sorry, you should have been told. I need you to restate each question in your answer."

Now the literary cowpoke looked worried. Abigail said, "When this is edited some of my questions may be taken out, so I need you to restate the premise before you speak."

Candida spoke up. "If Abigail asks you, 'What color is the sky?' don't just say, 'It's blue.' Say, 'The sky is blue.' If Abigail says, 'What's the subject of *No Other Troy*?' don't say, 'Sex and tacos.' Say, 'My new book, *No Other Troy*, is about sex and tacos.'"

Abigail smirked and Hamburger nodded. He looked like he was getting a sore neck from sitting twisted around like that, Bobby thought.

"Let's start again," Abigail said. "Mark, perhaps you could begin by saying something like, 'My novel *No Other Troy* is a bit of a meditation on the difficulty of reconciling a belief in the redemptive power of love with a Godless universe.' In your own words, of course."

This was clearly more than Hamburger had signed up for. He smiled weakly. As appalled as Bobby was by Abigail's club-footed manner, he was getting a big kick out of watching the professor wiggle. You can be the big sheriff of the Brown Faculty Club, but getting TV exposure means kissing some stinky ass.

Hamburger swallowed and tried again. He said carefully, "It's a tough thing to hang on to love in this modern world. Everywhere you look there's bombs goin' off, kids getting killed. In *No Other Troy* I'm looking at whether a man and a woman can make a safe haven for love in spite of all the fear and anger."

Bobby could see that Hamburger was struggling. He was distracted. Abigail was out of her chair and crouched next to the camera, mouthing something at him like a mom talking to a kid through a school-bus window. Finally he broke down and said, "What is it, Abigail? What do you want me to say?"

"Do not go gentle into that good night," Abigail orated as Candida stopped shooting. "Rage, rage against the dying of the light!"

"Uh, yes, that's the general idea," Hamburger said with some distress. He seemed to have decided he'd have a better chance of selling his book by going on *American Idol* and singing "The Impossible Dream."

"Can you say that?" Abigail asked.

"Say what?"

"Do not go gentle into that good night. . . . Rage, rage against the dying of the light. It's Eugene O'Neill."

The cowpoke looked like he was ready to slap leather. He said, "I'd kind of prefer not to ride in on someone else's pony."

"Our viewers will recognize the allusion. Let's give them a familiar thread to follow back to your work. Mark," she lowered her voice and said conspiratorially, "I want to give them a way in."

Hamburger was flummoxed. He clearly felt like a sap but did not know how to wiggle out of it. He took a breath and said, "It's man's bad break to be the only creature who knows he's going to die. Maybe that's why a writer writes. To push back the dark a bit. Leave a light on in the window. I don't know, I always figured it beat haulin' cotton."

He smiled and looked at the door. Abigail drummed her chubby fingers on her knee. The cowboy pressed on: "Everybody quotes Dylan Thomas on the dying of the light. We all start out raging, but in the end most of us go into the good night gratefully."

Bobby was fascinated. The poor slob had managed to drag Abigail's trout into his canoe. Of course, he still had to figure out some way to paddle back to shore. Abigail was drumming. It was a race now, before she stopped the tape and asked him to start again.

Hamburger took a quick breath and said, "In *No Other Troy* I'm trying to figure out if it's possible for one man and woman to forget all the bad news and day-to-day defeats that sink so many relationships and build a bridge together, skin to skin. It's hard to stay loyal to your allies in a cold world. Maybe in the end the communities that matter are the tiny communities of husband and wife, parent and child, lover and lover. If you let the heartbreak of the wider world take those relationships away from you, man, the rest of it will surely go to hell. That's what I'm gettin' at in *No Other Troy.*"

He stopped talking. Abigail looked at Candida. Candida nodded. Abigail smiled and said, "Very beautifully said, Mark, and so folksy, too. A gift for the colloquial! That's what *Harper's* said about you in 1988." She was glancing at her crib notes. "I wonder, is there a quote from Mark Twain we could drop in here?"

Bobby looked at his watch. It was an hour back to New Bedlam. He could not stay here any longer and watch Abigail torture this old cowhand. How could this silly woman be the top talent on a network he had to fix with minimal resources?

The man with the shaved head walked him out.

Bobby said, "How long is Abby going to keep Hamburger tied to the whipping post?"

"This will go on for hours." The man smiled. "Then we'll spend twice as long reshooting her asking the questions to an empty chair."

"Making her look smart, huh?"

"Oh yeah. We'll get all the Abigail reaction shots. Nodding, shaking her head, laughing, sympathetic, dubious. By the time we edit this you'll think Abby has an encyclopedia in her brain and the cross-examination skills of Perry Mason."

Bobby stopped at the foot of the steps and said, "You guys do a good job. It's appreciated."

"Thanks," the bald man said. "Listen, Candida is really good. If there's anything else you have going that she could get in on, I know she'd be open."

Bobby said he'd keep that in mind and got in his car and drove south toward the ocean. It hit him that maybe God was up in heaven having a good laugh at the fix Bobby found himself in. Maybe the Lord entertained the angels by making Bobby squirm the way Abigail Plum tortured poor Mark Hamburger. Maybe God was a TV programmer.

When he got back to the office he got pulled into a panic over a threat by a central Massachusetts carrier to drop BoomerBox unless King slashed its fees. He and Kenny dealt with that for two hours. Then he had to bury himself in HUT levels and cumes, statistical analysis and budget juggling. By the end of the long day he had forgotten Mark Hamburger's name.

Up in Providence, Hamburger had forgotten Bobby, too. He was drinking tequila in a College Hill saloon, working hard on forgetting Abigail.

Abigail Plum and her producers were beavering late into the night, shooting inserts. She had rewritten all her questions to anticipate Hamburger's answers, and to make it look like he was following and agreeing with her. The problem now was arriving at a shot of Abigail that Abigail liked.

The tech with the shaved head had raised his camera as high as the tripod would go, and still the monitor was revealing her extra chins. He put the tripod up on milk cartons, and she craned her face up at an angle. Finally, when she looked like a religious painting of a saint regarding the beatific vision, she pronounced herself satisfied and ready to roll tape.

The bald tech whispered to Candida, "Are we going to shoot the whole show like this, with Abby craning up at the ceiling?"

Candida shrugged and nodded. "It's her best and only angle."

part three
100 fathers

23.

D ash Ryan could not recall the name of the woman who was painting his face. She talked away at him as she moved around his head, jabbering happily in his right ear, then his left. It reminded him of a stereo demonstration record. When he and Pam were first married, they bought a big color TV console with the AM/FM radio and hi-fi. The salesman put on an LP filled with the sounds of race cars charging from the left speaker to the right and a foghorn singing call-and-response with a bullfrog. He remembered ducks quacking along in a procession from one end of the showroom to the other, and then scattering as a train barreled across the sonic landscape.

He could recall the smell of the aftershave on the salesman as he lifted those speaker doors off their hinges, uncoiled their cords, and positioned each five feet from the cabinet. This maneuver had been rehearsed so that just as he set the second speaker on the floor, the sound of the "1812 Overture" exploded on either side of the Ryans. Pam jumped and then covered her mouth with her gloved hand and laughed. They were sold.

Dash could remember sitting next to Pam on the green couch in the living room of their old house in Bethesda watching himself interview candidate Edmund Muskie on that TV. They never used the hi-fi much. Pam sometimes liked to play original cast albums when they had folks over, but neither *West Side Story* nor *My Fair Lady* took advantage of the home entertainment system's capacity for extreme stereo panning.

All these details Dash remembered precisely. He could recall the heft and ballast of the primitive remote control. To use it you had to stand directly in front of the TV's electric eye and aim like Marshal Dillon. He could remember details of the day they replaced their rabbit ears with a roof antenna. Craig Bjerke from the station came over on a Saturday and went up on the roof and hooked them up while Dash held the ladder and Pam brought out lemonade on a tray.

These images from decades ago were at his disposal, but Dash could not recall the name of the woman who was swabbing color under his eyes and slapping blush on the back of his hands and spraying what felt like gum in his hair, while chattering as if she were his closest friend.

Was she the girl who wanted to be a weatherperson and sent him résumés full of misspelled words? Or was she the one with the daughter at CNN and the son in jail? There were two or three regular makeup women on the show and it pained him that he could not remember any of their names. He saw them more than he had ever seen Craig Bjerke. Why was Bjerke still taking up space in Dash's memory? Why could he not record over that old tape?

"What do we want to do about the forelock?"

Dash looked in the mirror at the chatty woman, who was regarding the top of his head like a chess master. Dash began to answer but a voice to his right said, "Can you do something to keep it visible?"

It was his segment producer, Rudy.

"I could darken it up," the makeup woman said, and then added for Dash's benefit, "so it doesn't disappear in the light."

"I'm afraid it's even disappearing in the dark," Dash said with a rueful smile. Calling it a forelock had been kind of her. Dash's forehead had lately expanded like a balloon. The widow's peak that had held on for thirty years was in rapid retreat. His hairline had passed from Richard Nixon to Jack Nicholson to Jonathan Winters, and now only a few heroic strands held back the inevitable Hubert Humphrey.

"I'm afraid the peninsula is eroding," Dash announced. Rudy and the makeup girl laughed. They were relieved he could joke about it. Dash wanted to assure them he was above such petty vanity while hinting that his producer should be, too. He elocuted in a sonorous voice, "Nature's inexorable charge has worn down this fragile promontory."

"I can paint it in if you like," the makeup girl said and began brushing brown between the remaining hairs. Dash protested feebly not to bother, while secretly hoping it might work.

Rudy said, "I'm starting to lose it in the back, myself," and gestured to the crown of his head. Rudy was twenty-five and had hair like a mop.

"I suppose it's silly," Dash said, "but I was always glad mine went from the front and not the back."

"Oh yes, it's much better." Rudy smiled. He was pretape jolly. "It seems like guys who lose it from the back are bald, but guys who lose it in front are just balding."

"I know exactly what it is," Dash said as the girl continued to slap on color like she was basting a turkey. He held his punch line for an extra beat to get their attention. "Fellas who are losing it in back look like they don't know!"

Rudy laughed and shook his head and said, "That is great stuff! You should make that your next essay! I mean it! Let's do next week's on how guys really feel about losing their hair! It's a riot, Dash."

Dash smiled and said, "Well, that could be a good idea." Never in a million years.

The girl—the name Bonnie came into his head, was her name

Bonnie?—finished her camouflage job and asked what he thought. She had painted a tan landing strip on top of his head. Dash glanced toward his segment producer, who offered no opinion. Maybe it would photograph okay, but what would Pam think when she saw it? She'd notice straightaway. And if she did, others might. He would seem like a fool. He always wondered if Cronkite and Brinkley had used the switch from black and white to color to cover their midlife cosmetic strategies. Technology had afforded him no such opportunity. He told the girl to wash it off. The world had watched his hairline recede. It was too late to disguise it now. Pam always said that God arranged for us to lose our eyesight at the same pace that our spouses lose their looks.

He rose from the chair and thanked her for her ministrations. He was fairly certain now her name was Bonnie. Did he dare risk it? "You look wonderful, Mr. Ryan," she told him as she fixed his necktie. What the hell, let's be bold. "Thank you, B . . ." He held the consonant in the air and watched for some signal that it was appropriate, some smile, some flicker, but the girl's face looked puzzled and so he pulled out of his dive and called her "Beautiful," and she grinned and flapped her towel. He added, "All credit to your subtle magic," and he winked.

In the small black studio he greeted the cameraman and technicians and took his usual seat in the high director's chair in front of the fake wood backdrop. A tech came and clipped a microphone to his lapel. Dash lifted his jacket and the fellow snapped a small black box onto the back of his belt. He tugged down the coattail and tucked it under his butt and asked the teleprompter operator to scroll down his text. He read it out softly, dictating a couple of modifications as he went.

Rudy stood next to the camera and said, "We'll do it once straight through and then break it up, okay? Want to run through it once?"

"I don't mind if we start," Dash said.

Rudy smiled an exaggerated smile. He said to the soundman, "The Pro." Then he asked for quiet and counted down three-two-one.

Dash spoke into the glass eye.

"When I was a young man there was a lot of talk about the brows. Highbrow, middlebrow, and lowbrow. A highbrow read the classics in Latin and knew all about opera. A middlebrow went to the cinema and listened to Cole Porter and Duke Ellington. A lowbrow laughed at rude jokes and listened to rock and roll. Somewhere along the line we seem to have suffered from brow inflation. Cole Porter and the cinema are highbrow now. Dirty jokes are accepted in mixed company, and rock music is respectable. What used to be highbrow is now seen only in doctoral theses. What used to be middlebrow has become highbrow. The new middlebrow is the old lowbrow. What now passes for lowbrow used to be illegal."

Dash gathered his breath to go into his finish but Rudy took advantage of the pause and said, "Hold it there a moment, Dash. Sorry. Just a couple of things. I wonder if we need Cole Porter *and* Duke Ellington. What do you think about dropping one?"

"Okay, take out Duke."

"Would you mind if we kept Duke and dropped Porter? Diversity."

"Porter was gay, you know. Does that count?"

"This way you can say 'Duke' is highbrow now. That familiarity is nice. And really hit it hard when you say 'the cinema.' Sort of stick out your pinky on that, like you get a kick out of these snooty words for old-fashioned pastimes."

"The cinema," Dash said like a stage Englishman.

"Yes! Want to do it from the top again?"

"Sure thing."

"Okay, gang, we're going again. This time let's go from the top to 'knew all about opera.'" He said to the cameraman, "Right after 'read the classics,' I want to begin a slight push in."

So it went for the next thirty minutes. Dash's previous segment producer would have let him knock this off in ten minutes, but Rudy was young and full of ambition. Dash supposed he should be grateful. The young man would spend hours in the edit bay, assembling all his takes into the read most flattering to Dash, and put in all sorts of visual references and cutaways. There would be vintage film of Duke Ellington, perhaps a funny shot of an opera singer in a horned helmet, and video of some off-key rock or rap act from MTV.

MTV had changed the vocabulary of television. Even here, in the stuffiest old corner of the network news division, *Weekend Daylight,* the young producers were frightened to hang on a human face for more than five seconds without jumping to a shot of something else. Dash told friends from the old days that if he happened to say on camera that a boy at the ball game was eating a hot dog, they'd cut away to a one-second shot of a hot dog. To everyone over thirty-five the MTV vocabulary was one of many editing styles, and a silly one at that. To directors under thirty-five, it was simply the way TV was supposed to look. The new assumption was that the broadcaster's job was to click before the viewer could, to outdraw his remote control, to skip a second ahead of his tiny attention span.

Dash left the studio to the usual compliments from Rudy and the makeup woman and the usual silence from the crew. He went into the men's room and scrubbed away his tan. There were eight orange paper towels on the side of the sink when he was clean.

There were network stars not much older than Dash who wore their makeup all the time—even on airplanes and in the street. What began in their fifties as "No time to wash it off" became in their sixties a habit. They put on their war paint in the morning as soon as they shaved, struggling to look as they had when they first became anchors. They froze themselves in the face they had worn when they peaked. With each year their bodies shriveled and their heads dilated. In real life they looked like lightbulbs on sticks. But they did not spend much time in real life. They lived on television, and on television they looked ageless.

Those old lions might be snickered at by their staffs, but they were untouchable. They had their prime-time magazines and news specials. They had contracts worth millions of dollars. They put their names on ghost-written best sellers. They were in demand as commencement speakers and at journalism schools.

Dash had never cracked that club. He had been a local star as an anchor in Boston and D.C., and when he moved up to the network in the seventies he got plenty of airtime. He did some weekend anchoring, too.

He had no illusions about his prospects now. Doing essays on the weekend edition of the early-morning show was the last stop before the train ran out of track. There had been vague talk of finding a slot for him at the network's new cable-news franchise, but even that had stopped lately. He knew the deal. The cable channel was skewing old as it was. Advertisers had no interest. They wouldn't even want him off camera. He knew what the same grinning young executives who slapped him on the back at network functions would say behind closed doors when his name came up: "He'd just be in the way."

The hell with them all, Dash figured. "Hell" was as profane as he ever got. He had been trained as a young man to say "Shucks" if he hit his thumb with a hammer. In those days an on-air obscenity would kill your career. Now it was nearly accepted. He told himself he had had a good run. He looked forward to spending more time in the country.

But he felt so sorry for Pam. If they'd had kids it might have been different, but as it was she spent all of her enormous capacity for concern on him. She would be heartbroken for him if he were let go. It made him ashamed to think of it.

There was one card he had never drawn. He hesitated to do so now, but perhaps it was late in the day for pride. Pam's sister, Betty, was always going on about her boy Skyler's success with his cable channels in Rhode Island. Dash liked to think that his own modest celebrity had inspired the young Skyler to seek a career in broadcasting. Before Betty's divorce she and Dominic used to visit Bethesda with the boy, and once or twice Dash brought him to the station to watch him do the news. Young fellow like that, it had to make an impression.

Dash had also helped out Skyler's dad a time or two. Once, in the sixties, he'd quietly loaned Dominic five thousand dollars to get through a bad patch at his garage. A lot of money in those days. Dominic had paid it back with interest. As far as Dash knew, the sisters never found out. A man like Dominic, a prideful man, would not forget that sort of generosity or discretion.

He never wanted to call in that favor, but the humiliating prospect of waiting until he was out of work pushed him forward. When he got back to his office, Dash asked his secretary to find the phone number of King Cable in New Bedlam, Rhode Island, and see if she could raise Dominic or Skyler King.

He saw his reflection in the window of his office. He raised his chin and gave himself a stern glance. Authority. Experience. Wisdom.

Dash Ryan was not ready for the glue factory yet, by God. His assistant came over the intercom. "Dominic King on line one, Mr. Ryan."

See how quickly he picked up? Dash's reflection smiled strongly back at him. If he did make a switch, perhaps he'd try puffing up his hair.

24.

obby's assistant was at lunch and his phone was ringing. He picked up. It was the old man, Dominic King.

"I want you to come over here," Dom said as a salutation. "I got someone I want you to meet."

"Where are you?"

"The Red Tide," Dom said in a tone that implied that Bobby was stupid for asking. "It's lunchtime."

Bobby had already eaten, not that the old man would care. He had been in New Bedlam for five months and he'd developed a hatred for chowder, stuffed quahogs, and especially clam cakes—boiled grease cooked around what seemed to be a tennis ball. He also had some issues with the use of vinegar as a third condiment, along with salt and pepper. How Dominic ate that sludge every day without his arteries turning to Elmer's Glue was a mystery Bobby would commit to future generations of forensic pathologists.

Dom was seated with his back to the wall, side by side with a man of roughly the same age and much gentler features. Where Dominic was taut and leathery, his companion was pillowy. Where Dominic had hair the texture and thickness of a soapy Brillo pad, the newcomer had fair, feathery wisps struggling to cover a high freckled forehead.

Dom was dressed in a short sleeve black-and-white nylon shirt two sizes too big for him. His guest wore a blue blazer with a crest on the pocket, a pale blue dress shirt, and a red necktie that seemed to be strain-ing to hold back the evidence of a few extra trips to the dessert cart.

The soft man smiled up at Bobby. Dom did not; he dragged some bread through a puddle of olive oil and said while chewing, "This is Dash Ryan, you've seen him on TV."

He kept eating. Dash Ryan half stood, holding a cloth napkin on his crotch with his left hand while offering Bobby his right.

"Bob Kahn. Nice to see you, Mr. Ryan."

Bobby had long ago trained himself to say "Nice to see you," in-stead of "Nice to meet you," in case he was being introduced to some-one he had forgotten he had met before. He repeated Ryan's name so he would remember it.

The older man did look familiar, but Bobby could not place him. He looked at the center of Dash Ryan's face and tried to imagine the features with more hair and less padding. New York? Weatherman maybe? Something to do with news?

"It's great to meet you, Bob. I've heard a lot about you from Dom and Sky. And I've been reading a lot about you in the trades. Great stuff you're doing up here. I love that energy. I think you used to work with Howard Temple?"

"I did." Bobby smiled. The backstabbing bastard who fired him. "How do you know Howard?"

"He worked for me at ABC back in the seventies," Ryan said. "Smart kid he was, too. Always refilled my coffee without my having to ask."

Ryan lowered his voice like he was telling a secret: "Ambitious, too. The type to hang around the edit bay on Sunday night just to see how it was done."

Wow, Bobby thought, it was hard to imagine Howard young. Also hard to imagine him other than sedentary. Dash Ryan, ABC, trained speaking voice. Got to be news. His teeth weren't good enough to be anything else.

Bobby sat down and asked what brought him to Rhode Island. Dash said, "Partly to meet you." Uh-oh.

"Dash Ryan is a television legend." Dom sounded like he was reading a citation. "He's had it up to here with business-school pencil dicks telling him what to do. He'd bring a lot of class to our operation. You and me are going to talk him into making a jump."

Bobby wondered if he could get away with pretending to choke on a popcorn shrimp. The two old men had their eyes fixed on him.

Finally he said, "That's interesting, Mr. Ryan. What kind of role did you see for yourself?"

"Well, Bob." Dash Ryan looked from Bobby to Dominic to Bobby like a man sucking in enough breath for a long declamation. "I am getting a little weary of the network grind. I came up in the school of Roone Arledge and Don Hewitt. I do not appreciate a lot of what passes for news these days—"

Bobby tried to say that there was no news at King Cable, but Dash pressed on.

"Let me tell you something else, Bob." He looked at Dom and smiled a this-is-just-between-us-men smile. "Having to be up at four a.m. every Saturday and Sunday puts a little crimp in the love life."

Dash chuckled. Bobby smiled. Dom chewed.

"And the city is not what it used to be. My wife and I have deep New England roots. She has her family here. We have lately found ourselves talking about how great it would be to get a little place by the shore. I'd like to cut back on my load. Maybe work on a memoir. Yet here's my dilemma. I'm not the sort who could ever walk away from broadcasting altogether. I know your channels have no news per se, but I could imagine a role for myself as a sort of overall editorial consultant, help train the next generation, supervise content on some of the historical stuff—I caught a special you did on Eureka on medieval tapestries and it was engrossing, but I found myself thinking, Gee whiz, I could have really made a contribution to that. And I would be fine with doing the sort of on-air essays I do now on *Weekend Daylight.*"

He paused. For the first time Bobby saw a crack of anxiety in the confident facade. The old guy needed a job.

Dom cleared his throat. He leaned over and said to his friend, "Try the calamari."

Bobby got it. Dash Ryan was an old network guy put out to pasture on a predawn weekend show. He recognized him now. He sat on a stool and talked to the camera about how baseball was better when they used wooden bats, and whatever happened to doilies? The poor geezer never made the big money A-list anchormen command, never got the White House beat or the war assignment. Now he was approaching the last exit on the turnpike.

Bobby had known ghosts like this back at his own network. You'd see them in the elevators when you came to work on a weekend, walking the empty corridors in their makeup bibs.

Back then he would have jumped out a window to get away from an old plow horse like this, but having himself been sent to the glue factory by Howard gave him some sympathy. Maybe he could offer him a consultant's deal.

"I'm sure you know, Mr. Ryan, we don't pay anywhere near network money. This is a modest operation."

"I've done pretty well for myself, Bob," Dash said. "I did not blow my savings on the stock market." He smiled at Dom, who might have been asleep with his eyes open. "If it were about the Krugerrands I'd stay where I am. No, Bob, it's that I want to slow it down, breathe the sea air, but still keep my hand in the game."

At least he didn't say stop and smell the roses, Bobby thought. Ryan added with some determination, "I believe I still have a contribution to make."

Dom spoke: "So we put Dash on salary right away. The hell with these New York college boys he's working for. They want to try and enforce a contract, I'll put a contract out on them!" He bared his lower teeth, attempting a smile.

"Are you around tomorrow, Mr. Ryan?" Bobby asked. "It would be great if you could come by the office so we could brainstorm a little."

Dash said he'd be glad to. Dom shot Bobby a look that said, Don't try to wiggle out of this, smart guy.

"Great, then!" Dash said, clearly delighted. "Now, Dom, if you'll give me a lift to my nephew's place, I promised Skyler I'd come by and see his kids. Three! My God we're proud of that boy. Pam was worried he'd become some kind of playboy, but I always told her, that young man is solid! Let him sow his wild oats and he'll come home and make us proud!"

Holy smoke, Bobby thought. He's a relative, too! The King gene pool had endless tributaries. Who's going to show up next—Cousin Barnabas the vampire?

Dash watched Bobby's face for a sign, but the young man revealed nothing. Bland inscrutability. Dash did not want to have to beg for this job. Hell, he once paused during an interview with Buzz Aldrin, excused himself, got up, went in the men's room, and passed a kidney stone. Washed his face, came back, and finished the piece. What had this smug kid ever done?

Dash's view was that his skills were portable. A TV newsman's day-to-day life changed very little whether he was working for one of the big-three networks or a little station in Podunk. You went into the same kind of studio with the same kind of crew and talked into the same kind of camera. How many people saw it was really not a newsman's concern.

As they left the restaurant, Dom startled Bobby by laying a hand on his shoulder. He said quietly, "Dash is not the first network hotshot we've taken in."

Bobby walked back to the office shaken. What was he supposed to do with a sixty-five-year-old weekend news reader? Have him do historical commentary on the Comic Book Channel? Recreate Dan Rather's Greatest Hits for BoomerBox? Every time he began to drag these channels up an inch, one of the Kings came along and piled on another sandbag. This is not a business, he told himself, it's a rich family's indulgence.

He ran into Kenny coming out of the building as he was walking in. Kenny began to say he was heading out on an affiliate call but the white shorts and tennis racket gave him away.

Bobby asked what the deal was with Dom and Dash Ryan.

"Dash is here?" Kenny asked happily. "He was a real influence on Sky and me when we were kids. Knowing a real TV news guy probably put the first bug in us about getting into the biz."

"How is he related to . . . all of you?"

Kenny loved knowing more about a subject than someone else did.

"Dash Ryan is married to Betty's sister, Pam!"

"His mother's sister. So he's Sky's uncle."

"Well, uncle by marriage. He's not blood."

"Ah."

"Why, what does he want?"

"He wants a job."

"Doing what?"

"That's what I have to figure out."

"Ho ho! I ain't takin' him!"

"Thanks, Ken."

"Why don't you give him to Eureka. He and Abigail can discuss the underrated influence of Lady Bird Johnson together."

"I'm trying to grow these channels, Kenny. I can't have every King relative on the payroll."

Bobby immediately realized he had said too much to the wrong person. Kenny was no one's confidant.

"Give Dash to Annie," Kenny said as he left. "Let her figure it out."

So Bobby bushwhacked Annie King with Dash Ryan. She was nice as could be, talked knowledgeably about his work on *Weekend Daylight,* got all his references to old Broadway shows and film stars, and acted as if nothing would excite her more than finding a way to make Dash an important voice in the Eureka chorus.

Bobby then had to work out which pilots he was going to kill to pay the old brontosaur's salary.

Ann was far too canny to let her equanimity slip. She took Dash out for tea and listened to his dubious suggestions and ignored his dated name-dropping and as soon as they got back left him in Skyler's empty office and saw on her schedule the perfect sucker: Abigail Plum.

Ann could not imagine what else to do with an AARP network pontificator. Anyway, didn't Abigail claim to represent the intellectual wing of the King Cable constituency?

She waited until the next time Abigail slid into her office. Abigail was dressed in a deep green muumuu with a string of fat wooden beads around her neck. Had Abby made a necklace from an abacus? No doubt she had come here to pitch some untenable new idea. Ann wanted to head her off.

"Do you know Dash Ryan?" Ann asked. Abigail made a happy

face and opened her round mouth like a baby expecting a spoonful of ice cream. Why couldn't she just admit she did not know?

"He's a veteran network newsman," Ann explained. "Covered Watergate, Jimmy Carter. He does commentary on that *Weekend Daylight* show."

"Oh yes," Abigail said happily. "My dear friend Ramona does decorating pieces on *Daylight*. I know exactly the gentleman you mean. Very nice speaking voice, very masculine."

"I suppose it is at that. Well, listen. He's an old friend of my father and he's looking for a quieter life, and anyway, it looks like Eureka could have him if we want him."

Abigail's defenses went up. "Have him in which capacity?"

"Abigail, that's what I'd like you to help me figure out. Is there a way to make this character relevant to our audience? He has an awful lot of experience. I was hoping you would try producing him, see what the two of you come up with."

Relief moved across Abigail's features. Dash Ryan was not coming after her position. He was being put in her hands.

"I would love to work with Mr. Ryan, Ann. I so admire his lifelong devotion to the old verities of network news."

"Let's not make the verities too old, Abigail, okay?" Ann said. "We're all working hard to bring Eureka's demos down to a youthful fifty. We don't need Dash Ryan reminiscing about how much better soda pop tasted when it came in breakable bottles. Try to keep him in this century, alright?"

Ann realized she was talking like Bobby Kahn. She would never lower her standards, of course, but the ratings were up, the press was flattering, and she had to admit—she liked it.

As her penance Ann had to listen to Abigail pitch a miniseries she wanted to do called "AIDS and the Holocaust: Twin Tragedies."

"Abigail," Ann said, "I've got to confess, you've lost me. What the bloody hell does AIDS have to do with the Holocaust?"

"That will be the point of the series, Ann. We'll connect the dots between these two great modern tragedies of prejudice and persecution. Use each as a metaphor and jumping-off point to examine the other with fresh eyes."

"Yes, Abigail, but they have nothing to do with each other."

"You might be surprised," Abigail said with an air of unearned superiority. "Some experts feel that close examination might reveal that the ratio of gays to Jewish people persecuted in the Holocaust works out to be roughly proportionate to the number of Jewish people to gays infected with AIDS."

Boy oh boy, Ann thought, I'd like to get Sammy Bignose in here right now and see if he can say something even dumber than that. "Is there an angle here I'm not getting? Help me out, Abigail."

"Well, you might consider that in addition to its educational and public-service contributions, a series—or in fact even a single two-hour special—such as this would be a strong contender for a Peabody or even an Emmy award."

Bingo. Got it. Abby's been trying to figure out how to bag a Peabody, and she's studied the lists of past winners and decided AIDS is a winning topic, the Holocaust is a winning topic, stick 'em together and you double your chances. Always thinking. "I'd like you to focus your attention on Dash Ryan right now, Abigail, okay? If that works out we can talk about your next big project." Ann led Abigail down the hall to introduce her to Dash.

She returned alone to her office and locked the door. "I only pray," she said to the ceiling, "that they do not spawn."

25.

On Thanksgiving morning Skyler surveyed his handiwork and saw that it was good. Bobby Kahn was getting results. King Cable was running more like a professional business and less like the expensive playhouse of three spoiled children. The worst of the staff were being pushed out or, even better, drifting away of their own volition. The losers didn't like it there anymore. The people with potential were rising to the challenge. Even that weird black kid Boris Mumsy, who worked for Kenny, now made eye contact and said hello. Better than the internal improvements was the dawning external perception of King Cable as a legitimate business. When Skyler talked to local affiliates, they actually brought up Bobby's stunts. They admitted to watching some of the shows on Eureka and BoomerBox and even the Comic Book Channel. That had never happened before. In the past, if the affiliates mentioned the Kings' channels at all, it was to complain about having to carry them. Skyler was proud of himself. He had steered this whole enterprise in the right direction while navigating between the reefs of his crazy stepbrother and his insecure half sister.

What he had not counted on was the expanded presence of the old man. Skyler never expected Dom to pat him on the back and say, "Well done, son." That was beyond his capacity for generosity. The son did sort of hope, though, that the father would continue to stay away from a business he had always disdained. Sky had not counted on Dominic actually taking an interest in what went on at the TV channels. He didn't mind, exactly. He just didn't feel comfortable anytime Dom was circling the chessboard. It threw off Sky's game.

In the spacious and sunlit kitchen of the King family house, Annie was peeling carrots while Claudia and mother Betty performed taxidermy on a turkey with the assurance of Hawkeye Pierce removing shrapnel from a special guest star. Betty and Claudia were chatting about what the kids wanted for Christmas, how long to boil the turnips, and a woman they both knew who had just gone in for a routine physical and learned she had a tumor in her abdomen the size of a grapefruit.

Annie tried to take part in these conversations, but they jumped between topics so quickly that she was never quite sure who was who in their rapid-fire litany of tragedies and recipes. So she peeled and chopped and peppered.

She felt a little lonely and a little guilty. She could hear the lamentations of her mother back home in England when Annie told her she would be moving to Rhode Island for good after university.

"That business is a nasty little bribe," her mum had declared. "I'm sorry, darling, but you're a grown woman now. You should see that. Dominic gives each of his children a bauble, a shiny fishhook, and no one is strong enough to tell him, 'Thank you, no.' What an absurd old man he is, Annie! What do you want with an American television station? You don't even like television! I'm sorry, sweet, but it's Dominic's way of keeping his children under his thumb, of dragging you into his brutish world, of making you dependent on him."

Annie had brushed her mother off. She told her that Dominic had nothing to do with Eureka, it was a little arts channel in New England. It was hardly as if she were being tempted with Hollywood depravity.

Her mother didn't buy that. She had said, "Annie, why do you think he gave it to you to run? If he were truly generous, he would have offered to underwrite something for you in England. Remember when you and your friend from school asked him to loan you money for your film about India? Where was his generosity then? Dominic only gives gifts to bind people to him. He is a profoundly selfish man. I never wanted to discourage you from spending time with him as a child, Annie, I let you go there every summer, but now you are grown and you must see that he is not what either of us wish he were."

Annie's mother was not one to speak this openly. She didn't even like to sneeze in front of other people. Annie knew it was hard for her to say these things; she had to think there was no other way to stop her daughter from making a terrible mistake.

"I damaged my life by wanting to believe Dominic was better than he was, Annie," her mother had said. "That he might be capable of loving unselfishly. I don't want you to make the same mistake. He is your father and he loves you as much as a man like that is capable, but his kind of love demands loyalty oaths. His love is a mirror. There is no reciprocity in him. He will keep testing you until one day you fail, and then he will be unforgiving."

Annie had smiled and told her mother that she knew her father was a louse, she had known that since she was nine years old. "But he is my father and I am entitled to a share of what is his. I may not be as fragile as you think, Ma. There is a chance I might just get the better of the old bastard."

Her mother had smiled then and patted Annie's hand. Annie knew what she thought. No one ever got the better of Dominic King.

Kenny burst into the kitchen in a hunting coat, scarf, and gloves, carrying a steaming glass serving dish covered in tinfoil.

"Red hot! Coming through! Chef Boy-a-Ken's famous hamburg lasagna is in the house!"

Kenny slid his steaming plate onto the counter and turned to the women with the unburdened look of a man who had just chopped down a redwood and dragged it over a mountain. He leaned over and kissed Skyler's mother on the cheek. "Happy T-Day, Mamma Betty." He took off one of his gloves and grabbed a wad of stuffing. "Where are those little munchkins of mine?" he said, and ran off to play with his nephew and nieces.

Claudia hoped that Kenny would not get into another fight with little Jeremy over his portable PlayStation.

The kids loved Kenny. He was a grown-up who acted like a kid. He was happy to roll around on the floor with them when the other adults had all gone off to take naps or watch football. As a matter of fact, Kenny often wanted to keep rolling around on the floor when even the kids were sick of it.

It was strange for the other adults to remember that Kenny had once been married. It was long ago and seemed to have come and gone in a matter of weeks, but in fact he had been a husband a whole year. This was shortly after Kenny and Sky had made their first money and there was a general intuition that Kenny was going to settle down and normal up.

It was not to be. Kenny was barely back from his bachelor party when he began moaning to his pals about being tied down and missing his old rowdy ways and boy oh boy was he a heartbreaking Romeo back in the day. None of these regrets seemed especially sincere. The premises on which they were based were untrue anyway. Kenny was acting as he thought a young husband was supposed to act. He bought himself some sweaters and loafers and put on ten pounds. Having had no good paternal role models in his life, Kenny relied on old TV situation comedies for instruction on how a husband behaved. He aspired to be a cross between Darrin on *Bewitched* and Dick Van Dyke.

Dorothy was a nice girl who was happy to be married and have all that over with. She got a kick out of Kenny. He didn't want to talk about having kids yet, but that was okay. She liked her job as a legal secretary and had her own friends and they had years to start a family.

Kenny destroyed his marriage exactly 365 days after his wedding. It seemed to Sky that he had applied an almost architectural ingenuity to the effort, although Kenny always swore he had merely goofed up what he had intended to be an anniversary treat.

When Dorothy came home from work on the last day of March, her first wedding anniversary, she found that Kenny had filled the dining room with flowers and had a beautiful meal prepared. The meal was served on a new set of patterned bone china with matching serving platters, saltshakers, and butter plates. They ate using new monogrammed ("K&D") silverware with matching tea set and napkin rings. By the end of the meal Dorothy was so moved that Kenny could have proposed an anniversary threesome with a kangaroo and she would have said okay.

What he did instead was push back his chair, lay down his napkin, and come around to her side of the table. He reached into his pocket and took out a small package wrapped in gold paper with a silver ribbon. It was a bit bigger than a ring box, smaller than a wristwatch. Dorothy guessed earrings but she would have been thrilled with anything.

Kenny said, "Doro, I want you to open this, but before you do, I want to tell you something."

Dorothy blinked, smiled, and nodded.

Kenny said, "I love you and I love us together. I never, ever want it to change. All this is just the beginning of what I know is going to be decades and decades of shared love and life and laughter."

He seemed to be speaking less to her than to an invisible studio audience, but that was Kenny. That was the man she loved.

He went on: "Today we have been married one year. Our newlywed period is over. Now we get into the real marriage."

Oh my God, Dorothy thought, he wants a baby!

Kenny said, "I want to enter into this next period with total honesty and communication between the two of us." He was standing, she was sitting. He crouched down to look her in the eye. He ended up on one knee, a hand on the arm of her chair.

Kenny closed his eyes and nodded his head. "You know, Doro, I was quite the playboy before you stole my heart. The boys always said, 'No woman is ever going to put her brand on old Ken.'" He opened his eyes and smiled at her. "You proved them wrong. But, Dor, a man like me can't change overnight. I want to tell you with total candor, I have slipped a few times in this first year. I have not always been as pure in my actions as I would like to be. I want to make a clean breast of it, tell you everything, and give you my solemn, solemn promise that from this day forth, I will be entirely faithful to you and you alone, till death do us part."

Dorothy felt something move from her stomach up into her throat. What was he saying? That he flirted? That he had kissed someone else? Surely not—

"I had sex with Ruth Camocello. Nothing heavy, no emotion. It was when you were up at your sister's operation and I was horny. She has sex with everybody."

Dorothy felt like the room had filled with water. She fought for air. She said, stupidly, "Where?"

"Just in the car, in the parking lot of The Beachcomber. Hey, listen, she was so drunk I doubt she even remembers."

Dorothy stammered and looked away from him. She focused on the pattern on the new dinner plate. It was a thin blue double ring with a small gold eagle. It was masculine, like something you'd see in the captain's dining room on a cruise ship.

She said, "Is that the only time?"

"No." Kenny took her hand. "Well, that was the only time with Ruth, but there were a few others."

"How many?"

And here Kenny King launched into a recitation that might have been plagiarized from the memoirs of Caligula. Kenny detailed liaisons with waitresses, grocery clerks, and two of Dorothy's bridesmaids. He described such a litany of variations, combinations, and lubrications that he might have been reading from a medical book edited by Harold Robbins.

Dorothy swam through confusion, resentment, anger, humiliation, betrayal, and fear for her reputation. My God, it seemed that Kenny had bonked half the population of New Bedlam. Everyone in town must know. Everyone at the market, the restaurants, the church—they all knew and she did not.

"How could you do this to me?" she asked him.

"Honey, I didn't do it to you. I did it to me. None of those women meant anything to me. I have a kind of addiction, and I had to make sure. But now I've kicked it. I'm over it. I have not looked at another girl in a month, and I can look you in the eye and tell you that if you forgive me, I will recommit myself to this marriage, to fidelity, and to you. What do you say, Doro? Can you forgive me?"

She stared at him. He was struggling to look contrite, but what

Dorothy King saw vibrating under the skin of her husband's face was not contrition. What she saw was glee.

She leaned forward in her chair, leaned right into that horrible pink face, and she said, "You sick, selfish little shit! This is my anniversary gift? This is what you want to give me at the end of our first year together? I knew you were weak, but this isn't just weakness. You are mentally ill. You are a needy, selfish infant who wants what he wants when he wants it all the time. My sisters were right about you! They told me, 'He's empty, Dorothy. Look in his eyes, there's no one there!' I thought I could fill you up, but you are broken, Kenny. You are broken and you can never, ever be fixed!"

Kenny reeled back. His lips flickered but no words came. His face turned red and his eyes got wide and white, and then his face turned white and his eyes got red. He said, "You don't mean that. I've hurt you."

"You stupid, stupid little pig," Dorothy said, and she got louder as she said it. "You think you're some kind of ladies' man? You can't even do it right! You're the worst lover I ever had! I put up with it because I thought it was my *duty.* Now you tell me you've been inflicting yourself on every whore in town? Is that what I've been smelling? What infections have you given me, you diseased little monster?"

Kenny was wobbling on his feet, turning around and around very slowly. He pointed at the small wrapped package on the table in front of her. He said in a beaten voice, "You might want to open that."

He walked out the front door and she heard his car turn over and move down the driveway.

She sat for a while staring at the plates, tapping a butter knife, shivering. Finally she reached for the small package and peeled back the ribbon and opened the paper. There was a deep green jeweler's box inside. She opened it. A gold-emblazoned card was filled with Kenny's handwriting. It said, "APRIL FOOL! I have not slept with, flirted with, or looked at another woman since I met you. Feel better? I love you, Dorothy. Ken."

Dorothy stared at the card and tried to comprehend what had just happened. Was she supposed to feel bad now? Guilty? Relieved? God, her sisters were right. He was a sad, sick little creep. He had not been making her listen to his confession. He had been telling her his fantasies.

Did he fantasize now that this card would make her feel bad for what she'd said to him? Oh no, no. She was glad she said it. She would be glad to say worse.

She turned over the gold-leaf card and wrote Kenny a note. He found it stuck in a scoop of cold mashed potato on the new bone china. It said, "This is the end of our marriage."

Later on, Dorothy had her marriage to Kenny annulled. And she wasn't even Catholic.

That was a long time ago, and Kenny's marriage had been written out of King history. Now he was just lovable Uncle Ken, the only grown-up who knew how to play Yu-Gi-Oh! His own mother had long ago left New Bedlam for a third marriage in Pennsylvania. She, too, had been written out of history. Once the Kings took your picture down from the wall, you never existed.

The family sat down to dinner and Skyler announced, "Before we eat I want to demonstrate to you all a Thanksgiving miracle." He walked across the dining room, reached his hand into the butler's pantry, and turned a switch. All of the electric candles that lined the walls in glass bell jars lit up. Everyone oohed and ahhed. Those candles had not worked since Skyler was twelve. "That's not all," he said. He turned another switch and two ancient ceiling fans groaned to life. Now the family clapped.

"I thought those fans were purely ornamental!" Kenny said.

"Thank our new friend Bob Kahn for the home improvements, gang," Skyler said. "In addition to being a crack TV executive and very smart dresser, he knows how to turn a screwdriver!

"My next ambition"—Skyler took his seat at the head of the table and tucked in his cloth napkin—"is to get him up on the roof to fix the floodlights."

"Boy oh boy," Kenny said. "If we ever get sick of letting him work at the channels, he'll make a hell of a butler!"

Bobby Kahn was unaware of the praise being heaped on him. He was driving off the ferry that connected New London, Connecticut, to the north shore of Long Island, on his way back to Massapequa for the holiday. With luck he could get through dinner, avoid any family fights, and be back in Rhode Island by midnight. His mom would complain a little, but she knew he was busy. Thanksgiving was a bump in the road to Bobby, an interruption in what had become a consuming passion to turn King Cable into his personal and professional pedestal. It was all going to work. Bobby knew it. If Howard called today and said the network wanted him back, Bobby would tell him to blow it out his ass. He was running his own ship now, and he liked it. Better to be captain of your own ferry, he reckoned, than swabbing the deck on someone else's yacht.

26.

t was tough to teach Dominic King anything. His philosophy was, he knew what he needed to know and what he didn't know he didn't care about. Then Bobby explained to Dom about permalancers. When it sank in, the old man's face cracked into a smile like ice breaking across a frozen lake.

"Wait," Dom said. The two of them were seated at the only occupied table at The Red Tide. It was three thirty on a Tuesday afternoon and they were going over budgets for the new year. "You're telling me I can keep all of these people working full-time and I don't have to pay them any benefits?"

"In theory," Bobby said. Dom's enthusiasm worried him. "See, the government recognizes that television is a unique business. You need to be able to hire freelancers like camera operators, set designers, and makeup people to work a lot of hours for a limited period of time. But if the show they work on turns into a hit, that period could turn out to be years. More often, you only need them for a few days or weeks. If a show is suddenly canceled, you let a lot of people go and you will probably hire most of them again to work on something else. It's not like most other businesses where there is a reasonable assumption that you can accurately estimate and carry a fixed labor force over a long period. So both the government and the unions allow TV companies to keep certain categories of employees working full-time as freelancers, without requiring that you pay them benefits."

Dom glowed. "And how many King Cable employees could we designate as permanent—What did you call them?"

"Perma-lancers."

"What categories? Is it only cameramen and makeup girls?"

Bobby could see where this was going. "That's what it was designed for, but the law has been interpreted pretty broadly. If you call a job 'production,' almost anything can be—"

"The sissies?"

Bobby stopped. That was a new one. "Who are the sissies, Dom?"

"The freaks, you know, Batman and Robin there. Kenny's weirdos."

"Oh, the Comic Book Channel staff. Yes, certainly Todd and Albert who are on camera, anyone who is attached to a specific series. They probably should be considered freelance. I wouldn't do it with anyone who has a back-office job."

"Why not? Why wouldn't you do it with everybody?"

Bobby wished he had never started this. "Well, because A, it will piss off a lot of people if you arbitrarily take away their benefits, and B, if you abuse this loophole in such a blatant way that our resentful employees go to the Attorney General and bring to his attention how a law passed to allow gaffers to move between different series is being bent to cheat stenographers out of their medical insurance, you may get the government poking up your finances with a colonoscope."

"We still got stenographers?"

"Dom, don't get too greedy with this, okay?"

Dom smiled again. He liked this Jewish kid. He knew how to play the game. He told Bobby to make sure he started running this "perma-lance" routine on all new hires. Then they went through the rest of the budget. Bobby was looking for a lot of investment, a lot of new dollars. Dom liked that he wasn't vague about what he'd do with the money if he got it. He wasn't like Kenny and Sky when they asked for money, full of vague talk with no specifics.

Bobby put his ass right on the line. He'd say, "Dom, if you give me an extra two million for BoomerBox, I will use it for these acquisitions which will move the weekend ratings this much, which means we can add almost four million in billing by the end of the year. If you give me three and a half million, I can do that *and* boost CBC with a second-quarter tent pole that will give Kenny and his crew a new story to tell when they go out to advertisers and affiliates. If you give me five million, I can do all that plus come up with a new original series for Eureka, and have some extra money for marketing, which by two years from now will push your earnings up ten million across the board. It's your call."

That's what Dominic liked! The kid treated it like a business. You give me this much today, I'll give you back this much tomorrow. He put his projections down on paper. He put his pecker on the table. Dom respected that.

What Dom liked even more, though, was this perma-lance thing. That had implications across all his businesses. After all, were cameramen any more seasonal than car salesmen? Or limo drivers? Why shouldn't many of the employees of Dominic King's various enterprises be moved under the King Cable umbrella? Let them set up some lights or something to keep it all legit. Get Big Manny and Little Manny from the garage down here once in a while to oil the cameras.

Dom liked the television business.

Kenny walked by The Red Tide and looked in the window. The sight of Bobby sitting with the old man, working down the spreadsheets, stung a little. Kenny had always been the numbers guy in the operation. He did not go in and join them. He didn't want to risk Dom blowing him off, or putting him down in front of the help.

He went back to the office. He saw Skyler. "I just saw Dom and Bobby at the Tide. They looked like they were going to elope."

"That's nice," Skyler said. From the door of his office it looked like he was transfixed by the data on his computer screen. He was, but Kenny couldn't tell that it was a virtual tour of a resort in Barbados.

"Dom's taking a lot of interest in the channels," Kenny said.

"That's fine," Skyler told him. "The old man can smell money. We're doing something right."

"Yeah," Kenny said. "I guess that's good, huh?"

Skyler was paying no attention. Kenny left and Skyler didn't notice.

Dominic and Bobby walked back to the office. It was a winter day, windy and dreary. The cold weather was endless up here. This close to the ocean, there wasn't even much snow, just sleet and mud. It always seemed to be about to get dark. It was why the locals drank all the time.

"So!" Dom looked at Bobby with a slight wrinkling of the corners of his mouth. His face muscles seemed to be struggling to stop a smile. "Who was the girl?"

Bobby had brought a date to the King Cable Christmas party. Dom was introduced to her, but he was after more than a name.

"Kim. Kimberly DeCarlo."

"She's from here?"

"Yeah, she's from Newport."

"How'd you meet her?"

"Dom, why do you care how I met her?"

"Sensitive. Some big secret I'm not supposed to know about?"

"I met her, okay?"

"So you're settling down with a local girl. Nice."

"I'm not settling down, Dom. She's a girl I've been seeing."

Dom was delighted. He'd hit a nerve. He liked to know people's soft spots.

"So Kim DeCarlo from Newport. Does Kim watch your TV programs?"

"I didn't ask her, Dom."

"No? Very interesting. You meet a girl, you like her, you ask her out, she says yes, you bring her to a King Cable function, but in all this she never mentions if she knows the TV shows you make or what she thinks of them. Peculiar."

"I don't think she watches a lot of TV, Dom."

"Why is that? Is she a hi-fi buff? Or is this a purely physical relationship?"

"She's a schoolteacher, Dom. She teaches high school in Newport."

Dom's face darkened. He lost his enthusiasm for kidding Bobby. He tried to shift back to talking about work. Bobby was grateful, then confused. Dom was asking questions Bobby had already answered. It started to bug Bobby more than the needling had.

"Dom," Bobby said finally. "What is it? What's wrong with my going out with Kim?"

"None of my business," Dom said quickly. Without looking at Bobby, he began to slap his coat like he had lost his keys.

"What?"

Dom looked flustered. He said, "Don't ask me something if you don't want to know the answer."

Bobby was not going to get drawn into this kind of game. "Fine," he said. But as they approached the King Cable parking lot, it began to eat at Bobby. What could the old man possibly know about this woman whom Bobby had been dating off and on since the end of the summer?

Something about her being a teacher, or about where she lived? Bobby tried to imagine what Dom was not telling him. Did Dom know the girl somehow? Or her family? Had the old man screwed over Kim's dad in a business deal? That would be bad. Had he had sex with her mother? That would be terrible. Bobby had watched more soap operas than other men. He thought, What if Dom had had an affair with Kim! No, that was absurd, it was revolting. But God knows Dom has done a lot of revolting things. He sure was acting guilty, and guilt was not an emotion that often visited the old reprobate.

Bobby knew he would not sleep tonight if Dom did not tell him what was wrong, and if he did not get an answer now, Dom would never tell him. The old man went to unlock his car. Bobby took hold of his shoulder. "Don't bullshit me, Dom. What's the issue with this woman?"

The old man looked up, his brow wrinkled and his eyes averted.

"First, I don't know this woman," Dom said. "For all I know, she may be the exception to the rule."

"What rule?"

"The rule about schoolteachers."

Bobby felt like he was swimming through gravy. "I don't know what you're talking about."

"Look, you want to sleep with whores or can-can girls or stewardesses or the cocktail waitress at the Biltmore, that's your business."

"No shit it's my business."

"But have some respect for yourself, Bob. A schoolteacher!"

Bobby was confused. Did Dom think schoolteachers were nuns or something? Did he think Bobby was sullying some maiden?

"Dom, try to move into this century. What absurd proposition are you struggling to form?"

Dom looked at Bobby sadly, the way you'd look at a man who could not tie his shoes.

"I gotta say this?"

"Say what, Dom?"

"Schoolteachers are the lowest people in our society. You don't want to get mixed up with one. They're weaklings who have the good fortune to get an education and then are so cowardly they never want to leave the school. They are emotionally retarded ass-kissers afraid to step out into the real world."

Bobby looked at Dom with astonishment. No matter what absurdity you prepared yourself to hear come out of the old guy's mouth, he would still amaze you. "That's just about the silliest thing I ever—"

Dom put up his hand. "I told you you wouldn't want to hear."

"No, go on. Please. You're achieving a new level of Dom-nicity."

"It's a simple fact. What grade does she teach?"

"High school."

Dom turned his hands palms up, like that proved his point. He shook his head and said, "See, if you'd said kindergarten or first grade, I might have made an exception. But anyone who teaches high school has serious emotional issues. I mean, I can see if you got a blind mother at home and a father with multiple sclerosis and it's the only work you can get to buy them medicine. I can see that. If you're too ugly to get work in porno films or stripping, I suppose in that case it could be forgivable. But anyone who teaches high school because they *want* to must be either an arrested adolescent or frightened of the world or—and in my experience I have found this mostly to be true—they are bullies who want to lord it over kids who have no choice but to pretend to pay attention to them and who they can punish if they react in a normal human manner."

"Let me guess, Dominic. You did not get along well with your teachers."

"No, smarty-pants, I did fine. I recognized them for what they were. Weaklings who needed to be big shots in front of a roomful of children."

"And you apply this insight to every teacher. No exceptions?"

"I didn't say that." Bobby stared at him. Dom said, "There were a few good Nazis, too."

Bobby was speechless. Dom put a hand on his arm. "Look," Dom said, "I don't know this girl. You're right. She may be very nice. More to the point, she may give you sexual relief without any complications. Fair enough. But I think you should be wary of being trapped by someone like this."

"Someone like *what*, Dom? She's a schoolteacher, for Christ's sake! I can't believe that you of all people think that's a morally questionable profession!"

"Whoa, whoa. Me 'of all people'? Me of all people. What does that mean? Now you're looking down at me and mine?"

Bobby told himself to shut up and withdraw from this ridiculous argument. He said to Dom, "Don't turn this around. You are the one looking down on someone you don't even know."

"That's right, I don't know her," Dom said. He pointed at Bobby with his car key, making a little stabbing motion. "For all I know she may be Mother Teresa in the body of Marilyn Monroe. I hope for your sake she is. But I'll tell you this—nine out of ten schoolteachers are petty, insecure, jealous people who think they have the right to play God to a bunch of helpless kids. As a profession, I have more respect for prison guards. Even if they don't start out that way, teachers end up bitter because the kids go out in the world and make money and do something with their lives while the teachers stay behind and recite the same empty routine over and over until they die. They're like gerbils in a spinning cage, except a gerbil don't know it's a gerbil. A teacher does.

"They all end up the same—resentful of their students, jealous of the smart ones, hateful of the stupid. They only like the goody-goody butt-lickers who remind them of themselves."

Bobby was past being offended. He was amazed. Dominic King had wells of spleen like the oil reserves of Arabia.

Dom shrugged. "Okay, you asked, I told you. No offense to Kim from Newport."

"She'll appreciate that."

"I like the thing with the perma-lancers."

"You like it five million dollars' worth?"

"Could be."

"Okay, Dom. Thanks for lunch."

The old man drove off. Geez, Bobby thought as he went up to his office, what a nut. No wonder the King kids are all neurotic.

But the next Saturday night at Kim's apartment in Newport, some little seed from Dom's spiel worked its way into Bobby's throat. They had been to dinner and a movie and now she was grading papers while Bobby sat next to her on the couch watching highlights from a basketball game.

"This doesn't bother you?" he said.

"No, no," Kim said. She was wearing glasses and they both had mugs of hot chocolate. Bobby looked down at the pile of papers she had already graded that was between them on the couch.

"Mike Kennedy gets a C, huh?" he said.

Kim was working away at another paper. She said, "Uh-huh."

Bobby started reading Mike Kennedy's paper. The kid had written about religious allegories in *Dune, His Dark Materials,* and *The Hitchhiker's Guide to the Galaxy.*

"Boy," Bobby said. "This one has a future at the Comic Book Channel. Seems pretty smart for an eleventh-grader. You're a tough marker."

Kim said "Hmm" and kept working.

Bobby picked up another paper. This one was written by a girl named Maureen Thomas and it was titled "A Different Drum." Kim had given this an A minus. Bobby read it. It was earnest and heartfelt, an editorial in favor of going one's own way against the crowd in *To Kill a Mockingbird* and *A Separate Peace*. Bobby thought it was pretty lame.

Kim finished her last paper, took off her glasses, and put her hand on Bobby's neck. "All done," she said.

Bobby smiled and told her, "You work too hard."

She purred and tugged at the back of his hair.

"Hey, Kim," he said. "How come you gave that kid Kennedy a C and the girl with a different drum an A?"

"Her paper was better than his." She leaned forward and kissed Bobby's neck. Okay, he told himself, drop this right now. He put his arm around her shoulder and she nestled against him. The basketball report was over. He clicked off the TV. She began rubbing her hand up and down his shirt buttons.

He couldn't help himself. He said, "It just seemed from an outsider's point of view like the Kennedy kid's paper was a lot better than the girl's."

Kim pulled back and looked at him. She said, "Well, feel free to come in and substitute anytime."

"I'm sorry," he said.

"That's okay."

"I'm just curious. I really want to understand your job."

She studied him like she was trying to decide whether to give him the benefit of the doubt. Finally she said, "Okay, here's the thing. Mike Kennedy is a real little snot. His father's a big shot, he knows he can buy his way out of any trouble, buy his way into any college. He lords it over the other kids who follow him around because he has a truck and an indoor pool and a big estate where they all hide out from their parents. He's bright enough that he doesn't have to work hard. He does just enough to get by and expects all the teachers to treat him like a little prince, even though he does not even halfway exert himself. He probably wrote that paper on the school bus the day it was due."

"And the girl who got an A?"

"Maureen is a poor kid with no advantages who is really trying to do well, even though no one at home gives her any encouragement. She has a little sister she takes care of while her mother drinks. There has never been a book in any of the six cheap apartments she's lived in since she came to our school. She works harder than any student I have."

Bobby smiled. "Wow."

"So you see, Bob, Maureen's paper on *To Kill a Mockingbird* is an example of a real effort by a good kid in a tough situation. While Master Kennedy's survey of Dungeons & Dragons represents a half hour's work in front of the TV by a spoiled brat."

Bobby put his head back on the couch and contemplated that. Kim leaned against him cautiously. She kept her hands to herself. Who am I, Bobby thought, to criticize this woman who cares so much about reaching these schoolchildren? What do I contribute to society with my crappy TV shows? I make more money in one month than Kim does in a year. I should shut up and be grateful I met a nice girl like this and see if she still wants to go to bed with me.

Yet still a little red devil with a face like Dominic King's stood on Bobby's shoulder, sticking his pitchfork into the place where he should have held his tongue. Just as Kim was softening against him he heard himself say:

"But you know, Kim, it really isn't a teacher's place to grade her students' intentions, is it? I mean, it's great to give a good kid a break, but isn't it kind of inappropriate for you to dock the smart kid just because you don't like him? And if the poor girl earned an honest B, wouldn't it be better to give her the B she got fair and square than to make it an A out of pity?"

Kim pulled away from him and moved her mouth for a few seconds before any sound came out. When it did it sounded like this: "Inappropriate? You think my judgment about these students—about whom you know nothing—is inappropriate?"

Bobby was in it now. "Well . . . yeah. You're their teacher, not their priest. It's not your job to look into their hearts. You can't know for sure that Kennedy didn't knock himself out on that paper and that Maureen isn't just feeding you a sob story. Whatever's going on in these kid's personal lives is none of your business, really. Your job is to judge them fairly and give them the grade they've actually earned. Isn't it?"

Kim looked at Bobby with an astonishment that was quickly reconfiguring itself into fury. Bobby had no idea where that speech had come from. What did he care about the scruples of grading high-school term papers? It ran through his mind that if he had been subconsciously looking for a way to torpedo this budding relationship, Kenny King himself could not have done it better.

Kim was off the couch now, waving the English papers in front of Bobby's face, throwing them in the air and letting loose with a string of piercing admonishments. Bobby was too stunned at himself to make out many of the specific charges, although "conceited," "ignorant," "selfish," "arrogant," and "asshole" flew out of the tornado like tree limbs to whack him on the ass all the way down the stairs, into his car, and over the bridge back to New Bedlam.

When he pulled into the apartment complex where he lived, he was still not sure why he had done what he did, but he was pretty sure who was to blame.

"You go to hell, Dominic," he said.

27.

Spring was the season of miracles. Old stumps sprouted fresh flowers, broken limbs mended sweet with sap, furry new creatures came sniffing wide-eyed at the sweet air, and melting ice blessed fields long fallow. All down the Rhode Island shoreline cold men were once again filled with amorous affection for their neglected wives.

Pity poor California, Skyler King thought as he stared at the purple heather blooming in his garden. Never knowing the depths of winter, they would never savor the spring.

The miracles extended to King Cable, which finished the first quarter of the year (Q1 in the lingo of the entertainment industry) showing remarkable growth in every division. The substantial ratings success attained in Q4 had been parlayed into real monetizable momentum.

The "Kennedys, Cartwrights & Corleones" stunt had been a press bonanza. Skyler himself had been interviewed in *USA Today,* the *Boston Globe,* and by the Associated Press. Conan O'Brien had even made a reference to it in a monologue! It was exactly the sort of buzz that put King Cable on the map. They sent out highlights reels to carriers across the country. When Skyler went to call on affiliates, they met him with new respect.

After Sky put on the charm, Kenny came in with the bad news. If they wanted BoomerBox, they had to make room for one of the other

King channels, too. Either CBC or Eureka. Special incentives if you took all three—the King Bundle. Most basic cable operations still scoffed at that, but services in both Utah and Nebraska went along, and a large hole in King's upstate New York distribution got closed.

What was happening more and more, though, was that while it was still tough to win space on the lower numbers of the cable box, it was getting easier to wedge the King networks in on the new upper tiers and on satellite. It did not increase viewership very much, but it allowed Skyler to be able to tell potential partners and advertisers, "Between BoomerBox, Eureka, and CBC we are now available in thirty million homes."

Which was not a lie. Between them the three King networks were available in that many homes. What stayed unsaid was that twenty-nine million of those homes never turned them on.

Still, the prognoses were all positive. The success of the *Bonanza* stunt led to similar tongue-in-cheek histories of other TV classics. There was a four-night biography of the Cleaver clan from *Leave It to Beaver,* which mixed clippings from the original 1950s series with bits from the syndicated sequel that ran for several seasons in the 1980s and a made-for-TV movie that told the story of how Ward met June.

Boris Mumsy, the chubby black kid from the Comic Book Channel, came up with a weekend stunt for BoomerBox that made national headlines: "Who Slept with Who on *Gilligan's Island?*"

For that one they went to LA and shot host wraps with the well-known comedian Phillipe Jorge, who had a new movie coming out in which he played a sex therapist. Dressed in his goofy doctor's garb and with a poster for his new movie behind him, Jorge spent a whole afternoon taping thirty-second bits in which he started by elucidating the conventional wisdom that Gilligan was sleeping with Mary Ann, Ginger with the Professor, and the Howells with each other; moved on to posit that rich Mr. Howell had Ginger convinced that diamonds were a girl's best friend; and ended with a series of clips suggesting that from a close reading of the text one could reasonably construe that the Skipper and his little buddy Gilligan had a relationship based on rum, sodomy, and the lash.

BoomerBox was hot. It was not just Skyler and Kenny saying so. *Entertainment Weekly* put it in print for millions to read. When Kevin Costner tried to sue the channel to stop them from intercutting *Dances with Wolves* with suspiciously similar scenes from *F Troop*, the network reaped a torrent of publicity. In the end, Costner backed down and "Dances with *F Troop*" became BoomerBox's highest-rated weekend ever.

Skyler's self-confidence, sturdy even in the worst of times, was now so swollen that his wife worried that he would try to go over the Alps on an elephant. Had Skyler not said changes needed to be made? Had Skyler not crossed the continent hunting for executive TV talent and come back with Bobby Kahn slung over his mule? Had everything Skyler predicted not begun to happen? No time to slack now—the lessons proving so fruitful at BoomerBox needed to be applied to the other operations. The Comic Book Channel was doing better, but "The Life of Superman" in seven parts was not going to generate the kind of buzz King was getting a taste for.

And Eureka, Eureka. It was like dragging a horse to the vet. No matter what good ideas Kahn's team threw at them, Annie's factotums found a reason to resist. The best numbers they had were a stunt Boris Mumsy came up with when Annie insisted on sticking with her Shakespeare week—"Shakespeare *vs*. Tom Cruise," in which the Bard's greatest hits were put up against the best of Cruise and viewers were asked to vote on which superstar was more substantial. It was *Henry V* vs. *Top Gun, King Lear* vs. *Days of Thunder, Richard III* vs. *Mission:*

Impossible 2, A Midsummer Night's Dream vs. *Eyes Wide Shut,* and *Much Ado About Nothing* vs. *Cocktail.*

Annie had a fit when she realized that while the Cruise movies were being broadcast in their entirety, the Shakespeare flicks were cut down to greatest-hits reels. Apparently she felt this gave TC an unfair advantage in the polling. Cruise did win in the final tally, but so what? It got Eureka a mountain of PR and—as Sky explained to Annie's locked door—it was no indictment of Shakespeare, it was just a tribute to the higher-recognition factor of a big movie star. After all, everyone alive who knew who Shakespeare was also knew Tom Cruise, but not all Cruise fans knew Shakespeare.

As happy as Skyler was, Bobby Kahn was happier. How he loved to imagine Howard Temple sitting in the network lunchroom reading the press on Bobby's new success. Not that Bobby hogged the spotlight. He was too smart for that. He knew that the surest way to get your ideas accepted was to share the credit. When he had an inspiration— such as had happened last month with his notion to dub funny new soundtracks to classic foreign films for Eureka—he always did his best to push it into someone else's mouth and then loudly credit them with having a GREAT idea. No one ever spurned such a compliment or denied paternity when the whole room was clapping.

They were at a Eureka off-site to come up with some new series programming. Someone brought up the most boring cliché in the world: "We should have our own *Siskel & Ebert*–type show where we get two critics to talk about all kinds of movies, plays, recordings. . . ."

Bobby let it slide, he let it hang in the air while people talked in circles and then Chinless Mark Findle, in passing, mentioned that an old movie director from the seventies played the psychiatrist to the psychiatrist on *The Sopranos* and maybe there was something to be done about great directors who take acting roles, from John Huston to

Orson Welles. Bobby saw his opening and before anyone could see it coming jumped right in and said, "Now that is a GREAT idea, Mark!" Everyone looked up in astonishment, Findle most of all.

"If I hear what you're saying"—Bobby nodded at Findle with great sagacity and placed the tips of his fingers together, as if in prayer— "there's a germ of something special in putting two psychiatrists— maybe one's fat and one's thin, we'll figure that out—in putting two psychiatrists together and having them *analyze* celebrities. From a distance!"

Before the startled Findle could protest that he meant nothing of the kind, Bobby jumped up from the table and started circling the room. "I LIKE this." He grinned. "Wouldn't it be fun to see what they make of Madonna, drop a lot of German terms, look at clips of her peddling her *Sex* book one year, becoming a Jewish mystic the next? Talk about 'transgressive sexual disposition,' or 'a narcissistic compulsive disorder.' This is good, Mark, this is very good!"

Khefa from Research caught the bug. She threw in: "I don't think it needs to be two white men, though. There should be a contrast. Maybe it's, like, an Oprah-type lady therapist who's real touchy-feely and, like, a stuffy old German professor with a beard."

"Nice," Bobby said. "So there's tension between them, contrasting dynamics. Felix and Oscar, Sam and Diane. Gee, we could have some fun with this. Whoever's in the news, whoever's getting divorced, whoever's on trial. Imagine if we'd had this during O.J." He stopped and started again. "But then again, who says we can't do historic episodes, too? Analyze Hitler or Princess Diana? It's really a very fresh, very smart way to look at celebrity, isn't it?"

Who could resist such a vortex of enthusiasm from the boss? Especially when the subtext was "We have the big idea we were locked in here looking for; if you all buy in we can go home early."

By the end of the meeting Stinky Mark Findle was half convinced it really was what he intended to say. By next week he would be sure of it. This was what good management was all about. Bobby was getting the job done, making his staff look good, and—most important—making the bosses look good.

And if his success up here in New Bedlam could also in some small way contribute to making his old boss Howard Temple look bad down in New York, well, that would just be even karma all around, wouldn't it?

Spring was a time of miracles, all right. For the Kings and for Kahn, for the woodland creatures, for all who tilled the earth in Rhode Island and those who toiled on the sea.

One of nature's miracles, though, was causing consternation among some of the Kings' neighbors and indignation in the precincts of the Rhode Island Wildlife Protection and Natural Resources Conservation Authority.

The precious coastal freshwaters of New Bedlam were being choked. From all analyses, the phenomenon was not natural in its origin. Unlikely as it seemed, the evidence was washed up on the banks of the local streams and squirming in the net of Ranger Beth Baits Banger, the stern protector of the ecology who had frog-marched Dan Clancy off his own property when she shut down his excavation of the Native American burial ground.

Ranger Banger of the Rhode Island Wildlife Protection and Natural Resources Conservation Authority was a squat and rugged woman with a square head connected by very little neck to a stout and sturdy frame. In her green uniform—short sleeves, short pants, high khaki socks, lace-up Timberland boots, RIWPNRCA vented golf cap, and lime-green aviator sunglasses—she resembled one of those decommissioned sidewalk mailboxes that are painted green and reassigned to be garbage bins.

Ranger Banger served only one master—the environment of southern New England. You messed with that, you got a taste of Banger justice.

Her latest case was ugly. It brought out the avenger within. Incredible as it seemed, someone had introduced out-of-state carp into the fragile Rhode Island ecosystem. The fish—hungry, red, and as much as two feet long—were breeding at a rate that would startle a sultan. The streams, ponds, and wetlands of New Bedlam were choked with belligerent out-of-state wildlife. By all that was holy, Ranger Beth Baits Banger would track down the ones responsible and make out of them an example to visit terror on every enemy of nature in the Ocean State.

"All you rich bastards with your private hatcheries and contempt for nature's way," Ranger Banger vowed. She pronounced bastards "bas-tits" but her meaning was clear. This time you went too far. And this time you're gonna pay.

28.

I t was dark in Betty King's millpond, and so full of carp that Sammy
Bignose could not swing his waterproof flashlight without bumping into them. They wiggled around him like eels, nipping at his
flippers and rubbing along his wet suit. He could hear Kenny's voice
above the surface, shouting. He came up and raised his mask.

"You saying something, Ken?"

"I said, can you see their balls? I want to know if these fish are castrated as advertised or not."

"I think it's a pretty fair bet they're not, Ken. I mean, there's like
ten million of them and we only had a few hundred eggs at best."

"But can you see their balls? I want evidence! If we can show that
those touch holes in Arkansas deliberately sold us fertile fish and told
us they were barren, I got a big settlement coming."

Sammy knew it was useless to argue with Kenny when he got
like this.

"Hey, Ken!" Moe called. "How come Sammy's in the water with
the fish anyway? Why don't we just get a net and bring some of the
fish up here in the air and get a good look at 'em?"

Kenny looked at Moe. Then he looked at Sammy in the pond.
"That's a fucking good question, actually."

Sammy didn't want to admit that he just wanted to get back in
the water. He said, "From what I know of carp, Ken, the first thing

they do when you pull them out of the water is retract their genitals. Examining them in their natural habitat gives us our best shot of assessing the disposition of their gonads or lack thereof."

"That makes a certain amount of sense, I suppose," Kenny said. "Given that if a giant hand came out of the ocean and dragged me in, my own balls would probably retract pretty quick. I guess my only question, then, would be A, how come you can't find any fish balls down there in their so-called natural habitat, Prince Namor, and B, since when do you know ANYTHING about carp?"

There he goes with the sarcasm again. Sammy sighed. He put down his mask and submerged.

A figure was approaching Kenny from behind. Moe, speaking into the hose, tried to give a warning. "B-b-b-batter—B-b-b-batter."

"Moe, you swamp dweller," Kenny said, "what are you trying to tell me?"

"Batter up!" Moe said anxiously. "Batter up!"

Kenny turned around to see Natural Resources Conservation Authority Ranger Beth Baits Banger striding toward him like John Wayne. She had replaced her everyday green golf cap with a more formal Smokey the Bear hat. Her camouflage Jeep was parked at the end of the driveway.

Beth had hated Kenny since ninth grade, when he missed no chance to make fun of her stern manner, rugged build, and unfeminine aptitude for sports. It was Kenny who first called her "Baited Beth," and Kenny who had branded her "broad-shouldered across the rear end," a hurtful description that stuck all through secondary school, and which had been abbreviated by Kenny's cronies to BATRE, pronounced "Batter." How many times when she was at the plate in a girl's softball game or close to a winning score in field hockey or even trying to work her way through a math problem at the black-board in front of the class was her concentration shaken by some mocking Woody Woodpecker voice calling, "Batter up!"

Sometimes they added a stutter for effect. "B-B-B-Batter up!"

All these years later, here they were again. "Ranger Beth!" Kenny said with fake delight. "What brings you out to our little King commune? Come to smell the new sap?"

"Mr. King." Beth spoke in a firm and official voice. "I have here a warrant with your name and the names of Mr. Skyler King, Miss Ann King, and Mrs. Elizabeth Koenig King."

"A warrant? For what?"

"Mr. King, I believe you should take this warrant to your attorney and not discuss it with me or any other person who might have to testify against you in court."

"Okay, Beth. Thanks. Now what the hell are you serving me a warrant for?"

"Carp, Mr. King. The Rhode Island Wildlife Protection and Natural Resources Conservation Authority has evidence that you or someone in your family knowingly imported and provided breeding space for a strain of illegal and dangerous carp with reckless disregard for said carp's effect on the environment of the waterways of this state."

Kenny had the sociopath's gift of being able to look anyone right in the eye and lie without blinking. He said, "Beth, I swear to God, I don't know what you're talking about."

Just then the seas parted and the goggled head of Sammy Bignose broke the surface like Moby Dick.

"Kenny!" he shouted, breathless and oblivious to Beth Banger's presence. "Look at the rig on this one!" He was waving in his hand a wiggling fish half the length of a Volkswagen tailpipe. "This daddy fish right here could populate Indian Lake with baby carp and have enough sperm left over to fill the Rocky Point pool!"

Beth Baits did something Kenny had never seen her do in all the years he'd known her. She smiled.

29.

obby and Dom drove back to New Bedlam from a meeting at
the State House in Providence.

Dom had introduced Bobby to four state senators who
looked like extras from *Goodfellas*. This fella can get you tickets to any
event at the Civic Center, Dom said as Bobby shook hands with one
legislator. This guy can hook you up for the Red Sox. This one can get
you out of having to hook up to the city sewers if you buy a house
with an old cesspool. They were like the Knights of the Round Table,
Bobby thought, each with his special gift.

Bobby had no intention of ever calling on any of these pols but
appreciated the tour of the zoo. He knew it was a sign of Dom's mostly
hidden paternal instinct, and he accepted it as a compliment.

Their meetings done, they were negotiating their way out of a
side street when a Ford station wagon cut them off. Dom reacted as if
the other driver had leaned out the window and spit in his face.

"A woman!" he shouted. "It's got to be a woman!"

"Careful there, Dominic," Bobby said as he followed the Ford
onto the main road. "Someone might mistake you for a sexist."

"Sexist," Dom said. "That's a fag word. Lookit, there she is at the
red light. Pull up and I'll prove it to you."

Bobby came to a stop behind the station wagon. It was indeed a
middle-aged woman. He was about to say, "Fifty-fifty shot," when he
saw Dom jump out of the car and hustle up to the driver's side of the

Ford. Bobby could not believe it. Dom tapped on the window. The startled woman lowered it an inch.

"How come you're in such a hurry to get to the red light?" Dom shouted at her. He pointed up at the traffic signal. She looked at him blankly. Dom bellowed, "You wouldn't let us pull out because you were in such a rush to get to the red light!"

The woman looked in her rearview mirror at Bobby. He shrugged. She closed her window and gave Dom the finger. He shouted at her, "No class! You got no class!"

The light turned green and she roared off. The car behind Bobby honked. Dom took his sweet time sauntering back and getting in.

As they got onto the highway Bobby said, "That was useful."

"It's always a woman," Dom said. Another tutorial had begun. "You watch. Anytime a driver denies you a simple courtesy, cuts you off for no reason, won't give an inch, it'll be a woman. Men don't behave like that."

Bobby sighed. "You're painting with a broad brush, Professor King."

Dom had an endless well of such wisdom. What really bothered Bobby was that these bigoted simplifications seemed to prove out. He was afraid that every discourteous driver he encountered for the next month would turn out to be a woman. He was still having trouble shaking off an observation Dom had made four months earlier: "You ever notice how every time one of these news shows does a piece on a hundred-and-ten-year-old man or the oldest person in such-and-such a town it's always a black or an Indian?"

Bobby did not want to get drawn into that one. He said, "I guess they have good genes."

"Nah," Dom had told him. "It's all bullshit. These people ain't one hundred sixteen years old. But they were all born back when only white people got birth certificates. You got all these con artists, eighty years old and claiming they rode with Custer. I saw one, I swear, 1975 he claimed he was at the Alamo, and the local newsgirl is so stupid she asks him if he still has dreams about it."

Bobby did not know if Dom actually believed his theories or if he thought it was funny to challenge the liberal sensibilities of the younger generation. The old man had many obnoxious qualities, but Bobby doubted he was really a bigot. He was too smart for that. Still, it bothered Bobby when he heard a morning-show host promise an interview with the last survivor of Teddy Roosevelt's Rough Riders, and, sure enough, it was an African American man who looked not much older than Red Foxx.

"You come up with anything for Dash yet?" Dominic asked as they drove.

Shit, Bobby thought, I'd rather talk about hundred-year-old Indian woman drivers. "Annie's got Abigail Plum working on it," he said. "We're trying to figure out how to use him at Eureka."

Dom gave Bobby a suspicious look. "Figure it out."

Despite Bobby's best efforts to stall, the veteran network newsman Dash Ryan had accepted a contract with King Cable, quit his job in New York, and moved with his wife to Rhode Island. Bobby could accept the bite out of his budget, but he dreaded putting Dash on the air.

When he got back to the office, Bobby asked Ann if there was any progress with Dash. She said there was movement, but she wasn't sure she would call it progress. She asked if Bobby wanted to see the tape.

"Sounds ugly," he said.

Ann said he could judge for himself. They went into the conference room. Ann put in the tape and the screen lit up with a shot of Dash Ryan leaning over a saddle, apparently dressed as Roy Rogers. They watched what seemed to be the sound from one channel with the picture from another. A resonant broadcaster's voice was making a point about civility in public discourse, but the visual was of an uncomfortable old man dressed up as a cowboy.

"When I was a schoolboy," Dash intoned, "one of the first lessons we learned about democracy was that our great debates were conducted in a civil manner. It was one of the cornerstones of our republic. The rule was simple: 'I disagree with what you say, but I will defend to the death your right to say it.' Where has that gone? Listening to our political rhetoric today, it seems to me that the unstated code is, 'If I disagree with what you say, I will stoop to any slander, insult, or dubious testimony to destroy you.'"

Dash continued speaking in this vein, quoting Daniel Webster and Will Rogers, but all Bobby could focus on was the big cowboy hat sliding up and down on his little head. The tape ended. A voice behind them said, "What in the holy hell was that?"

Bobby and Ann turned. Kenny had entered the room while they were watching. Ann said, "Bob, I am not going to put this on Eureka. We have bent pretty far to accommodate your vision of a wider audience, but this—this is ludicrous."

Annie had indeed been trying to be a good soldier. *Head Shrinkers,* in which Felix and Oscar psychiatrists diagnosed celebrities from a distance, had become the highest-rated series on the network, which was not saying much but at least spared them the embarrassment of having Abigail's *FootNotes* be their number one show.

After much lobbying from Bobby, Annie had finally given in and agreed to pilot an outside pitch for a series called *Fertility Clinic,* which Annie hoped would be a serious study of couples using new technologies to conceive, but on which Bobby had privately prodded the producers to emphasize sex and recrimination.

Bobby knew Annie was fighting her instincts for the good of the team, but Dash Ryan in a ten-gallon hat was too much.

"Don't worry, Ann," Bobby said. "No one's ever going to see this. What did Abigail claim she was trying to do?"

"She said she was trying to reach out to the Red State mentality," Ann said. "She claimed she was carrying out your mandate to broaden what we think of as our constituency."

"Yeah," Bobby said, "Abby's a real visionary. Look, it's obvious sabotage. She wants to hog the Blue States—where we're actually seen—for herself and turn Dash into a clown. I've got half a mind to suit her up as Annie Oakley and see how she likes it."

Kenny suddenly exploded with laughter. "She dressed Dash as a cowboy!" He wailed with delight and laughed for another sixty seconds, until he began choking and weeping. Bobby smiled. He looked at Ann. She was smiling, too.

"Okay, okay," Bobby said. "It doesn't solve our problem. What do we do—"

Kenny interrupted. "Don't let Dom see the tape! He'll want to put Dash up on a horse and have him introduce *Bonanza*."

They were all laughing now.

"Okay, okay," Bobby said. "But what do we do with Dash Ryan? Dominic wants us to find a place for him and I have no idea where it could be."

A figure appeared in the doorway. "I'll take him," said Boris Mumsy.

Boris had grown a goatee. It was Mephistophelian. It wrapped his soft chin in an arrogant spear and jutted upward into his cheeks like twin forks. Bobby was not sure if Boris had actually lost weight, or if the shadows and architecture imposed on his face by the zigzagging beard only made it look as if he had. Certainly he had found a barber who could flatten the lumps of his hair, so that the top of his head, which had once resembled a collapsing stack of mashed potatoes, now had the even plane of an aircraft carrier. Boris had replaced the T-shirts that accented his bulk with a smart brown sports jacket that provided him with shoulders. The oversized black kid who couldn't look you in the eye had transformed himself into a tall and imposing African American television executive.

As soon as he opened his mouth, though, you knew he was from the Comic Book Channel. Boris said, "He can host the Jack Kirby *Star Wars* show."

Ann looked at Bobby. Maybe she was off the hook. Bobby said, "Remind everyone what that is, Boris, will you?"

Boris's eyes fluttered but his voice was as firm as a politician delivering a practiced stump speech. He faced Ann and said, "Suppose I told you that Jack Kirby, the comic-book genius behind *Captain America* and the *Fantastic Four,* created *Star Wars* and never got credit for it?"

Ann said, "I might say you are generous with your use of the term *genius.*"

Kenny wanted to jump in, but Boris held the floor. "In 1971 Kirby created *The New Gods,* three entwined comic books telling the story of a war in outer space."

Ann had a look on her face that Bobby read as, "If this will get me out of having to find Dash a job, I'll endure it."

"Unless Kirby had a Wookie in there, I don't see the connection, Boris," Bobby said.

"Okay, get this. The evil gods live on a black metal planet that looks just like the Death Star. They are ruled by Darkseid— pronounced 'Dark Side'—a big black metal villain who bears more than a passing resemblance to Darth Vader, who you will recall was always trying to pull Luke over to the dark side."

"I'm not buying it, Boris," Ann said.

"Wait, I'm not done. Now, Darkseid is himself kind of an update of Kirby's greatest Marvel villain, Doctor Doom. Doctor Doom wore a complete suit of robot body armor under a medieval cape and robes because his face had been blown off in an explosion. It's documented that the first time the actor who played Luke Skywalker saw the Darth Vader suit he said, 'Oh, it's Doctor Doom.'"

"So what are you saying, Boris? Which do you think Darth Vader is based on—Doctor Doom or Darkseid?"

"Well, both, they're very similar. Kirby's greatest Marvel villain and Kirby's greatest DC villain were both big half-robot guys with deep voices who walked around making their minions tremble while they hatched their plans for conquest."

Bobby did not even ask how Boris knew the comic-book characters had deep voices. He let him go on.

"Okay, here's the hook. Apocalypse is the Death Star. Darkseid is Darth Vader. Luke Skywalker's name is an awful lot like one of Kirby's young heroes, Mark Moonrider. But that's not the killer. One of Kirby's three comics, *Mister Miracle,* is all about Scott Free, a young man who escapes from Apocalypse and joins the war against Darkseid. Now get this—halfway through the series comes the shocking revelation that sets comics fandom on its ear." Boris paused for effect. Bobby thought, this poor kid learned to talk from reading the letters pages of comic books. Boris announced: "Scott Free finds out that Darkseid is his father!"

"You're almost there, Boris," Bobby said, "but not quite."

Boris's eyelids stopped fluttering. He looked at Bobby.

"What was the supernatural power that gave the heroes strength in *Star Wars,* Bob?"

"Well, that would be the Force, Boris."

"Yes. There was a similar supernatural power that the New Gods called on for power in times of stress, Bob. It was their religion and their power reserve."

"And what was that called, Boris?"

"Bob. It was called the Source."

Boris let silence hold the room. One could almost hear Darth Vader's heavy breathing echoing through the office.

Bobby did not share any of Boris's moral indignation, but he knew a *Star Wars* special could get big ratings on the Comic Book Channel. And it was possible that they could get away with claiming fair use of clips from the *Star Wars* DVDs if they called this a "news" documentary. Have to talk to the lawyers about that. Hard to claim a first-amendment news privilege for the Comic Book Channel, but perhaps they could team up on this with one of the Providence broadcast channels. It wasn't like those guys had any standards, and it could provide a legal shield.

The key thing was getting Dash Ryan, an established network newsman, to host the goofy thing. That would give it credibility. That would give it profundity. Most important, that would give Dash Ryan a job.

Bobby looked at Ann. He said, "I'm not saying I buy it completely, but it's as solid a case as *The Da Vinci Code,* and that's done pretty good numbers. And think about it, if the *Star Wars* people do sue us, that will give us more publicity than we could ever afford to buy."

Ann shrugged. Whatever unhitched Dash from her ankle was okay with her.

Bobby considered the whole big idea. It made a lot of sense. Dash Ryan, with his years of network hard-news credentials, was exactly what Boris needed to sell this *Star Wars* doc. In fact, Dash was exactly what the Comic Book Channel needed. He was a grown-up with professional television experience. He could impose some order on Kenny's staff.

His age was not going to affect the demo, either. You could put Barbara Walters in a nude wrestling match with Regis Philbin and the

Comic Book Channel would still repel older viewers like a *Grand Theft Auto* video game with an Eminem soundtrack.

Kenny had a spring in his step as he headed back to his office. He couldn't wait to run off some copies of Dash in his Hopalong hat. He was surprised to find Skyler sitting behind his desk, his feet up on a vintage copy of *Cerebus the Aardvark* number one, for which Kenny had just coughed up five hundred dollars, and issues one to three of *Giant Size Man-Thing.*

"What's wrong with you?" Kenny said.

"Nothing wrong with me," Skyler said coolly. "Might be something wrong with my mother, though, when she arrives back here for the summer and finds out she's under indictment." Skyler held up two summonses, one addressed to him and one to Betty.

"Want to explain what you've done to us this time, Ken?"

"Hey, it was Betty's idea," Kenny insisted. Skyler stared at him like he might punch him on the ear. "She asked you to help her clean out her millpond and you blew her off!"

"What did you do, Kenny?"

"Nothing you need to know about."

"It's my *mother* this time, Kenny. What did you do?"

"Look, they can't prove anything. I'm going to fight this. I already talked to Gus Flynn. He's going to take the case."

"Oh no," Skyler laughed softly. "No, no, no you are not. You are going in there and talk to the judge and tell him you did this, by accident."

Kenny started to protest, but Skyler raised his hand and dug his heel into the rare comic book. "Listen to me, Ken. We have a lot going on right now, a lot of balls in play. I will not have the high rollers I am talking with about investing in this company pick up their newspapers and read a human-interest story about how the wacky

King family of New Bedlam, Rhode Island, are denying under oath that they populated the town drinking water with giant flounder."

"Carp!"

"Do I care, Kenny? Oh fuck no I do not. Listen, go in there and beg for mercy, say it was a mistake, say you were only trying to stock a fishing pond on your own property, plead insanity if you want to. I have a feeling they'll buy that. Pay whatever the fine is, pay to clean out all the coastal waterways and old Miss Quigly's swimming pool, spend whatever needs to be spent, but MAKE THIS GO AWAY. Fast. And quiet. Make this go away."

Kenny did what Skyler told him to do. He sulked about it, but he did it. He got off with making several generous donations to the local Democratic Party, paying a five-thousand-dollar fine, and offering to lead a fund-raising drive to buy a bathysphere for the URI School of Oceanography.

Moe Notty and Sammy Bignose were not called to give testimony.

Everyone forgot about the Great Carp Caper, as Betty called it when she told the story, with one exception. To Ranger Beth Banger justice had not been served. To Ranger Banger the rich kid had bought his way out of trouble again. Now nasty little Kenny and his two finger-sniffers would be even more flagrant, more arrogant, more prone to pollute the soil and befoul the waters.

Beth Baits Banger took this one personally. From here on in she would keep a watchdog eye on Kenny King. His kind thought they could get away with anything. That made them sloppy. Next time that redheaded fink broke the law, he would find Ranger Banger on his ass like cheap toilet paper.

She would have to think of a better simile. She had time.

"Laugh all you want, spaz-boy," Beth muttered to herself as she watched Kenny drive away from the courthouse. "I'm comin' for ya."

30.

W ho Wrote *Star Wars?*" was more than the most successful program the Comic Book Channel had ever created. It was the highest-rated program they had ever run, beating out the record set two months earlier by the *Batman* movie marathon. "Who Wrote *Star Wars?*" generated international buzz. *USA Today* ran a column comparing characters from Kirby's comics with characters from the movies. Publicists for the films went into spin control, which gave the whole controversy a second life. It was a marketing dream.

As Bobby expected, the *Star Wars* people had denied King Cable licenses to use excerpts from their movies in the show. Bobby took a deep breath and let Boris and his team grab clips straight from the *Star Wars* DVDs. He claimed the fair-use protections granted to news organizations and insulated himself by making the news division of Providence Channel 11 a titular coproducer of the special. In exchange for lending legal cover, Channel 11 got four excerpts introduced by one of their newswomen to use during sweeps week. The Comic Book Channel got a layer of legal protection and a promotional push from the news broadcasts.

It was all that Bobby had hoped for, and fortune burnished his dreams. Bobby had not anticipated how much Dash Ryan would bring to the *Star Wars* project. First, he was an active and enthusiastic editor, working with Boris's team like a wise professor and guiding them around landmines in the production. Beyond that, he was a warm and avuncular presence on-screen, laying out the story of Jack "King" Kirby and his creations like he was saving Private Ryan.

It was the presence of Dash, even more than *Star Wars,* that sold Channel 11 on becoming King Cable's partner on the production. Channel 11 took Dash's borrowed gravitas and did something Bobby had not expected: They syndicated their "Who Wrote *Star Wars?*" segments, complete with credit to and plugs for the Comic Book Channel special, to stations in thirty-six states.

For Dash Ryan, it was a personal vindication. His name might not mean a lot to the young upstarts at the old network, but there was a whole nation of local news organizations thrilled to have him on their air. And look what his arrival meant to King Cable! Overnight, he gave them their greatest success.

Kenny and Skyler looked at the numbers and looked at each other. All across America TV viewers were hearing about this great *Star Wars* exposé on their local news channels. All across America they were being enticed to go to the Comic Book Channel for the whole story. And all across America citizens were clicking up and down their remote controls and discovering that their local cable service did not offer the Comic Book Channel. They were calling their operators and complaining. That most of the calls came from viewers whose parents paid the cable bills did not much matter. This was a rare groundswell, and the Kings moved quickly to take advantage.

Skyler lobbied to offer the Comic Book Channel to any system that wanted it, at a discount, and wrap up as many deals as he could before the moment passed. Kenny said no.

Kenny said that now was the time to play tough with their fellow cable operators. Make them pay full price for CBC and make them take Eureka or BoomerBox to get it. Skyler said that was nuts, they'd lose two-thirds of the potential new distribution. Kenny said no, they'd get at least half, and they'd get it for multiple channels, not just CBC. Skyler told Kenny he could try it his way west of the Mississippi, where King Cable had almost no presence. He wanted to protect and extend their base in the East, and he wanted to get on to as many satellite services as he could, as fast as he could.

Kenny perfected his pitch for the Comic Book Channel and took it on the road. At a meeting in the conference room of a Holiday Inn in St. Louis, he was lecturing five midwestern cable distributors on the essence of his channel's appeal. He could read the room and he knew he was not getting through. To these people it was another pitch in a life full of pitches. Kenny's strength as a salesman was his complete lack of shame. If he had to make a fool of himself to close the deal, no problem. He had had plenty of practice.

"I heard what you said to Roger when I was out of the room, Tony," Kenny said to one of the distributors. "You said this is a channel for geeks. Well, guess what? You're right. It is. I'll say it to anyone who wants to listen."

Here Kenny took off his jacket, climbed up on the conference table, and planted his feet wide apart.

"THE COMIC BOOK CHANNEL IS A NETWORK FOR GEEKS!" he cried, his fists on his hips. He looked down at the impassive businessmen. They were like him and his family, former house builders and supermarket owners who had bought in at the right time and now controlled local cable empires. They were used to being wined and wooed. They were used to being bribed and browbeaten, too. Kenny King standing on a table yelling did not move them.

Kenny tore open his shirt. He had a Superman T-shirt on underneath. "I AM NOT JUST SIMPLE KENNY KING, BOY TV EXECUTIVE!" he cried. "I AM SUPERGEEK!"

He lowered his voice to its normal squawl. "I am a geek and I speak for millions and millions of other geeks out there in your territories. We are glad to be geeks! We think geeks are cool! You guys went to high school, right? What was the percentage of geeks to good-looking, popular kids? Fifty-fifty? Higher? Go take a walk around your local mall! How many people do you see who look like the cast of *The O.C.*? Like the people on *Lost*? Right! Not so many. Now, how many geeks do you see? HUNDREDS!"

Kenny strolled up and down the conference table with his hands in his pockets, essaying an insincere aw-shucks routine.

"But I'll tell ya a little secret, gang. Geeks ain't nerds. No no no, don't make that mistake. I am a comic-book geek because I WANT to be. I like it! Roger, I seem to recall that you're a bit of a sports geek. Yeah? And you, Antoinette, you still a cooking geek? Tony, still got that airplane hanger full of old cars? Guess you're what we might call an automobile geek."

Kenny reached the end of the table and jumped down to the floor. He barely missed kicking over a pot of hot coffee.

"You guys are missing the boat," Kenny told the middle-American cable operators. "You've got all these channels chasing the cool kids. You've got Fox and the CW and MTV and two dozen more, but you're not doing anything for the geeks. And guess what? There's just as many of us as there are of them! Is our money no good to you? Has not a geek credit? Don't you want our eyeballs and our advertising and our subscription fees? 'Cause if you don't, I guess we geeks will have to get out our charge cards and call our satellite providers and recite the geek mantra: 'Scotty, beam me up!'"

Kenny's pitch struck a nerve. Cable operators in the western United States began signing up for the Comic Book Channel in impressive numbers, and to get it they took BoomerBox and sometimes

Eureka, too. Skyler's soft sell for the eastern United States worked fine, but Kenny's hard bargain in the west worked better. Between the two of them, they more than doubled the company's reach.

By the autumn of Bobby's second year at King Cable, Boomer-Box and the Comic Book Channel were in fifty million homes, and Eureka was closing in on thirty. Dash Ryan was moving from channel to channel like Robin Hood. Boris Mumsy, the attic of useless knowledge, was his Friar Tuck.

Boris produced and Dash hosted a series of popular shows for BoomerBox that revealed the hidden connections between characters in different TV series. Using crossover episodes from old shows, Dash demonstrated how Lucy and Ricky were friends with the Williams family on *The Danny Thomas Show,* how the Williams family had been arrested in Mayberry by Sheriff Andy Taylor, and how Sheriff Andy's universe extended to *Gomer Pyle, U.S.M.C.*; *Mayberry R.F.D.*; and even the short-lived and little-seen *New Andy Griffith Show.* Given that Lucy had once been visited by Superman, the conclusion was that Gomer and Sgt. Carter lived in the same world as Clark Kent and Lois Lane.

Dash hosted similar connect-the-dots specials tying *All in the Family* to *The Jeffersons, Maude, Good Times, Gloria,* and back to *Archie Bunker's Place,* and showing the little-known link between *The Dick Van Dyke Show, Friends,* and *Seinfeld* through crossover episodes of *Mad About You.* These family-tree specials were popular on their own and drove up viewership of reruns that no one had previously cared about.

Like an Alistair Cook for idiots, Dash Ryan loaned his voice of reason to subjects as obscure as any Jesuit argument about the number of angels on the head of a pin and as trivial as the number of nuts in a Snickers bar.

The Comic Book Channel scored near–*Star Wars* ratings with an investigative special showing the influence on Harry Potter of a Vertigo

Comics series called *The Books of Magic,* about a twelve-year-old English boy with big glasses and a mop of black hair who learns he is destined to be a great wizard and is carried away from dull suburbia to be trained in the dark arts.

They even figured out a way to sprinkle some of Dash's magic dust on Eureka. Boris and Dash cooked up a weekend stunt based around the premise that each U.S. presidential administration for the last fifty years was reflected in the hit TV shows of its time. Dash compared Eisenhower with *Father Knows Best,* JFK with *The Defenders,* the Johnsons with *The Beverly Hillbillies,* the return of Nixon with the revival of *Dragnet,* and so on, up through Ford and *Happy Days,* Carter and *The Dukes of Hazzard,* Reagan and *Dynasty,* Bush Senior with Dana Carvey–era *Saturday Night Live,* Clinton with *Sex and the City,* and Bush Junior with *Fear Factor.*

Best of all, Bobby continued excerpting Dash's specials and syndicating them to local news channels around the country. The local channels loved the bits, Dash gave even the silliest a veneer of respectability, and the King networks got endless free promotion on broadcast, which drove up their ratings where they had distribution and drove up pressure on local cable operators to add them where they had none.

By the end of Bobby's second winter in Rhode Island, the whole television industry was buzzing about King Cable. Bobby ran into his old boss Howard Temple at the bar of a New York hotel during Up-Front week. Howard looked like he had aged ten years.

"God, Bob, people at the network can't believe what you've done with those channels. I mean, every time I pick up a magazine, there you are. The Boy Wonder. It's so great to see it. I'm proud of you!"

When Howard fired him Bobby fantasized about something like this, but now that it was real he felt no satisfaction, not even much vindication. He just felt kind of bad that Howard seemed so beaten and sorry he had wasted a lot of energy on anger and guilt.

The older man asked Bobby if he had time to join him for a drink. They got a couple of glasses of scotch, old-network style.

"Bob," Howard said after polishing off one glass of whiskey and motioning for a second. "I want you to know I have rubbed their faces in what a mistake it was to let you go. Every time one of those nitwits brings up the need for us to think outside the box and learn from the cable channels, I remind them that they forced me to fire the best new thinker we ever had."

Bobby knew it was horsecrap, but he appreciated the gesture.

"Don't let it bother you, Howard. You did me a favor. I've found my place."

"You brought Dash Ryan up there, too, didn't you, Bob? God, who would have thought? He's older than I am, you know. I worked with him when I was first in the business. Wonderful man. It's incredible what you've done for him over there."

Oh my sweet mother, Bobby thought. Howard wants me to offer him a job. He must have finally run out of sidekicks to kick over the side, and now they're coming for him.

"Dash is a special talent," Bobby said. "He was another guy the networks thought was used up. I hear the bean counter who let him go is now selling drive-time on a radio station in Trenton."

It was a cruel thing to say, but Howard deserved it. Bobby wished his old boss no ill, but there was no place for him at King Cable. Let him find his own lifeboat or let him sink. Bobby paid for the drinks and left Howard at the bar.

31.

King Cable's prosperity brought all sorts of rewards. The Kings had been rich for years, but now their television business was outperforming all of Dom's other companies combined. The old man was amazed. Skyler and Kenny had proved to know something after all.

There were generous bonuses for the key executives, four of whom were Kings themselves. Dash Ryan made double what he had expected, and also found himself in lucrative demand as a voice-over man for commercials. Nine months with the Kings and he had passed his last year's compensation at the network.

Dash polished and perfected the sort of prosecutorial outrage he had developed for his indictments of the *Star Wars* and Harry Potter creators. He found that this new voice-of-the-people indignation not only raised his q ratings, but it also got him speaking engagements and college lectures offers. Pam was thrilled. She told her sister, Betty, that if they had known how much better life would be in Rhode Island, she would have made Dash move up the coast years ago.

Boris Mumsy was handed two hundred thousand dollars. He put it toward a house at the end of Main Street, which he had customized into every twelve-year-old's fantasy palace. He had a comic-book room, with shelves full of Mylar-bagged back issues and a display case for his collector's items. He had a video room with a flat-screen TV and alphabetized science-fiction and supernatural DVDs, including every episode of *Buffy the Vampire Slayer, Alias,* and *Twin Peaks.* He had original comic-book pages and comic-strip panels framed on his walls, and above the fireplace in his living room hung the centerpiece of his home—a specially commissioned and ornately framed painting of Conan the Barbarian by fan-favorite Conan artist Barry Windsor-Smith.

Bobby found himself with a bonus check as big as his annual salary. He was touched. At the same time, Skyler offered him a three-year extension on his two-year contract with a big bump and escalating stock options and profit sharing. He was practically offering to have Dom adopt him and make him the third brother. It was a great deal, but Bobby hesitated. He was not 100 percent sure he wanted to promise his whole future to King Cable. The success he'd experienced and the attention it brought him had spurred offers from all over the TV industry. He was not at all sure he would ever want to return to being someone else's deckhand, but part of Bobby was still the kid who loved the big networks, and he was not prepared to say he would never go back.

So successful a business demanded a professional level of talent, and Bobby, Skyler, Kenny, and Ann made a lot of hires and more than a few fires. They quit relying on old Dom's local lawyers and put some established entertainment attorneys on retainer, along with bringing a woman Bobby knew from the network in-house. They got smart kids out of film school and gave them production jobs and experience worth more than money. Bobby even got Skyler to spring for a proper in-house editing system, which saved money over the long haul, curtailed reliance on outside facilities, and meant they could keep production going around the clock.

There was a new ad-sales team, too. Two men and a woman, all of them young, blond, attractive, and aggressive. Annie nicknamed them The Hitler Youth. They brought gaming and computers and soft-drink clients to the Comic Book Channel. They brought Lifestyle Accounts, from automobiles to vacation packages to mobile phones, to BoomerBox. And if Eureka was still skewing "old," they used that to make it a home for all the liquor companies that younger demo channels could not touch. The Hitler Youth were a potent force. They were all as ruthless as Kenny and as pretty as Sky.

The younger Kings were chickens when it came to firing people they had known for years and would run into around town. Bobby took on the role of bad guy. He got rid of Stinky Mark Findle and hired an acquisitions chief from American Movie Classics. He brought in a young woman from Boston with real marketing experience to oversee the willing but inept Abe Tottle. As in any enterprise that had long been dormant and suddenly caught fire, Bobby found that some of the King Cable holdovers were anxious to grow and had the talent to do so, some had never wanted to work hard and left when the culture changed to demand it, and some sad cases were just not good enough to keep around.

Bobby Kahn fired people. He didn't like it, but having been through it himself and come out stronger, he no longer lost sleep over it, either.

On a frozen February Monday when Bobby should have been observing the Low Impact rule, he was in the middle of arguing with Ann over their contradictory notes to the producers of *Fertility Clinic*. She was still fighting for a high-minded documentary about reproductive technology, and he was pushing for sex.

"Fiona and Cindy have the best story, Bob," Ann insisted for the fifth time. "It's poignant, it's timely, and it will get us the kind of attention you are always looking for."

Bobby needed some coffee badly. "Look, Ann, the lesbians can be part of the show but they can't be the focus of the show. I mean, come on, they're not the most attractive people in the cast. John and Mary Jane, that's who people want to see naked. They're young, they're hot, and she seems to be some kind of exhibitionist. She practically dragged the crew into the room with her while the doctor put her in the stirrups. That's great TV! How can you not want to use that?"

"I would say that if we put that scene on Eureka, we are skating pretty close to pornography."

"Oh, please! It's not pornography if you can't SEE anything. It's a medical examination! Anyway, once he starts working on her, where does the camera go? To her face! Her face, Ann. This is all about emotion, this is all about storytelling, this is all about making a connection between this woman and our audience. We can't talk about this anymore."

It was at this point, a point when Bobby was distracted and overwrought, that his door swung open and Kenny walked in with Dominic King and a pretty young woman carrying a tape recorder.

"Surprise inspection!" Kenny called out. Bobby and Ann stopped arguing.

"This girl's doing a story on me for the paper," Dom said. "She wants to talk to you."

Ann headed for the door. "Maybe you'll have time to call me later, Bob," she said.

"Uh, okay," Bobby said. Dom looked pretty dapper. Perhaps he had his eye on making this young journalist the fourth Mrs. King. Kenny was swanning around like a ballerina, trying to work himself into the article. The reporter stuck out her hand.

"I'm Daphne Rufo-Callahan," she said. "I'm doing a profile of King Cable for the *Rhode Islander Sunday Magazine*. I've spoken with Mr. Ryan and Skyler King and Mr. King. I've been hearing a lot about you."

It struck Bobby as funny to hear an attractive, well-dressed professional woman say "Rhode Islanda," "Mista," and "Skyla." Bobby had developed a native's ear for the different New England accents. On Long Island, where he grew up, the word *harp* was pronounced "hawp" or "horp." In Boston it was "hahp." In Maine it was "hap." But in Rhode Island it was—remarkably—"hop." In Rhode Island the muscle that pumped one's blood was a "hot" and an intelligent person was "smot."

By local standards, Daphne Rufo-Callahan had the speaking voice of Winston Churchill. Bobby talked to the reporter for twenty minutes, with Kenny sitting beside him throwing in comments and Dom drifting in and out of the room, scaring people every time he wandered into the corridor.

Daphne Rufo-Callahan asked the usual questions about Bobby's background and the three channels and how they came up with their ideas for shows. This being a local magazine, she asked a few questions about how Rhode Island compared with New York and Los Angeles as a creative center and as a place to live, and Bobby pretended New Bedlam gave those other media towns a run for their money.

She asked if it would be okay if her photographer came up and took a couple of pictures of Bobby in his office. Sure. A bored-looking bearded man chewing what must have been a whole package of gum came in and clicked off ten shots of Bobby at his desk, Bobby on the phone, Bobby and Kenny showing Dom some paperwork, and Bobby by the window with his arm over Dom's shoulder.

Bobby could not wait for the people from the *Rhode Islander Sunday Magazine* to get out of there and give him back his office so he could make sure Annie was not on the phone with the producers of *Fertility Clinic* undermining his orders.

He was right to be concerned. Annie was in with Skyler, impugning Bobby's scruples, intellect, and understanding of the audience. She went from mocking his mispronunciation of the word *misanthrope* to railing against what she insisted was his sexism and antigay bias.

Skyler thought she was acting like a spoiled kid who was not getting her way. "You know, Annie," he said, "it's got to be possible for someone to disagree with you without it being evidence of their basic corruption."

Annie made a startled noise, something between a laugh and a gasp. Skyler usually went out of his way to treat her concerns with respect. Sometimes he was the only one who did.

"Listen, sweetie," Skyler said, "I need to be very frank with you about this. You have to be careful not to react to any criticism or opinion contrary to your own as proof that the other person is morally wrong. If anyone fails to see the world exactly as Ann King does, then that person is either unethical, weak, or stupid. You and Bobby are having a disagreement about how to edit a television program. That is something he knows a lot about, and he has proven that to us. You are not fighting over how to cure cancer. You are my only sister, but on the matter of how to edit a television show, my feeling is that Bobby's instincts are usually right, and I would suggest you accept his instincts here and move on to something more useful."

Annie only looked hurt for an instant. She smiled and said she'd give that some thought, thanked Skyler for his time, and left the office.

She was shaken, and angry with herself for being shaken. Skyler's tone of patient condescension cut to the bone of her insecurities about her place in the family and how her opinions were received. It cut to her sense of whether she was regarded as a real King. She knew her reaction was irrational, and that made it worse. Maybe she was just a rich young girl being indulged by reluctant relatives. Maybe Bobby Kahn was the real boss of Eureka and everyone knew it but her.

Right now Bobby Kahn was having his photo taken with her father for one more story about how the programming genius from New York City had turned around the once pathetic King Cable. No one had asked Ann to be in the photograph. No one had even considered it.

She was ashamed of her smallness and jealousy. She walked down the hall and looked into the room where her father and Bobby were posing in front of the picture window, their arms around each other's shoulders.

32.

Skyler had one thing on his mind: how best to monetize the rapid growth of his company. He was quietly talking to the banks about bringing in some big-time partners for King Cable, perhaps an existing satellite company, formulating a merger. He was feeling out some venture capitalists about putting one or more of the networks on the market. What might the Comic Book Channel fetch as a spin-off? What was the value of all three of the King networks to Disney or GE?

Skyler was in a race against technology. The companies that measured TV ratings were about to introduce minute-by-minute ratings to replace the old method of counting viewership by the quarter hour. It would no longer be possible to sell advertisers the illusion that the entire audience who watched a program were also watching the commercials. Now the sponsors would be able to tell how many people clicked to another channel during the ads and would want the prices they paid cut accordingly. This was the latest in a string of blows to the TV ad-sales model that began with the introduction of the remote control and continued through TiVo, time-shifting, and video-on-demand. Put that together with a shift in distribution away from cable and the writing was on the wall. Skyler had seen it coming. He had brought in Bobby Kahn to make his family business attractive enough to sell off before the cable industry collapsed. The clock was ticking.

The chairman of the multinational entertainment conglomerate NOA, a smiling black man named Al Hamilton, sent his private jet to chauffeur Skyler to New York for a get-to-know-you lunch. On the same trip he had a meeting with a Wall Street hotshot about moving the other way—hanging on to the channels and spinning off the cable company itself. With all the new distribution systems coming, this might be the last time a cable system had any real value.

Then there was the straight route, a simple Initial Public Offering. Take King Cable and all its networks and assets and offer shares on the stock exchange. Get in on the windfall if they privatize social security.

So many ways to go, so much money to be made. Skyler was not one to boast, but when he returned to New Bedlam he was proud of himself.

Claudia came back from church with the Sunday newspaper. "The piece on your father is in," she said. She came into the room holding the magazine supplement to the Sunday newspaper. She held it up for Skyler to see.

The cover was a photo of Dominic standing in front of a blue window with Bobby Kahn. Bobby had his arm around the old man's shoulder. They were both smiling. The headline said "The Old/New Face of Cable TV." The subhead read "How a veteran Rhode Islander teamed up with a young buck from NYC to launch a television empire."

"Why is Bobby Kahn on the cover and not you?" Claudia asked. "Doesn't he work for you?"

"Hey, sweetheart, it's all PR. Let me see that article."

Skyler leafed through the pages. There was a big picture of Dom and Dash leaning together on a TV camera, and a smaller photo of the two of them as young men, apparently taken at Dash's wedding.

Skyler noticed that his mother had been cropped out of the shot. He recognized what was left of her arm. Type reaching across the page, separating the photo from the body of the text, said: "The King of Cable—How Dominic King Went from TV Car Salesman to the Man Who Owns the Channels." The text was the usual oatmeal about how Dom fought his way up in Pawtucket and had a vision when cable TV appeared that it was the future. He had apparently told them he got the inspiration one night when he checked into a hotel in Denver on a business trip in the 1960s and saw cable for the first time. Skyler chuckled. Not one aspect of that sentence was true, including that Dom had ever been to Denver.

There was a picture of Dom, Skyler, and Annie with a caption that read "Dominic with his two children, Skyler and Ann. They work for him running his stations." Oh boy, Skyler thought, wait till Kenny sees that. He'll drive a snowplow into the *Rhode Islander's* printing press.

That's when Skyler realized he had not seen any mention of Kenny in the text at all. He skimmed through again. Nothing. Boris Mumsy got a mention but not Kenny. He went to the jump page. Good, there was a picture of Kenny and Bobby showing Dom some spreadsheet that he was pretending to read. The caption said "Chief Programmer Bob Kahn (center) presents boss King with the new schedule while a staffer looks on."

"Oh my God," Skyler exhaled. "A staffer." He called out to his wife. "Claudia!"

Her voice came back from the bathroom. "What is it?"

"Is the phone machine on?"

"I think so."

"If it rings, don't pick up, okay? I don't want to talk to Kenny."

An hour later the phone rang in the King Cable studio, the black room on the first floor of the Victorian house on Main Street.

A young engineer picked up while eating a sandwich.

"Studio."

"Who is this please?"

"This is Steve. Who is this?"

"This is Mr. King, Steve. Mr. King of King Cable. Is there a crew in the studio right now?"

"Uh, yeah. We're shooting promos for *Swap Shop*."

"Who's in charge down there?"

"Boris."

"Put Boris on, please."

Steve yelled very loudly right next to the receiver. "BORIS! MR. KING WANTS TO TALK TO YOU!"

Boris came across the studio and picked up the phone.

"Mumsy here. Oh, hi Ken."

"Hello, Boris," Kenny said in the unnaturally even voice of a pilot talking to the tower from a crashing plane. "I'm coming down to the studio to tape something and I would very much appreciate it if you would clear the decks for me for a half hour or so. I won't need a lot of time. Just tell the crew we are going to be shooting a couple of five-minute segments, very simple, just a man on a stool in front of a blue screen. One camera, very clean. And we'll need a prompter and someone to type in some copy."

"Well, I can run the prompter, Ken. Who's coming in to do the piece? Dash Ryan?"

"No, Boris. As a matter of fact, I am coming in to do a little piece. I've written a couple of editorials and I want to try them out on camera."

"Ah," Boris said. "And Bob Kahn's cool with that?"

There was a gurgling sound in the phone, as if it had fallen into a toilet. When Kenny's voice came back, the self-control of the trained pilot had been replaced by the tone and timbre of a werewolf.

"BOBBY KAHN IS NOT THE PRESIDENT OF THE COMIC BOOK CHANNEL! I AM THE PRESIDENT OF THE COMIC BOOK CHANNEL! I OWN THE COMPANY THAT OWNS THE COMIC BOOK CHANNEL! BOBBY KAHN WORKS FOR ME AND SO DO YOU!"

For a moment Boris Mumsy forgot he was a well-tailored television executive and became again an eye-fluttering fat kid with a mouth full of Reese's. He closed his eyes. He steadied himself. And when he spoke, he spoke calmly.

"Didn't mean to imply otherwise, Ken. Just hadn't heard about it. Come on down, we'll be here."

Twenty minutes later Kenny King was in the studio, passing out copy and seating himself on a low stool. He refused Boris's offer of makeup, which was probably just as well. Kenny's face was redder than his hair, and perspiration was coming off him like a sprinkler.

Boris fed the text into the auto-cue while Kenny drank six paper cups of water and gathered himself for his on-screen debut.

"How do you want to slate this, Kenny?" Boris asked.

Kenny looked at him with suspicion.

"What do you want to call it?"

"Oh." Kenny's eyes were still burning but he forced his mouth to make a smile. His little teeth lined up along his lower lip like a tiny white fence. "Call it, 'The Angry Man.'"

The next day, Monday, everyone at the King Cable office was talking about the piece in the *Rhode Islander.* The cover with Dom and Bobby smiling was even taped up behind the counter of the diner across the street. Someone had written across the top in Magic Marker, "Butch and Sundance." Someone else had added in pencil, "Thelma and Louise."

Bobby didn't understand why a local article was causing such a fuss. King Cable or the individual networks had been written up all over the country, in *Entertainment Weekly, TV Guide,* even *Time* and *Newsweek.* But boy, put it in the Sunday supplement of the state's single big newspaper and it was like Dom and Bobby had gone to Mars and come back with a cure for crabs.

Annie was drinking tea from a PBS pledge mug and listening to Abigail Plum critique the quotes attributed to Bobby.

"You'd certainly get the impression from this that we were all eating with our fingers until Bob Kahn arrived and showed us how to use silverware," Abigail said as her finger traced the margin of a photocopy of the *Rhode Islander* story. She flipped to the next page. "Gee whiz. 'I saw a need,' 'It was obvious to me,' 'I always felt,' 'It hit me that if I.'" She looked up at Ann. "If Bob would just train himself to say 'we' every time he wants to say 'I,' he would come off so much better."

Annie looked through her own copy of the story. "Ah, you missed one. Here's a 'we.'" She smiled and looked at Abigail and read her the line. "'When I saw the list of shows in development the week I arrived, I knew we had a lot of work to do.'"

Boris was waiting in Bobby's office when he arrived.

"Hey, Boris, you get those promos wrapped?"

"Yeah, sure. Listen, Bob. I'm in a funny position here. Kenny is my boss, you know?"

"Why, what's wrong with Kenny?"

"Uh, do you know about 'The Angry Man'?"

"What's that, another superhero I missed growing up? Sounds

like—what's the other guy's name—not Kirby. Ditko! It's a Ditko character?"

Now Boris was really uncomfortable.

"Okay, Bob. Listen, Kenny's my boss. He started CBC, he owns it, it's his channel. I knew that when he hired me. I'm just on the payroll around here."

"What has he done?"

Boris closed the door. He put a DVD into Bobby's machine. "Check this out."

The picture came on. It was a shot of the head and shoulders of Kenny King fidgeting in front of a blue screen.

"Can you fix the color?" Bobby asked. "He looks all red."

"He was all red," Boris said.

Kenny looked to someone offscreen and then went into a rapid-fire tirade.

"Hey, true believers, I'm Kenneth King and I am ANGRY. I am MAD. You know what I'm ticked off about? Right here." Kenny held up a copy of an old issue of *Spider-Man* in which the web-swinging wonder is pinned under a huge piece of machinery while the room around him fills up with water.

"Now what am I mad about? I'll tell ya right now. You all know this classic Spidey story, right? The 'Master Planner' saga? The Webhead's finest hour? Well, I say PHOOEY! Let's look back at that classic story."

Kenny stared at the camera blankly. Boris explained, "There's supposed to be cutaways here, he wants to pan over the pages of the comic book." Bobby nodded. Kenny seemed to get a cue and began raving again:

"The plot is that Peter Parker's sickly Aunt May needed a blood transfusion and because she had some rare type—Z-negative from all the times she almost dies, I think—she had to get the transfusion from a close blood relative. Peter was selected. Only no one else knows Peter had radioactive blood. 'Cause he was bit by a nuclear spider! Only when Aunt May gets this blood she doesn't start climbing walls—she falls over in a coma. So now Peter gets Dr. Kurt Conners, aka the Lizard, to make her the world's only batch of radioactive blood-curing formula. For some reason, though, Dr. Connors can only make one bottle of the stuff, there's no more. So what happens? On the way to the hospital the serum is hijacked by Dr. Octopus, who brings it back to his secret lair on the bottom of the Hudson River. Spidey goes on a rampage to get back the serum, beating up every crook in town until he finds out where Doc Ock's HQ is. He goes down to the bottom of the river, knocks on the door, and then fights Dr. Octopus and every henchman in the five boroughs to get back the serum. Then, just when he thinks he's won, Doc Ock blows the roof off the place and the whole river comes pouring in while Spider-Man is trapped under ten tons of giant machinery."

Kenny finally took a breath. So did Bobby. "Wow," Bobby said to Boris, "this is horrible."

Kenny started in again: "After two whole issues lying under the machinery weeping, in what three generations of fans have called Spidey's greatest moment, our hero summons every last reserve of strength he never knew he had and with a heart-tearing, pulse-pounding, bone-popping moment of desperate resolve, Spider-Man HEAVES the giant machine off his back, grabs the magic remedy, and swims up through the collapsing building to the hospital, where he gives the formula to the grateful doctors. Aunt May is plugged in, the serum works, and no one on the medical staff makes any connection between Spider-Man and the bruised, battered, soaking-wet Peter Parker who appears a moment later to hold his aunt's hand.

"Right? Do we all agree on the gist of this classic adventure? Well, you know what I say?" Here Kenny held up his mint copy of *Spider-Man* number 33, February 1966, and tore it in half. There was an audible gasp from the crew in the room. Watching it again in Bobby's office, Boris blanched and covered his mouth.

Kenny came back redder than ever. "BECAUSE IT'S ALL WRONG. Spider-Man got in this mess because Aunt May needed a transfusion from a blood relative. Only there's one thing they forgot. PETER PARKER AND AUNT MAY ARE NOT BLOOD RELATIVES. Her name is May PARKER, right? Her husband was kindly Uncle Ben Parker, right? You know, old Mr. 'With great power comes great responsibility.' Well, do the math, kids. Ben Parker was the brother of Peter's dad. May Parker is no blood relation to Pete. She's only his AUNT BY MARRIAGE."

Bobby looked at Boris.

Boris said, "Kenny has some family issues about who's blood and who's not."

"Ya think?"

Kenny was on-screen, summing up his thesis with unnatural calm.

"The so-called greatest Spider-Man story ever told was based on an entirely false premise. How does that make you feel? A little cheated? A little annoyed? Or perhaps like me, a little ANGRY!"

The camera pulled back, as if recoiling in horror. Kenny said, "Till next time, I'm Kenneth King. The ANGRY MAN."

Neither Bobby nor Boris said anything for a while. Then Bobby said, "What does he want to do with that?"

"He intends to put it on the air."

Bobby had no idea what to say. "Well, that can't happen."

"You tell me, Bob."

"I mean, even as a concept, it's ridiculous."

"Yeah."

"How much was that comic worth, that he tore up?"

"Hundreds."

"Well, he has it to spend, I guess. You know what the scariest part of all was?"

"Watching his veins expand like that?"

"No. 'Till next time.'"

33.

obby went to Skyler's house to complain about Kenny.
He played him "The Angry Man." Skyler shook his head
and winced. "Well," he said, "Ken always wanted to be a
superhero. Angry Man—able to raise his blood pressure in a single
tirade."

Skyler went into a monologue in which he attempted to peel
back for Bobby the layers of his stepbrother's psyche.

"What you have to appreciate about Kenny, Bob, is that even
though he lies all the time, he's not functionally a liar."

They were sitting at Skyler's dining room table, which he had
been using as a desk. When Bobby came in Skyler had closed four
folders and turned over a few sheets of paper.

"How does that work, Sky?" Bobby asked.

"Well he's such a *bad* liar that he doesn't fool anyone. He achieves
no deception. So for all practical purposes he's not a liar at all."

Bobby filed that away and pushed on. "The lying is not my problem, Sky. I don't care about that. The trouble now is that Kenny
wants to put his craziness on the air. You saw his 'Angry Man' routine.
It's like seeing Kenny with his skin off. It's not attractive. We can't allow that to be broadcast on the Comic Book Channel. Not now, not
when things are finally going well."

"Well, tell him."

"I have told him. He says it's his channel and, of course, he's right. That's why I'm here. I need you, and your father if it comes to that, to back me up here."

Skyler rolled that around in his head. Bob was a great executive, but if he thought Skyler would ever bring Dominic into a fight over the channels he still did not have a complete read on the King dynamic.

Bobby saw Skyler wasn't going to speak so he kept going. "It was bad enough when he insisted on talking to journalists and giving interviews. But at least that's not hurting us on the air. But this 'Angry Man' embarrassment is on the network!"

"Here's my advice to you, Bob," Skyler said. He leaned forward. "Let Kenny win this one. Yeah, I know, it's bad television. So what? It's five minutes long. Run it once in the early morning and again at midnight. Whenever it will do the least harm."

"There is no good time to run something that bad."

"Agreed. But sometimes you give on a small one to win the big ones. Look, Bob. You're a lot smarter than Kenny. You can outtalk him and outthink him. You can outpolitick him, too, if you want to play it that way. But I would only ask you to consider this. He is the president and major shareholder. He did start the channel. He dreamed it up, as lame as it was before you came in to fix it. Spot him one, once in a while. Let him win one. It's like you're playing basketball against a midget. You can beat him every time, but if you do he's going to get mad and not want to play with you anymore."

Bobby bit his fist. "You're not going to back me on this."

"No can do, kid. If you want to go and try and line up Dom and Annie and make it an issue for the board of King Cable, I guess you could. But, boy, that is a lot of ammunition to expend on killing a tsetse fly. My bet would be that if you let Kenny do this for a few weeks, he'll get it out of his system and you'll never hear from 'The Angry Man' again."

Bobby got up. "Okay."

Skyler looked at him and thought, It better be okay, bud. You go to Dominic with this and you're off the list forever. But all he said was, "Thanks, Bob. Hey, what's going on with that surgery show you told me about for Eureka?"

"We're working on it. Lots of legal hoops to jump through, finding the right cool doctor with the right kind of practice, getting around hospital regulations, liability insurance, finding a patient who is articulate, good-looking, and has an emotional story *and* does not mind being cut open on TV. It's a lot of land mines, but we'll get there."

"I'm counting on it." Sky got up to walk him to the door. "You signed your new deal yet?"

"Almost. Still working on some details."

"Any problems, you come to me."

"Sure."

Bobby walked out of the beach house, waved to Skyler's wife, and got in his car. How the hell did Annie come out of that family? he wondered. She's like Marilyn Munster.

Two things he knew for sure. "The Angry Man" was going to get a time slot so bad anyone who accidentally saw it would think it was a Veg-O-Matic commercial. And he was not going to sign a new deal with King Cable until it spelled out in black and white that he had absolute control of all programming and scheduling decisions on all channels. He was not going to stick around this fish-smelling Hooterville for another three to five years if any member of the extended King family could walk in anytime and ruin his work with their personal ego-jerks.

Bobby had been getting calls from all over, even the old network. Some kid he'd never heard of from the West Coast asked if he wanted to be considered for a position running their new cable division. It was pure delight to tell him no thanks, but if they needed someone to save prime time, let him know.

By the time he got to his apartment Bobby had decided on his terms to re-sign at King. He would assume the presidency of all three channels with complete control of everything that went on the air and veto power over all hires and fires. The Kings could give themselves any title they wanted, oversee all the backroom functions, and reap the lion's share of all the financial rewards. Oh yeah, and if they sold any or all of the channels, Bobby got to walk with a full payout and a taste of the sale.

The Kings were going to pay for making Bobby swallow Kenny's baboon act.

He needed to unwind. He drove to a health club on Route 95 and had a workout and a swim. The pretty girl who worked behind the juice bar who he sometimes flirted with was not on duty. So he lay by the side of the pool and listened to the filter swish around. He was almost asleep when he felt his cell phone vibrate and grabbed for it in his breast pocket.

But he had no phone because he had no pocket because he had no shirt. He was lying on a towel on a beach chair by the pool. Yet he swore he felt the phantom buzzing over his chest as sure as he was lying there. He did not have his mobile phone, but he felt it vibrating like an amputated limb.

The object of Bobby's anger was at the Hungry Horse Tavern with half of his usual complement of toadies. Sammy Bignose was off at some IMAX film about giant squid, so there was only Moe to listen to Kenny's latest script.

"You know what I'm angry about today?" Kenny recited as he looked at the college-ruled spiral notebook in front of him.

"Don't say 'today,' Ken," Moe said. He was trying to suck the garlic off a piece of garlic bread.

"What do you mean?"

"Well, they might run your piece at night, right? So you shouldn't say 'today.'"

"What do I say?"

"Say 'now.'"

Kenny tried it. "You know what I'm angry about NOW?" He looked at Moe. That was good. "I'm fed up with the Incredible Hulk's whiny alter ego, Professor Bruce Banner. I mean, what is wrong with this guy? Every time he finds himself being thrown out of an airplane, or dropped manacled into a tank of hungry sharks, or standing in front of a Cuban firing squad, what does he do? He starts to turn into the mighty Hulk. Right? And what does this great genius SAY whenever he is about to DIE and he starts to turn into a giant, invulnerable, eight-foot monster with super-strength? Huh? He says, 'Oh no! Not here! Not . . . NOW!' What is THAT about?"

He looked up at Moe. "Whadya think?"

"It's good, Ken. It's really good. I never thought of that before about the Hulk. Hey, Ken. How come he's Bruce Banner in the movies and Bruce Banner in the comics, but on TV he was David Banner?"

Kenny was proud of his depth of knowledge and tutorial gifts. "Well, Moe, the official reason given by the TV producers was that alliterative names like Bruce Banner and Peter Parker and Reed Richards are too comic-booky and unrealistic."

"And giant green monsters weren't?"

"My response to that is, then why did you hire Bill Bixby to play him, huh?"

Kenny lowered his voice. "But between you and me, I once asked

Smilin' Stan Lee himself for the real lowdown at a con in Boston, and you know what Stan the man told me?"

"What?"

"You can't repeat this."

"I won't."

"Stan told me that the TV people told him that the name Bruce had 'homosexual overtones.' "

"No way."

"Yes."

"What about Bruce Willis?"

"Bruce Springsteen."

"Bruce Wayne."

"Well, Moe, we might have to give him Bruce Wayne."

In a booth across the room, hidden by an electric Budweiser sign but keeping close watch in a large mirror over the bar, Ranger Beth Banger was studying every grimace and snicker that flitted across Kenny King's face. What were he and his toupeed sack-whacker planning now? Was their laughter directed at the legal system that let them slip through its fingers? Laugh on, you fish-smuggling sicko. I'm up your ass like a rubber glove.

Half an hour away, at the Midland Mall in Natick, Rhode Island, Ann King was sitting behind a one-way window in a tiny green room watching a dozen bored Rhode Islanders talk about what they looked for in an Arts and Entertainment TV channel.

Khefa from Research was running a focus group to gather insights into the likes and dislikes of potential viewers of Eureka. They had been locked in this hidden closet for three hours with nothing but a box of doughnut holes and the piped-in opinions of a group of people who had nothing to do but hang around the mall on Friday night and go off into a cinderblock room for four hours for ten dollars and all the Kool-Aid they could drink.

The first rule of focus groups is that the leader cannot tell the civilians what they are there to talk about. To give them any such information is believed to taint the scientific accuracy of the experiment. So the first tedious ninety minutes were spent nudging and prodding the participants to talk about their tastes and habits until one of them mentioned something that could be used to push the conversation toward the hidden topic. It took this group forty-five minutes just to bring up TV, and another half hour to get them on to cable channels.

"I like those makeover shows," one woman said. She was wearing stirrup pants and a Grateful Dead T-shirt. She seemed ready to go further, perhaps even touching on something that might be of use to Eureka, but a man with long sideburns interrupted her to say, "Them things is all fixed. The only thing that's real on TV anymore is hockey."

Ann reached for the jelly-filled Munchkins.

A single King Cable employee was engaged in useful work that dreary evening. Boris Mumsy was locked in an edit bay, making final revisions to a special that he already knew would premiere high and repeat forever. "Betty & Veronica: Madonna/Whore" examined all the evidence on each side of the fifty-year argument "Which was the virgin and which was the slut?" Did Archie and Reggie's endless fascination with the bitchy Veronica mean she was putting out or holding back? Did they ignore girl-next-door Betty because they could have her anytime, or not at all?

Boris knew it was a barrel of baloney. He also knew it was great TV. Boris had learned a lot about making television since Bobby Kahn came to town. One thing he learned was that successful TV executives never admit to one another or to anyone else that they are making garbage. If you have a hit reality show devoted to mocking a gorgeous woman for being hilariously stupid, you always say, "Isn't she adorable! There's something so sweet and real about her that the audience just loves." If you have a series devoted to making fun of a bunch of fat kids trying to play sports, you look at the screen and say, "I love their determination! When poor Howie fell into that mud pile and all the kids laughed at him, my heart was breaking." The truth was that you, as producer, probably paid an intern to push Howie into the mud pile and plan to use that shot for the tune-in promo. But etiquette demanded that you never, ever cop to it. Successful TV executives did not drop their masks. In that way, Boris thought, they were much like supervillains.

Boris knew that "Betty & Veronica: Madonna/Whore" achieved a level of panting stupidity that promised great ratings. He had worked hard to dumb it down to the point where it would carry its audience across all commercial breaks. And he knew that when the ratings came in Bobby would look him right in the eye and say, "Great writing on that one, Boris. Smart, smart stuff."

Bobby left his gym and drove to a restaurant on Federal Hill in Providence to have dinner with Dominic King. It was an unusual nighttime meeting, and far from New Bedlam. The old man had something on his mind.

"What do you think about Skyler talking to people on Wall Street about King Cable?" Dom said when the veal arrived.

"I don't know anything about it," Bobby said. "That's above my pay grade." He thought of all the papers on Skyler's dining room table that he turned over when Bobby came in. He was working on taking the company public. Bobby realized he had to tread carefully. Dom stared at him like he was taking an X-ray.

"I hate this stock-market, going-public, IPO shit," Dom said. "It's killing this country."

Dominic King—patriot, Bobby thought. There's a new one.

"My attitude toward business is very simple," Dom declared. It was tutor time again. "I spend a hundred dollars to make a product, earn two hundred selling it, that's good business. Am I wrong?"

Bobby shook his head.

"Television, ladies' gloves, automobiles, rides to the airport. It's the same principle."

"Well," Bobby said—and he was talking only because he was not in the mood to sit quietly and play protégé—"TV's a little different because you have nontangible goods, intellectual property—"

Dom cut him off. "What crap. Intellectual property. Same rule applies in all businesses: It ain't who thought of it that owns it. It's who paid for it that owns it. Am I wrong?"

Bobby shook his head. Dom continued. "Once Wall Street gets a hold of you, making a hundred percent profit every year ain't good enough. Now, I made a hundred percent last year, I gotta make a hundred fifty this year, I gotta make two hundred next year, I gotta make three hundred the year after that. Wall Street is not about profit, Wall Street is about growth. And when the growth stops, your company loses all its value. Even if you're still making a good profit on a good product, your company loses all its value." Dom was chopping his veal into tiny pieces.

Bobby began to say, "Well, yeah, because people invest—"

Dom cut him off. "I understand the reasons!" A bit of veal flew off his lower lip. "I know WHY it works that way, but it's a bad system! It causes companies to fire workers when they are making a solid profit, it forces cutbacks in quality to give the illusion of growth! It takes away a man's ability to decide what is best for the company he built and puts him under the scrutiny of outside directors and government agencies!"

Ah, Bobby thought, we have reached the root of Dom's aversion. The old man likes money, but not as much as he likes control.

"There was a good chain of supermarkets up here," Dom said, wiping his mouth. "Macnie's. They got bought by a big chain. The chain got bought by some public company. Suddenly these grocers had to show growth every quarter. For a year or two they did okay, then they started to leave the peaches out an extra day. Save a little that way. Then they cut back on the cleaning crews. Every other night instead of seven times a week. The store started to be a little dirty. The lettuce isn't so fresh anymore. People stopped shopping there. Now Macnie's is gone."

Dom waved for the check. "That happens every time. We got a good solid business here. You should be proud. Skyler should be proud. Don't let him screw it up by bringing in Wall Street."

Bobby nodded. He offered to pay the bill. The old man waved him away.

Dom had calmed down. He had made his point. He trusted Bobby to carry out his wishes with discretion. He said, "This get-rich-in-the-stock-market scam is bullshit anyway. Don't all these investors know that for someone to win, someone else has to lose? They hear about some stiff making a million dollars—where do they think the money came from? I mean the actual dollars, where do they think they came from? The mint went into overtime? No, if you got a million bucks you didn't have yesterday, it means somewhere somebody who had a million bucks don't have it anymore. Someone wins, someone loses. Who says you'll always be the one who wins?"

Dom stood up to leave. "It's the same as the Indian casino."

Neither Dom nor Bobby saw Sammy Bignose sitting at a booth

near the bathroom with his mother and his sister. They were celebrating Mrs. Bigenos's birthday with a dinner in Providence after a trip to the IMAX theatre.

Sammy had only caught a bit of what Dom was telling Bobby, the parts where Dom raised his voice. He caught enough to know that Dominic was telling Bobby not to let Skyler do something the old man didn't want him to do.

Bignose relayed this intelligence to Kenny, whose resentment over the *Rhode Islander* story was inflamed by the news that Bobby the big shot was eating with the old man at a fancy restaurant. Kenny sure didn't get an invitation. Kenny could hardly wait to tell Skyler that Dominic and Little King Kahn were making plans to shut down Sky's strategies for growing the company.

Kenny chuckled. Sky likes to think he's unflappable, but when he finds out that their employee Bobby is sneaking around with Dom trying to interfere with Sky's financial initiatives, ol' Sky will flap like a parrot in a propeller.

34.

T he *Rhode Islander* article, for all the ill will it stirred in the Victorian house on Main Street, New Bedlam, was responsible for one remarkable event. In March, Dominic King received a registered letter on gold leaf informing him that he had been granted membership in the Rhode Island Hall of Fame. This honor, much coveted and closely guarded, was bestowed once a year on a small group of the state's most prominent educators, legislators, sports figures, broadcasters, and accomplished native sons.

It was the kind of thing most people who knew Dom would have expected him to scoff at, but in fact he was thrilled. Skyler told his mother that it surprised him to see the old man so excited to be honored by the very sort of people he'd spent his whole life hating. Betty said, "But that's exactly why, Skyler, don't you see? He was always the little boy outside looking in. Now they've invited him into their party on his terms. It was not that Dominic never wanted to be part of the Big Shot club. He just wanted them to come and ask him. He thinks this proves he was right all along."

Kenny was more impressed by how much the Rhode Island Hall of Fame was charging for tables at the induction banquet.

"They called me to ask how many tables I was buying!" he said to Skyler in a panic. "Did they call you? Did you see what these fat cats want us to pay? This is all a scam, like 'Who's Who in American Cable Broadcasting'!"

"The company will buy the tables, Ken," Skyler said. "It's a legitimate expense. We'll invite business associates and our key executives and whoever the sales force wants to butter up with liquor and lobster. Don't be a tightwad on this, it's the old man's moment of glory."

"About time," Kenny said.

"I'll say."

"Hey, once he gets in, can he nominate other people?"

"I have no idea. Who did you have in mind?"

"Well . . . like us for example."

"I'm touched, Ken. Forget it. You're not getting in until you're very old and very respectable."

Kenny went looking for Sammy Bignose and Moe. He found them in the basement, in the heat of a passionate argument.

"It doesn't count, Moe!" Sammy Bignose was saying. It took a lot to snap Sam's patience with his Sancho Panza, but Moe seemed to have reached that limit.

"It does count! I got you! I got you!"

"Kenny!" Sammy implored when he saw the boss. "Back me up here. What are the rules for April Fools'?"

Kenny just looked at them. April Fools' Day was a touchy issue with him ever since it ruined his marriage. He finally said, "I tell you a lie and then if you believe it, I say, 'April Fool!' Like last year, when I told you I was making you a vice president. You should have seen your face."

Sammy said to Moe, "What you did doesn't count!"

"Does so, I got you good!"

"Wait, wait," Kenny said. "What did you say, Moe?"

Moe grinned. "I come in from lunch, right, and I says to Sammy, 'Hey, Sam! I just had a chicken sandwich at the Hungry Horse and it was pretty good.'"

Kenny looked at him. "Yeah?"

"And he believes me, and I wait a minute and then I says, 'April Fool!'"

Kenny grinned and looked from one moron to the other. "I don't get it."

"There's nothing to get." Sammy sighed.

"I fooled him!" Moe said. "I didn't have the chicken! I had a egg salad! Get it? April Fool!"

"Oh, man, Moe," Kenny said. "What did your mother drink while she was pregnant? Listen, you two. This is serious. The phone bill just came in and once again there's a couple of hundred bucks in 900-number sex-line calls from my phone. This isn't funny anymore! These phone bills go to general accounting and into the public record of this company. Anyone on the board or even a newspaper reporter could examine these. The FCC could even get involved. It is not a joke. If you are doing it, stop it now. If you know who's doing it, stop them. If you don't know who's doing it, find out and make sure they eat poison, okay? Got it?"

Sammy and Moe nodded and looked at the floor. They were trying not to laugh. Kenny started up the stairs. He paused and said, "Hey, by the way, Eureka's doing a special on porn stars and Bobby and I are going down to New York to have dinner with a few of them. We need a driver. One of you can come along."

The two goons shoved each other and rushed to Kenny's side. He looked at them both and said, "April Fool!"

The Rhode Island Hall of Fame induction dinner was held at Rhodes on the Pawtuxet, a banquet hall not far from the state airport in Warwick. King Cable bought almost half of the fifty tables for the event. Among the other inductees were a famous radio announcer and children's show host, the editor of the *Rhode Islander,* a Newport-born comic who had made it big in Hollywood, and a woman from the Rhode Island School of Design who had found acclaim in Europe making sculptures out of kitchen utensils.

The cocktail party was a who's who of local celebrities, politicians, and power brokers. Dominic arrived early with Annie on his arm. He had had a haircut and was wearing a new tuxedo. Lean and suntanned, he looked like a real mogul. Bobby thought the old man smiled more in his first ten minutes in the room than he had in the last decade.

Annie looked like a screen star from the golden age. Bobby approached them as Boris Mumsy was engaging Dom in an argument about why the Cartwrights never changed their clothes.

"It was for continuity, Mr. King," Boris insisted. "They shot the outdoor scenes on location all at once and the indoor scenes later. They had to match. That's the only reason. It wasn't supposed to be because they each only had one set of clothes."

"My point is they were frugal!" Dom insisted. "They didn't throw their money around on fancy duds!"

Bobby took Annie by the arm and moved her away. "You look amazing," he said.

"Thank you, Robert. So do you."

"Now, explain this to me, what does induction in the Rhode Island Hall of Fame actually entail? I mean, is there a physical hall you can go visit, like Cooperstown?"

"I have inquired after this very point," Ann said. She snagged a glass of champagne from a passing tray. "Apparently what membership in the Rhode Island Hall of Fame gets you is your name engraved on a plaque from Emblem & Badge, for which you pay through the nose, and a pewter cup of some kind if you are flush enough to spring for that after you've paid for your plaque and your table, and—here is the

end of the rainbow—you get your picture hung somewhere, not necessarily in a public place but somewhere, in the Providence Civic
Center."

"Very nice," Bobby said, stealing a sip of her drink.

"But here's the bad news," Ann said.

"There's a catch?"

"Here's the catch. The Providence Civic Center is no longer called
the Providence Civic Center."

"Oh no? So where will they hang Dom's picture now?"

"The Dunkin' Donuts Center."

"Egad."

"It's not exactly Mount Rushmore. Then again, my pop is not exactly Abe Lincoln."

Bobby thought champagne and Annie went together well. She almost seemed flirtatious. He said, "Hey."

"What?"

"Can you and I go out together next weekend and talk about
nothing to do with work?"

"Robert, what else is there?"

"When the ratings came in for *Shakespeare's Secrets,* you promised
to take me horseback riding. That was last year. You still owe me."

"I owe you, eh?"

"You do."

"Well, if I owe you—"

Kenny, with his supernatural instinct for bad timing, stuck his
face between them. From the smell of him he'd skipped the champagne and gone straight for the hard stuff.

"Fuckin' Dom," Kenny said. "He doesn't change."

Bobby and Ann gave him a go-away look, which he ignored.
Kenny said, "I go up to congratulate him and tell him how proud I

am and he says, 'What's wrong with you, you look like shit.' I say, 'I'm just getting over bronchitis; I got out of a sick bed to come pay tribute to you.' And he says, 'See, I told you not to go running around without socks.' Unbelievable. Since we were kids, anytime one of us got sick, it had to be because we failed to do something Dom told us to do. Couldn't be anything else."

Skyler joined them. "What are we talking about here?"

Annie said, "Our father's special bedside manner. If someone gets ill, it's because he or she did not listen to his advice."

"Oh yeah." Skyler smiled. "Dom never bought the germ theory."

The three of them were then off comparing childhood stories. Bobby was not included. He backed off, figuring he'd fix the date with Annie later on.

"Whenever I'd get a stomachache," Skyler was saying, "he'd try to feed me a Hershey's bar. He'd always say, 'It got the U.S. Army through the Battle of the Bulge!'"

Bobby drifted around the room. Dom was complaining loudly to the editor of the *Rhode Islander* and several horrified guests that no one was allowed to say a word against queers getting married, but light up a cigarette and people treat you like Lee Harvey Oswald.

Bobby backed away from that homily. He found Abigail Plum looking tentlike in a pastel dress, talking literature with a thin, long-haired man in a blue suit with no tie.

"Bob," Abigail said. "Do you know Mark Hamburger, our resident great novelist?"

"Mark, oh yes, I do! We met when you were taping *FootNotes*. How are you?"

"Bob, I'm well. People really liked that program, you know. I got calls from all over the country. You ran it quite a lot for a while."

"Yes, yes we did."

"You haven't run it in a bit now, though."

"No, well, you know, you have to rest them. Don't want to burn 'em out. How did you like the show yourself, Mark?"

"I never did watch it, Bob. Don't like watching myself on TV. Makes me self-conscious."

"Well, you should try and force yourself sometime. You came off great."

Bobby moved toward the bar, hoping to find a pretzel. He was starving and it looked like dinner was a long way away. He spotted Mr. and Mrs. Dash Ryan greeting well-wishers and chatting with fans.

"I'm doing Dom's induction speech," Dash said to Bobby on the sly. "You want to give it the once-over?"

Bobby ran his eyes down the copy. Dom the deep, Dom the profound, Dom the generous, Dom the visionary. Looked fine to him. Pam Ryan suddenly stiffened and grabbed her husband's arm. She said, "Oh my word."

Bobby followed her gaze. A big burly man with a red nose and red hair and a black tux with a green flower in his lapel was entering the room, shaking hands and patting shoulders. With him was a woman who looked to be about seventy in a slightly crooked brown wig and the stoop of someone who carried jugs of water on her back.

"Lord have mercy," said Dash. "I didn't think he'd come."

"Well, he's on the Hall of Fame board," Pam said. "He had to come."

"Well, let's go say hello and make the best of it."

Bobby said to Pam, "I've met that man, remind me what his name is."

Pam whispered, "That's Dan Clancy, dear. He and Dom don't get along."

Of course, Bobby thought. Fancy Dan Clancy of Clancy & Cianci.

Dom's rival. Big of him to show up, but so what? He went and asked Kenny for the lowdown.

As usual, Kenny had the dirt: "Clancy and Dom hate each other," Kenny said, "but that's not the awkward part. The awkward part is that Dom once rode the snake with Mrs. Clancy."

Bobby looked at the old woman again. She was shaped like a question mark.

"Oh, don't tell me that," Bobby said.

"Oh yeah, this could yet turn into an interesting night," Kenny said and took another swig of his drink.

Dinner was called and the swells from the cocktail party made their way to their tables. Bobby was seated with Boris and other key King staff at a table close to the family. He looked around the room and saw that the Clancys were seated on the other side of the hall.

The dinner took a long time coming. It was some kind of fish. The menu said Cape Cod halibut but Bobby was sure it was carp. It was so cheap now, local restaurants were trying to sneak it in all over.

The speeches, nominating and acceptance, for and from the other inductees, went on longer than the Comic Book Channel's *100 Greatest Superheroes Countdown*. One man got up and talked for thirteen minutes about the lessons he learned in kindergarten, and he was only there to induct someone else.

Finally it was Dominic's turn. Dash Ryan climbed to the podium and said, in reference to how long everyone had been sitting, "As Caesar said to Cleopatra, 'I did not come to make a speech,'" which got an appreciative laugh. He then threw away his text and improvised a tight four minutes about how Dom responded to whatever historical moment he was in and made the most of every opportunity that came his way.

"He's a man who hates false sentiment and will drive fifty miles out of his way to avoid a compliment," Dash concluded. "But I'm sorry, Dom, we've got you trapped tonight. You're not getting out of here until you listen to me say it for all the people here. We who know you best, love you most. You're your own man, you're one of a kind. Dominic Coutu from Pawtucket, welcome to the Rhode Island Hall of Fame."

Everyone clapped. Kenny tried to start a standing ovation. Bobby leaned over to see that, to his amazement, Dom was wiping a tear from his eye. Annie was crying and smiling at the same time. Boy, Bobby thought, you think you know people. . . .

Dominic made his way to the podium, looked around, nodded, sniffled, and gathered himself to speak. He fished a paper out of his jacket and put on some black horn-rim glasses Bobby had never seen him wear. He cleared his throat.

"Thank you, Dash," he said. "That was very kind. I guess you finally read the fine print in your contract." He looked into the audience. "Dash and I married sisters, you know. The Koenig girls. He was smart, he held on to his. I was stupid." He seemed to lose his thoughts for a moment, then he gathered himself.

"I want to thank all of you and the Hall of Fame for including me in such honored company. It's very nice. I want to especially thank my children. My daughter, Ann, my English rose, the most beautiful woman in the room. I saw some of you guys looking at her. Let me make it clear—you want to ask her out, you come talk to me." There was laughter. Annie blushed. "I'll say no, but you come talk to me. My son Skyler and his wife, Claudia, and their kids, my grandchildren. Hi, Maudie, Amy. Jeremy, you look bored, go play your video game, it's okay, pal."

Aw hell, Bobby thought, he's not going to mention Kenny. He looked at the family table. Kenny was staring into his plate, forcing a smile.

Dom went into his text.

"You remember, back around 1990, the Soviet Union collapsed. You all remember that. The Cold War? Eastern Europe was freed. 'The Collapse of Communism.' It was a big deal, it was in all the papers. Why did this happen? Was it the Polish pope, was it Solidarity? The Russian people? *The Gulag Archipelago*, the Chernobyl explosion? Was it Reagan with his Star Wars?" Dom stopped and looked up. "Oops, I'm not supposed to say 'Star Wars.' We might get sued again."

People laughed. Charming Dom, who knew?

"I've been in business my whole life. I've fixed cars, I've sold cars. I've run coin laundries and a limousine service. I've been a small businessman and I've been a pretty big businessman. Fifty years on, I have an opinion about why in a century that began with most of the world under monarchy, and went on to experiment with socialism, fascism, and communism on grand scales—even tried a little theocracy here and there—the only thing that worked, the only thing that prevailed, the only system people actually wanted was capitalism. You want to know why?"

"We like money!" someone yelled. Bobby looked. It wasn't Kenny. Kenny was sitting somberly watching Dom speak.

"You said it." Dom answered. "Capitalism wins out every time, not because it's the best system. Someone said a benevolent monarchy is the best system, and speaking as a King myself, I have found that to be true." Laughter again. "No, capitalism always wins out because it is the system that most closely fits with human nature. Simple as that. It's like Darwinism—it's not right or wrong, it's just what we are. You got a big house? I want it. I got more than I need? I still want it all. You got a good-looking wife? I want a better-looking wife. And maybe a girl on the side, who knows?"

Some of the audience were uncomfortable, but most of them seemed prepared to vote for Dom for governor. Dan Clancy was looking at his watch. Mrs. Clancy was either drunk or she'd had a stroke.

Dom finished up. "I am a businessman. No more, no less. I offer the public goods and services they want at a reasonable cost to them and a reasonable profit to me. I won't steal from you, but I will try to get the best deal for me and for my family. If you do the same, we should all make out okay.

"It's not the way of heaven, but we are not angels. We are women and men. And if the Almighty has a problem with that, I say, Hey— you made us like this, don't complain." Dom turned to the bishop, who was seated at the rostrum. "Sorry, your eminence.

"I appreciate this honor very much. Some of you I have known for years, some of you I have known for a short time. Some of you I would like to get to know better. I am very proud to be a Rhode Islander. And I am proud that you consider me worthy to join the Hall of Fame."

Dom left the podium to great applause. It took him ten minutes to make it back to his table, with all the handshaking and compliments he had to wade through. Kenny and Ann were effusive. Claudia kissed him on the cheek and he rubbed his grandkids' heads before Skyler gathered them up and said he had to get the children home to bed, great job, Pop, good night.

Most of the room had come for other people, and they were quick to get their coats on and move out. Dom's contingent hung on awhile. When the headwaiter came and said to the core group that they had to clear the room, the King company headed for the cocktail lounge, which was still serving. Dom took everyone's orders and bellied up to the bar. He called for a Jameson's and Coke on the rocks and turned to see he had parked himself right next to Mr. and Mrs. Dan Clancy.

Clancy looked at Dom as a bull looks at a matador. He breathed in and out and then said, "Very nice speech, Dominic. Welcome to the club."

"Thank you, Dan," Dom said. He looked at Mrs. Clancy. "Hello, Cynthia. It's good to see you."

The woman had a voice like all the cigarettes in the world. "Hallo, Dom. Nice tawk."

It was a little awkward but okay. "Were you looking for a Jameson's, Dom?" Dan Clancy asked. He slid a brown drink toward Dominic. "Please, tonight of all nights—let me buy you a drink."

Dom looked startled. Then he looked something like embarrassed. He lifted the glass and nodded to the man he had hated since he first saw him. "Thanks, Dan," he said, and he took a swig.

Dom felt a chip of something tiny and hard brush by his teeth and against his tongue. He almost spit it out, but he didn't want to look like a slob in front of Clancy and he didn't have a napkin, so he swallowed it.

Dash Ryan moved in to rescue Dom from Fancy Dan by getting between them and asking Clancy about the Catholic Charities Appeal. Bobby was trying to firm up his date with Annie when she said, "Just a minute, Bob," and moved to her father's side.

"Dad? Are you feeling all right?" Dom had his hand to his mouth. He took it away and it was red. He brought out a handkerchief and put it to lips. His mouth was bleeding.

Ann steered him to a chair. Kenny and Pam Ryan swooped in.

"I think I cut my tongue on something," Dom said. "Gimme that Coke bottle." Kenny reached past the Clancys and grabbed the half-empty bottle of Coca-Cola used to make Dom's drink.

The rim of the glass bottle was cracked off. "I felt it in my mouth, but I thought it was a piece of ice," Dom said, turning the bottle in his hand. "I swallowed it."

BILL FLANAGAN

Pam Ryan was signaling for Dash to call an ambulance. No one else was thinking that far ahead. Dom looked at his white shirt. There were speckles of blood on the front. His mouth was filling up. Kenny told him to put his head back. Annie said no, lean forward. Bobby said there had to be a dozen doctors in the room. Pam said a rescue squad was on the way. Boris said it would be quicker to drive him to the hospital. Dom said something no one could understand. He was gurgling.

Annie said, "Dad, what is it?" She leaned to his mouth. He said, "Make sure you get my plaque."

They carried Dominic out of the room on a chair, like a Jewish bridegroom. As he left, he looked at Dan Clancy, who raised a glass in his direction with an expression that might have been concern or might have been a salute. Dom was sure it was something else. Dom was sure it was "I got you."

288

part four

reservations

35.

t wasn't that Skyler was scared of hospitals. He had the emotional detachment to walk through halls of the sick and grieving without it impinging on his equilibrium at all. What bothered him about hospitals was the feeling they gave him that nobody really knew anything. The piles of paper in what were surely the wrong places, the closets overstuffed with materials the staff had given up any attempt to identify, the abandoned pushcarts and orphan dinner trays and misplaced clipboard medical charts gave him the impression that here was the institutional ineptitude of the Registry of Motor Vehicles married to the responsibilities of God.

He had his father's room number written on the back of a business card. He walked up and down deserted corridors trying to find some pattern in the digits and letters along the way. It struck him that any second-year assistant manager at the Portsmouth Ramada Inn could do a better job organizing a floor plan.

He looked into an unmarked room and saw an old man, unshaven and wheezing on a respirator. Two failing flowers in a cheap plastic pitcher leaned toward him as if straining to hear what he said in his sleep. It looked like he would expire before they did. It was a double room, and the plastic curtain between beds had been pulled back to reveal a toothless man in the next bed staring desperately at the ceiling and gumming the air. It must be a trade secret, Skyler thought. We must take away their dignity intentionally, to make them seem less like us. It makes us feel safer when they go.

Skyler heard Kenny's voice, as distinctive as a crow. He followed it to a room on the other side of the nurse's station. Kenny was abusing some chubby candy striper in a hairnet who apparently spoke no English and was treating Kenny as she would a horsefly.

"This is not his chart!" Kenny was wailing at the nurse's aide, at Annie, and at anyone within the sound of his braying. "You cannot give the wrong medicine to a patient in critical condition and walk away like you gave him curly fries instead of hash browns! This is our father here! Get it right!"

The nurse's aide left, muttering sounds that Skyler was pretty sure were not a real language.

Kenny did not let her leaving interrupt his rant.

"This is why hospitals get sued!" he announced. "What if I hadn't happened to be here! What if that bat-faced incompetent had fed Dom the wrong dosage of someone else's medicine? What if she comes back and does it again?"

"He looks so little," Annie said.

For a moment Skyler thought she meant Kenny, but of course she meant Dom, who did indeed look as shrunken as a mummy under his thin hospital blanket. A yellow tube was taped to his nose and a drool-catcher hooked over his lower lip. A green screen was bleep-bleep-bleeping along on a monitor on a cart beside the bed, and a bag of some orange nutrient was hanging from a rolling hat rack, connected by a hose to a needle in his arm.

"No change in him?" Skyler asked.

"Betty said he was talking this afternoon," Annie said. "But she couldn't understand what he was talking about. It was probably nonsense."

"And they still can't say exactly what happened?"

"Apparently the trauma of swallowing the glass set off a heart attack," Annie explained. "When he came in the doctors were working on one thing, they did not immediately realize the other had happened. We lost some time."

Annie felt like an actress who had been summoned to the stage before she had time to memorize her lines. She could not swallow that she might be at her father's deathbed. It was not because she loved him so much she could not bear the thought of his dying—like everyone who knew Dom, she had imagined his death on more than one occasion without it seeming like an entirely unpleasant prospect. But she was not done with him yet. She knew a day would come when they would say good-bye, but she was not ready for it to be now.

Skyler was taken aback. The old man was worse than he expected. He wondered how long he had to stay. He tried to think of some excuse to get out of there without seeming like a heartless prick.

What was unknown to the antsy Skyler and the trepidant Annie and the angry Kenny was that the nurse's aide Kenny had insulted had unintentionally switched the bag containing Dom's intravenous medicine with the bag holding his urine. She confused the in tube with the out tube. While his children stood around him, piss was dripping into Dom's bloodstream, where it would swim to his brain, causing dementia before it filled up his heart and killed him.

No one would ever know this. After Dom was dead the same nurse's aide would pull out the needles and roll up the tubes and never realize she had done anything wrong.

"Good thing I came by when I did!" Kenny announced. "This place is a goddamn monkey house!"

If his heirs had known that Dom could hear their voices, they might have taken that occasion to whisper, "So long, it's been good to know ya." Instead the old man was being sung out by Kenny's tirade. Then again, that was probably Dom's kind of tune. Kenny's voice was to him like the rattle of a tailpipe on an old car. He heard it but he paid no attention.

His mind was on other things. Dom felt like he was floating down a long tube. It didn't feel bad, it didn't feel good, it just was.

His throat was kind of scratchy, which made him think of when he was a kid and had his tonsils out. He remembered a dream he started then, a dream about riding a white pony in the woods up in Cumberland. He couldn't tell if it was a real memory or a dream memory, but he was glad to have it back.

For a minute or two Dom was a little kid again. He and his brother, Frank, were throwing bottles off the train trestle. They hit the top of a Buick and the Frenchman driving it got out and threw rocks at them. Frankie hit his windshield with a quart bottle of Warwick Club Fruit Sherbet and the two of them got their asses out of there.

That was good fun. Like the time when they was a little older and the plainclothes cop picked them up for setting fire to the grass in Roger Williams Park. The cop, some Irish dick, decides he's going to talk them straight, acts like Bing Crosby in a movie, drives them all around gassing about civic duty and what kind of men they want to grow up to be and how he's been where they are now and sometimes all a kid needs is some-one to believe in him enough to give him a second chance. Dom's so scared he's pissing his pants, but Frankie's polite, yes officer, no officer, thank you officer. And the cop eats it with a fork and he says, Okay boys, I'm gonna give you that second chance, and he pulls over the car and lets them out and smiles and waves, and as he's driving away, Frankie picks up a brick and chucks it right through his back window.

Did they fuckin' run that time!

"What do you figure he's thinking about?" Kenny said.

"I don't know," Skyler said. "Probably where he left the combination to the strongbox."

"He looks peaceful," Annie said, studying him. "He's remembering something that made him happy."

Kenny came over next to her and looked at Dom.

"He does look kind of happy."

"Where do you think we go when we die, Skyler?" Annie said.

"We'll never know," Skyler said quietly. "Waste of time guessing."

"All those people who've been declared dead and revived say the same thing," Kenny said. "You pass through a tunnel toward a blinding light, and you're aware of relatives and people who love you standing around, welcoming you, helping you along."

"Yeah, I heard that," Skyler said.

"You don't believe it?" Annie looked at him. She had never heard Skyler talk about anything profound.

"I think it's a birth memory," Skyler said. "During the trauma of going out you remember the trauma of coming in. The tunnel with the bright light at the end, that's the birth canal. The relatives standing around welcoming you in—that's your parents and the doctor. I think that's all it is."

Ann thought about that.

Kenny said, "Or maybe it's an argument for reincarnation. Maybe you die and go right back down the chute and are born again."

Skyler really wanted to get out of there.

Dom was seeing visions as the urine pumped through his brain. He saw his mother hanging out the wash. He saw his childhood girlfriend, Susan, sticking out her tongue to reveal a square of Tootsie Roll Fudge. He saw Skyler's mother, Betty, sitting on a swing in a sundress.

He heard Annie's distant droning about Jesus, like a radio coming from another room. Even now, it meant nothing to Dom. It was all a con designed to scare widows out of their money. If God was real He could look Dom in the eye and explain Himself or He could go away and leave him alone. One thing he would not tolerate was judgment. Dom's attitude had always been "Who is God to judge me?"

When Dash and Pam Ryan arrived, Skyler said, "Well, it's getting pretty crowded," and took off.

Annie fell asleep in the sticky plastic chair and woke up when the eleven o'clock news was on. Dom seemed to have settled down, so she kissed him on the cheek and went home.

Kenny stayed all night. He didn't know why. It wasn't like he thought Dom was going to wake up and say anything to him, and it wasn't like anyone was there to give him any credit for it. He just felt like staying.

At two in the morning a priest came by and said hello. Kenny knew him. Father Rick, the hospital chaplain. He was locally famous for being a stand-up guy, bright and dedicated and widely admired. It was said in New Bedlam that Father Rick took himself off the fast track for bishop back in the eighties because he refused to cover up the usual sex scandals. Instead, he asked the diocese to assign him to the sick and dying. He'd stayed at the hospital ever since. He was respected for that, and for looking just like Glen Campbell. Rumor was, he even signed Glen Campbell's autograph from time to time when he was out of town and not dressed as a priest.

"Ken," Father Rick said in greeting. "How's the old man holding up?"

"See for yourself, Father. I don't think a fourth marriage is in the cards."

"You want me to give him extreme unction?" Kenny looked at him like the priest was proposing an enema. Father Rick explained, "The Sacrament of the Sick. Last Rites."

"Oh, I don't know. He wasn't really a churchgoer, Father."

"Up to you, Ken."

"Yeah, sure. Go ahead."

The priest stuck some oil on Dom's forehead with his thumb and mumbled some prayers and then stood and looked down on the unconscious old man. He looked over at Kenny, who had no idea what to do—say "Amen"?—and said warmly, "Okay, Ken. We got his passport stamped. You might want to go home and collect some Z's."

"Yeah, pretty soon, Father. Thanks."

An intern who looked about fifteen appeared at the door.

"Doctor," said the priest.

"Father," said the intern.

Father Rick said to Kenny, "You can't do any more here, Ken. Go home and sleep," and he left.

Kenny turned to the doctor, who was glancing at Dom's chart without interest and making little checks in the margin with a fancy ballpoint pen.

"He seems to have settled down," Kenny told the intern, who had not asked. "I caught one of the nurses giving him the wrong medicine, but I think they've got it right now. Made a big difference."

"Uh-huh," the young doctor said. He had rings under his eyes. "You family?"

"Stepson."

"Looks stable. No need for you to be here."

"Yeah, that's what Father Rick was saying."

The intern pursed his lips at the mention of the priest's name. "If the patient lives, God gets all the credit," the intern said. "If he dies, the doctor gets the blame."

Then Kenny and Dom were alone for the rest of the night.

36.

Sammy Bignose and Moe worried about Kenny attending the dying Dominic like loyal dogs locked outside their master's sickroom. Sammy knew what it was like to watch your dad waste away. His own father had died of prostate cancer when Sammy was a kid.

"You know what the worst thing about dying is, Moe?" Sammy said to his companion.

"Pretty much everything, I would think," Moe said.

"The worst thing is that it comes at the end of your life," Sammy explained.

Moe contemplated that. He and Sammy were sitting on a green wooden bench in a little park near the King Cable office. Sammy was dressed in a wet suit, his goggles loose around his neck. Moe was eating a banana. It occurred to Moe that if dying did not come at the end of your life, it would not be dying. If it came any other time, it would just be getting really sick. But he did not press Sammy.

Sammy elucidated anyway: "See, it's bad enough to be in pain all the time and have tubes up your nose and a hose in your dick and lose all your hair and have people come in and goggle you."

Moe took another bite of banana and listened.

"But what really stinks is that you can't look forward to having the pain stop and getting out of there because you know the pain's only going to stop and you only get out of there when you're dead. And how can you look forward to that?"

Sammy had clearly thought about this a great deal. He continued, "If you went through all that and then got, like, two weeks of feeling healthy at the end, it wouldn't be so bad. But it just gets worse and worse and then you're dead. It's like if a movie is really good but it has ten minutes that are really bad, it's okay if the ten bad minutes come in the middle—it's still a good movie. But if a movie's really good and then the last ten minutes are terrible, it wrecks the whole thing."

Moe said, "Like when you're watching a TV show and then the guy wakes up and it was all a dream. I hate that. Except sometimes he looks and there's like a mystical amulet or a tomahawk or something from his adventure in his bedroom and he says, 'Or *was* it?'"

Sammy looked at Moe. He said nothing more. They both sat on the bench, contemplating the futility of existence. Then Sammy said, "I'm going back in," and waddled off into the water where Moe watched him slowly disappear.

Sammy had a big secret. He would never tell his mother or his sister. He would never tell Kenny or Moe. Lately when he went underwater Sammy could hear the fish talking to one another. They didn't have much to say, mostly "food, food, food" or "warm, warm," but it was still impressive to an outsider. A couple of times he woke in bed in the early morning, just before the sun came up, and was sure he could hear the thoughts of people down the road going to work and getting dressed.

Sammy believed he was developing telepathy. He tried to turn it off and on in the office and was not certain if he was really reading people's minds or just making stuff up. Once he stared at Annie when she was writing in a notebook and he was sure he heard her voice in his brain saying, "I like men with beards." That startled him so much that he got up and went outside.

Another time he sat in the diner across from the office staring at people as they ate, and although he mostly didn't pick up anything at all, a man came in delivering cases of Pepsi and Sammy heard clear as a radio, "No one will ever know I buried the money under the tool-shed." Sammy got his car and followed that guy's truck all the way back to 95.

He was not sure what this new power meant. At times he was not sure it was even real. But he did know that if he could hone his extrasensory talents, he would use them for the good of all humanity. Until then, he would spend as much time as he could underwater, testing them on fish.

37.

I n the old Victorian house, Annie had canceled all her meetings but one. She was obligated to come into the office to see Sarah Planter, an old school friend who had come all the way from London to pitch her on a documentary.

Under the circumstances, it was a subdued reunion. Annie invited Abigail Plum to join the two old schoolmates in Annie's office. Sarah Planter put a tape into the player and Ann turned off the light. There was a loud beep and a band of colors came across the screen. The film began.

Three middle-aged Pakistani or Indian women with very dark skin sat primly in a row with their heads erect, wearing Mona Lisa expressions and bright saris. Behind them was a green cinderblock wall and a row of lockers or file cabinets. The women's eyes followed an unseen interviewer, who was standing out of the shot next to the camera. They told their stories like children reciting a lesson.

A scroll at the bottom of the screen translated them into English. They told how they had become prostitutes in Mumbai's brutal red-light district. All three had been sold as wives to much older men when they were twelve or thirteen. The men had sex with them, used them for a year or two, and then sold them to pimps for use as whores.

They now worked out of the slum brothels, which were not whorehouses as whorehouses are thought of in the West. These are tiny two-room hovels that resemble fortune-teller booths, with rows of dirty sheets hung from the ceiling to provide a suggestion of privacy. The men who come there are usually so drunk they don't care who sees them doing what.

The prostitutes work in these rooms until age, disease, or beatings cost them their value. Two of the three women said they were HIV positive, the third did not know. Although free condoms are supplied by the health authorities, men will pay twenty-five rupees to have sex without a condom, five rupees more than the price of sex with one. A rupee is worth about one cent American.

All had young children. They and their children slept on the sidewalks and in the gutters. They have to pay five rupees a night for the privilege to local gangsters. The women said this was fair, why should they and their children expect to sleep for free?

The camera followed the women out of the well-lit room into a dark street, past children playing in abandoned cars, and into a garish, winding alley of wooden huts, tents, and tiny windowless shops, all dedicated to the sale of women, men, eunuchs, and children for sex.

The three women pointed out the storefront quacks selling illegal prescription medicines, AIDS cures, and HIV tests, which they administered with safety pins. The women recited their tribulations pleasantly, like schoolteachers talking about the horrors of the Civil War.

Sarah Planter's voice off camera asked who watched their children while they were working, and the women pointed the camera toward the swinging saloon-style doors of a bright yellow room in one of the few buildings bigger than a hut.

Annie made a mental note that this felt too set up and should be edited out. The power of this presentation was its matter-of-factness. Any moment obviously staged would dilute that power.

The camera followed the women into a bright room filled with beautiful little girls, all dressed in colored T-shirts and skirts and jeans, eating rice and painting pictures. When the guests arrived, a woman in charge called the children to attention and they all lined up in neat rows, grinning and giggling. They introduced themselves by name, someone turned on a tape player, and they leaped into an elaborate Bollywood dance routine, bumping into one another, laughing, spinning, clapping, and occasionally falling down.

A tiny girl missing two front teeth ran into the arms of one of the prostitutes, who picked her up and told her she had done a wonderful job.

Sarah Planter got up and turned off the tape. Abigail turned on the light in the office. Annie wiped her eye and cleared her throat.

"Remarkable, Sarah," Abigail said. "What did you shoot with? Sony 150?"

"Panasonic AG-DVX 100A," Sarah Planter said.

"Really! It looks great."

"Shoots at 24p so it looks like film, mini DV stock, works well in low light."

"How big a crew?"

"Three of us, although Paul, my soundman, got sick the second day and Jenna and I did most of the work without him."

Annie broke in: "How can they live like that?"

"Here's the thing," Sarah Planter said. "To them, that's just life. They don't have any sense of injustice. They love their children, they go to work, they have little feuds and little alliances with their neighbors and coworkers. They have good days and bad days."

Annie shook her head and motioned toward the black TV screen.

"Here's what I've decided about the human race," Sarah Planter said. She said it with an air of cartoon seriousness, to make fun of her-self for making such a grand pronouncement. "Some people are wired from a very young age to be worriers, some of us are wired to be happy, some are wired to be brave, and some miserable. Whether you find yourself living in a mansion or a ghetto, your disposition will adapt to it."

"George Costanza on the airplane," Annie said. The other two women looked at her without comprehension.

"It's a character on *Seinfeld*," Annie explained. "Throughout the series he was always miserable, could not keep a job, dumped by every girlfriend, a real drip. In the final episode all of his dreams came true, he sold a television show to NBC, and they offered him a private jet to fly to Paris for a holiday with all his friends. He got on the jet and was unhappy with the size of his seat. No matter how much money he got, George was always going to be George."

Sarah Planter nodded at the story but Abigail was amazed.

"Since when do you watch American sitcoms?" Abigail asked Annie.

"Since the Wrath of Kahn descended on our network, darling. Like ancient amphibians, we adapt or die. This week I'm watching the complete second season of *Will & Grace*."

Annie turned her attention back to Sarah Planter's film.

"It's wonderful, Sarah. And it's important. How do you see this happening?"

"We'd like to shoot for six months, one week a month," Sarah Planter said. "Go back and follow these mothers and their children through what we think of as a school year. We want them to emerge as people like us, dealing with mundane parent/child dilemmas in this grotesque context."

"Will these children escape that life?" Annie asked.

Sarah Planter shook her head and said, "Some might. Most won't. These girls are in constant danger of being stolen, kidnapped, and sold into slavery, too. Because of AIDS there is a market hungry for younger and younger girls. There is a myth in Asia and Africa that AIDS can be cured by sleeping with a virgin. As soon as they hit eleven, they have to look over their shoulders all the time. There are little boys, their brothers, who try to protect them, but sometimes the boys betray them, too."

"That can't be," Annie said.

"That is the world," Sarah Planter told her. "We all live knowing that someday bad things are going to happen to us and someday we are going to die. As long as it's not today, we put it out of our minds. They do the same."

"Eureka must make this film," Annie said. "How much do you need?"

Sarah looked at Abigail, who looked straight back at her with an expression that suggested nothing. Sarah said, "If we had seven hundred fifty thousand we could cover every base, follow the side roads, the doctors and relief workers."

Abigail saw the *FootNotes* budget being sucked up into an Indian brothel. She said, "I don't think we can go that deep."

Sarah Planter said, "Look, tell me what you can afford and I'll tell you what we can do. A lot of it has to do with how many days each month we shoot, and how many of the mothers and children we follow."

"I'm sure we can find four hundred thousand," Annie said. "Maybe even five if we had to."

"I can do it for five," Sarah said quickly.

They went to lunch then and talked more about Asia. Sarah Planter had come from the same place as Annie. Now she lived in Thailand and devoted her life to serious work.

They ate salads and went through a bottle of wine. Annie kept getting up to check with Kenny at the hospital. No change.

The women talked about all the awards this film would win and the good it would do. How could Americans see this and not want to help? They had to find some call-to-action to incorporate; perhaps Eureka could even adopt that school and solicit donations to help protect those girls. Was there a scholarship program they could fund?

When they returned to the office Annie insisted that Sarah come upstairs and meet Bob Kahn. Abigail came, too.

They knocked on Bobby's door and he motioned for them to come in. He was sitting across from Boris Mumsy, and they were talking to a speakerphone.

"Help me here, Eddie!" Bobby was saying. "When I said I need big movies I did not mean *Ghost World* and *Crumb*! Come on! We want . . ." he looked at Boris.

Boris recited, "Both *Punisher's* would be good. Any window we could get on *Hulk* or *Superman Returns*. *Hellboy* would be terrific. *Constantine*. Is it too early to make an offer on *The Dark Knight*?"

The voice of the Comic Book Channel's new head of acquisitions came back out of the box.

"Those are major Hollywood movies! We are not going to get a *window* on these for the money we have! A lot of studios are wary of dealing with us since the fights over *Star Wars* and *Harry Potter*. I am using all my leverage and connections to make deals for very little money with people who have no motivation in the world to cut us any kind of break. I got you one Marvel movie already—that was a miracle. Don't expect miracles every time!"

Bobby rolled his eyes and Boris smirked. Bobby said to the box, "You got us *Howard the Duck,* Eddie! That does not count! I appreciate that it's a hard job. That's why they call it work. Please get back in there and use all your charm and acumen to get us at least one decent play date on some movie someone somewhere might actually want to watch. Thank you!"

Bobby clicked off. He said in a low voice to Boris, "I almost wish we still had Stinky in that job. Some neutron farts might be a good negotiating tool." Boris laughed.

"Bob Kahn," Annie said, "this is Sarah Planter. Boris. Sarah has just shown Abigail and me the beginning of a remarkable film about Indian sex workers and their children."

"There's an Indian burial ground right next door, you know," Bobby said to Sarah. Boris disappeared from the room as if by vaporization.

"It is about women in India," Annie said. "Bombay."

"Mumbai," Sarah Planter corrected.

"Sounds interesting," Bobby said without conviction. "Is this a theatrical?"

"No, actually . . ." Sarah Planter said and trailed off.

"We're looking at it for Eureka," Annie explained.

Bobby became more alert.

"We've been looking for a big event," Annie said. "Well, we've found it. Based on what Sarah has showed us, I am prepared to commit a substantial part of our development budget to funding this documentary."

"Ah." Bobby was getting concerned. "How many parts is it? Is this a miniseries? Do you see this anchoring a weeklong stunt?"

Annie let that hang in the air. Sarah Planter said, "I have conceived the film so far as a single piece, about ninety minutes. I suppose we could consider breaking it up, if we shoot for nine months, we might have three separate hours, each covering three months—"

"Wait, wait," Bobby said. "How long do you need to shoot this? When would it be ready for air?"

"Well," Sarah went on, "depending on the budget, we hoped to shoot one week a month from this September or October until spring. That is all undetermined, of course—"

Bobby said, "So this is really two years away, if you're talking about a summer stunt."

The three women nodded. Bobby said, "Well, I'll have to look at it. We've been talking about doing something on harems, maybe as a series, so this could be the kick-off for that, I suppose. If I had faith that our acquisitions department could pull in *Pretty Woman* or *Risky Business* or maybe that comedy where Melanie Griffith plays a hooker, we might get some traction out of this. Prostitutes get ratings."

Annie's face flushed.

"This is not a Happy Hooker movie!" she said. "It's a serious documentary about women who are sold into sexual slavery as children, struggling to survive and raise their own daughters in a brutal environment. Bobby, this is the most important program Eureka has been involved with. It is a serious film about a serious subject."

If Bobby was moved by Ann's argument or thrown by her determination, he did not show it. He said, "A year ago I would have said go for it. But we are finally turning the corner with Eureka. We are looking at our seventh consecutive quarter of growth and all the demos are trending young. Finally. We need to keep moving in the right direction, Ann. Now I'll look at the tape. If I think it can be a fit with us, great. Nothing would make me happier than to take on some big subjects. But I have to be frank. If I think this is something that will hurt Eureka, I'm not going to say otherwise."

He said to Sarah Planter, "It won't even be good for your film to get shown on a channel with the wrong audience. It would end up in a bad time slot and nobody would know about it."

He said to Annie as she left, "How's your dad doing? I tried to go by this morning but they said it was family only."

"No change," Annie said and hurried out the door.

The three women went back to Ann's office. Sarah Planter was used to this kind of reaction. She dealt with it all the time.

Annie was angry and embarrassed. Maybe it was her father's illness that made her especially emotional, but she did not think so. She thought Bobby Kahn was turning into a proper little prick.

Abigail Plum was surprised that Bobby would be tone-deaf to Ann's mood. The day Annie's father was in the hospital dying was not the day to say no to her. Abigail knew they mocked her behind her back, but she didn't care. She protected her domain by being alert to all the subtle signals the King siblings gave off. Abigail had noticed that while Bobby was brilliant at what he did, he sometimes seemed to be missing that instinct. Abigail had a great many conceits, but she never forgot to bow to the Kings. Bobby seemed to believe that success had made him one of them. That was a miscalculation Abigail would never make.

As dysfunctional as they were, the Kings were a family. Flabby Abby had understood from the first what Bobby seemed to miss; all of the employees of King Cable, no matter how successful or important they might be, in the end were hired help.

38.

Dominic King's children were standing around his bed arguing about whether to turn off his respirator.

"I think as long as there's a chance, we should hold on," Ann said.

"My heart's with you, Annie," Skyler said. "But face it, he's gone already. This is inevitable. The sooner we make the call, the sooner we can begin to heal."

Kenny was red-eyed. He had been maintaining a bedside vigil. "You know something, Skyler," he said. "Between the three of us, I bet we could come up with nine or ten compelling reasons to kill the old bastard. But I don't think 'closure' is one of them."

Skyler got glum and went outside to check his phone messages.

Annie looked at Kenny. He was distraught and exhausted. God, she thought, he needs it more than I do. And neither of us is going to ever get it now.

She said to him, "It's not like keeping him here is a hardship on anyone."

"That's right," Kenny said. "If Dom can't take it with him, he's going to do his best to spend as much of it as possible on the way out."

She smiled. She had not told her mother Dominic was dying. She was not prepared to deal with the reaction. If Mum pretended to be sorry, it would be too tempting to call her a hypocrite. And if she said she was glad, well, Ann might have a hard time forgiving her for that. She didn't want to lose both her parents.

"Hey," Kenny said, "Did you see the numbers on 'Gomer/Gump'? Point nine nine on a Sunday night at nine p.m. Maximum HUT time."

"Remind me about HUT again."

"Homes Using Television. A number like that in that time slot means the show will have legs forever."

"I didn't know about *Gomer Pyle*. We didn't have that in England."

"Oh yeah, well, Forrest Gump was a total rip-off. The small-town idiot who always wins, the marines, the whole thing. This can be bigger than the *F Troop/Dances with Wolves* stunt, and that was a monster."

"It's great, Ken."

"Yeah. We're doing okay. I'm glad the old man lived to see it."

Annie looked at her shrunken father and said, "What was he like when you and Skyler were kids?"

"Him? Same mean bastard, but tougher to run away from. Listen, here's my big emotional scene with Dom. I'm fourteen, right? Skyler's my best friend. I'm over at the King house all the time. I think these people walk on water. One day I decide to bunk school and I tell a couple of my buddies we can go to my house. My mom's at work. So I head over there with these guys Dennis and Alan, I unlock the door, and I hear this yelping and banging coming from the back of the house. I think it's a burglar. I go crashing in there, all ready to attack like Daredevil or the Blue Beetle, and there's my mom having sex with Skyler's dad. My mom looks like I just pulled out a gun and shot her. My two pals come running in behind me and they're totally unhinged. I mean, they didn't even know which end the thing went in and this was not, believe me, the best visual introduction to the

wonders of reproduction. It was . . ." He looked for a word. He settled on "hilarious."

Annie was appalled. No wonder her mother resisted the lure of
New Bedlam so strongly. She began to reach out to touch Kenny and
then felt awkward and withdrew her hand.

"So Dom looks up calm as can be and says, 'Hey! You punks are
supposed to be in school! Close the door and wait for me in the living room. Now!'

"Well, what are we gonna do? We do what we're told. We go sit
on the couch, and I gotta tell you, Annie, I was shaking. I mean, all
the rest of it was bad enough, but I knew that the second Dennis and
Alan got out of there the whole school was gonna know. There was no
way to keep this quiet. I guess Dom knew, too, cause he didn't even
ask or threaten or anything. He walks out into the living room in his
high pants and white undershirt and he says, 'Now you three see what
you get when you sneak out of school! How do you think this makes
Kenny's mother feel? Huh? You think this is what she deserves? You
two, what are your last names?'

"They tell him. He says, 'Okay, big shots, that's who I thought
you were. Well I got news for you. One of your mothers used to go
out with a Chinaman before she met your old man. I ain't gonna tell
you which of you's mother it was because I'm a gentleman. This Chinaman was a friend of mine from the war and guess what? He gave
her a dose of the creeping crud. I never told her I knew about it and
I never told her husband 'cause I think he's an okay guy. But if you
two little ass-lickers make this kid here or my boy Skyler feel bad
about this, if I hear about any dirty jokes or name-calling, if I find
anything written on any lavatory wall referring to Kenny's mother, I
am going to not only tell you two which of your mothers was a Chi-

naman's slut, I am going to tell every person you know and your father, too. Now get out of here before I put my foot up your ass.'"

"And the story never got out?" Ann said.

"It was all over town in six hours. That's why he and Betty split. The old man was incapable of apologizing. Hell, if I hadn't barged in, Dom and my mom probably would have kept the whole thing secret and he'd be married to Betty today and you wouldn't exist in this universe."

She looked at him. He said, "You're welcome."

He sighed and continued. "But because of Dom's warning, it wasn't as tough for me or for Skyler as it might have been. Kids mostly felt bad about it, I think."

Skyler came back in. "Reminiscing about life with Father?"

"I was just telling Ann about Dom's man-to-man talk with Dennis Joli and Alan Farnum."

"Oh that." Skyler laughed. "And you wonder, Annie, why I want to pull the plug? I remember not long after that, Dom was worried I might be following in his footsteps, I think. He sat me down and gave me the lecture on The Unwritten Law. You ever get that one?"

"Tell me."

"He says, 'Sky, you gotta know about The Unwritten Law. This is true in every state and most places in the world. Any man can take a gun and shoot any other man who he finds out has slept with his wife, and no jury will ever convict him.' Now, aside from making me wonder how Dom had gotten along without being riddled with bullets, I missed one important aspect of the lesson. I didn't realize he meant you could get away with shooting someone who sleeps with your wife while you're married to her. I thought he meant you could shoot anyone your wife ever slept with, even before you met her! I was scared for years that some girl I went out with would get married and tell her husband about me and he'd come put a slug in me. I mean, hell, I think I was twenty-three before someone set me straight."

Kenny began laughing. He laughed until Ann and Skyler caught the bug and began laughing with him. They laughed like all the dead people laughing on all the old TV shows.

39.

Dash Ryan was coming in from getting the Sunday paper when Pam met him at the door.

"Honey," she said. "Dominic just died."

Dash had to sit down in his chair and catch his breath. After a moment he said, "Who called?"

"Kenny King just phoned. He said it happened around four a.m. He wanted to wait to call people until a decent hour."

"We better get over to Betty's."

Kenny had been working the phone all morning. He had called Sky right away and Betty not much later. Betty said she would wake Ann. He spent the hours between Dom's death and seven a.m. placing a death notice and talking with the obit writer, alerting the funeral home and the cemetery, filling out the hospital forms. Then he started calling Dom's friends. He called his own mother, too. Now remarried and living in Pennsylvania, she would want to know.

He did not call Bobby Kahn. Ann would tell the staff. Bobby Kahn was not family. He was an employee. Time he realized that.

Kenny told everyone that Dom passed calmly, that he almost seemed to be smiling, that he must have been having a nice dream. That was a lie. What really happened at the very end Kenny would never tell.

At three forty-five Kenny was sleeping in the chair when he woke up to find Dom tearing at the tubes in his arms and nose. He had a wild look in his eyes, like an animal in a trap. Kenny leaned over and tried to talk to him and tell him to leave the tubes alone, but Dom grunted and snapped his dry mouth at him and kept pulling at the plastic and tape.

Kenny stood there staring at him. What a tough old buzzard he was, what a fighter. Most of his brain had shut off. From the cerebral cortex to the frontal lobe, the battery was dead. All the neural blocks were open, the inhibitors, the learned behavior, the habits that passed as manners. Most of Dominic King was gone, but what was left was going down swinging. His reptile brain was thrashing and spitting all the way out the door.

The nurse came in and gave him a shot, and he died a little while later. Kenny stayed in the room with him for a while. "You might not have done right by me, old man," he said to the body. "But I did right by you."

The three Kings had their usual argument over what kind of funeral to give him. Annie wanted a two-day wake and full church service and graveside prayers. Kenny wanted a burial followed by a memorial with speeches. Skyler wanted whatever was quick.

Betty King came up with the compromise. She got the funeral home to put together an abridged, two-hour deal where people came and shook hands with the family and said a prayer by the casket for the first hour, and then a minister came into the room and said the Lord's Prayer and invited anyone who wanted to get up and say a few words. One-stop shopping.

Dash Ryan delivered a brief reworking of his remarks at the Rhode Island Hall of Fame. Dom's lawyer told a funny story about Dom loaning the boys money to start the cable business, and two different characters from the car lot told heartfelt but confusing stories about Dom's various methods of convincing skeptical consumers to invest in questionable used cars.

There was a pause while the room waited to see if anyone else was going to get up. Skyler shook his head. Annie was too weepy. Bobby Kahn, seated in the back row with people from work, considered going up; he had a few words in mind. But something in the restrained greeting he got from all the Kings when he paid his condolences made him stay seated.

He was surprised to see a confident, well-dressed black man stride up to the lectern.

"I know a lot of you don't know me," he said. "My name is Boris Mumsy and I work for the Kings at their television company. I won't be long. I wanted to share with you something I just learned. See, Mr. King used to come by my desk and talk to me sometimes. It was a little scary at first." People laughed. "But I got used to it. Anyway, there was this Italian word he used a lot, and I'd heard it my whole life but I never knew what it meant. Now there seem to be a lot of Italian people here today." He looked around. Another laugh.

"Maybe one of you will know this word. It's the name of a great tree, and for those of you who care, it was the name of Che Guevara's motorcycle. It's a word in Italian that means 'Mighty One.' Who knows what the word is?"

There was a mumbling from the congregation. A couple of hesitant guesses. Boris shook his head no.

"The Italian word I learned from Mr. King was *ponderosa*." Now people got it and laughed. Someone clapped.

Boris said, "And I was so inspired by this, I went on the Internet and pulled down a very obscure poem. The little-known words to a familiar song." Boris took a piece of paper from his jacket and

317

unfolded it. Kenny King appeared at his side wearing a black cowboy hat. Kenny handed Boris a white ten-gallon Stetson, which he
put on with great formality. People tittered. Sammy Bignose and Moe
Notty shuffled up to the front of the room looking meek. They put
on cowboy hats, too. The four men cleared their throats and looked
down at the words on the paper Boris held in his hands. Then they
began to sing:

> *We got a right to pick a little fight—Bonanza!*
> *If anyone fights anyone of us, he's gotta fight with me.*
> *All for one, one for all, that's our family creed.*
> *We got a right to pick a little fight—Bonanza!*
> *If anyone fights anyone of us, he's gotta fight with me.*

Some of the old people in the room looked confused or offended,
but most people applauded.

Kenny stepped forward. "Now there's a lot more verses about
Hoss and Joe and Adam know, but you get the idea. Dom loved that
old TV show. And I kind of think it was because he was himself a
ponderosa. He was a mighty one."

It occurred to Bobby to go outside and check the black sign with
the little white plastic letters and make sure this was Dom King's funeral. It seemed from the eulogies that he might have stumbled into
the memorial service for Edward R. Murrow.

Kenny and his crew walked back to their seats. The congregation
reached to touch him and shake his hand as he passed. When the
party got up to move to the graveyard, Annie leaned over to him and
whispered, "Are you sure *ponderosa* is Italian? I think it's Spanish or
Portuguese."

"Annie, please," Kenny whispered back. "I'm trying to say my prayers."

Ann sat back and looked at her father's casket. She asked herself if she believed in heaven. She decided it didn't matter. Even if this world is all there is, it's still a good deal. If this is it, it's plenty.

40.

T he Saturday evening after Dom was buried, Skyler made reservations for himself and his sister at a fancy Vietnamese restaurant in Boston. It was a lavish place, dominated by a great gold Buddha the size of a seated King Kong.

"Never go to a Chinese restaurant with Kenny," Skyler said when they were seated.

"Why? What does he do?"

"Have you never seen it? Oh, little sister, it's mortifying. He imitates the waiters! I swear he doesn't even know he's doing it, it's part of that five-year-old he keeps so close to the surface. An Asian man will come up and say in an accent, 'You like drink?' and Kenny will squint his eyes and nod and say, 'Ah so, yes, velly much, please.'"

Ann laughed and shook her head. "No, he doesn't do that, I don't believe you."

"Ah, it gets worse. Italian, Mexican. Kenny is New Bedlam's man of a thousand voices. Once when we were in college we were coming home from a Grateful Dead concert and we stopped at a soul-food place in Roxbury. Ann, I swear, he was doing Amos and Andy. We barely got out of there with our lives."

Ann smiled and said, "He is such a horrible little man. How did we get stuck with him?"

"We'll have treasures in heaven, I'm sure. Listen, Annie. That's kind of what I wanted to talk to you about. It's going to take a while to settle Dom's estate, but the gist of it is pretty obvious. You and I will get some of the other businesses, the car lots and such. There are tax reasons to keep the corporations Dom formed for those companies intact, and in some cases there are other partners, other beneficiaries, outstanding bank loans. We'll work through all that. I'm in favor of divesting ourselves of those businesses eventually and letting them go on without us."

"I would be inclined to agree with that. Will those men who worked for him for years be all right?"

"Oh yeah, Dom took care of everybody. I'd be very open to offering the key people at those companies a chance to do a management buyout if they want to."

"Okay."

"Now, King Cable. With Dom gone, it's all ours. You, me, and Kenny. That includes the house, too. I asked Betty and she does not want it. As far as she's concerned, she traded that place for cold hard cash and she's still glad. So my thought is, if you want the house, buy me out. If you don't want it, I'll buy you out."

"What about Kenny?"

"Well, he's never lived there. It's not his house in any way, shape, or form, except that he happens to own a third of King Cable and for legal reasons we put the house in the company name."

"I'm not sure Kenny sees it that way. He's always over there, cutting the grass or working on the pond."

"Hey, Kenny's way of working on the pond almost got us all thrown in jail. Please. I'm not trying to cheat Kenny, but you and I control two-thirds of the votes now. We can override Kenny anytime we want. And I would very much like to get the family house separated from the TV company as soon as possible. In the next six months we are going to be fielding some very lucrative offers on King Cable.

Everything from straight buyouts to partnerships to mergers to going public and selling stock. I want to get the family house out of the business before it ends up listed as part of some portfolio."

"I agree with that," Annie said. "But Sky. I've thought about this a lot. I want to give Kenny the house."

Skyler looked at his sister. "Yeah. Sure. Is that before or after you elope with Sammy Bignose?"

"Sky, I mean it. Kenny has gotten the least of any of us, and it means so much to him. I don't expect him to be in my life much in the future, and if you end up moving out of King Cable he'll be out of yours. Let's not pretend we're going to remain close with Kenny when there's no business tying us together. You avoid him as much as you can now and you're partners!"

"Well, all that may be true, Ann, but it doesn't mean I want to give him my family home!"

"Come on, Skyler. Your family home is the home you and your wife live in with your children. You haven't spent two consecutive hours at the house in five years."

"Untrue. Anyway, what do you mean by *give* it to Kenny? You don't mean that literally, do you?"

"Why not? Who says we have to make money on everything we do? We're rich enough, and from what you just said about stock offerings and merger opportunities, we're about to get considerably richer. If you're not going to live in the house and I'm not going to live in the house, let's give it to someone who would love to live in that house more than anything in the world."

Skyler had no place to run to. The spring rolls had not even come yet.

"Come on, Sky," Annie said. "Keep it in the family."

They passed the rest of dinner talking about other things. Skyler said he had a plan to turn the legal department into a profit center: "Why should they get away with not generating revenue?"

Bobby Kahn's contract came up, too. Skyler said they had offered him the deal of a lifetime, five years all-in, big raises, great incentives, profit sharing, but he turned it down. He wants to be president of all the networks with veto power over anyone else's ideas, including the Kings.

"He has a high opinion of himself," Annie said.

Skyler looked at his sister coolly. "I like Bobby," he said. "I've always stuck up for him."

"You have," Annie said.

"But I do wonder if we have not gotten the best out of him."

Ann said nothing. And that quickly Bobby Kahn was skinned a second time.

They did not talk about Bobby any more that evening, but while driving home Sky tried to talk Ann out of wanting to give the family home to Kenny.

"Annie," he said. "Giving Kenny the house is a sweet gesture, but come on. It's *Kenny*, for God's sake. Do you want to drive by there and see Moe Notty's face in the upstairs window?"

"There's something you need to know, Skyler," Annie said. "Something I only learned after Dom died. Now don't get upset, but strictly speaking you and Kenny and I are not the only people with a claim on King Cable or the house or any of the rest of it."

Skyler stared at the road ahead. He said, "That's not true."

"Listen, Sky, it's not a big deal unless we make it one, but . . ." Ann hesitated. This was like dropping the bomb on Hiroshima. "Skyler, Dominic never actually divorced my mother."

Skyler skidded his car across two lanes. Ann screamed. He drove straight off the highway into a truck stop and put the car in park. He turned to her and said, "WHAT?"

"I didn't know it myself until I called to tell her he had died. She doesn't want anything, Sky, it's just . . ."

"Annie, what are you talking about? That is impossible! Dom was a very smart businessman, and I might add extremely paranoid. There is no way he just *forgot* to divorce your mother. I'm sorry, but she's wrong. Either that or she's trying to rope you into pulling some scam, which I have to say, given the history of this family, would not—"

"Skyler, shut up!" Annie was not angry. She just needed to get him to pay attention before he hyperventilated. "Look, I didn't expect this, but here it is. They went through the divorce in England, but there were still unsettled issues and he was back here and she was there, and he got angry with his own lawyers at one point. I don't know exactly why, but he never signed the papers and neither did she. I suppose if either one of them had wanted to get married again they would have, but neither of them did."

"But she took settlement money from him."

"No, Skyler, believe it or not, she didn't. My mother lived perfectly well without any of the King money."

"Except now you're telling me she owns half of everything!"

"For the moment. I'm sure she'll work it out in a fair way. She may just sign it all away on principle."

"That's a hell of a principle."

"But until then, we find ourselves in an awkward position."

"We sure do."

"Which is that my mother and I together own, what, 50 percent plus 18.8 percent. We own 68.88 percent of King Cable. You and Kenny have 18.88 percent each."

Skyler looked like a man watching his barrelful of dreams slide over Niagara Falls.

"What do you want to do, Annie?"

"Well, first, if you think about it and agree it's a good idea, and if Betty really doesn't want the place, I'd like to tell Kenny we are giving him the family home and grounds."

Skyler let out a long breath and put his car back into drive. Fucking Dom, he thought. Always had to have a pistol in his pocket and Big Casino up his sleeve.

They drove in silence until they hit the Rhode Island line, and even then all Sky said to Annie was, "I hope you don't regret this when you grow up."

41.

obby had spent the weekend in Long Island with his mother. He'd never needed a Low Impact Monday so badly.

When he got into the office, his assistant said Skyler wanted to see him. Bobby returned a couple of phone calls first and then went down the hall. Skyler was sitting with Kenny and the company lawyer and the head of Human Resources.

Thank God, Bobby thought, we're finally going to settle my contract.

"Gang," Bobby said in greeting. "Is this a happy meeting or a sad meeting?"

"Sad meeting, Bob," Skyler said. "Look, we've been going around and around on what you want out of your new deal and we just can't get there."

"Well, that is bad news, Sky," Bobby said. He was looking for a cup of coffee. "Because I'm getting a lot of calls from New York and Los Angeles. I don't want to leave King Cable, of course, but you guys are going to have to come up with—"

Skyler interrupted. "We think you should leave, Bob."

Bobby laughed. "Thanks for the vote of confidence, Sky! No, listen. Let's take half an hour to work through the points and figure out a way to make us all comfortable with this. Maybe I can wait until year two for the title change."

Kenny's mouth was pushed into a smile, but his eyes were trying to launch out of their sockets. "No, Bob. We're not interested in going forward on a new deal with you. Sorry. You're a good guy and you've done great things for King Cable, but it's best for all of us now if we move on."

Time stopped. Bobby's ghost stepped out of his body and looked at the frozen room and himself standing there, in jeans and sneakers, no tie, corduroy jacket. He looked at Skyler and Kenny and the two new factotums, all in tailored jackets and slacks, all ruthlessly efficient. Oh my word, Bobby thought. I am being fired. It's happening again. He floated back into his body and he felt like a door slammed on him. It's happening again.

"Skyler," Bobby said. "You gotta be kidding. There's nothing I have done that has not worked out better than we ever hoped."

"This was not an easy decision, Bob," Skyler said.

"I can't help notice, Bob," Kenny said, "that your emphasis is on 'I.' 'What *I've* done.' I like to think the success of King Cable was a great team effort, Bob. You were a fine quarterback, but we're taking you out of the game."

Bobby looked around the room, hoping to find some way to slow things down or delay this argument until he had time to think clearly, to marshal his defense. He said, "Where's Annie?"

"Annie has taken herself off the executive committee," Kenny said, "and out of the decision-making process."

"She's handing over her seat on the board and the leadership of Eureka to Abby Plum," Skyler said. "You don't want to get Abby in here, do you, Bob?"

Bobby was wobbly. The lawyer got up and gave him her chair. He sat on the arm; he wasn't staying.

"Can you give me a few weeks," he said, "before this is made public? I want to make sure I get the best new deal I can wherever I decide to go."

"Absolutely," Skyler said, and he said it so the others in the room would know he meant it. "We know how in-demand you are out there, Bob. I have to say, it made this easier. I mean, how long could we expect to hang on to you anyway? You're going to do great."

"Yeah," Bobby said. Kenny was staring at him with a resentment Bobby could not begin to fathom. "Okay, well, I guess that's it. See you around the quahog bed."

Bobby walked out of the building without returning to his office, got in his car, and drove the back way to the King house. He knocked on the door and no one answered. He went around to the side porch and let himself in. The ceiling fan he had fixed was spinning. He clicked the wall switch off and on. The lamps he rewired were still working.

He walked through the house yelling for Annie. He heard her voice upstairs. "Bob? Hello?" She came down the stairs wearing striped men's pajamas. She was drying her hair with a towel. She was puzzled to see him.

"What the hell, Annie?" he said, standing at the foot of the stairs looking up at her. "Your brother just fired me! You're okay with that? I mean, what the hell?"

"Oh, Bobby." She came down the stairs but not all the way. She remained three steps above him. "The final decision was only made yesterday. There's no conspiracy."

"But you went along with it."

"Doesn't matter now. I'm leaving Eureka, and Rhode Island. I don't want to be a television executive, Bobby."

"Well, I guess you have that luxury," he said. "I still need to work for a living."

"But why limit yourself? You're young and you're bright and

you have some money. You could do anything. You could go somewhere you've never been, see what other people are like. They might surprise you."

Oh good, Bobby thought, I need a little condescension right now.

"I need a job, Annie," Bobby said. "I have about one week to grab one of the deals being dangled in front of me by TV companies who don't know I just got fired. If I wait, I'm finished forever."

He looked at her like he had never seen her before. Then he said, "You don't have any idea what you're walking away from. Television is the most important medium there ever was or ever will be. Every other form of entertainment—drama, comedy, sports—has been absorbed and transformed by television. Politics, government have been transformed by television. Nothing else you could ever do with your life would matter more than what you can do by staying here. You and I could run Eureka together, Annie. We could make it something great."

"You know what I've decided television does, Bobby?" Ann said. She moved down two steps and they were eye to eye. "It makes people greedy, horny, and hungry. That's it. That's what it's there for. To make people crave things they don't need."

"Don't forget angry," Bobby said. "TV does a good job at angry, too. But you've done all right by it, Ann. Your TV money will pay for a few trips to Thailand."

"Yes, it will. My father was a capitalist and a very hard man. But you know what they say: 'Behind every great fortune there is a crime.'"

"Mario Puzo."

"Balzac."

"So now that I don't work for you anymore," Bobby said, trying to smile, "at least I can ask you out."

"You'd have to come to Mumbai."

"Sure," Bobby said. "Someday."

He had a lot to do. He had to start working the phones, alert the headhunters. It was starting to sink in, and it was okay. He had been through this before. Things happen for a reason. Suck it up, make a classy exit.

"Listen, Ann," he said. "I know I was a jerk sometimes, but no hard feelings. I always respected you. I'm sorry for any misunderstandings."

Annie put a hand on Bobby's shoulder. "Listen, genius," she said. "Not every disagreement is a misunderstanding."

Bobby drove back down the King driveway for the last time, past the old barn and the lost cars and the carp pond. "Never fails, never fails, never fails," he said to himself. "The people who own the airline always decide they can fly the plane."

Bobby remembered something he used to think about when he was a little kid. The universe is infinite, right? And no two things are exactly the same anywhere.

Well, if that is true, if there is an infinity of tiny variations, then everything that could exist must exist somewhere. So somewhere out in the cosmos there is a planet with a real Lucy Ricardo, and somewhere there is a real Ben Cartwright, and somewhere there is a planet where Bobby Kahn is married to Annie King and they are running their television empire together.

And if you keep extending this logic, somewhere there is a planet where we are all the TV characters and people sit down at the end of a long day and watch our adventures. In some distant galaxy an alien race is weeping at Dom's funeral, laughing at Sammy and Moe, and rooting for Bobby and Ann to stop fighting and fall in love just like Luke and Laura and Sam and Diane and Ross and Rachel.

That's my theology, Bobby thought as he drove down Main Street, New Bedlam. My whole life is a TV show designed for the amusement of people on another planet.

42.

nnie had finished boxing her possessions and packing her bags. She was flying overnight to London to see her mother and then on to India to produce Sarah Planter's film about sex slavery and the children of HIV.

She had been startled when Kenny let her know, in a friendly but obnoxious way, that she was not welcome to store her belongings in what was now his house. That also meant clearing her clothes out of what had always been her bedroom.

Annie had assumed that even with ownership of the house transferred to his name, Kenny would be gracious enough to continue to treat the place as a family home. Foolish assumption. Gratitude was not in Kenny's vocabulary. Ann tried not to hold it against him. She remembered a line she learned from an episode of the *Mary Tyler Moore* show: "When an elephant flies, you don't complain if he doesn't stay up too long."

Kenny's good behavior during Dom's last days was as much flying as that little elephant would ever do. As soon as Kenny took over the house, he began turning it into a shrine to a boyhood he had never lived. He had a big oil painting of Dominic made from an old photograph and he hung it in the living room in an ornate frame with a little portrait lamp on top. Kenny liked it so much that he then had the same kind of portrait done of himself, put it in the same kind of frame, and hung that right across from Dom's. Kenny's picture might even have been a little bigger.

At the cocktail receptions and community events Kenny took to hosting at the homestead he liked to stand before Dom's portrait with a drink in his hand, a single woman at his side, and raise a toast to his old dad—friend, protector, father, pal—the best any boy ever had.

Skyler negotiated a settlement with Annie's mother, and then sold King Cable and its three booming networks to the multinational NOA for four hundred million dollars and three years' use of a private jet. Sky kept a consulting title and they gave him an office in Manhattan, which he never visited. NOA began moving key operations of Eureka, BoomerBox, and the Comic Book Channel to New York and laid off a lot of the old employees.

Boris Mumsy was one they kept. He moved to SoHo, lost seventy-five pounds, and started dating a CNN weekend anchorwoman. They sometimes ran into Bobby Kahn at industry functions.

One day on the beach Skyler saw his son watching *Dragonball Z* on a handheld PlayStation. He said to his wife, "I think we cashed out of the cable business just in time."

Moe and Sammy Bignose were paid off by the new owners of King Cable. Kenny put them on salary as his assistants. His share of the NOA buyout made him so rich he could afford to pay for playmates. Kenny's new business inspiration was to sell farts as downloadable ring tones. He knew teenage boys would go for it, and he and Sammy and Moe spent many happy hours recording demos in analogue and digital, genuine and simulated. They considered bringing in Stinky Mark Findle to lay down some extended rippers but were concerned about contending with him over copyrights. Mostly Sammy and Moe hung around Kenny's house and put his comics in alphabetical order and played video games and broke things and tried to fix them.

There was one bad incident when a big raccoon got in the barn and started eating Kenny's comic-book collection. Kenny sent Sammy and Moe out to capture the beast, and after a number of failed attempts they managed to lure the raccoon into a big steel lobster trap. They called Kenny out to the barn to see a huge, wet, foaming, screeching monster clawing at the cage and baring its yellow fangs at him.

Kenny wanted to get a shotgun and blast the racoon right there, but Sammy had borrowed the lobster trap from his uncle and could not return it shot full of holes or caked in bloody fur.

So Kenny decided to drown the raccoon in the trap. He got a rope and lassoed the cage and began dragging it over the King's great lawn and down to the sea with the wailing, leaping, panicked animal inside. It took a long time and Kenny suffered some rope burns along the way, but he made it to the wet sand and began hauling the trap, raccoon and all, inexorably toward the water.

The raccoon was screeching, the ocean was roaring, the sand was soggy, and Kenny was cursing and shoving and trying not to get his fingers bit off. Moe and Sammy stood on the hill looking down at the gruesome tableau, feeling something close to existential dread.

A troop of Girl Scouts were having a picnic on the beach. They all began pointing and weeping and shouting to the scoutmaster to make the bad man stop hurting that poor raccoon. The scout leader approached Kenny and was rebuffed so rudely she took out her mobile phone and called the police to report a madman loose on Arnold's Neck Beach, trying to murder an animal.

The police patched the call through to the Rhode Island Wildlife Protection and Natural Resources Conservation Authority. Ranger Beth Banger jumped in her Jeep and sped to the scene.

She parked on the crest of hill that looked down at the private beach. There she saw a maniacal, wild-eyed, and soaking-wet Kenny

King trying to drag a steel cage into the surf on a rope, while a dozen hysterical Girl Scouts pulled the trap the other way and an adult woman, no doubt the den mother, stood at the water's edge waving a mobile phone and screaming for the girls to come back.

Beth reached under her car seat and withdrew a tackle box from which she pulled a Taser—a stun gun. Not much need for this kind of weapon in the wildlife-protection business, but occasionally a ranger came up against a dangerous animal that had to be put down. Beth turned her weapon up all the way and strode down the hill to the ocean like The Man with No Name.

Her face was firm but her thoughts were flying. "That little twat," she thought, "is violating environmental, coastal, animal-cruelty, and shell-fishing equipment statutes all at one time, in front of a dozen unimpeachable witnesses. Let's see him bribe his way out of this one!"

Up close she could see the raccoon, panicked, bouncing around the half-submerged cage with its claws and teeth spread wide. Kenny King, up to his knees in the surf, was wearing almost exactly the same expression. Beth ordered the troop leader and the little girls back up the beach. She splashed out to where Kenny was hauling and cursing and screamed at him, "Kenny King! Kenny King! Stop this right now! Release that animal or I will use force to make you!"

Kenny seemed to not know she was there. The waves were whacking them, the rope was burning his hands, the Girl Scouts were screaming, and the raccoon was snapping and gnashing. Beth grabbed him by the arm. She remembered his real name.

"Kenny DuBois! Let go of that rope right now, that's an order!"

No one had called Kenny by his mother's name in years. It shocked him. He looked at the ridiculous woman holding his arm, soaking wet in her green Smokey the Bear hat.

He said, "B-B-Bite me, B-B-B-Baited B-B-Beth."

She raised her Taser and pulled the trigger. A needle on a wire shot out from the gun and planted itself in Kenny's shoulder. Electrical current ran up the line and juiced Kenny like the Lindbergh baby kidnapper. It had not occurred to Beth that firing an electrical charge into someone while they were both standing in the ocean might make a moderately dangerous technology borderline lethal. Kenny went over like the Hesperus. He twitched and shuddered and flopped into the waves.

"Holy shit!" Sammy Bignose shouted from the hill. "Beth shot Kenny!"

Beth yanked the line and the metal dart came out of him like a fishhook. Moe and Bignose came running into the water and helped Beth haul the convulsing Kenny onto the sand.

They dropped him on the beach with his teeth chattering, his fingers twitching, and his eyes blinking open and closed like a venetian blind.

Lying in the mud with a mouthful of vomit, Kenny saw Beth Banger calling for an ambulance and a squad car while the liberated raccoon bounded back up the beach to Kenny's barn to finish eating his comic books as the Girl Scouts sang "Born Free."

43.

Bobby Kahn was in an expensive and pretentious fish restaurant attached to a trendy hotel near Central Park West. It was barely noon and the place was almost empty. In order to make sure no one saw them, his small party was seated not in the street-level room where other diners were served, but at one end of a large table at a private dining room upstairs.

Bobby was sitting with the headhunter Tom Jackson, who had negotiated this powwow with Masonic secrecy. A woman attorney he had never met from his old network's HR department was there, and the network's Chief Financial Officer—the austere consigliere of the boss of the boss of Howard Temple, the man who'd fired Bobby Kahn two years before.

The CFO was a compact man with small eyes and small wire-rim glasses and a bald head that emerged from the rim of a tight black crew cut like a Fabergé egg on a velvet pedestal.

The woman was thin to the point of emaciation, which made her look older than she probably was. She had spiky, frosted hair. They both had the restrained positivity of insurance brokers about to tell you that the company had decided to go ahead and reimburse you for that accident two years ago after all.

A waiter came and placed large bowls in front of each of them. Each bowl was empty except for a little chunk of lobster that looked like a tissue sample, a tiny bit of celery, and garnish standing up like the feather in Robin Hood's cap. With ceremonial boredom the waiter poured a muddy bisque into each bowl from a little silver cup and then went away.

"So, Bob," the CFO said. He was speaking intensely in a near whisper. "You know the network has been through a bit of a rough ride this season."

Bobby sipped his bisque. "I've seen the press."

The CFO, the attorney, and the headhunter all made the same little wince, as if someone had pulled their hair.

"A lot of that is just the cycle," the CFO said. "And I trust your discretion. We are making changes. We will be putting in place a new President of Programming and Production to run the whole operation. Someone's got to fix prime time. Bob, we think you are the man."

Everyone stared at Bobby. Bobby chewed his bit of lobster and swallowed it and took a drink of water. He let the offer go down slowly.

He asked them, "What about Howard Temple?"

The attorney spoke for the first time. She said, "Howard doesn't know yet."

Bobby nodded. This is how it was done.

The CFO spoke up. His voice was a little louder now. "Howard will be well taken care of, Bob. You needn't worry about him. Now let's be honest. Folks at the network know that the wrong man was fired two years ago. We should have asked you to step into Howard's job then. Frankly, he blamed you for his own shortcomings and we were dumb enough to fall for it."

The headhunter spoke. "It's understandable, the way things were represented at that time, that the brass would be deceived. Luckily we now have the evidence of Bobby's superb performance in cable." He lowered his voice and his eyes. "And of course, how poorly Howard has done without Bobby to lean on."

Bobby allowed all this talk to float over him. They were using almost exactly the script he had imagined when they shoved him out the door. He didn't say a word. He just nodded and took another spoonful of soup.

The CFO and the lawyer and the headhunter looked at Bobby and looked at one another and looked at Bobby again. Then the CFO said, "Bob, come home."

Bobby swallowed and said, "Absolutely."

Then everyone smiled and shook hands.

The waiter appeared and asked if they were all satisfied.

"No offense," Bobby told him. "But this is the worst chowder I've ever had."

The waiter began to apologize, but Bobby told him not to worry, it was a good lunch anyway. The CFO laughed. He thought it was strange, though, that Bobby had said "chowda."

They paid the bill and got their coats and shook hands and walked out of the restaurant. The CFO had a car waiting and the headhunter waved for a cab. The HR attorney was heading south and Bobby walked along with her. He was telling her about his new apartment when he saw a face he knew coming toward them, waiting to cross the next street. It was Howard Temple and it was too late to avoid him.

Howard saw Bobby and smiled and began to call out. Then he saw the HR woman and his mouth froze in mid-formation. Right then he knew. The "walk" sign came on and they approached each other like a prisoner exchange at the Berlin Wall. The woman from HR pretended to be talking on her cell phone. Howard was turning red. He said, "Bob."

Bobby nodded. He couldn't make a smile. He hurried to the other sidewalk. When he got there the HR woman put away her cell phone and said, "That was awkward, but he won't think anything of it."

Bobby thought that was the silliest thing he ever heard. "No. He knows," he told her.

Bobby felt no triumph at all, no satisfaction. Seeing Howard reminded him of how awful it felt to get fired, that was it. He was surprised that achieving the vindication he had dreamed of did not make that bad feeling go away.

At that moment he felt a lot of sympathy for Howard. But he was sure he could get over it.

44.

Annie woke in the dark and for a moment thought she was in her old bedroom in New Bedlam. After days of quick naps in train seats and nights of reading through insomnia, she had finally made accord with her exhaustion and fallen into twelve hours of bottomless sleep. She came out of it like a baby chick pushing through an eggshell. She put her feet on the soft rug. She felt her way to the wall and parted the thick curtains and white scrim to reveal a floor-to-ceiling double-door window that curved up at the top like the dome of a minaret.

Orange light shone on her. The sun was rising on the Arabian Sea. She pushed open the windows. They swung out above a cobblestone road, five stories below, already filling with bikes and taxis, merchants and tourists, and sailors making their way home to the armada of tugboat-size ferries, trawlers, and fishing boats strung together in the harbor. A little boy was nudging along a weary dog. Six dark men huddled over a chunk of board, playing dominoes. Four Pakistani men in Nehru caps posed for a photo snapped by a tourist in Bermuda shorts and a fanny pack. On a patch of grass under a palm tree, a handsome young man was doing martial-arts exercises, bare-chested.

Indian ladies in pink and white dresses led a carnival line of children holding hands. Two dozen weather-beaten rowboats were lined up like a sagging picket fence. One dark man was pressed against the corner of a wall, surreptitiously peeing under a sign that said "Welcome! Fort Cyrus Yacht Club."

Gulls and pigeons competed for crumbs and nested in the frames of her window. Annie got what was left of a croissant from the night before and let them have it. The sun was already baking her face. She looked out at India.

The hotel room was tastefully posh. The chairs, desk, and headboard were made of the same ribbed wood. Skyler would have known what it was. Betty always said her son knew the cost of everything and the value of nothing. A marble-topped table was laid out with a peach and a pomegranate and a small crescent knife. The voices in the street got louder. There was laughter.

The bare-chested boy under the palm tree was doing push-ups now, preparing for his idea of manhood. In the distance enormous construction cranes were rising like dinosaurs from a swamp. A new century was being raised. It was where Annie belonged.

She had made her way from Rhode Island to London to Paris to Rome to Mumbai. As she traveled her doubts fell away like winter clothes. Now she was moving unburdened. Thank God she had not stayed in England as her mother wanted, or taken her father's house as her own, or tried to bend her talents to fit at King Cable. It was hard to believe she had ever been tempted. How could she have spent her life in television? She didn't even watch television.

She had gotten a shock last night, when she arrived at this hotel. She went into the club room to get some toast and tea and found a few guests watching television. It took her a while to notice the program. It was *Lookers,* the dreadful reality show that had gotten Bobby fired from the network and sent him to King Cable. She saw his name come up at the end: Executive in Charge of Production. Ann thought about how Americans complained about countries like India taking their telemarketing jobs. But look what America takes in return: They colonize imaginations.

From this distance, America looked strange. They had spun the dream of democracy into an ambition that everyone, rich and poor, clever and dull, eats the same bad food and watches the same bad TV shows. The rich just ate the bad food in nicer rooms and watched the bad television on bigger screens.

The best Ann could hope for Bobby Kahn now was that he never find out what he missed.

She caught herself. Easy to sit in judgment on a terrace above the world. Let's see how she held up after she joined Sarah Planter's film crew in the slums of Bombay. She might end up back in New Bedlam asking Kenny for a room.

She remembered something Dash Ryan had told her when she was leaving town, the day Kenny was arrested for trying to drown a raccoon and Skyler had to leave an investors' meeting to bail him out of jail. Dash and Pam were the only ones to show up at the train station. Pam gave her a box of cookies for the journey, and Dash said, "Remember, honey. Every great traveler starts out expecting to come back."

Annie looked out at India. If this world is all there is, it's plenty. She got dressed and went off to work.